London Waiting

M.A. Maggiano

ISBN: 195043351X
ISBN-13: 978-1-950433-51-3

This novel is a work of fiction. Names, characters, places, and incidents either are the product of the author's imagination or are used fictitiously. Any resemblance to actual persons, living or dead or locales is entirely coincidental.

Cover design by Pro Designx.

Published by Poetic Justice Books
Port Saint Lucie, Florida
www.poeticjusticebooks.com

<u>Other books by M.A. Maggiano</u>

Roman Interlude
Return of The First

<u>Books by M.A. & C.M. Maggiano</u>

Valkyrie: Guardians of the Lost

CONTENTS

ACKNOWLEDGMENTS

I'd like to give special thanks to my fellow author R. J. Blacks who floated an idea to me for a plot change to my first book, Roman Interlude. I filed that idea away for future reference, and London Waiting is a direct result of that discussion.

Thanks to all the members of the Morningside and Treasure Coast Writers Groups who helped critique my work along the way. And especially my final editor Kris Haggblom whose review helped tighten up the storyline.

London Waiting

~ A Novel ~

Part I

"The holiest of all holidays are those
Kept by us in silence and apart;
The secret anniversaries of the heart."

Henry Wadsworth Longfellow
Holidays

Chapter 1

Sara Ferguson got the call from Columbia Presbyterian Medical Center at 2:53 p.m. The person working the emergency room admissions desk called Sara to inform her that Mrs. Rose Cavendish was there and was being treated.

Sara grabbed her coat and purse and headed to her boss' office to let him know she had a family emergency. "Jeff, I'm sorry, I've got to leave. My grandmother's had a stroke, and they've taken her to Columbia Presbyterian."

Jeff Charles, senior partner and co-founder of the agency, shot up from his seat. "Go! Don't worry about anything here. We'll cover all your accounts. Do you need anything? A ride?"

"Thanks, Jeff, no, I don't think so. I'll get a cab out front."

"Okay, I'll call security and see if they can snag one for you before you hit the street."

"I appreciate that. I'll call in later once I find out what going on."

Jeff helped her with her coat. "Sara, don't worry about this place. Go! Do what you have to do, and once things settle, call me and let me know what you need."

Sara nodded, picked her handbag up off Jeff's desk, and rushed out the door.

* * *

SARA BOLTED FROM THE ELEVATOR when the doors opened in the lobby and ran to the exit. Her long legs allowed her to cover the distance quickly. Maneuvering through the crowd, her fluid movements made it look as if she was once again on the soccer field attacking the goal, her brown hair dancing in rhythm behind her. As she ran, she scanned the area ahead, looking to avoid anyone who would impede her progress. As Sara pushed her way through the revolving door, she saw a uniformed guard from building security standing by the curb next to a waiting yellow cab.

"Ms. Ferguson?" he asked as she approached.

"Yes."

"This cab is ready to take you to the hospital. I've already given the driver your destination as Columbia Presbyterian. Is that correct?" asked the guard as he opened the rear door.

"Yes, thank you so much," said Sara as she climbed into the back of the waiting cab.

"I hope everything turns out okay for you, Miss," offered the guard as he closed the cab door.

Sara acknowledged the sentiment with a wordless nod.

Sara leaned forward in her seat, "How long do you think it will take to get there?"

"Maybe very quick, Miss. Traffic not very bad now," replied the turbaned driver.

"Thank you, please go as fast as you can," urged Sara as she flopped back in her seat.

"Yes, Miss, very quick, Chakar will do his best," replied the driver as he maneuvered the vehicle from lane to lane, trying to move as fast as possible.

Sara looked out the cab window, lost in thought. Nothing can happen to Nan; we've only got each other left in this world. What would I do if she died? Trying to put a brave face on this event, Sara confirmed to herself that Nan couldn't die. She's British, and she wouldn't stand for something like that happening unscheduled.

Yes, that's right, Nan is a survivor. She came to America after the Second World War. Nan had survived the London Blitz, worked a job in a defense factory at sixteen to save the money for passage to America. Once the war ended, she did just that. When Nan arrived in New York in July nineteen forty-five, she was eighteen years old, widowed, not two shillings to her name, and three months pregnant, as she often told Sara. But she had survived. Nan gave birth to Sara's mother, Sophia Rose McDonald, on New Year's Day, nineteen forty-six. In nineteen forty-seven she had once more found love and married William Cavendish, who again left her as a widow in April of fifty-three. Nan told Sara that much like her first husband, William, also died during the war. But William died in Korea during the infamous Battle of Pork Chop Hill.

Nan had been through hard times, but now she had a comfortable life. She said Grandpa Bill, as she called him, had made several smart investments in the short years they were together. Nan always told Sara that people would have called Grandpa Bill a dreamer, but Nan always said he was a visionary who saw the future. Nan told Sara people laughed at his investments in Polaroid and IBM, but he had been correct, and now Nan reaped the benefits of his vision.

"Very quick, Miss," called out the driver as he pulled to the curb in front of the emergency room entrance.

Sara snapped out of her daydream when he called out. She paid the fare with her credit card and added a good-sized tip before exiting the cab. Once inside the hospital, she looked for the check-in desk and approached the young woman who was filling out forms. "I'm Sara Ferguson; I got a call saying my Nan...sorry, my grandmother, Mrs. Rose Cavendish, was being treated here."

"Let me check. Yes, Mrs. Cavendish is here. She's being treated in room four. I'll take you back. If you go through those doors, I'll meet you on the other side."

Sara did as instructed and followed the woman after she was through the doors. It was just a short walk to the room, and Sara wasn't prepared for what she found once she entered. Nan was on the bed and looked very old and frail, nothing like the way she looked this morning when they had coffee before Sara left for work. The left side of her face was drooping. Sara looked at all the wires, tubes, and monitors hooked to her grandmother and began to cry.

"Nan, I'm here," she said, as she walked to the bed. Sara picked up her grandmother's hand and held it in hers. "Nan, can you hear me? I'm here, can you open your eyes?" There was no reaction and Sara continued to talk to her grandmother. "Please open your eyes, Nan, let me know you know I'm here," Sara pleaded. There was no response.

Sara released her grandmother's hand, removed her coat, and prepared to stay for the duration. Then she went to find a nurse or doctor who could give her an update. At the nurse's station, she located the RN who was seeing to Nan and introduced herself. "I'm Sara Ferguson, Mrs. Cavendish's granddaughter, what can you tell me about her condition?"

The nurse pulled the chart. "Your grandmother was unresponsive when they brought her in. The person who called the ambulance reported it appeared she had suffered a stroke because her speech became slurred and she had trouble moving the left side of her body before she collapsed."

"Was it a stroke?"

"Yes, Ms. Ferguson, it appears she has suffered a stroke. The doctor ordered an MRI, and confirmed it as an ischemic stroke, a blood clot has stopped the blood supply to a large part of her brain."

"Can that be treated?"

"We're trying. Once the CAT scan confirmed the clot, the doctor prescribed a clot-dissolving medicine which can increase her chances of recovery. We're waiting to see if it works on your grandmother," replied the nurse as she closed the folder. "We're checking on her every few minutes to see if there is progress. So far, there's been no improvement. The doctor may have to look for an alternative method to remove the clot."

"Alternative method, what's that?"

"By surgical removal, or by the use of a catheter to break up and remove the clot from the artery so the blood flow can return to normal."

Sara trembled, "That sounds dangerous. Does it work?"

"We've had an excellent success rate." Replied the nurse as she tried to reassure Sara. "Let's go check on her and see if the medication is having any effect."

The nurse led the way back to the treatment room, and Sara again picked up her grandmother's hand. "Wake up, Nan," she whispered.

"Mrs. Cavendish, can you hear me? Can you open your eyes for me, dear?" asked the nurse in a louder tone than Sara had used.

"Come on, Nan, please open your eyes. It's me, Sara, I'm here with you." Sara began to cry again as she continued to hold Nan's hand. She kissed her grandmother's palm then squeezed her hand three times in their secret code, which meant, "I love you."

Sara felt the gentle pressure as Nan tried to squeeze back as she opened her eyes.

Chapter 2

Nan managed a weak, lopsided smile as she tried to squeeze Sara's hand harder. Nan made a slurring sound as she tried to call her granddaughter's name. "Sharrraaa."

"Yes, Nan, it's me, Sara. Shhh, don't talk. I think the medicine is working."

The nurse leaned over the bed, trying to get the readings off the instruments attached to the old woman while she talked to her. "Hi, Mrs. Cavendish, nice to see you awake," she said with a warm smile. "Do you know where you are?" she asked.

Nan nodded weakly, "Hoass-ptal," she mumbled.

"That's right, you're at Columbia Presbyterian. My name is Jenny, and I'm your nurse. They brought you in about two hours ago. You've had a stroke, and the doctor's given you medicine to dissolve the blood clot. It appears to be working since you have regained consciousness. Do you understand what I'm saying?"

Rose Cavendish replied with a slight nod then closed her eyes.

"Nan?" said Sara.

"It's okay, Ms. Ferguson, her vitals are good, she's gone to sleep. The body is doing its job right now as the medicine continues to dissolve the clot, and now it decided she needs sleep. You can stay with her, and I'll be back in thirty minutes. I'm on shift until midnight; if you need anything, just use the call bell."

"Thanks." Sara settled into the chair next to the bed and watched the lines move across the monitors, the soft beeps emanating from the machine were hypnotic in their rhythm. Every fifteen minutes, there came a hissing sound as the machine inflated the blood pressure cuff on Nan's arm. Sara focused on the numbers as they rose and fell. "One thirty-two over seventy-nine," Sara said aloud. "That's a good reading. Now it's just a waiting game."

Sara jumped when something touched her hand.

"Ms. Ferguson," said Jenny, "It's almost midnight You've been asleep for a few hours. Why don't you go home and come back in the morning?"

"But what about my Nan?"

"Your grandmother is resting comfortably. It appears the medication has done its job and dissolved the clot. The sensory tests we've done on her show she is not responding better. There isn't much else you can do here tonight."

"Can I speak to the doctor before I leave?"

"I'm sorry, Dr. Randell left for the evening after he reviewed the latest information on your grandmother's condition. He ordered another CAT scan for the morning to see what effect the clot had on her brain."

"What's that mean? Is my Nan going to have brain damage?"

"Ms. Ferguson, if you'll accompany me to the nurse's station, we can let your grandmother rest while we talk."

"Okay," replied Sara as she picked up her handbag and followed the nurse out into the hallway.

After a short walk, the nurse explained to Sara what she could expect. "Ms. Ferguson, at this point, we can't be sure whether your grandmother has sustained any brain damage. You saw that the clot has affected the speech center of her brain. So, putting it simply, when the clot cuts off the blood supply, that part of the brain no longer gets oxygen. The brain suffers from the loss of oxygen and in severe cases dies."

"So, she's got brain damage is that what you're telling me?"

"No, Ms. Ferguson. Please keep calm. What I'm saying is that you saw your grandmother can talk. But her speech was slurred. While the medicine has dissolved the clot, the impact on her speech and possibly gross or fine motor skills will more than likely remain for a while until her brain relearns these things."

The nurse reached out and placed her hand on Sara's shoulder. "Given time, it's possible your grandmother may make a full recovery. However, I don't want you to get the impression that just because the clot has dissolved that your grandmother will hop out of bed and walk out of here like nothing happened."

Sara nodded. "Okay, I understand. I'm just worried about her. She's the only living relative I have left in this world."

"It's fine, I understand. Now, why don't you go home and get some sleep? Your grandmother is resting, and we'll see she has a restful night. You should do the same."

"Perhaps you're right. I know she's in good hands. I'll be back in the morning."

"That's good. We will admit her to the Intensive Care Unit as soon as they process the admission paperwork. When you come back in the morning, check with the front desk for directions to the ICU."

"Thanks, I'll do that. I'll just say goodbye to Nan, and I'll be on my way." Sara replied as she returned to the treatment room. Sara leaned over the bedrail and kissed her grandmother's forehead. "You rest and get better, Nan. I'm going home for a while. I'll be back in the morning," she whispered.

Sara left the emergency room and made her way to the main entrance and exited onto the street. She wanted to walk to sort things out, so she turned right and headed down Broadway.

As she began to process to process everything that happened, she asked herself the first question. "Why on earth did they transport Nan all the way up here to Columbia Presbyterian Medical Center? We have hospitals closer to where we live. In fact, Columbia Presbyterian Hospital is only minutes from us on 116th Street. Strange. Maybe Nan was visiting friends. I must ask next time we speak."

Five blocks later, Sara stopped at a Dunkin Donuts south of 160th Street and got a large coffee to go.

As she sat by the window, she took out her phone to call for an Uber. Seven minutes later, a white Toyota pulled up in front of the donut shop. She threw her coffee cup in the trash as she exited the store.

Once Sara took her seat, the driver confirmed her destination. "East Ninety-fourth and Park Ave. Is that correct?"

"Yes, that's right."

* * *

WHEN SARA ARRIVED HOME, the concierge greeted her as she entered the lobby. "Good Evening, Ms. Ferguson, how are you?"

Sara sighed, "Hi Charlie, not doing well. My grandmother had a stroke. She's up at Columbia Presbyterian Medical Center."

"Oh, Miss, I'm so sorry to hear that. Did you say the Medical Center?"

"Yes, I don't understand why they brought her there. The only thing I can think of is she must have been uptown, and that was the closest place to bring her."

"I'll keep her in my thoughts. Would you mind if I told David when he comes on shift? Everyone here loves your grandmother. She's a wonderful woman."

Sara nodded. "Sure, you can tell David. Now, if you'll excuse me, I've got to get some rest."

"Of course, Miss, if there's anything we can do, please, just call down and we'll do whatever we can to help."

"Thanks, Charlie. I'll keep that in mind. Goodnight."

"Goodnight, Ms. Ferguson."

* * *

THE ELEVATOR CHIMED as it reached the fourteenth floor. Sara exited and turned right. The thick burgundy carpet under her feet reminded her she was almost home. Sara placed the key in the lock, opened the door, and turned on the small table lamp as she entered. The low-wattage bulb gave off a glow in the otherwise dark rooms. Apartment 1401 was a large corner unit overlooking Park Avenue and had been Sara's home for the past fifteen years. Ever since that awful day when Nan had been there to pick her up from school. Sara remembered that day as if it were yesterday. She was thirteen years old, and Nan tried to explain why she was picking her up. Sara thought, for a woman whose life was a chronology of stories of the death of loved ones, it must have been difficult for her grandmother to tell her both parents had died in a car accident on the New York Thruway.

Sara walked through the darkened rooms running her hands over the furniture, thinking about the times she had spent with her grandmother. Nan had given Sara a comfortable life and perhaps overcompensated in several areas trying to make up for the fact they were the only family each other had. Sara walked over to the small bar in the room's corner where she poured a healthy shot of brandy into one of the Waterford balloons Nan had set up. "Nan always said, 'A little taste of brandy makes me think clearer.'"

The brandy warmed Sara's throat, but her thinking didn't become clearer. Instead, it focused on something she never thought about, and that was that Nan was getting older, and the day would come when she was gone. Seeing her grandmother in the hospital had brought Sara to realize the old woman wasn't immortal, and perhaps in a short time, Sara would be alone in the world. Her last surviving relative gone.

Sara put the glass down on the table and stood. Defiant, unrelenting, she made her declaration. "No, nothing can happen to Nan. It can't, and I won't allow it." Then she realized she had no control over her grandmother's destiny and she began to cry.

* * *

SARA WOKE UP ON THE COUCH where she'd fallen asleep, and saw it was 3 a.m. Sara knew there was nothing else she could do tonight. She went into the bathroom, washed her face, and changed out of her work clothes and into her soft cotton sleep tee. As she sat on the side of her bed, she chose to do something she hadn't done since she was thirteen. Sara stood, turned around and kneeled at the bottom of the bed and prayed for God to send someone to watch over her grandmother.

Chapter 3

Sara was already awake when the alarm went off. She had been lying there, alone with her thoughts for some time. She came to realize her fear that Nan would someday pass away was no longer just something that would probably happen years from now. She had never given any thought to the fact that Nan was in her late eighties. The woman's character, demeanor, and outlook on life always made her seem younger than her years. However, when Sara first saw her at the hospital yesterday, the impact was startling.

The apartment seemed unnaturally quiet as Sara filled the coffeepot. She began to call out for Nan, then realized there would be no answer, so she just went about her morning rituals in silence. No one to talk to, no one to share a pot of coffee with, no one to wish her a good day when she left for work.

Before she left for the hospital, Sara called the office to check in with her boss. She dialed Jeff's direct number and was surprised when his executive assistant answered.

"Good morning, Mr. Charles' office, may I help you."

"Hi, Candice, it's Sara Ferguson. Is Jeff in?"

"Yes, Sara, he's been waiting for you to call, I'll buzz him."

"Thanks."

Once she had placed the call on hold, the executive assistant pressed the intercom.

"Yes?"

"Sara Ferguson is on two-two-six."

Without even saying thank you, Jeff Charles, co-founder of one of the top advertising groups in New York City, mashed the button with the blinking light. "Sara, what's going on? How's your grandmother?"

"Hello, Jeff, I haven't been there yet today, they sent me home last night."

"How was she last night?"

Sara went through the whole series of events from arriving to find her Nan comatose, to the medication beginning to work, and their brief conversation before she went back to sleep.

"So, she responded to the treatment. That's always a good sign."

"Yes, that's what the nurse said. She said the areas of the brain that were affected by the blood clot would take a while to regenerate. With therapy, she should be able to retrain other parts of her brain to develop any skills she lost."

"Again, that's great news. Now, how are you holding up?"

Sara sighed, "I'm dealing with it. It was bizarre being here, alone, last night. This morning I had to remind myself that Nan wasn't here. There's never been a time when she's not been here."

"You know you didn't have to be alone; you could have stayed with me."

"That's kind of you, Jeff, but I think it's best if we don't start back down that road again."

"Are you sure? You could stay in the guest room, that way you wouldn't be alone. I'd be here with you, and you would have me close by if you wanted to talk."

"Thanks again, Jeff, but I don't think so. Given our history, I think we both know that talking wouldn't be the end of our interaction if I stayed. Besides, you're still married."

"Okay, but Charlotte and I are separated. That's why I'm living on the west side."

"Separated doesn't mean divorced. Sorry, Jeff, I'd rather not. It'd be best for everyone involved." Sara changed hands with the phone as she looked around the room for her iPhone. "Listen, I've got to go now. I'm headed back to the hospital. I just wanted to let you know my situation. I probably won't be in for the rest of the week."

Jeff knew he'd lost the battle, so he gave in to Sara's wishes. "All right, that's not a problem. I'll ensure your accounts are covered. Keep in touch and let me know if you need anything."

"I will."

"If you change your mind, you know where I live. No need to call first."

"Yes, I do. I'll keep that in the back of my mind. Thanks, Jeff. I'll check in again when I know more. Bye."

Sara hung up and thought about her past relationship with her boss. It had started as a fling; both of them were out-of-town visiting a client in Chicago. There were late hours, take out dinners, while they worked shoulder to shoulder on the new ad campaign, the constant revisions using the *Praise and Polish* technique for review. It was a classic workplace romance. After the final pitch had been made, and the client signed the contract came the celebration. The party, the drinks, and the admiring glances across the room that said, "You're great" and "We did it."

Then came the first kiss. Which led to another, which in turn led to their first intimate evening at the Ritz-Carlton. The three-day wrap-up that followed the pitch gave Sara more time to spend alone with Jeff. No one seemed bothered that it took three days to accomplish what was typically completed in four to six hours.

When they got back to New York, things were low key. Working lunches. Late-night meetings. They frequented different hotels to avoid being repeatedly seen in the same ones.

Their romantic trysts never turned into overnight stays. They both had an image to keep, and Jeff had already been through one messy divorce. He wanted to avoid another.

It was Sara who broke it off. Jeff had made overtures about them being together, but that was all it ever was. Although he'd promised, Jeff never followed through to give his full commitment to their relationship. Since he got to enjoy the pleasures of the flesh without the cost of another messy divorce, everything seemed to be working out fine for him.

* * *

SARA STEPPED FROM THE ELEVATOR and saw Winston, the day shift concierge standing by the front doors. Winston was Nan's favorite of the three men who worked the desk. She said it was his military bearing. Sara supposed Nan just liked soldiers; after all, she married two of them.

When he heard the elevator doors open, Winston turned to see who was getting off. The six-foot-tall, retired Marine drill instructor tipped his hat and greeted her. "Good morning, Miss Sara, I'm sorry to hear about your grandmother."

Sara offered a weak smile. I guess by telling Charlie he could tell David about her grandmother, it was implied that he could pass that information on to Winston. There were few secrets here in the building called Highgate.

"Good morning, Winston. Thank you. I'm going up to the hospital now."

"You going all the way up to the Medical Center? My, my, how come Mrs. Cavendish is way up there?"

Ah, thought Sara, the secret is out. "No idea, Winston. The only thing I can think of is that she must have been uptown for some reason when she had the stroke. I'll have to ask her once she can talk better."

"Please tell her we're all asking about her. Would you like me to get you a cab, Miss?"

"Yes, please, and you can be sure I'll tell her you send your best wishes."

"Very well, Miss Sara. I'll be just a minute," said Winston, tipping his hat again, as he headed out the door.

Sara watched Winston as he walked out into the street and flagged down a taxi. As she watched him direct the cab to the curb, she could imagine him in a Marine uniform. His Smokey the Bear, Drill Instructor hat low across his eyes as he shouted commands at his troops.

Once the cab pulled to the curb, Winston waved for Sara to come outside. With another small smile, Sara mumbled, "Yes, Sir, Drill Sergeant, Sir," as she approached the front door, which he held open for her as she exited Highgate. He followed Sara to the cab opening the rear door for her. "Thank you, Winston," she said as he closed the door.

Sara told the driver where she wanted to go, sat back in the seat, and wondered what condition she would find her grandmother in. There had been no calls from the hospital, so Sara assumed things hadn't had a significant change. Maybe Nan had just slept most of the night.

* * *

SARA ARRIVED AT THE MEDICAL CENTER and followed the directions she had received at the front desk to the ICU. Checking in at the nurse's station, Sara found Nan was in room five.

Afraid of what she might find, Sara moved to where she could peek in the door. As she watched her grandmother, she thought some of the droop had disappeared from her face, and she seemed to be awake.

Sara gathered her courage, put on a bright smile, and walked into the room. She walked to the bed and put her hands on the safety rail. "Hi, Nan, how are you feeling?"

The old woman offered a lopsided smile back. Even though it looked like her face had almost returned to normal, she still lacked muscular control on her left side. Without words, Nan struggled to raise her hand. Sara took the old woman's hand and brought it to her lips, and she kissed it before placing it against her cheek. "I love you, Nan. Hurry up and get better."

Nan pulled her hand back as she tried to point at Sara. "Whooo are yoou?" she slurred.

It stunned Sara, and she took a moment to reply. "It's me, Nan, Sara, your granddaughter."

Not happy with the answer she had received, Nan asked again, "Whooo are yoou?"

Fear took over, and Sara answered again. "I'm Sara, Sara Ferguson, your granddaughter. We've lived together for fifteen years, ever since my mother and father died. My mother was Sophia, your daughter."

Rose Cavendish took her granddaughter's hand and touched her fingers to her chest. Looking at the young woman at her bedside, she again tried to express what she needed to ask as she shook her head. "Nooo, inshide, whooo yoou inshide?"

Now Sara was scared and began to cry. "Nan, I'm Sara, inside I'm Sara. Don't you remember me?"

Rose nodded, which confused and frightened Sara even more. "Sharrraaa, yesssh," she struggled to say, which gave Sara hope, but once more she attempted to ask the question Sara hadn't answered to her satisfaction. "Sharrraaa, whooo yoou inshide?"

Tears were streaming down Sara's cheeks as she tried to answer. "Nan, I don't know how to answer your question. Inside I'm Sara. For as long as I can remember, I've always been

Sara." Closing her eyes, she prayed, "God, please make her better." A gurgling sound stopped her prayer.

Sara noticed the facial droop had reappeared, Nan's eyes rolled back in her head, and her tongue lolled out the corner of her mouth. Alarm bells went off in the room. "Nan! Nan!" Sara screamed as the medical team rushed in.

"Miss, you have to leave," said one nurse, pushing her out the door.

Sara tried to protest, "No! She's…"

"It's not an option, Miss. Leave! Now!"

Sara left the room. She moved to the end of the hall so she could watch the activity and see who was coming and going. One of the nursing assistants told her to leave the ICU and go to the waiting room. She accepted and left.

Sara took a seat in the corner of the couches. She closed her eyes and said a silent prayer asking God to spare her grandmother. It was a selfish one, asking for Nan to be made whole again because she was all Sara had. But that was all she had to offer.

Chapter 4

A tall man in green scrubs came into the waiting room and walked over to where Sara was sitting with her head resting on her pulled up knees. "Miss Ferguson?" he asked in a soft voice.

Sara opened her eyes and saw a doctor squatting next to her. She took a breath before answering, "Yes."

"Miss Ferguson, I'm Dr. Randell. I'm sorry to say your grandmother has passed away."

Sara didn't respond. She sat motionless; her eyes glazed over as if in a trance.

The doctor stood and took a seat next to her. "Miss Ferguson, your grandmother suffered another stroke. Unlike the first one that brought her in, this was a hemorrhagic stroke. It appears she had an aneurysm burst in her basilar artery."

Without looking at the doctor, Sara said, "She's gone." The doctor understood it not to be a question. "Did she suffer?"

"No, I'm sure she didn't," Dr. Randell offered. "She was unconscious when I arrived, and she never came to. It all happened in a matter of minutes."

"That's good, I wouldn't want her to have suffered. Can I see her?"

The doctor nodded, "Yes, if you wish. Just give us a few minutes to remove all the medical equipment. A nurse will come and get you."

Sara tugged on his scrubs. Her voice sounded robotic as she asked. "Can you take me?"

"If that's what you want. I'll come get you when we're done."

"Thank you," she said, in that same flat, emotionless monotone, as she looked at his face for the first time. "Dr. Randell, why did she die?"

In the seven years George Randell had been a neurosurgeon, he'd forgotten how many families he had informed that a loved one had passed away. As the notifying physician, he'd learned through many mistakes how to interpret the questions of a grieving family member. George Randell, M.D., discovered the answers they sought were often philosophical and not medical in nature.

"Everyone has a time to die. Tonight was your grandmother's time. She was allowed to see you and talk to you one last time."

Sara listened to the words of the man she had met only minutes before. Looking back toward the doctor, Sara said, "Yes, I did get to talk to her, but I don't understand what she was trying to say. What did Nan mean when she asked me who I am inside?"

"Sorry, I can't answer that for you, but you did get to talk to her, and she knew you were by her side. The fact you were with her when her time came is something to be thankful for."

Sara released her hold on the doctor, pulled her knees to her chest, and wrapped her arms around them, pulling herself into a ball.

"I'll go check on how they are progressing with getting your grandmother prepared. I'll be back as soon as everything is done."

Sara nodded, her face buried against her thighs.

Ten minutes passed before Dr. Randell returned to find Sara in the same position she had been in when he left. "Miss Ferguson, we're ready."

Sara uncurled herself, stood, and looked at the doctor. Nodding she was ready, she was led back to room five. The door was shut, and the privacy curtains had been drawn closed.

She stopped at the door. Dr. Randell noticed her strength seemed to have ebbed, and she began to swoon. The doctor placed his arm around her waist to support her weight. "You don't have to go in there if you don't want to."

Sara shook her head, "No, I have to do this. I need to see her."

"Would you like me to stay with you?"

"Yes, please, I feel like I'm going to faint, but I have to do this."

Dr. Randell slid the door open and pushed the curtain aside so they could enter. The lights had been lowered, and all the machines turned off. The doctor helped Sara closer to the bed. Not wanting to rush, he realized she was determined to go all the way to her grandmother's bedside. The safety rails had been lowered, and Rose Cavendish lay in quiet repose, eyes closed.

"I love you, Nan," she said as she reached out and took her grandmother's hand. "I love you, and I'm going to miss you. You've been there for me for more than half my life. Thank you for everything you've done for me."

Sara smoothed a section of her grandmother's hair. Turning to the doctor, Sara said, "She wasn't a vain woman, but she never went out without making sure her hair was perfect."

Randell nodded and remained silent.

"Okay, we can go now. I've seen her and I know she's at peace."

Dr. Randell led her out of the room and to the nurse's station. "You'll have arrangements to make. If we can help in any way, just let us know. We'll keep your grandmother here until you can have her moved. If you can wait a bit longer, we'll see to it that you are given your grandmother's belongings."

"I can do that. I don't think there's anything else I can do at the moment."

* * *

SARA DIDN'T HAVE ANY IDEA what to do or who to call to have Nan taken care of. Then she remembered Nan telling her if anything ever happened, Sara would need to call Mr. McDougal, Nan's lawyer.

Sara wasn't ready to go home after receiving her grandmother's belongings, so she went to the hospital cafeteria and got a cup of tea. After taking Nan's cell phone from the old woman's purse, she hit the button to turn it on and entered Nan's passcode, which she assumed was 1945. Whenever she had to use a four-number pin, that was what she chose. Nan said she would always remember the year she immigrated to America.

The phone sprang to life and Sara opened Nan's phonebook. "I wonder if Mr. McDougal's number is in her phone?" After pressing the "M," she scrolled through the names. Mary McDonald O'Riley, Nancy Madison, Mickey's Market, Fran Muller. "Not here," she said, "maybe under 'L' for a lawyer." Once again she pushed the appropriate letter and scrolled through the names. Martin Lamb, Claire Larson, Betty Linkowski. "Hmm, not there either," she mumbled.

After thinking about the situation for a few minutes, Sara just decided Nan would have the lawyer's number in her telephone book back at the apartment. Since she decided to leave that task until later, she scrolled through the names one by one.

When she came across the "I's," she saw a group of listings starting with ICE. "Ah, Nan had In Case of Emergency numbers listed. Let's see what's here." The first one was ICE1-

Sara; the second was ICE2-McD. "McD? McDougal? That has to be the lawyer," she said as she pushed the button to dial the number.

The polished voice of a career receptionist answered, "Good afternoon, The Law Offices of McDougal, McDougal, and Slone. May I help you?"

"Good afternoon. My name is Sara Ferguson, would it be possible to speak to Mr. McDougal?"

"I'm sorry, to which Mr. McDougal are you referring? Michael or Joseph?"

"I'm not sure, Mr. McDougal is my grandmother's lawyer, and she told me in the event of an emergency he was to be contacted."

"Thank you, may I please have your grandmother's name."

"Cavendish, Mrs. Rose Cavendish."

"Thank you. You said your name was Ferguson. Is that correct?"

"Yes, Sara Ferguson."

"Thank you, Ms. Ferguson. Please hold."

Sara held the phone to her ear and waited. Mindlessly stirring her tea, she wasn't aware of how long she had been on hold.

The line clicked as someone established the connection. "Ms. Ferguson, this is Michael McDougal, how may I help you?

"Mr. McDougal, my grandmother left instruction to contact you in an emergency."

"Yes. What's happened?

"She passed away about an hour ago."

The line went quiet, and Sara wondered if she had lost the connection. "Mr. McDougal, are you there?"

The lawyer didn't answer for a moment, then Sara heard him exhale.

"Yes, I'm here. I am sorry, Ms. Ferguson, where did this happen?"

Sara remained disconnected from the events and spoke in the same robotic tone she'd used with Dr. Randell. "They brought her to Columbia Presbyterian Medical Center yesterday. She'd had a stroke. They treated her, and it looked like she was responding to the treatment, then she had a second stroke today, which killed her."

"Ms. Ferguson, are you at the hospital now?"

"Yes, I'm in the coffee shop. I called because I'm not sure what to do next. I know arrangements have to be made."

"Yes, don't worry about that at the moment. Please stay where you are. I'll be there in thirty to forty minutes. How will I recognize you?"

"I'm wearing a pale blue blazer and matching skirt. I'm in the back corner opposite the cashiers, I'll wait for you here."

"Thank you. I'm on my way. Again, please don't worry about anything."

Chapter 5

While she waited for Mr. McDougal to arrive, Sara got another pot of tea and an order of dry toast. Food was the furthest thing from her mind, but she knew she needed to eat something. Lost in thought about everything that happened in the past two days, she didn't notice the man who walked up to her table.

"Ms. Ferguson, you're still here?"

Sara looked up and saw the neurosurgeon's friendly face. "Dr. Randell, what are you doing here?" she said, a note of surprise in her voice.

The doctor realized her mind was elsewhere. He smiled, looked around, then pointed to his hospital badge. "I work here. I noticed you sitting here. It's obvious your mind is a thousand miles away. Are you all right?"

"Yes, I'm doing okay. I was thinking about my grandmother. I'm waiting for her lawyer to get here. Nan had Mr. McDougal's number in her ICE list." She said, pointing to the phone on the table.

"That's good. Now you have someone who can help with everything that needs to be taken care of."

"Yes, I do. Excuse me for being rude, doctor, would you care to sit down?"

"Sure, but only for a minute. I have to get back upstairs. I stole a few minutes to get a large black coffee." Raising the cup to eye level, he added, "The life's blood of the hospital's medical staff."

"I don't mind coffee, but I can't drink it black."

"Neither did I until medical school. After the first semester, I only drank dark roast, black. Guess I needed the higher-octane rating to keep me going."

"Well, it looks like it paid off. You graduated."

"I did. I wish I could stay longer, but I have to get back."

"Thanks for stopping and saying hello, Dr. Randell."

The doctor raised his coffee cup in a salute and walked away. "Take care of yourself, Ms. Ferguson."

"Thank you, doctor, you too."

* * *

MICHAEL F. MCDOUGAL, ESQ. ARRIVED closer to the forty-minute mark. Sara noticed him as he entered the coffee shop and scanned the area looking for her. He must have been in his early seventies. A full head of silver hair still had traces of black streaked through it, a remnant of younger days. His gray eyes matched the color of his single-breasted, two-button suit. He was carrying a black topcoat over one arm and a briefcase in the opposite hand. The lawyer walked straight to Sara's table, "Excuse me, are you, Sara Ferguson?"

Sara nodded, "Yes, I am."

"Good afternoon, Ms. Ferguson, I'm Michael McDougal. May I sit?"

"Yes. I'm glad I could contact you. Nan always said you were the person to call in an emergency. I wasn't sure where to get your number, but Nan had it on her phone."

Once he'd taken his seat opposite her, the lawyer put his briefcase up on the end of the table. "Ms. Ferguson, first off, please allow me to express my condolences for your loss. I've known Mrs. Cavendish for over forty-five years, and I've been her lawyer for the past forty."

"Thank you. I had no idea Nan had a lawyer all these years."

Mr. McDougal smiled, "That's a story for another time, Ms. Ferguson. But for now, I've brought some papers to go over with you. Your grandmother wanted to ensure if anything happened to her, everything would be seen to. By that, I mean someone would take care of all the arrangements that needed to be completed."

The lawyer took out two folders and placed them on the table. "Mrs. Cavendish told me years ago that she had determined life was a contract only issued daily. Since you were thirteen when your parents passed away, she wanted to protect you and ensure wouldn't be troubled by having to figure out what to do."

McDougal opened the first folder and removed a two-page document. "To ensure this was the case, your grandmother signed a durable power of attorney, which gave me the power to manage her finances and health care during the years you were a minor. The document remained in effect even after you gained your majority. If for any reason you were unable or unwilling to do so the document protected all parties involved. Now that she has passed away, this document is no longer valid."

After he replaced the document back in the folder, he passed it across to Sara, who asked, "Nan, was a pretty smart woman, wasn't she?"

"Yes, she was, she learned quite a lot from the school of life. And after what happened to her in her lifetime and finally losing her only daughter, she saw the effect it had on you at that young age. After that, everything she did was to protect you in every way possible."

McDougal lifted the other folder as he prepared to impart on the rest of the required information to his new client.

"Before I go any further, please allow me to ask, may I call you Sara?"

"Yes, of course, you may. Even though we've just met, it's clear you know a lot about me."

"I do, your grandmother adored you. When we would meet, she was always telling me about you and what accomplishment you'd achieved since our last meeting."

"I had no idea."

"You can be assured that's true. Now, back to what I was saying. If you notice, this folder is sealed. This is your grandmother's Last Will and Testament. In it, she names me as the executor of her estate. Do you understand what that means?"

"Yes, I think so. It means you take care of settling all her affairs and I guess that means including making the arrangements for her funeral."

"Correct, however, regarding her funeral. Since you are now an adult, if you're willing to do so, I would like your input on the arrangements."

"I'd like to do that. After everything she's done for me; I want her to know how much I loved her."

"Thank you, Sara; I'm sure your grandmother would appreciate knowing you helped with the details. Someone from the office will contact you in a day or two to discuss what needs to be done. We have your home number on file. May I also have your cell phone number?"

"Certainly," Sara replied as she recited the number.

McDougal copied the number onto the legal pad in his briefcase. "Now, back to the will. I have to file it with the probate court to go through all the legal loopholes. Once that's done, you'll be notified when the reading will be conducted.

"There is only one final bit of business to discuss, and it's quite simple. As of now, my law firm represents you. Your grandmother insisted on that final piece. She wanted to be sure you had legal representation should the need arise."

"Mr. McDougal, that's very kind. However, there are two things I'd like to say. One, I'm not sure why I'd need a legal firm on retainer, and two, I'm pretty sure I can't afford you."

The silver-haired attorney smiled, showing a perfect set of white teeth. "Sara, I told you, your grandmother wanted to protect you. This was the last thing she could do to achieve that goal while she was alive. As for the cost, the estate will cover that. Again, please allow me to assure you there's nothing to worry about. Everything will be taken care of."

"Okay Mr. McDougal, if Nan trusted you with her legal affairs for over forty years, I'm sure I can, too."

McDougal slipped the sealed folder back into his briefcase, closed the lid, and snapped the latches shut as he stood. "Sara, I'm sorry we had to be introduced this way. However, it was nice to finally meet the granddaughter Rose Cavendish spoke so highly of. I'll be in touch as needed. Someone from the office will call about coordinating the funeral arrangements."

"Thank you, Mr. McDougal."

The attorney gathered his coat and briefcase. "Sara, can I drop you off at home on my way back to the office?"

"No, thanks. I think I want to sit here a bit longer before I leave. There's no one to go home to. It was lonely in the apartment this morning."

"I understand. I'll leave you then. Before I go, let me give you my card. I've written my private number on the back. If you need anything, don't hesitate to call me."

"Thanks, I'll put your numbers into my phone."

"Well then, now I'll say goodbye, Sara. I'll see you soon."

"Goodbye, Mr. McDougal."

After the lawyer had gone, Sara went through the cafeteria line once more and bought another pot of tea. As she poured another cup, she thought about the last part of her conversation with Mr. McDougal. I've got a lawyer. Why would I need a lawyer? I don't know, maybe there's something I don't know about that will require legal help. I guess I'll find out when the will is read. And he said the estate would cover the legal fees. Sounds like Nan had more in the cookie jar then she let on. But hey, after coming to America with not much else but the clothes on her back, and the unborn baby in her belly, who am I to judge. Good for her.

The hours passed as Sara sat there, thinking about everything she could remember about her grandmother. Her smile, her laugh, and most of all, her determination that everything would turn out well.

When she looked at her watch, Sara realized it was now 8:00 p.m., where had the time gone. I might as well face the inevitable she thought, it was time to leave. Sara took the folder McDougal had given her and placed it in her purse. It felt as if she had to force herself to stand so she could put her coat on. After she got it buttoned, she placed her phone in her pocket, grabbed her bag, and left.

As she exited the hospital, the cold air felt good on her face. As she looked around for a cab, Sara once again thought about going home. "No reason to rush," she said to herself. "No one there, not even a cat to check on." Sara pushed her hands deep into the pockets of her coat as she began walking in the direction of home. As she had done last night, her mind once again ran through things that still made no sense. The most puzzling was what Nan had been doing uptown. It doesn't matter, she thought. Nan was close to a good hospital, she was brought here, and they helped her. It was just her time like Dr. Randell said.

After walking ten blocks, Sara was getting tired. It had been a mentally tiring day for her. Now her body was feeling the effects of that mental exhaustion. She stepped off the curb and tried to flag down a cab. The third one she hailed stopped to pick her up.

Sara tossed her bag onto the seat as the burly driver turned to address her through the Plexiglas partition. "Where to, lady?" he asked, his Brooklyn accent evident in every syllable.

"The Highgate on Ninety-fourth and Park Ave."

"You got it."

As the cab made its way down Broadway, Sara mindlessly looked out the windows. Everything was a jumble, no reason for the placement of the buildings. The storefronts mixed into new and old architecture, a mishmash of stone, steel, glass, and neon. Sara had no place to go and was in no hurry to get there. Thinking about her situation, she had a change of heart. She knocked on the Plexiglas. "I've changed my mind. Take me to Seventy-second and Central Park West instead."

"What address?"

"I'm not sure, but I know the building. I'll show you when we get there."

The driver let out a sigh as he looked into the rearview mirror. "Okay," he said, repeating the location.

Chapter 6

Sara directed the driver to a building in the middle of the block. After paying the cabbie, she got out and looked up at the tall structure. *Go on*, said the little voice in her head. *You know you don't want to go home and be alone. You're going to have enough nights of that.*

Sara entered the brightly lit lobby and walked up to the concierge desk in the center of the marble and polished brass entrance.

"May I help you?" asked the uniformed attendant.

"Yes, please ring Mr. Jeff Charles. Let him know Sara Ferguson is here."

"Is he expecting you?"

"No, he isn't, but I'm sure he'll see me."

"Yes, ma'am. Just a second, please," The concierge retrieved Jeff Charles' name from the computer and dialed the phone number, his eyes roaming over every inch of Sara as he waited for an answer. "Good evening Mr. Charles, this is Phillip at the front desk. Sorry to bother you sir, but there's a Sara Ferguson here to see you."

Sara removed her coat and turned her back to the desk. The mirrored wall allowed her to see what was happening behind her . Sara noted the attendant continued checking her out as if she would be on the menu.

"Yes, Mr. Charles. I'll tell her. Goodnight sir," he said and hung up the phone.

Sara turned, giving the older man a sly smile as if to say I saw you checking out my butt.

The concierge smiled sheepishly. "Mr. Charles said to send you up. Apartment 1202."

"Thanks," said Sara as she walked off toward the elevators, exaggerating the sway of her hips for the benefit of the nighttime attendant.

***

JEFF ANSWERED THE DOOR wearing tan slacks and a cream-colored polo shirt, he gave Sara an inviting smile as she walked past him into the apartment.

"Let me take your coat," he said as she passed. Sara willingly handed it over as she looked around the apartment for the first time.

Sara made her way over to the couch and collapsed into the seat. She looked up at the man who was both her boss and ex-lover. "This is a nice place."

"Thanks. Can I get you a drink?

"A dirty martini?"

"One dirty martini coming up." Jeff went to the bar, grabbed a bottle of Stoli, and began to prepare the drink. "After our conversation this morning, I'm surprised to see you."

"Well…" Sara took a deep breath, pressing her hands into her knees as she looked around. "I'm surprised to be here. I was on my way home, but I changed my mind and told the cab driver to bring me here."

Sara watched Jeff's face brighten as she told him she'd made a conscious decision to be here.

He came from behind the bar with Sara's drink in his hand, "I can understand that. I guess there's no one waiting at home and you didn't want to be alone. I'm glad you came."

Sara took the drink from his hand, put it to her lips, and swallowed half. A grimace replaced her calm expression. "Yes, I didn't want to go home and be alone. There will be enough of that from now on. I didn't want tonight to be the first."

Jeff looked perplexed. "Sara, what do you mean from now on? What's happened?"

"My Nan's gone." Tears began to roll down her cheeks. "She passed away this morning not long after I got there. She had another stroke. The doctor said it was quick, and she didn't suffer."

Jeff put an arm around her, "Why didn't you call me? I would have come to the hospital to be with you."

Sara shrugged. "I don't know. I didn't want to be around people, so I just sat in the cafeteria drinking tea for most of the day. Besides, I had to figure out what I needed to do. They told me I needed to make arrangements."

Jeff tried to hug her, but Sara resisted. "Sure, the funeral arrangements. Don't worry about that. I can help you sort all that out."

Sara turned in her seat, reached out to touch her ex-lover's face. "Thanks, Jeff, that's sweet of you to offer. But my lawyer is taking care of everything for me."

"Your lawyer?" He laughed. "Since when do you have a lawyer?"

"Since about four o'clock. Mr. McDougal was Nan's lawyer, and she arranged for him to be my lawyer now that she's gone."

"McDougal?" asked Jeff. "Do you know his first name?"

"It's Michael."

Jeff tilted his head and had a curious look as he asked. "Michael McDougal, of McDougal, McDougal, and Slone?"

"Yes, that's him. He came to meet me at the hospital after I found his number in Nan's phone. Do you know him?"

Jeff shook his head. "Not personally, but definitely by reputation. I've dealt with some of his underlings, about five years ago, when we had some contractual issues."

"Were they any good? Have I got a good lawyer?"

Jeff smiled and nodded, "Oh yeah, they were good all right. The group who came to the meetings from McDougal's firm weren't even partners, they were his second string. They ate my legal team for lunch. We lost the negotiations and wound up giving the client everything they wanted."

Sara smiled at the thought of her boss being bested by her lawyer's second string. "Well, I guess that's a good thing. By having him and his firm as my lawyers, that is. Although I have no idea why my Nan felt it was important for me to have a legal team on retainer."

"Neither do I, but how are you going to pay these guys? They don't come cheap, and I'm pretty sure they don't do *pro bono* work."

"That's another mystery. Mr. McDougal said Nan's estate would take care of the cost. I'm guessing she was better off than I knew. She always told me Grandpa Bill had made some profitable investments back in the fifties. Maybe there's one or two more I don't know about."

Jeff moved closer to Sara on the couch and tried to pull her closer, once again, she refused.

"Jeff, please, I didn't come here for sex. I came because you were kind enough to offer me a place to stay, so I wouldn't be alone. Now if you can honor that offer, I'll stay. If not, please have your concierge call a cab to take me home."

Jeff removed his arm from her shoulder, raising his hands in a sign of surrender. "Okay, I get the picture. I'm sorry I tried to make a move on you just now. Yes, I can honor the offer of you staying in the guest room." Rising from his seat, he moved to the couch on the other side of the coffee table.

"What can you, or should I say, what are you willing to share about this conversation with your lawyer?"

Sara finished her drink and wiggled the glass, showing Jeff it was empty and hinting she wanted another. "Not much, he explained that Nan had some kind of Power of Attorney that would have let him take care of everything for her if it needed to be done while I was little. And that she had a will, which needs to go to the probate court."

Jeff was behind the bar making a second dirty martini for Sara, "I guess that's standard stuff. You've told me you were only thirteen when you went to stay with her. It's obvious she didn't want you put on the street if anything happened to her." He said as he continued stirring her martini, "As for the will, that's just normal practice."

"That's what he said. And we also talked about the funeral. He asked me if I wanted to help make the arrangements. I said I would like that, and Mr. McDougal said someone from the firm would get in touch with me."

Jeff handed Sara her drink. "Listen, I know this has been a rough couple of days for you. Please don't worry about coming back to work until you're ready. There are things you will need to do that will require time. After the funeral, we can talk about you returning."

"Thank you, Jeff. That's very kind. Now if you don't mind, will you point me to the guest room, I think I want to lie down for a while."

"Certainly," he said, rising from his seat and offering Sara his hand to help her up. "Right this way. He led her down a short hallway and opened the door at the end. Turning on the light, he allowed Sara to enter. "You can stay here. There's a bathroom en suite," he added, pointing to another door. Everything you need should be there." Turning to leave, he pointed to the other end of the hallway. "That's my room if you need anything. If you decide you're hungry, the kitchen is through the dining room. Please make yourself at home. Try to get some rest. I'll see you in the morning."

Sara gave him a kiss on the cheek before he left. "Thanks again, Jeff."

"Sure, no problem," he said with a smile.

Sara closed the door as Jeff left. As he walked down the hall, he heard the click of the lock being set on the guest room door.

Chapter 7

Exhaustion caused Sara to enter a state of REM sleep. Dreams flooded from her subconscious as she saw doctors, lawyers, hospital staff, Jeff, and other people from her office: everyone moving about in a live-action play that made no sense. Everyone was in the wrong place, their roles all jumbled.

Jeff was behind the nurse's desk. Mr. McDougal had shown her to the guest room. It was Dr. Randell who answered the phone at the agency this morning when she'd called Jeff to tell her Nan was in the hospital. But when she told him why she was calling, he laughed and said, "No, she's not. She's in the morgue!"

Sara woke with a start. She sat up, cuddling herself as a chill passed through her. Perspiration flowed from every pore as she cried. The realization that Nan was in the morgue played on her mind. She tried to rationalize that this was where the bodies of the deceased were kept until someone claimed them. It didn't help.

As she slipped out from under the covers, Sara's felt the plush carpet under her feet. The plush robe on the end of the bed offered a warm comfort as she donned it and went into the adjoining bathroom. Tired eyes looked back at Sara as she realized last night's fitful sleep had not helped her regain her usual level of energy.

Hunger pangs reminded Sara she'd not eaten much of anything in almost two days. Sara unlocked the bedroom door and made her way through the apartment looking for the kitchen. She found it by following the smell of fresh-brewed coffee, expecting to find Jeff waiting for her. It surprised her he wasn't home. The coffee had just finished brewing when she walked in, so Sara assumed he'd just left. Next, to the coffeemaker, she found a note.

> Sara,
>
> Sorry, I had to leave. I have international calls to make, and my notes and proposals are in the office.
>
> I tried to wait for you to get up so I could see how you are doing this morning.
>
> Make yourself at home; the fridge is stocked so please help yourself. I'll call the apartment later today to see if you're still there.
>
> I don't know what you would like to do, but if you want to stay here for a while, you'll find a keycard and a door key on the hall table. I've told the concierge I may have a friend staying so no issues there and like I said you've got a key.
>
> Jeff

Sara considered Jeff's offer. It was a kind gesture, but could it remain platonic? Would she feel a physical need for someone? Would Jeff press the issue now that he claimed he was separated with no hope of reconciliation with Charlotte?

People have done stranger things in the name of money. And Jeff had already lost millions in a previous divorce.

Sara knew she couldn't make this a long-term arrangement but decided to stay one more night. Just until she got the call from Mr. McDougal's office about helping with Nan's funeral details. After she poured a cup of coffee, Sara opened the fridge to get some milk and scan the shelves to see what was available.

Sara opened the drawers in the fridge and discovered Jeff had a large assortment of things from the local deli. She decided the lox with cream cheese, tomato, lettuce, and onion would be nice on a bagel. As she looked around the kitchen, she found a bag of fresh onion and garlic bagels next to the coffeemaker.

Once Sara assembled the sandwich, she took it to the dining room table along with her coffee. Feeling ravenous, she devoured the food and thought about making another one. "No, that's enough for now. I'll eat again later. I've got things to do." Since she was staying another night, that meant she'd have to go back to the apartment and get clean clothes and her personal items.

After she dressed, Sara took the key card and apartment key from the hall table and placed them in her bag. She rode the elevator down to the lobby, exited past the morning concierge and walked out onto the street. It was a beautiful day, sunny, and a gentle breeze was blowing, so she walked for a while. Sara turned into an entrance to Central Park. Sara walked when she needed to think. It was one more thing she had picked up from her Nan. The old woman often went on long walks to clear her mind. She said being out in the open helped her think things through. When Sara was younger, she always found it was funny that Nan said she needed to be outside where it was noisy to think better

Sara had always preferred the quiet when she had something to ponder. She couldn't study with the radio or TV on like other people did. She never knew why she changed to being a person who needed noise, it just happened. Perhaps it had to do with getting older and having more things on her mind. It happened to her when she was in college. She found her mind wandering onto different subjects when she would sit in the library trying to study. As she tried to study for the marketing exam, she would think about the statistics course.

Everything became jumbled in her head, and that's when her grandmother suggested she try to find a place to study that wasn't quiet, but rather a noisy environment. Sara was a skeptic and split the difference. She found a semi-quiet place to study, the coffee house on campus. Conversations between the patrons were hushed as the barista called out the orders. Much to her surprise, the noise helped her focus. The next day she tried the student commons. More noise made it easier to focus. Sara concluded that since there was so much rattling around in her head, her subconscious had to work on filtering out the noise. Allowing her to suppress all the other things that were going on. From that day on, she always went to noisy places when she needed to think.

Today, the one thing she needed to think about was Nan's funeral. Her first thought was which dress Nan would be buried in. Maybe something long, like the robin's egg blue one she'd worn to the last formal occasion given by Jeff's agency. Or perhaps the wine-colored dress she had gotten at Christmas. Sara decided she would go through Nan's wardrobe later today. She would need to make a list of everything she would have to give away. Sara continued to walk as she thought about what Nan would like. What kind of flowers should there be? Maybe hydrangeas, those were one of Nan's favorites. Who would show up at the funeral? Nan had a few friends, but she wasn't an A-lister on the society circuit. The best Sara could figure it would be a small affair. Maybe just her few friends, and of course Mr. McDougal would be there. As she finished thinking through all those items, she emerged from the park and hailed a cab for the rest of the trip.

Chapter 8

The taxi let Sara out in front of her building where Winston was again on duty. He opened the door as he saw Sara approach. "Good Morning, Miss Sara, how are you this fine morning? How's Mrs. Cavendish coming along?"

Sara's face told him things were not well. She looked at the taller man and gently shook her head. "Nan died yesterday. She had another stroke while I was there. She never regained consciousness."

"Oh, Miss Sara, I'm so sorry to hear that. We'll miss your grandmother. We all liked her."

Sara offered a weak smile, "Thank you, I appreciate that."

Winston lead her to the elevator and pushed the call button. "If there's anything we can do for you, please let us know. Would it be all right if I told the others?"

"Yes, please do. I'm sure they would like to know."

As the elevator chimed and doors opened, Winston offered a final smile. "Thank you, Miss."

Sara pushed the button for the fourteenth floor, and the doors closed. As the elevator carried her to her destination, Sara removed her key from her purse, as she prepared herself to enter what she could no longer think of as *their* apartment. But in her mind, it would always be theirs. As she applied the key to the lock and walked in, Sara thought about things she didn't want to even consider. Disposing of all Nan's clothes. What about her bedroom furniture? What should she do with that?

And what about the apartment? It was a large unit with three bedrooms, three and a half baths. What would she do with all that space? Should she stay here? Could she even afford to live here? Sara realized she had no idea how much the rent was because she'd never been asked to contribute to their expenses. Nan had always covered everything, and Sara had been free to keep every penny she earned.

Sara placed her coat in the hall closet, then walked into the kitchen and turned on the electric kettle to make tea. As the water boiled, Sara prepared the teapot by tossing four Twinings English Breakfast tea bags in. "Nan loved her tea," she said to herself. Sara remembered not long after she had come to live with her grandmother, Nan sent her to the store to buy tea. Since her mother had not been a tea drinker, Sara understood nothing about tea, and her Nan hadn't given her any specific brand. Once she looked at the choices, Sara got a box of Red Rose Tea. After all, she knew Nan's name was Rose, and she thought she'd like that.

Proudly showing her choice to Nan, Sara could tell she wasn't fond of her granddaughter's selection. However, she put on a brave face and brewed the tea. The next time Sara returned to the store, Nan gave her a specific brand name for what she wanted. She had also told Sara if she couldn't find it to ask the clerk because she knew the store stocked it regularly. From that day on it has always been Twinings, unless it was unavailable.

After she poured the boiling water into the teapot, she replaced the lid and covered it with a tea cozy to help keep it hot while it steeped. She carried the tray containing the pot and her cup into the living room and set it down on the coffee table. After filling her cup, she sat back on the couch and looked around the apartment. Since she was Nan's only living relative, Sara thought everything in here would become hers, yet none of it felt like it was hers.

After her parents died, Nan brought Sara's bedroom furniture to the apartment. She hoped that having something familiar in her room would ease Sara's transition. Having her own room with her own furniture gave Sara a safe surrounding where she could retreat to if she felt the need to be alone. As expected, during those first months, there were times Sara went there to cry as she tried to figure out why her parents had died.

When Sara turned sixteen, Nan had taken her furniture shopping for adult furniture. She allowed Sara to choose what she wanted, which was a set of contemporary design with a queen-size bed. That was the only thing in the apartment that Sara considered hers.

Sara rose from the couch, took her cup, and walked into her grandmother's room. She walked over to the dressing table and took a seat. The bedroom was the largest of the three, furnished with pieces Nan said were Regency Period. "What am I going to do with all this furniture? Maybe if I leave the apartment for a smaller place, I can sell it to the new tenants." As she continued wondering what to do, she heard her cell phone ring.

Sara returned to the living room to retrieve her phone from the table where she'd left it. The number on the caller ID wasn't familiar to her, so Sara didn't know who was calling. "Hello."

A woman's voice asked, "Is this Ms. Sara Ferguson?"

"Yes, it is."

"Good morning, Ms. Ferguson. My name is Janet Collins. I'm from Mr. McDougal's office; he asked me to contact you about assisting with the arrangements for your grandmother, Mrs. Cavendish."

"Yes, Ms. Collins, I've been expecting your call."

"Ms. Ferguson, would it be convenient to meet today to discuss what you had in mind for your grandmother's service?"

"Yes, I'd like to ensure everything is covered and I think beginning right away would be a good thing."

"I agree. Would you like to meet at your apartment, or would you prefer another location?"

"The apartment will be fine, Ms. Collins, in fact, I'm here now, so whenever you're available, I'm free to meet."

"I'm available now, helping you take care of the arrangements is my primary focus. Again, if it would be convenient, I can be there in an hour."

"Okay, I'll expect you then. Thank you, Ms. Collins," said Sara as she broke the connection. "That was fast," said Sara as she looked at the now silent phone. "Mr. McDougal said someone would call, and she said this was her primary job at the moment." Sara pondered that thought for a moment. "Hmm, maybe having a lawyer isn't such a bad thing."

* * *

THE HOUSE PHONE RANG, and Sara answered it.

"Miss Sara, there's a Mrs. Janet Collins here at the desk; she says you're expecting her."

"Thank you, Winston. Yes, I am, please send her up." Sara noted Winston had said, "Mrs. Collins."

"Yes, Ma'am, I will, thank you."

A knock on the door a few minutes later alerted Sara that her visitor had arrived. When Sara answered the door, she got her first glimpse of Janet Collins. Sara judged the woman to be in her mid-forties. She wore her blond hair in a shoulder-length style that complemented the shape of her face and brought focus to her blue eyes. It also gave her a very professional look. The skirt of the blue pinstriped suit she wore was cut knee-length, and Sara was sure she didn't buy it off the rack. She carried her coat over her left arm and a slim leather portfolio in her left hand.

"Ms. Ferguson, I'm Janet Collins," said the woman, offering her hand.

"Nice to meet you, Mrs. Collins," said Sara shaking the offered hand. "Please come in."

"Thank you. Ms. Ferguson, since we will be spending a lot of time together over the next few days, please call me Janet," she said with a smile.

"And you can drop the Ms. Ferguson, too, and call me Sara."

"Wonderful. Shall we begin?"

"Yes. But before we start, would you like a coffee or tea?"

"Thank you, tea would be nice," replied Janet placing her coat and portfolio on the couch.

"Just give me a minute, and I'll get a pot started. How do you take your tea?"

"With lemon, if you have it, if not, just milk."

Sara smiled. "We have lemon. Nan can't live without her lemon tea in the afternoon." Suddenly as she realized she had just said *we* and *Nan can't,* Sara stopped what she was doing.

Janet had heard Sara's words and noticed the change in the young woman's mood. "Here, let me give you a hand with the tea, and then we can talk about what you would like to see for your grandmother's service."

Sara showed Janet where the cups were while she got the teapot ready and put water in the kettle. Sara took a lemon from the fridge, cut it and placed the slices on a plate. Once the tea was ready, Janet carried the tray into the dining room and set it on the table. As they took their seats, Janet reached to turn the handle towards her, "Allow me," she said, removing the tea cozy from the china pot.

There was something soothing about a cup of tea. Sara relaxed as she drank.

Sensing Sara had recovered from her distress, Janet got up and went to retrieve her portfolio from where she had left it earlier. Mrs. Collins returned to the table, moved her cup to the side, and placed the black leather folio in front of her and undid the zipper. "Sara, please let me begin by asking you, do you know where your grandmother wanted to be buried?"

Sara shook her head, once again she began to get upset as she realized she didn't have a clue about any of Nan's wishes for when she passed away.

"That's okay, don't worry. I gather Mrs. Cavendish never had that conversation with you in the past."

"No, we never did. Before Nan had her stroke, she'd never been in the hospital in the fifteen years we lived together. I never thought about the possibility of anything happening to her."

"Don't worry about it. That's why I'm here. Mrs. Cavendish made her wishes known many years ago when you were younger, and Mr. Mc Dougal created the durable power of attorney for her."

"So you know where she wants to be buried?"

"Yes, it was your grandmother's wish she be laid to rest with her late husband, Capt. William Cavendish at the Cypress Hill National Cemetery in Brooklyn."

"That would be nice. Nan didn't have much time with Grandpa Bill in this life. The thought of them being together for eternity sounds like something she would like."

Janet nodded as she removed a folder from her folio and handed Sara a yellow legal-size envelope. "This is the deed to the cemetery plot. We'll need this to have the gravesite opened so your grandmother can be interred there. I'll ensure it's given to the funeral home. That way, they can handle all the arrangements for the actual burial."

Sara and Janet spent the next hour going over other items that needed to be discussed. Much of it was what Sara had thought about earlier. What dress, what kind of flowers, did she want a priest and church service?

"Your grandmother wanted Jacobs Funeral Home to conduct the funeral. We've contacted them, and they have already picked your grandmother up. If you're up to it, we can go pick out the casket when we've finished here, or we can do it tomorrow." Janet Collins closed her folio and looked at the young woman who seemed overwhelmed by the number of details that had to be seen to. "Or if you'd prefer not to deal with that, I can take care of for you."

"No, I don't want to delegate that decision, I'd like to choose the casket. We can go there once we've finished here. I have nothing else to attend to today."

Sara cleaned off the dining room table and brought the teacups, teapot, and plates into the kitchen. After emptying all the liquid out, she placed them in the sink to be washed. When she returned to the dining room, she looked around checking to see if there was anything else she needed to do before she went with Janet to select the vessel that would hold her grandmother's mortal remains. Not seeing anything that needed to be done, she turned to Janet. "I think that's everything. I'm ready to go."

"Sara, before we leave, may I suggest we gather the clothing you want your grandmother dressed in. That way, you will not have to go back there again until the funeral."

Sara nodded her agreement and walked into her grandmother's room. She chose the robin's egg blue gown and the silver shoes she'd worn with it. She placed the items into a large garment bag, Janet helped Sara zip it up and to fold it in half using the little loop designed to slip over the top of the hanger.

* * *

DAVID JACOBS MET THE TWO WOMEN when they arrived at the funeral home. He accepted the garment bag from Sara, unhooked it and placed it on a coat rack. He then invited Sara into his office to fill out the required paperwork. Once that was completed, he led the women into the showroom containing a selection of caskets from which Sara could choose. Sara looked at her choices. As she saw the range of models to choose from, she thought, this is like shopping for a car. Steel, bronze, mahogany, the selection seemed endless. Mr. Jacobs showed her around, providing information about the casket materials and the pros and cons of each. Sara was getting a different education today. Since Sara wanted to make a wise choice, she asked the undertakers advice. Janet Collins remained close by to ensure the undertaker didn't push the most expensive products on Sara when lesser ones were just as adequate. Even though Janet had been told money wasn't an issue, her primary job was to protect the interests of their client.

The funeral was to be in two days. Nan's viewing would only be one day. The burial would be the next morning after a service at the Church of the Holy Trinity. Nan wasn't religious but attended the Episcopal services at Holy Trinity on the holidays and to remember the anniversaries of those who had been taken from her before their time.

Sara was exhausted when she returned to the apartment. It was still early in the day, and she hadn't yet gathered all the things she needed to take to Jeff's for her overnight stay. "I think I'll lie down for a while," she said to herself. Going into her room, she closed the door, sat on the bed, and kicked off her shoes. She took her phone, set the alarm to wake her in two hours, then placed it on her nightstand as she lay down,

Chapter 9

When the alarm went off, Sara awoke to find herself in her own room, in her own bed and couldn't help but wonder if it wasn't all just a bad dream. As she walked out into the empty apartment, the quiet confirmed it wasn't.

Sara packed her small overnight bag, and once again felt the silence she now thought of as the new normal.

Charlie, the swing shift concierge, greeted Sara as she exited the elevator. "Ms. Ferguson, I'm so sorry to hear about your grandmother. Winston told me she'd passed away."

"Thank you, Charlie, yes she's gone. I still can't believe it. When I walk around the apartment, I expect to see her. Her not being around will take getting used to."

"Miss, may I ask when the funeral will be? Winston, David, and I would like to send flowers and if possible, attend the church service for your grandmother."

Sara gave the concierge the information.

"Thank you, I'll pass that on to the others. May I hail you a cab?"

"Yes, thank you. I'm going to stay with a friend. I can't face being all alone in that big apartment just yet."

"I can understand that. If you will excuse me, I'll go flag down a taxi for you."

"Thanks, Charlie."

Since the evening rush hour was in full swing, it took Charlie a few minutes to hail a cab. Once he succeeded, he motioned for her to exit the building. As she entered the taxi, he tipped his hat, "I hope you have a good evening, Ms. Ferguson." Sara offered a tired smile as the concierge closed the taxi door.

* * *

THE RIDE TO JEFF'S APARTMENT didn't take long, so Sara never had a chance to make herself comfortable in the back of the taxi. Sara paid the fare and got out in front of Jeff's building. As she walked to the building's entrance, she reached into the side pocket of her purse. She removed the keycard needed to use the elevators and palmed it in her hand. As she walked into the lobby, she noticed the same concierge that had been on duty last night was there again. His smile brightened at the thought of interacting with this tall beauty again. Sara dashed his hopes as she walked by the desk flashing the keycard on her way to the elevators.

The man behind the desk offered a smile. "Have a good night, Miss."

Sara returned his smile, "Oh I will, you can count on it," she said in a sexy tone. When the elevator doors closed, she looked at her reflection in their polished surface. "Why did you say that? You do know nothing will happen? I don't know, maybe because I saw him checking out my ass last night like I was up for sale at the meat market. I hate when guys do that."

It had been a long day, and Sara was tired, but her comment to the concierge had put her in a mischievous mood. Both her head and her heart knew she didn't want to have sex with Jeff, yet her inner self wanted to do something that would give him hope. Sara thought about that rationale and realized she was angry at the way Jeff had strung her along for months. He'd always promised to leave his wife but never made good on it. If he had, then they would probably be together, and Sara wouldn't be facing the prospect of spending lonely nights in the large apartment.

Sara removed the apartment key Jeff had left for her as the elevator chimed its arrival on the twelfth floor. If he were home, it would be clear that Sara had taken the offered items and he would expect her to return. She used the key and undid the lock. As she opened it, Sara could see the lights were on. The unmistakable aroma of curry was in the air. Looks like he's ordered in, she thought. Well, that's good because I am hungry. Sara placed the key back on the hall table as she walked into the living room. "Honey, I'm home," she said with a wicked smile.

Jeff came out of the kitchen wearing a silk smoking jacket over lounge pants. He was shirtless, a diamond-encrusted *Chai*, the Hebrew symbol for Life, hanging from a heavy gold chain around his neck. "I was wondering when you would get here," he said with a broad smile, a sign he'd heard her greeting. "Looks like you've had a busy day. I hope you're hungry. As you can tell by the smell, I've ordered Indian. I know how much you like it."

"Yes, curry, the national dish of England as Nan used to say." Sara realized this was the first time she'd referred to her grandmother in the past tense. Maybe she was coming to accept that Nan was gone. Regardless of that fact, she still had no intention of allowing Jeff in her bed. At least not anytime soon. Who knows what will happen down the road.

Dinner went well. Jeff listened to Sara download everything that had happened. How she had gotten the phone call from the lawyer's office about assisting with the arrangements. Then meeting Janet at the apartment. Selecting the clothing for her grandmother's burial. The location of the funeral home for the viewing and the church where the funeral mass would be held. Sara talked about how strange it felt selecting the casket and even the fact that Nan would be laid to rest in the National Cemetery with her husband, Bill.

"Sounds like you've got everything covered. Sounds like the person from McDougal's office had everything under control."

"Oh yes, Mrs. Collins is very organized."

"Mrs. Collins, *Janet* Collins?"

Sara smiled at her boss, "Do you know her? Let me guess. She was on the team McDougal sent to do the negotiations you lost."

"Yes, we've met. In fact, Janet Collins was the *lead* counsel on McDougal's team. So yes, once again, my dear, you have an outstanding legal team behind you."

"Well, that's good, although I still don't understand why Nan thought I needed legal representation."

Jeff shrugged his shoulders as he stood and collected the dirty dishes. "You'll probably find out when they read the will. Could be something in there your grandmother wanted you to have help with."

"Could be. But you said Mr. McDougal's firm is a high-priced powerhouse. What on earth would need that kind of representation?"

Jeff finished rinsing the dinner plates and placed them in the dishwasher as Sara covered the leftovers and put them in the fridge. "No clue, Sara, maybe Nan owns a diamond mine in South Africa," Jeff offered in a laughing tone.

Sara wasn't pleased with Jeff's mocking of what she considered a serious question. Okay wise guy just you wait, she thought with a smile.

Noticing her smile, Jeff leaned against the dishwasher and crossed his arms. "Well, we've eaten, the leftovers are in the fridge, and the dishes are done. Now what?"

Sara moved closer to Jeff and reached out touching his arm. "Since everything's done, I guess it's bedtime."

Jeff offered a smile that matched hers. "That sounds good."

Sara's smile widened as she stroked his arm. "Glad you agree," she said as she turned her back on her host. "Goodnight, Jeff. I'll see you in the morning."

From the moment Sara walked into the apartment and said, "Honey I'm home," she was sure Jeff figured she'd wind up in his bed. Now she left him standing there wondering what went wrong.

As Sara walked down the hallway to her room, she remembered Jeff's comment, "maybe she owns a diamond mine." Geez, Jeff, you certainly can be a grade 'A' asshole.

When Sara closed the bedroom door, Jeff once again heard the click of the lock being set.

Chapter 10

The next two days seemed to drag by. Sara had returned to the apartment and decided she would not tempt fate by staying with Jeff any longer. Resigned to the fact she would live in the large apartment alone until she either found a roommate or moved, Sara, put on a brave face and accepted the challenge. "Come on Sara, if Nan was brave enough to immigrate here as a pregnant widow with very little money, you can certainly work up the courage and be brave enough to live alone."

Sara agreed with herself, took her coat, and left for the funeral home where she would sit and watch as Nan's friends paid their final respects. Janet Collins had wanted to send a car to take Sara to the funeral home, but Sara refused and took a cab.

As she exited the elevator, Sara noticed an unfamiliar face behind the concierge desk. The man smiled as Sara approached the counter. "Hello," she said to the stranger. "Where's Charlie tonight?"

"Good evening Miss, Charlie asked for the night off, he said he had a funeral to attend. My name is Walter, I'm filling in for him tonight, and I'll be here tomorrow daytime too, covering for Winston. He's going to the same funeral tonight and then to the burial service tomorrow. I guess it was someone in the building that passed away."

Not wishing to play the sympathy card and get the whole "I'm sorry for your loss," from a stranger, Sara just confirmed that fact. "Yes, that's correct; a longtime resident has passed away. I'm headed to the funeral myself."

"She must have been one special lady. If the entire concierge staff, the cleaning, and maintenance staffs are taking off, they must have thought the world of her."

"Yes, I'd agree, Mrs. Cavendish was an original. She was one of a kind."

"May I hail you a taxi?"

"Yes, thank you, Walter."

"Not a problem, I'll be just a minute," said the stand-in concierge as he exited onto the street.

* * *

SARA ARRIVED AT THE FUNERAL HOME before the official viewing hours began. David Jacobs met her at the door and took her into the large chapel. As they walked in, Sara hesitated. The open casket had been set atop a carved wooden platform at the end of the room. Sara could see her grandmother's head raised above the rim of the casket.

After taking a deep breath, Sara convinced herself this would not differ from viewing her grandmother's body in the hospital. Sara nodded. "Okay, I'm ready."

As she got closer, Sara could see Nan's face. She looked like she was sleeping; her face and body lay in quiet repose. Dressed in the blue gown, she looked as if she were ready for the ball and had a short rest before leaving.

Mr. Jacobs stood at the foot of the casket. He smoothed several of the pleats in the lining of the split lid. "We've done our best to take good care of your grandmother. I hope you will agree."

Not sure what he meant, Sara just nodded. She recalled the death of her mother and father. This wasn't the same. Because of the crash and the fire that followed, her parent's caskets had been closed. Now, for what Sara knew would be the last time, she looked at the woman who had cared for her for most of her life.

Sara reached out, touching her grandmother's hand. The stone-cold flesh startled her, and she withdrew her hand. "Nan, I'm sad that you're gone. Hopefully, you and Grandpa Bill are together again in heaven, dancing the night away."

Mr. Jacobs directed Sara away from the platform and to the row of high-backed chairs in the front row. For the first time, Sara's focus was beyond that of the casket, and she noticed the large flower displays on both sides of the casket and down the sides. "Who sent all the flowers?" she asked.

"Many people and organizations," replied Jacobs. As he led the way, he offered to show her the cards of condolences on the displays. The first was from Michael McDougal, another was from his law firm. Likewise, she found a lovely arrangement from Jeff and another from the agency. There was one from someone named Thomas Moskowitz, another from a Robert Fleming. On the other side of the room, she read the card on a large arrangement of red roses, "With My Deepest Condolences, Walter Fitzsimmons." I have no idea who these people are. Then, she saw one that made her smile. It was from Winston, Charlie, and David. The card read, "We will all miss your smiling face, but we know heaven is a bit brighter now you're there." The last one was signed, "With Love and Respect, The Highgate Staff."

Sara got teary as she read the sentiments on the cards attached to the flowers. Sara scanned the flowers and thought I don't know who some of these people are. But since they took the time to send flowers, Nan obviously had dealings with them. Even though I don't know them, they must have respected her.

Michael McDougal and Janet Collins were the first visitors to arrive. After paying their respects to their former client, they took up seats alongside their new one.

Sara wasn't sure what to say to the two lawyers. What do you say to someone attending a funeral? Gee, doesn't she look good? Sara decided the best thing to do was just acknowledge their presence. "Thank you for coming, and thank you for the flowers, they're beautiful."

"You're welcome. I'm glad you like the flowers, Janet made the call to the florist," replied McDougal.

"There are flowers from people I don't know. Do you have any idea who they could be?"

"I'm not sure, I'll look and let you know." McDougal got up, walked over to the large floral sprays to read the names on the cards.

Janet moved closer to Sara, taking the seat vacated by her boss. "How are you holding up?"

"I'm making it. One foot in front of the other as they say."

"That's good. I'm sure the events of the past few days are still a shock to you. You'll have lots of time to figure out what's next after this is all finished and things settle down." Janet smiled as she placed her hand on top of Sara's. "I know you think everything in your life has changed, and you feel lost. The best advice I can give you is don't worry. Everything will work out."

"Thanks, Janet, you've been very helpful over the past few days. Will you still be around after tomorrow?"

The older woman nodded, "Of course. Mr. McDougal and I will be there to assist or provide guidance and recommendations for whatever you may need."

"The first thing I'm going to need is a realtor to help me find a new apartment."

McDougal had returned just in time to hear Sara's last comment. "A realtor? I wouldn't rush out and plan on moving just yet."

"I was thinking about that the other night, that apartment is so big, and I have no idea how much the rent is."

"Sara, don't worry about it right now. I can assure you, your grandmother thought of everything in the event something happened to her. I've told you how detailed her Durable Power of Attorney had been. The rest of the planning she left in place was just as detailed. With all that planning, don't you think your grandmother wouldn't have also given consideration to where you would live when she passed away?"

Sara stopped and considered the lawyer's remarks, then breathed a little easier. "I didn't think about it in those terms, but now that you mention it, yes, I guess she would have also taken care of that, too."

As McDougal sat, he continued, "There is no need to worry about the apartment or the rent until after the reading of the will. After that date, if you decide to move, I'm sure Janet can help you get a realtor. But there's no hurry."

"Mr. McDougal, my head is just so full of things I think I have to do, but it sounds like Nan already planned everything out."

"Again, Sara, please don't worry about the details. Everything is being seen to. Have you considered going back to work?"

"Not really, I thought I'd be looking for an apartment and moving and doing whatever else needed to be done after tomorrow. Now that you tell me to just relax, I guess I can do that. Maybe I'll mention it to Jeff when he shows up tonight."

"Perhaps that's best," added Janet. "You have to develop a new routine now that your life has changed. It would be good for you to do this soon."

Sara nodded, "Yes, you're right.. Mr. McDougal, did you recognize any of the names on the three flower arrangements?"

McDougal shook his head, "No. I'm afraid I didn't. If they sent flowers, perhaps, they'll stop by and pay their respects. Then you can find out who they are."

"I guess we'll see, I am curious."

* * *

FOR THE NEXT TWO HOURS, people filtered in and paid their respects. Sara knew two by name because they lived on the same floor as she did. Others she knew by sight for the same reason, they lived in Highgate.

Winston followed the other two concierges into the chapel, bringing up the rear like a drill instructor ensuring his troops were following orders. They took turns, offering a prayer to the woman who always gave them a warm and open smile when she saw them before stopping off and paying their respects to Sara.

Now it was Winston who led the group and acted as their spokesman. "Miss Sara, again, please let me say how sad we are at your grandmother's passing. She always said hello and took a moment to ask how we were doing." The former Marine reached out to his two companions. As he put his arms around the shoulders of the other two, he continued, "All three of us will miss Mrs. Cavendish, and we hope you will not be leaving Highgate anytime soon."

"Thank you, Winston. It was nice of you to come. I appreciate the flowers the three of you sent. They're beautiful, and the card made me cry. I met Walter this evening. He explained he was filling in so all three of you could come by tonight. He also told me he'd be doing that again tomorrow so you could attend the funeral mass. That's very thoughtful of you."

"It's not much, Miss Sara, but it was the least we could do," replied Winston. "We'll find seats in the back and stay for a while if that's okay with you. And we'll see you at the church in the morning."

Sara rose from her seat and hugged all three of the men. "Thank you again. You're welcome to stay. I'll look for all of you tomorrow."

The three men retreated to the back of the chapel, tipping their imaginary hats as they took up seats in the last row.

Jeff showed up a half-hour later. Sara introduced him to Michael McDougal. After shaking hands with the lawyer, Jeff was gracious enough to say hello to Janet Collins. He asked how she'd been, and they exchanged pleasantries for a minute before McDougal cut in. "Sara, Janet and I will leave now. The limo will pick you up at Highgate at 10:00 a.m. and bring you here for the last viewing, and then it will take you to Holy Trinity for the funeral mass. We'll see you there."

"Thank you, Mr. McDougal, and thank you, Janet," she said, as she gave the woman a hug. "I'd have been lost without your help. I'll see you in the morning."

"You're welcome. I'm glad I could assist and make things easier for you. Goodnight, Sara."

After saying goodnight to the two lawyers, Sara took Jeff's hand and asked him to sit next to her. As he did, he looked around the room at the flower displays and the people sitting in the chapel.

"Who sent all the flowers?"

Sara pointed to the displays, and she recited who had sent them. "That's yours, and the one next to it is from the agency. Thank you so much. It was very nice of you to send a personal one, too."

"Given our history, I felt it was something I had to do."

Sara continued, pointed to the three which had come from people she had never heard of. Then on to the two that came from her lawyer and his firm. Finally, the two sent by the three concierges and the rest of the staff at the apartment building.

There wasn't much conversation between Sara and Jeff as the night went on. Several of Nan's friends came to say goodbye to their friend. However, if any of the three mystery men came by, they never made their presence known. Sara never saw anyone she thought could have been them.

As the night went on, Sara took Jeff's hand. "Mr. McDougal thinks I should consider going back to work after the funeral."

"What do you feel about that idea? Do you need more time to sort things out? You can take whatever you need, you know that."

"According to Mr. McDougal, there's nothing to sort out until after they read the will. He said I don't have to worry about moving until then, either. After everything is over, I can decide what I want to do. I guess she left money to pay the bills while her will goes through probate. The apartment rent is paid."

"That's good, it's one less thing to worry about. You know the offer is still open if you want to move in with me."

"Please, Jeff, don't start. I've already made it clear, that's not going to happen."

"Okay, but you can't blame me for trying."

The wall clock showed it was 10:00 p.m. Mr. Jacobs walked into the chapel and informed the few remaining visitors it was time to leave. He made his way to the front of the room and came over to speak to Sara. "Miss Ferguson, once everyone has left, you can have a few minutes in private to say goodbye if you wish to do so."

"No, that's okay, I'll save my goodbye for the final viewing in the morning."

"As you wish. Goodnight, Miss Ferguson," said Jacobs as he took his leave.

Jeff took Sara's hand and helped her up from her seat. "Are you hungry? Would you like to get a bite to eat or maybe some coffee?"

Sara nodded, "Yes, I think I could eat something. I don't remember the last thing I ate."

"Not a problem, what would you like?"

"I'm not sure yet, how about we find a twenty-four-hour diner? Whatever I decide I want, I should be able to get."

* * *

SARA COULDN'T DECIDE if she wanted breakfast, lunch, or dinner, so she ordered a mix and match combo of all three. Onion rings, a mushroom, pepper, and spinach omelet, an order of buffalo chicken wings and a strawberry malt. Jeff opted for coffee and a fried egg sandwich with swiss on a bagel.

Jeff watched his former lover as she sat in the booth. He noticed she was avoiding eye contact and sat, head down, looking at her hands as she picked at her fingernails.

"Earth to Sara, come in Sara," he said in an attempt to get her to smile.

"Sorry, I guess I was a million miles away."

"I'd say so. The order you gave the waitress was the most words you've spoken since we got in the car to come here. Are you okay?"

Sara shrugged, "Don't know."

"Maybe McDougal is right. You should come back to work. That will give you something to do. If you work on a new pitch, you will have other things to think about. And it'll get you out of the apartment."

"You're right, Jeff. Working will fill my days and my nights if I let it." Sara raised her head so she could look at his face and gave him a smile. "That's what I'll do. Tomorrow's Friday, I'll be back on Monday. Maybe I'll stop in over the weekend and catch up on what's happened while I was out. Can you have all my account files left on my desk?"

"That's the spirit. Sure, I'll have everything updated and left for you. That way, you can see the status of all your accounts."

Now that she had agreed to move forward and return to work, Sara felt as if they had erased one more problem. She felt good about her decision and was ready to devour the food she had ordered.

When Jeff dropped Sara off at Highgate, it was 1:00 a.m. David was on duty and welcomed her home. "Hello, Miss Ferguson. It was a nice wake. I've never been to Jacobs before, but I've heard he's excellent. Your grandmother looked beautiful. I know you must have heard this a hundred times already, but I'll miss her."

"Thanks, David, it's always nice to hear you'll miss her. I'll miss her too." As Sara continued past the desk, heading for the elevator, she thought, I guess people really do compliment the dead on how good they look.

Chapter 11

Sara was already waiting in the lobby when the black Cadillac limo pulled up in front of the door. Walter was standing by the entrance waiting for it to arrive.

As she exited the building, Sara saw that the sky was overcast, and it looked like rain. Halfway to the funeral home, the heavens opened, and many people scurried for cover. The smart ones just pulled out their umbrellas and went about their business.

Sara's limo pulled into one of the spaces marked off as reserved for the funeral procession. The black Cadillac hearse was already there as was a silver Bentley. An attendant from the funeral home walked up to the limo carrying a large umbrella and opened the door for Sara.

As he led Sara to the door, another usher opened it and showed her into Mr. Jacobs' office. Michael McDougal and Janet Collins were already there. Sara figured that the Bentley sitting in the reserved space must belong to the older lawyer.

Both men stood when Sara entered. "Good morning, Miss Ferguson," said Jacobs. "Everything is ready."

"Thank you, Mr. Jacobs."

"Good morning, Sara. How are you feeling this morning?" asked McDougal.

"I'm okay, I guess. I didn't sleep well last night. I keep thinking I'm going to wake up and find this has all been a bad dream. But now the reality of it all has set in, and I realize it's not."

Janet stood and moved to Sara's side. "It's always hard to deal with a loss. You'll be okay, just try to relax and take a breath. We're all here to help you."

Sara closed her eyes and took several deep breaths. The extra intake of oxygen helped calm her, and the tension she felt ebbed. She opened her eyes and looked at the funeral director. "I'm ready to say my final goodbye."

Mr. Jacobs led the group into the chapel and escorted them up to the open casket. Michael and Janet said a quick prayer then retreated to give Sara a private moment. Mr. Jacobs stood near the foot of the casket, close enough to react in case Sara became distraught.

Sara again reached out to touch her grandmother's hand. She knew what to expect this time and didn't recoil when she felt the cold skin. "Goodbye, Nan. I love you so much, and I will miss you. Thank you for everything you've done for me, thank you for being there when I needed you, and thanks for being my friend." Sara closed her eyes and said a silent prayer for her grandmother. "They're all together again," she said in a soft voice.

Sara took a deep breath and turned toward the funeral director, "Thank you, Mr. Jacobs, I'm finished. We can go now."

Jacobs nodded, "Please follow me. We'll go to the car while my assistants secure the lid on the casket."

Sara followed his lead as they left the chapel. "Mr. Jacobs, I wanted to tell you, my grandmother looked very nice. Thank you for taking good care of her."

Jacobs presented Sara with a gentle smile, "Thank you for the kind words, Miss Ferguson. We do all we can to ensure the last memory you have is as pleasant as it can be under the circumstances."

As she walked past the two lawyers, Sara turned to the woman she now thought of as her friend. "Janet, would you ride in the back of the limo with me? I'd prefer not to be alone."

"Of course, I will."

"Thanks. Mr. McDougal, I would have asked you, but I'm guessing the silver Bentley that's parked out front in the funeral line is yours."

"Yes, you're correct, that is my car. But I can leave it here if you would prefer."

Sara shook her head, "No, that's okay, Janet has helped me through everything so far. I'll be fine with her by my side."

The rain continued to fall, and two assistants held large umbrellas over Sara and Janet as they exited the building and walked to the limo. Once seated in the back of the Cadillac, both women sat in silence as they watched the casket containing the mortal remains of Mrs. Rose Cavendish loaded into the rear of the hearse for the trip to Holy Trinity Church.

* * *

WHEN THEY ARRIVED AT THE CHURCH, Janet instructed Sara on the protocol used for funerals. The casket was unloaded first, then the family entered and took their place in the front pew. After the service, the priest would lead the procession out of the church. The casket would go first, and Sara would fall in behind.

Sara was glad she had asked Janet to accompany her in the limo. She was sure the driver would know the proper procedures of when to open the rear door. The last thing Sara wanted to do was look like a silly child who didn't have a clue about how to act.

The rain had stopped. No umbrellas were produced as Sara walked from the limo to the church. Sara estimated there were twenty-five to thirty people present for the service. Some of them were people she had seen last evening, but there were others she didn't recognize. *I wonder if the people who sent the flowers are here.*

Sara tried her best not to cry during the service, but her attempts were unsuccessful. When the music started, and Sara heard the first chords of "I Dreamed a Dream" from *Les Misérables,* she lost all control and fell into a period of uncontrollable sobbing. Nan had taken her to see *Les Miz,* and they both cried through most of the play. Now Sara listened to the words and thought how appropriate they were for Nan and Grandpa Bill. *They only had a short time together, and after he was killed, she never considered marrying again. Nan must have loved him very much. But loving him was not something she often talked about.*

Sara regained control of her emotions by focusing on other things. *It was the same as she did when listening to music.* Concentrating on something else allowed her to stop crying and filter out everything happening around her.

Sara stood, watching the casket roll by on its way back to the hearse. *Oh my God, I zoned out and missed most of the service. I have to keep it together for the rest of the day,* she thought as she stepped into the aisle and walked back to the waiting limo.

A sea of umbrellas awaited Sara as she exited. The rains had returned with a vengeance. "Janet, this rain is horrible, what happens if it's this bad at the cemetery?" asked Sara as they got into the back of the Cadillac.

"Don't worry, Michael watched the forecast. He's arranged to have a marquee set up over the gravesite. We'll be okay. Are you okay?"

Sara took her arm, "Not really but I'll get through this. I want Nan to know I could do this for her."

"I'm sure she's watching and is pleased with how you're dealing with this."

"I hope so. I can't remember ever seeing her cry. Even after Mom and Dad died. I'm sure she did at some point, but never in front of me."

Janet offered a reassuring smile. "You're doing fine. I've seen people who had to be sedated to get through a funeral. You're a lot stronger than you think you are."

"Okay, I can hold on."

* * *

THE MARQUEE HAD SEATING for twenty people and was closed on three sides to keep the rain from blowing in. Nan's casket was sitting on the device used to lower it into the ground. Mr. Jacobs was standing inside the marquee handing everyone who entered a long stem red rose.

As Sara approached, he held out the offered flower. "I will ask everyone to place these on the casket at the end of the service," he said.

"Thank you, Mr. Jacobs," replied Sara as Janet took her flower and led Sara to the front row of seats.

Michael McDougal arrived a few minutes later and took the seat on the other side of Sara. He and Janet now provided support on both sides should the need arise.

While they waited for the priest to arrive, Sara glanced at both her lawyers. "Thank you for helping with all the arrangements. Everything is very nice."

Michael offered a nod as a sign of acknowledgment. "I'm sorry we couldn't have given you better weather. I'm afraid we had no control over that."

"No, that's true. However, you saw to it the marquee was provided to keep us dry. That in and of itself is something to be thankful for," said Sara.

The Reverend Oswald arrived and began the service. Sara proved to be stalwart and didn't cry during the service. When the priest asked for the family and friends to place their flowers on the casket as a final goodbye gesture, Sara proceeded to the front, setting the rose in the center of the casket's lid she kissed her fingers and put them next to the flower. "Goodbye Nan, I'll never forget you. You will be in my heart forever."

* * *

MICHAEL MCDOUGAL LEANED INTO THE OPEN DOOR of the limo. "We've arranged to have a small luncheon for everyone who attended the service. Are you up to attending?"

"Yes. Thank you for taking care of that as well."

"You're welcome. I'll see you there."

The limo left the cemetery and began the trip back to Manhattan. As she rode along the wet streets, Sara remembered how her lawyer came to the hospital as soon as possible after she called the firm. "Mr. McDougal is very nice."

With a broad smile, Janet replied, "Michael, yes, he's a sweetheart to work for."

Sara giggled a bit, "But I've heard you don't want to face him in court."

"That's true, I'm glad to be on his side of the aisle when we take a case to court."

Sara looked at the woman sitting next to her, tilted her head, and offered a smile. "I've heard you're no slouch, either."

Janet laughed, "Thank you. Sounds like my name may have come up in conversation between you and Jeff Charles."

"Sure did. When I told Jeff Mr. McDougal was now my lawyer he asked what his first name was. When I told him, it surprised him to find out the firm now represented me."

"I'm sure he was."

Sara continued, "He told me his company lost a big dispute with a client whose legal counsel was from McDougal, McDougal & Slone."

"Yes, we were."

"Then, when I told him you were helping me sort out all the details for Nan's funeral, he told me you were the lead counsel for the client."

"Guilty as charged," replied Janet.

"Good," replied Sara with a sharp nod. "Jeff is a nice guy most of the time, but he can be an obnoxious ass. Like when we were talking. I told him I had no idea why Nan thought I needed a legal team with the reputation of your firm behind me. Do you know what he said?"

Janet shook her head, "I wouldn't have a clue. However, judging by your attitude, it must have been something you took exception with."

"It was. Jeff said I needed you because maybe Nan owned a diamond mine in South Africa."

Sara's revelation slightly startled Janet, but her professional experience allowed her to recover in an instant. Sara hadn't noticed her surprise. "Well, I'm not sure why your grandmother wanted us to represent you," she lied. "But I can tell you, I'm sure your grandmother does not own a diamond mine, or a gold mine, or any other mine anywhere in the world."

"See, I told you he could be an ass."

* * *

THE LIMO LET SARA AND JANET OUT in front of Vesuvio on West 4th street in Manhattan. The maître d` greeted them as they entered the restaurant. Janet informed him there should be a reservation in the name of McDougal.

Carlo, the maître d`, didn't need to check the reservation book, he'd been expecting them. "Yes, of course. If you will follow me please."

Sara's eyes roamed the space. Like many restaurants in the city, cozy was the word of choice used as a quant way to describe cramped. Behind the bar, an assortment of pictures of famous patrons were jammed together covering the wall.

Once they had taken their seats. Sara noticed small *reserved* placards on several tables in the back. "How many people are you expecting?"

"Michael had them plan for twenty. I guess we'll see who shows up."

Voices behind Sara caused her to turn to see who was coming in. She saw Mr. McDougal talking to Winston, who had Charlie and David with him. Sara was sure they had been at the church and the gravesite, but she didn't remember seeing them there. I really was out of it, she thought.

McDougal and Winston were laughing like they were old friends when they got to the table where Sara and Janet were waiting. "I found these three degenerates out on the sidewalk," said the lawyer with a laugh. "They don't look like they've had one good meal between them in a month."

"That's not true, Charlie found half of a perfectly good pizza in the trash last night," laughed Winston as he put his arm around Charlie.

Sara couldn't hide her surprise as what was unfolding before her. "I guess you know each other."

"Yes, Miss. Mr. McDougal's been coming to Highgate for years to meet with Mrs. Cavendish."

"Really, I wasn't aware of that."

Mc Dougal smiled, "When I had something to discuss with your grandmother or if I had to get a signature I would drop by."

"Geez, Nan seems to have more secrets than the CIA."

"Let's just say your grandmother was interesting," said McDougal. "Winston, you and the boys can sit at any of the tables marked reserved. Order anything you want. But no doggie bags," he said with a grin.

* * *

AFTER EVERYONE ARRIVED, there were only two empty seats at the reserved tables. Orders for drinks were taken first then they decided what they would eat. Sara chose the veal scaloppini, Janet the risotto with shrimp and asparagus, while Michael selected stuffed veal chop.

As they waited for the food to arrive, Michael began the conversation. "Now that the funeral is behind you, what are your plans? Are you going back to work?"

After taking a sip of wine, Sara put her glass down. "Yes, I've spoken to Jeff. He's had all my account files updated and put in my office. I told him I'd start back on Monday, but I plan on going in tomorrow or Sunday to review everything so I can jump right in on Monday."

"That sounds good. The best thing you can do it to get used to the changes in your life and setting up a new routine for yourself."

"I agree," added Janet. "People hate change, so embracing it and moving forward is much better than resisting what you have no control over."

Once he had finished his veal chop, Michael continued the conversation. "As someone I hope you will view as a friend, I'm glad you're ready to move on." McDougal leaned forward on the table, allowing himself to get closer to Sara, so he could speak in a lower tone. "Now, as your lawyer let me tell you what's happening with the legal matters. I've had your grandmother's will submitted to the probate court. We've dotted all the i's and crossed the t's. All is in order from our end. It usually takes several weeks to probate a simple will."

McDougal crossed his arms before him on the table and continued. "Since you are your grandmother's only living relative, there should be no one coming forward to contest the will. While the document is more complicated than a simple will and has several codicils to the original document, I still don't expect there to be any issues. I would guess that we'll receive the *Letters testamentary* from the probate court within four to five weeks. That document gives me as the Executor the authority to administer the estate. Once we get that, we'll schedule the reading."

"That's fine," replied Sara. "You've already told me I need not worry about moving until after the reading. I can get back to work and sort out my life."

"Exactly," replied McDougal.

Chapter 12

Sara went to the office on Saturday morning to review the status of her accounts. When she walked in, it surprised her to find several other people were already there. Three other creative directors were working on something in the main conference room. It looked like some people from the art department were there also changing the presentation graphics.

Not bothering to hang up her coat, Sara just tossed it over the chair by her desk and sat down. The stack of accounts Jeff had left for her were sitting in the center of her desk. Each folder had a sheet attached with a handwritten list of notes to let Sara know the most current status of each one.

After reading the notes, she smiled. Jeff had been true to his word. Each account had been serviced as he said they would be when she left for the hospital on that first day.

* * *

FOUR HOURS LATER, after she had reviewed all of her accounts and made her own notes about their status, Sara was ready to leave. She gathered her belongings and headed out the door.

As she walked past the conference room, Willie Davis, one of the art directors, stopped her. "Sara, it's good to see you. We were all sorry to hear about your grandmother."

"Thanks, Willie. What are you guys doing here on the weekend?"

"We've got to make a major change to a pitch. The client wants to use cats. Don't ask." He laughed. "Why are you here? Are you back?"

"Yes, I'll be back in on Monday. I spent a few hours catching up on the events of the past week."

"It'll be good to have you back. See you then," said the art director, offering a hug.

Sara accepted Willie's hug and smiled. "It'll be good to get back. I've got to keep busy, and I've missed all of you." Sara waved goodbye as she walked to the elevators.

* * *

THE APARTMENT AT HIGHGATE FELT EMPTY. The door to Nan's room was closed. Sara hadn't been in there since she went in with Janet Collins to pick out the clothing for Nan's funeral. Sara had tidied up the apartment, putting things away that reminded her of Nan. Her reading glasses generally on the side table by the couch, the shawl she used to wear over her shoulders when she was reading or watching TV. Even the book she had been reading had been returned to the shelf.

Sara didn't want to remove all traces of her grandmother from the apartment. What she wanted to do was not be reminded at every turn that Nan wasn't there. Sara looked at a picture of her and Nan at her graduation from NYU. There was also a photo of them after Sara led her high school team to win the NYC soccer championships. On the credenza, there were ones of Nan and her mother and father. Only memories remained. Happy times to be remembered as life goes on.

* * *

MONDAY MORNING WAS SUNNY AND WARM as Sara headed to the office. *This is the first day of my new reality. Work, home, errands, gym, cooking for one,* this was Sara's new life. She was ready to tackle it head-on.

As she checked in with Alice, her administrative assistant, she found her schedule for the day would be a busy one. Good, at least I'll be occupied and won't have to sit here thinking about how to keep busy. When she opened the door to her office, she found a large flower bouquet on her desk. A small balloon on a pick stuck into the arrangement said: "Welcome Back." Removing the card envelope from its holder, Sara read the sentiment.

Sara,
We're all glad to have you back.
With our Love
Jeff, Bill & Martin

Relieved that the partners had sent the flowers, Sara placed the card back in the envelope. Keeping Jeff at bay will be a chore, she thought as she set her handbag down on the credenza. As she reflected on their situation, she concluded, it's not that I don't like him, I don't want to be used. If he ever divorces Charlotte, maybe, you never know what could happen. But for now, he's just an employer, colleague, and friend. Nothing more.

Sara's phone buzzed. She noticed it was the internal intercom and picked up the receiver. "Hello."

"Good morning," said Jeff.

"Good morning, to you, too."

"Glad you're back. I hope you found everything I left for you. Did you come in over the weekend?"

"Thanks and thank you for the flowers. I'll thank Bill and Martin later." Sara sat and placed her elbow on the desk leaning forward. She flipped through the stack of folders on her desk. "I came in on Saturday. I found all the files and the notes. Thanks again, that was very helpful. I was here for about four hours and got caught up. Alice handed me my schedule when I walked in. I've got quite a full day. Is that your doing?"

Jeff laughed, "Yes, it was, I figured you'd prefer to be busy. One of those appointments is possible new business."

"You're right, I prefer to be busy. And working on trying to get new business is always exciting."

"Okay, I just wanted to say welcome back. We'll talk later."

"I better get to it then. I'll catch up with you after the meeting and let you know what's going on," Sara said before she hung up the phone. "That went well, I'm surprised he didn't ask me out to lunch," she said to herself.

The hours passed quickly and that pleased Sara. The meeting with the potential clients also went very well. Both company executives were fans of some past campaigns Sara had produced and wanted her to be their primary creative director if they went with Charles, Jasper, and Williams.

The prospect of getting a new account was always exhilarating. Often, trying to take the clients ideas and creating something that would be successful in selling their product was a challenge. However, it was usually more of creating and selling the clients on your ideas because you knew what caused buzz and moved product.

Lost in thought, Sara typed and edited her notes on the fly. She didn't hear her office door open.

"Knock, knock," said Jeff. "How was your first day back?"

Sara leaned back in her chair as she turned from the computer terminal. "Good. It was a good day. I'm finishing up a memo for the partners about the possible new work."

"Did you slay them?"

A smile developed while Sara batted her eyes at the boss. "It didn't take much, they were fans of C, J, & W, and my past account work when they walked in the door."

"Do you think they'll sign with us?"

"They liked the ideas we threw out based on their desires. They liked the basic premise of the different pitches we talked about showcasing their products as the 'you really need this in your life,' so I'm hopeful. I know we can deliver what we talked about. So, as long as they are just as wowed by the final pitch as they were with our verbal descriptions, I think we've got new clients."

"Looks like you've had an epic first day back. What's the budget?"

"When you set me up to meet with these folks did you know they are getting ready to break out of the east coast market and go national?"

Jeff nodded, "Yes, that's why they came in, they wanted to go big. So, what's the budget?"

Sara picked up her yellow legal pad and wrote something on it. "You know what sounds fantastic right about now?" she asked.

Jeff smiled at the possibility he would enjoy her company for the evening, "Umm, a lobster dinner?"

Sara shook her head. "No. Here's what I was thinking—Charles, Jasper, Williams & Ferguson," she said as she turned over the yellow pad so he could read what she had written.

"Four point seven million!" Jeff laughed.

Sara turned the pad around again so she could see the writing. "Oops, sorry, I got distracted," she said, as she wrote something else and turned the page back around. "I meant to say *forty-seven million*, and that's just for the first year."

Jeff sat in the chair opposite. "That's my girl. I knew you'd bring these guys in. That deserves a celebration. So, how about that lobster?"

"So…how about that name change?" she replied.

"You land this contract, and that'll be the top agenda item at the next directors' meeting. Promise. Now can we go eat?"

Sara shook her head. "Sorry, I can't. I've got to finish the memo for the partners' meeting. Then I'm going home, it's been a long day."

"Hey, the memo can wait. You've got to eat."

"Jeff, I'm sorry, I hope you can understand, I can't commit to a relationship with you right now. Maybe, if things change, but for now it's just business. Can you live with that?"

"I don't have a choice, do I?"

"No, you don't."

"Okay. Good work on the initial pitch today. I'll expect the memo for the meeting. Have a good night, Sara. I'll see you tomorrow.

"Goodnight, Jeff," she said as he stood up and began to leave. "Jeff?"

"Yes," he said, looking over his shoulder.

"I am sorry."

"Me too," he said as he walked out the door.

* * *

THE WEEKS PASSED AS SARA REMAINED BUSY on creating the content for the advertising campaigns for the new client. Jeff had kept his distance and remained professional in their interactions. That made both Sara's personal and professional lives easier to deal with.

Janet Collins had called twice to check in with Sara to see how she was adjusting and if she needed anything. They set a date to meet for coffee one afternoon. Sara was glad to have company for a change and found it easy talking to the older woman. Janet always ensured the conversation remained light. Sara spoke about work since there wasn't much else in her life at the moment. That was okay. Talking about what she was doing made her happy and took her mind off other things.

Then Janet tried to broach the subject of Sara's home life by asking, "How are you doing at home? Have you gotten into a routine with cooking and cleaning?"

Sara went quiet. It took a long time before she answered. "I eat out a lot. I've kept the apartment clean," she said, as nervous laughter punctuated her speech. "No one's there to mess anything up. I don't go in Nan's room. Haven't been in there since you were at the apartment."

Janet reached out and covered Sara's hand with hers while offering a reassuring smile. "Okay, sorry, let's change the subject." The rest of the afternoon passed quickly. Janet dropped Sara back at Highgate when they finished.

* * *

SINCE SARA HAD BEEN BUSY WITH THE FINAL EDITING and artwork approvals for the new campaigns, the reading of her grandmother's will was the furthest thing from her mind when Michael McDougal called her office.

"Mr. McDougal, how are you?"

"I'm doing well, Sara, thank you for asking. The reason I'm calling is to inform you I've received the *letters testamentary* from the probate court this morning. We can now set a date to read the will. When would it be convenient for you?"

"Has it been that long already?" asked Sara, thinking the lawyer has said it would take five to six weeks to clear probate.

"Yes, it has. It's been six weeks since your grandmother passed away. Time moves by, doesn't it?"

"Yes, it sure does. Listen, Mr. McDougal. I know this is important, but I'm up against a hard deadline for a big campaign. I've got forty-seven million dollars of new business riding on these presentations. If I can clinch this account it could mean a partnership for me. I've got to make the final pitches next Friday and possibly Saturday if I need to adjust. Is there any way we can do it next Sunday?"

"We can wait until then if that's what you want to do," said the lawyer with a hint of amusement in his voice. "That won't be a problem. I'll have Janet contact you and set up a time."

"Great, sorry to cut this short, but I'm swamped. I'll wait to hear from Janet. Talk to you soon, Mr. McDougal."

"Good luck on pitching the campaign. I'll see you next Sunday," said the lawyer as he hung up.

That was interesting, she thought. I guess large clients are nothing to him. After all, he runs around town in a Bentley that must cost about three hundred thousand dollars.

Part II

*In completing one discovery we
never fail to get an imperfect
knowledge of others of which we
could have no idea before…*

Joseph Priestley

Chapter 13

Janet Collins called on Thursday to inquire if 1:00 p.m. Sunday would be an acceptable time for Sara to be at Mr. McDougal's office. After Sara agreed to the time and place, Janet told her a car would be there to bring her to the office.

***

IT WAS 12:20 P.M. WHEN SARA walked through the lobby of Highgate. She expected Winston to be on duty since his regular days off were Monday and Tuesday. However, Walter, the stand-in concierge greeted her. "Hello, Ms. Ferguson, nice to see you again. May I get you a taxi?"

"Hello Walter. I see you're here again. I hope Winston isn't sick."

"I wouldn't know miss. I got a call last night asking if I could do the morning shift here." He smiled as he continued, "And I said yes, I enjoy working at Highgate, lots of friendly people here."

"Yes, I guess there are, and no thank you, I don't need a taxi, I'm being picked up."

"Ah, that must be the black Lincoln Town Car that stopped in front of the door, he waited for a second then left, he's probably gone around the block. I'll flag him down and check if it's here for you."

"Thanks, Walter, it looks like a nice day out there. I'll come along."

The concierge tipped his hat. "Yes Miss," as he led Sara to the door and opened it.

The black limousine had made its trip around the block and again stopped in front of the apartment building. The *livery* designation on the bottom of the car's license place confirmed the vehicle was from a commercial car service. Walter walked to the front passenger door as the driver lowered the window. "Are you expecting someone?"

"Yes, I'm supposed to be picking up a Ms. Ferguson," replied the driver.

"Okay, wait here." Walter straightened up and hailed Sara, "This is the car you were expecting Miss," he said, as he opened the rear door for her.

Sara slid into the back of the waiting limo. "Thanks, Walter."

"My pleasure, Ms. Ferguson," he said as he closed the door.

* * *

WHEN SHE ARRIVED AT THE LAW OFFICES of McDougal, McDougal & Slone, Sara was ushered into a large conference room where everyone was seated around a large table. Michael McDougal stood to welcome her. "Good afternoon, Sara, it's good to see you again."

Sara responded to the lawyer's welcome. Distracted for the moment, she didn't take much notice of who was in the room. "Hello, Mr. McDougal. It's nice to see you, too. So I guess today's the day."

"Yes, it is. I believe you already know everyone here," he said, directing Sara's attention toward the others.

Sara looked across the table and saw Janet and smiled. Her expression changed to a mixture of mild surprise and confusion as she scanned the next four faces. The last one caused her to pause as if saying why are you here? Turning to the lawyer, she nodded. "Yes, I know everyone here. I can understand why Winston, Charlie, and David are here." Turning back to the lawyer she continued, "But I must admit, I'm confused why Dr. Randell is here."

McDougal understood her question. "Sara, I think I may have said to you that your grandmother was rather interesting. Perhaps unconventional would be a better word. Everything will come to light as I read the will, and the codicils contained within."

Sara shook her head as she looked around the room again. "Why do I feel like I'm going to need a drink before this is over?"

"Perhaps we should start with one," offered McDougal. "As a toast to the remarkable Mrs. Rose Cavendish."

Sara sat before replying, "I think that's a better idea."

Dr. Randell added his opinion, "I agree, because I've got no idea why I'm here. I didn't *know* Mrs. Cavendish."

"All will soon be revealed. Then everyone will understand why you are here. But let's have that drink first," said McDougal as he walked to the cabinet and picked up a silver tray containing seven crystal double old fashion glasses, an ice bucket and a bottle of twenty-five-year-old Macallan Scotch.

McDougal removed the lid from the bucket. "Would anyone like ice?"

Everyone declined. Winston coughed and gave McDougal a look much as if he had asked who wants ketchup on their filet mignon.

McDougal laughed. "Sorry, but it's only polite to ask."

McDougal poured the drinks. Janet helped distribute the glasses around the table. Once everyone had theirs, they stood and waited for McDougal. "Ladies and gentlemen, please raise your glasses in a toast to the indomitable Rose Cavendish. This world is a little sadder without her. Here's to you, Rose."

"To Rose," the group responded as they took a drink.

"If you will please take your seats, we'll begin," said McDougal.

As Sara sat, she again scanned the faces thinking she'd figured out what was about to happen. She was wrong.

"Ladies and gentlemen, before I read the contents of Rose's will I want to give you a bit of insight into what you're about to hear. To some of you, it may seem strange, perhaps even bizarre, and I will admit it was for me. I've been a practicing attorney for over forty years, and I've never had a client instruct me to place a codicil in their will with the beneficiary to be named at a later date."

As he opened the folder that lay before him on the table, McDougal looked at Sara and Randell. "Doctor, it is for this reason that you're here. Mrs. Cavendish had me add this codicil five years ago."

George Randell still didn't know what was going on, so he just sat and listened to the lawyer.

"This strange codicil, is, in fact, legal and binding. It states that if Mrs. Cavendish should be hospitalized and should pass away from circumstances related to the reason for her hospitalization, I could name the attending physician as a beneficiary to Mrs. Cavendish's estate. That is if it is deemed that said physician acted in my client's best interests."

Dr. Randell was speechless and just nodded his understanding.

McDougal looked the doctor in the eye. "And that, Dr. Randell, is why you have a seat at this table."

"Mr. McDougal, strange doesn't even cover this situation, but thank you for believing I did my best for Mrs. Cavendish."

The senior partner turned his attention back to his current client as he continued, "Sara, now that I've explained why Dr.

Randell is here, we can begin. That is unless you have questions."

Sara had no words. She'd heard about the reading of a will and had seen it being done in the movies so she had come into the room with the preconceived idea of what would happen. Again, she was about to discover she was wrong. A single nod was her reply to McDougal she sat and listened.

McDougal began reading, "I Rose Cavendish being of sound mind and body hereby declare this to be my Last Will and Testament..." After reading through all the boilerplate legal jargon, McDougal got to the first of two codicils.

"If it is the opinion of my legal counsel that the physician attending me at the time of my death acted with professionalism and in my best interest, I hereby bequeath said physician whose name will be added and notarized below, the sum of fifty thousand dollars."

"You must be joking," said Randell. "I didn't do anything to deserve that."

"Dr. Randell, were you the attending physician when Mrs. Cavendish passed away?" asked Janet Collins.

"Yes, I was, but–"

McDougal cut him off. "Were you the physician who made the pronouncement of death and signed the death certificate?"

"Yes, but still that doesn't warrant this," Randell protested.

Janet Collins cross-examined with another pointed question. "Dr. Randell, were you the one who informed Ms. Ferguson of her grandmother's passing?"

"Jesus Christ! What is this, an inquisition? Yes! Yes...I'm the one who told Ms. Ferguson. It was my job. Any doctor would have done those things."

McDougal attempted to calm the physician, "Dr. Randell, there's no reason to be aggressive. Mrs. Collins and I only attempted to point out that according to the terms of the codicil we have determined that given my client's circumstances you acted in Mrs. Cavendish's best interests and are deserving of the amount bequeathed you."

"I'm sorry for my outburst. But I felt like I was on the witness stand. Now, I can understand the rationale behind the questioning. I guess all I can say is thank you."

"You're welcome. Now as for the second codicil. The parties named in this one are Mr. Winston Clemons, Mr. Charles Wilkins, and Mr. David Owens who have faithfully provided concierge services for the deceased. The three individuals aforementioned having been faithful and trusted employees of the building known as Highgate are hereby bequeathed the following amounts. To Mr. Winston Clemons, who had been designated Senior Concierge, I leave the sum of one hundred thousand dollars. To Mr. Charles Wilkins and Mr. David Owens, I bequeath to each the sum of seventy-five thousand dollars." McDougal looked at the three men, "Congratulations gentlemen, it's obvious Rose Cavendish thought a lot of each of you."

Winston looked at the two men who accompanied him, then at Sara and finally McDougal. "Umm, I'm… Eh… We're… Excuse me, could I get another taste of that Scotch?"

"Sure, not a problem," replied McDougal, as Janet went to the cabinet and brought the bottle to the table.

"Help yourself," she said.

Winston opened the bottle and turned to his two compatriots. "Anyone else need a shot?"

They both nodded.

Sara sat, stunned to silence as she tried to put all the pieces together. Every time she thought she had it figured out, she was hit with another unexpected event. Mr. McDougal had said Nan was worth more than I knew. But how much more? She had just left three hundred thousand dollars to these four men. What could be left?

Chapter 14

After he finished his drink, Winston raised his hand. "Mr. McDougal, may I ask a question?"

"You may. What's your question?"

"You said Mrs. Cavendish gave us the money for being faithful and trusted employees of Highgate. Do we have to tell the people we report to about this gift? Because they may want to tell whoever owns the property about us getting this money?"

"That's a good question. We'll look into that later. There may not be an issue since it was a gift," replied McDougal with a slight smile.

"Now, for the main part of the will. To my only surviving relative, my granddaughter Sara Ferguson I leave the remainder of my property and possessions. Included herein are the properties known as Kensington, Somerset, Stratford, and Highgate."

Sara was confused. She paused for a moment, then blinked before repeating the last name McDougal had mentioned. "Highgate? How could Nan leave me Highgate? It's not a condo, it's an apartment building."

"That's correct, it is. So are the other three. You are now the owner of the apartment building known as Highgate."

Sara tried to speak. Unable to do so, she attempted to stand. As she struggled to focus on her lawyer, she began to feel unsteady as her world went black.

Chapter 15

When Sara came to, she found herself on a couch in someone's office. Dr. Randell was sitting in a chair by her side.

"Welcome back. How do you feel?"

"Woozy. What happened? Did I faint?"

"You suffered a *syncopal episode*."

"A what?"

"You fainted," replied Randell with a smile.

"Well, I guess I'm lucky there was a doctor in the house. Can I sit up?"

"Yes, but take it slow. Here, let me help you."

Dr. Randell helped Sara sit up. He then handed her a glass of water. "Drink this while I go tell Mr. McDougal you're awake."

Sara did as she was told and sipped the water. "What happened?" she asked herself. "Do I own Highgate? Is that what he said? And there's more?" Sara tried to stand and found that was a bad idea as her legs still felt rubbery, and she sat back down.

As she looked at her reflection in the mirror across the room, Sara verbalized what was running through her mind. "Nan you were full of secrets. Now I guess I understand why Mr. McDougal told me not to worry about the rent for the time being and that I shouldn't be in a hurry to move until after the reading of the will. And why he told Winston he'd check. The guys had no idea that Nan owned the building. Neither did I. And three more?"

Sara was laughing to herself when Dr. Randell returned with Mr. McDougal. "What's so funny," asked the lawyer.

"I was thinking about when you called, and I told you I didn't have time to come in because I was working on a deal that could be worth forty-seven million to the agency."

McDougal took a seat next to his client. "I can understand the position you were in. Now you're in a different position. How did the pitch go?"

"Great, we signed the client to a multi-year contract."

The lawyer tilted his head. "So, what do you think, are they going to make you a partner?"

Sara shrugged, "I don't know. Jeff said if we got this work, a partnership would be top of the list for the next board meeting."

"I wouldn't worry about that. If the partners don't give it to you, you can *buy* Charles, Jasper & Williams and change the name to Ferguson and Company."

McDougal changed his focus to the physician, "What do you think, Dr. Randell, is Sara okay to continue?"

"She seems to have recovered, but I'd leave the decision up to her. She's had quite a shock already, and it seems there's more to come."

"What do you say Sara?" asked McDougal. "Are you ready to go on? The good doctor is correct; there is a lot more I have to go over and tell you."

"Yes, I want to hear the rest," said Sara as she tried to stand again. Still finding herself unstable, she held the doctor's arm as McDougal led them back to the conference room.

Once they had returned to their seats at the table, Winston looked across at Sara. "Miss Sara, I don't know what to say. We expected nothing like this from your grandmother. We were all surprised to get the call telling us to be here."

"Winston, don't worry about it. As we've all learned, there's been a lot of surprises so far, but we're not done yet."

McDougal had picked up the legal document again and was prepared to go on. "May I continue?"

His client nodded, "Yes, please go on."

"As I was saying, your grandmother left you the four apartment buildings, Kensington, Somerset, Stratford, and Highgate. She also bequeathed you the rest of her personal property and financial holdings. You and I will talk about those later. Simply put, everything your grandmother had is now yours."

McDougal placed the will back into the folder and closed the cover, then continued to address those gathered around the table. "Now that I have completed my duties as the Executor of the will, and all parties have been informed as to what Mrs. Cavendish has bequeathed them, you are all free to leave—that is —everyone except Sara. Gentlemen, if you will follow Mrs. Collins out, she will ensure we have your correct contact information. Tomorrow someone from this office will contact you to make arrangements for payment of the funds Mrs. Cavendish left you."

One by one, each of the four recipients of Nan's generosity stopped and said goodbye to both Sara and her lawyer. Charlie Wilkins was the last person to exit the conference room and closed the door behind him.

Michael McDougal placed his forearms on the table and interlaced his fingers. "Sara, I'm not even going to say I understand what you're feeling because I don't. As your grandmother's lawyer, I knew a lot of what would happen here today. However, I must admit there are still a lot of unknowns."

The lawyer opened a smaller folder attached to the cover of the larger one, removed a sealed envelope, and placed it on the table. "If you're up to it, there's one more thing we have to do today. The last part of the will only concerns you and this," he said pointing to the legal-sized packet in front of him. Before he could finish, Janet returned to the conference room and took her seat.

McDougal picked up the envelope and held it toward Sara. "Do you want to go on, or shall we call it a day and pick up again in the morning?"

"Nan always said, good or bad, it's better to find out now. Let's continue."

The lawyer gave her the instructions that accompanied the envelope. "Janet will take you to the office next door where you alone will read what is inside. Take as much time as you like to read, reread, and digest its contents." McDougal stood and again held the envelope out to Sara. "When you've finished, please come down to my office. I will be waiting to answer any questions you may have. That is provided I know the answer. As I said, there are many unknowns left to discover. Oh, there is one last thing."

Sara looked up, "What's that?"

McDougal waved the envelope as he gave her the final bit of information. "This is the first letter. Your grandmother told me there are others that you will receive in time."

Sara took the envelope from the lawyer's hand and followed Janet Collins out of the room.

Chapter 16

Sara sat in the office where Janet Collins led her. She stared at the envelope Mr. McDougal had given her as she tried to fathom the events that had unfolded. His words ran through her mind as she turned the sealed document over in her hands. "This is the first letter; there are others that will receive in time."

The first letter? After listening to her grandmother's will, Sara was in shock as she realized why Nan insisted she have legal representation. Now, this. Sara picked up the letter opener Janet had placed in the center of the desk blotter when she showed her in. She inserted it into the corner of the envelope and sliced it open.

She removed the contents, unfolding the three pages she found within. Her grandmother's handwriting filled the unlined pages. Nan's perfect cursive style printing caused Sara to cry. She put the letter down on the desk and removed tissues from her purse to dry her eyes. She regained her composure and picked up the letter.

Dearest Sara,

I know what you have just experienced might seem like something from a 1950s English melodrama much like we used to watch on Saturday afternoons when you were younger. However, I can assure you what is about to unfold in your life is real and will have a significant impact on your future.

Allow me to begin by telling you there is much about my life you do not know. Many of the facts you believe to be true are works of fiction or perhaps only partly true.

Many years ago, before I left England, two people made a promise to each other that they would keep the secret that bound them together. Both parties agreed to certain things and to date neither of us has gone back on those promises. It was promised that each person would take this secret to their grave and by doing so, the terms agreed upon so many years ago would remain in force.

Since Mr. McDougal presented this letter to you at the reading of my Last Will and Testament, it should be evident I have done as promised.

Having protected this secret for over sixty years, I have given much thought to what would happen upon my death. Since I know at the time of this writing the other person involved has not predeceased me, I have decided my death does not release me from my bond. Therefore, this will not be a dying declaration where I will expose the details of the agreement or what the secret entailed.

While I am unable to give you the details, I have decided I can give you some clues to help you on your quest. I am sure the contents of my will surprised you. Just as I am sure you were also not aware of the arrangements I put in place many years ago to protect you in the event something happened to me while you were young.

Michael McDougal is a good friend, and a trusted confidant. He will provide you with any assistance you should need in the future. He will also offer to accompany you while you discover the other revelations about my life and affairs in New York. Listen to him because in the forty-five years we have been friends he has never given me bad advice. I will admit, there were times I did not listen, believing I knew better, and I can assure you I regretted each of those decisions. However, Michael never judged, and he continued to advise me until my death.

Now, back to what I was saying. After you make the rounds in New York, you should have more information that will serve as clues. When you reach that point, I want you to contact Mary O'Riley. Mary is an old and dear friend. We talk weekly so I can only hope nothing has happened to her during the time we have not been in contact. She knew not to call if I did not call her first.

Nevertheless, she also knows who you are and that one day, you would be calling. I hope you have access to my cell phone; Mary's number is in there. If not, *you will find it in the small white phone directory I kept in my dressing table.*

Be mindful of the time difference when you call. Mary lives in Mayfair, London. When you contact her, please tell her what has happened to me, then arrange to fly to England and meet her.

I cannot stress how important this first meeting is. If anything should happen to Mary before you meet, I am afraid the first, and perhaps the most important part of the British portion of the puzzle will be lost forever.

Sara, I have left you with the means and resources to do what it is I ask of you. You may believe the task I am about to ask you to undertake sounds simple. I am sure you also believe you already know the answer, but you will find the truth buried under a series of lies and falsehoods. The task, my darling, is this.

<u>Find out who you really are.</u>

Love,
Nan

* * *

AFTER SHE READ THE LETTER a second time, Sara remembered the last conversation she'd had with her grandmother. "Nan was asking me who I was inside," she recalled. "This is what she was trying to tell me. Find out who you are inside. I kept telling her I was Sara, but according to

Nan's letter, there's more to the story of Sara Ferguson that she wants me to find out."

Sara refolded the letter and placed it back in the envelope. Her mind was racing as she thought about the details of the letter. Since Nan is telling me, I have to go back to the beginning. I'm guessing there's a lot more to her story than I ever knew. I lived with her for fifteen years, and I'm in shock to find out what I've learned so far. I'm not sure what else there is but if it's as fantastic as today was, I'm not sure I'm ready to handle it.

***

ENVELOPE IN HAND, Sara left the borrowed office and walked down the hallway to Mr. McDougal's. His secretary had been given instructions to show Sara in once she arrived. As Sara appeared in her doorway, she rose from her seat, and ushered their client down the hallway. When they arrived at the senior partner's door, she knocked.

"Come in."

"Mr. McDougal, Sara Ferguson is here," intoned the secretary

"Good, show her in."

With a nod, the secretary opened the door wider.

Sara entered the large office, taking a seat in one of the upholstered chairs in front of McDougal's desk. Sara sat in silence as if trying to put together the right words before speaking. McDougal set the tone with gentle prodding. "Have you read the letter?"

"Yes, I've read it twice. When you read the will, I was in shock. I never knew Nan had amassed such a fortune. We never had serious conversations about money." Sara looked at her lawyer as she raised the letter from where she held it in her lap.

"Now that I've read this, the shock has been replaced by confusion."

"Unlike before, when you learned about the property, I think I can understand the confusion you're feeling."

"Do you know the contents of the letter?"

McDougal nodded, "Most of it, but not all. I know your grandmother wanted me to accompany you when you went to collect the rest of the information about your inheritance."

The look of shock again appeared on Sara's face, "The rest? You mean there's more?"

"Yes, there is. If you recall, there is the entire financial aspect of your grandmother's estate. Tomorrow morning we have an appointment to meet with Robert Fleming at Citibank. We'll be going downtown to his office in Tribeca."

"Yes, sorry I'm not with it. I don't think I've fully recovered from my fainting spell." Sara closed her eyes and moved her head around as she tried to focus. As she opened them, Sara made eye contact with McDougal, "Robert Fleming… Where do I know that name from? Who is he?"

"He sent flowers to the funeral home. I'm sure you read the card."

Sara thought back, "Yes, that's right, there were three flower arrangements from people I didn't know. I asked you if you knew that names and you told me you didn't have any idea. Why did you lie to me?"

"I'm sorry, Sara, at the time I wasn't allowed to divulge any of the information contained in the will. As the Executor of her estate, I had to follow Mrs. Cavendish's directions which were not to tell you. They were the same directions that didn't allow me to inform you that there was no need to worry about moving because you were now the owner of the building."

Sara frowned, "Okay, I get it, you had a duty to your former client that needed to be completed. So, this Mr. Fleming is from Citibank. I assume he's a banker of some type."

"Correct."

"Okay, I guess a better question would be: what business did he oversee for my grandmother?"

"He's a wealth management specialist. He takes care of one of your grandmother's accounts. Which are now yours."

"One of her accounts? Mr. McDougal, how many did she have?"

"Several, that I'm aware of."

Closing the cover of the folder, Sara's lawyer brought the conversation back to where it had been. "Now back to the whole issues of *other* accounts. You've already said you remember there were flowers from three names you had never heard your grandmother mention. Those three men work in the three offices we need to visit. We must go to each one to arrange for everything to be transferred over to you. I can tell by your face you're still in shock from hearing all this. I *can* empathize with what must be going through your mind at the moment."

McDougal rose from his chair, walked around his desk and took the seat next to his client. "I'm sure having received all this information at once is overwhelming. It must be difficult to rationalize just how your grandmother had maintained so many secrets over the years or why she even felt she had to."

Sara slumped slightly in her chair as she removed the letter from the envelope. "That's not the half of it. You said you knew some of what was in the letter. Are you aware of the task my grandmother wants me to undertake?"

"No, I'm not. The only facts I was privy to concerned assisting you with all the legal matters required to transfer all your grandmother's assets into your name. Now that we have completed the reading of the will, and obtained copies of your grandmother's death certificates, I can assist you with that. If you should require further help, we can certainly take care of anything you want to be done."

"There may be more that needs to be done. Please read this," she said, holding the folded pages out to the lawyer.

McDougal put on his reading glasses and unfolded the pages. As he read the letter, his facial expressions changed. First, he showed an interest in what he had read, stopped, and made eye contact with Sara as if saying you may be right. Then a smile appeared, and Sara surmised he had been reading about advising Nan and her not listening. As he read the last part, a serious look replaced the smile.

Once he'd finished, he removed his glasses, and returned the letter to Sara. "Find out who you really are? That's a rather cryptic clue for a task. I would think the entire portion of the letter about the secret and the promise plays a huge part in that task." Folding his glasses and replacing them in his jacket pocket, he continued. "I can tell you until this moment I had no knowledge of the personal information or of her task for you. Also, the name of Mary O'Riley is unknown to me."

Sara smiled, "Well, I guess I wasn't the only one Nan kept secrets from. Now I don't feel so bad."

"After reading the letter, I have to agree with you. Rose Cavendish was a wonderful woman. I'm glad to have known her, but she kept things to herself. As we continue to put your grandmother's affairs in order and visit the names she had provided, I think we will both get a better insight into who your grandmother really was."

Nodding, Sara thought about that. "But will it help me find out who I am? I'm quite happy being who I am at the moment. I'm not sure what would be achieved by finding out Nan's secret. But I'll do as she asked."

McDougal stood up. "I'm not sure either, but I'll do anything I can to assist. Right now, I think you should go home and rest. It's been quite a day of discovery for you. I'm not sure what information or surprise Mr. Fleming will provide tomorrow, but we shall find out together. I will pick you up at your apartment at 10:00 a.m."

"My apartment," said Sara in a hushed voice. "Mr. McDougal, would you like to know something? After Nan passed away, I was wondering what would happen to the apartment, now I guess that point is moot."

Her lawyer smiled, "Yes, Sara, I guess it is. Now, let's get you out of here. I'll call a car to take you home, and I'll see you in the morning."

"10:00 a.m., I'll be ready. Thank you for everything."

"You're more than welcome. Have a good night, Sara."

* * *

DURING THE RIDE HOME, Sara couldn't help thinking about the revelations that came during the reading of the will. The two codicils Nan had added later in life were a nice touch. She could understand why Nan had included Winston, Charlie, and David. But the second was just plain weird. Even Mr. McDougal admitted he'd never seen anything like that. However, he was sure Nan had all her faculties when she did it. To have a codicil drawn up, leaving a sum of money to a person to be named later was beyond strange.

Sara wondered what she would say to Jeff when he called tonight. She reviewed several mock conversations in her mind and she smiled and chuckled.

"Hi, Sara, how did it go today?"

"Oh, Jeff, hi, it went well thanks for asking."

"So, what happened? What did your grandmother leave you?

"Oh, not much, just four Manhattan apartment buildings, for starters. Mr. McDougal is taking me down to Citibank in the morning to see what else there is."

Sara laughed out loud, "Well I'm not sure what tomorrow will bring, but I'm betting when I find out, I'm not going to need to be a working stiff anymore even if they make me a partner. Thanks, Nan, you were always there and looked out for me when I was young. Now, I find out you've left me a fortune. I never would have dreamed this in a million years."

Chapter 17

McDougal's silver Bentley was parked in front of Highgate when Sara arrived in the lobby. Since it was Monday, Winston wasn't on duty, so once again Walter greeted her. "Good morning Miss Ferguson, I hope you're well today. Your ride is waiting for you, I told him he could park in front," he said.

Sara smiled. "Good morning Walter, it seems you're becoming a regular here at Highgate."

"Yes, Ma'am, I do like it here."

Sara nodded, "Yes, it is nice, have a good day, Walter."

"You too, Miss," he said, almost tripping over himself as he rushed to open the front door.

Sounds like he's bucking for a job, thought Sara, I'll bet one of the other three told him I own the building. My, my, how different life has become in the past twenty-four hours. Last week I was running myself crazy trying to get two pitches done hoping to be offered a partnership. Today I'm headed to Citibank to find out what else is in Nan's estate.

Walter opened the front door of the Bentley and allowed Sara to enter. As she slid across the slate blue Connolly leather surface, Sara looked at the lavish interior of this hand-built car as the door closed.

"Good morning, Sara, how are you?"

"Nervous."

"Okay, I can buy that, but there's no reason to feel that way."

"Maybe not, but I'm still nervous."

McDougal moved the transmission lever into drive and pulled into the flow of traffic. "I hope your nerves will calm down and you'll get used to it. This is just the first stop."

Sara didn't answer. As the lawyer drove them to their destination, Sara watched the scenery go by. She hadn't lost her eye for detail as she looked at the ad campaigns splattered across the city. She began laughing as she looked out the window.

"What's so funny?"

Turning in her seat, Sara answered. "Advertising. I was looking at the ads and thinking about my phone call from Jeff Charles last night."

"And why is that amusing?"

"Well for starters, the first thing he asked was if I was coming in today. He wanted to talk about the new account I signed last week."

"Obviously, you told him no."

"Obviously. And I told him you and I still had legal things to do, and I might not be in all week."

"I'll assume he didn't like that answer."

Sara shook her head. "Nope, he wanted to know how I would follow through with the clients. I told him I hadn't given it much thought and didn't know. So then he started with the whole 'well that's not how a person chasing a partnership would approach it.' Then I told him maybe I'm no longer interested in a partnership. That sent him over the edge."

"What did he say to that?"

"That's when he became curious and finally asked about the will. I said to him. 'Jeff, you know where I live, right?' 'Of course,' he said, 'I've dropped you off and picked you up there. Well, Nan left it to me,' I told him."

"Did he understand what you meant?"

"No, he said pretty much what I said yesterday. He said, 'You told me Highgate wasn't a co-op.' I explained that he was correct. To which he asked, 'so how did she leave you an apartment?' I'm sure you can fill in the rest."

"You explained she left you the *building*."

"Bingo. Then he went quiet. So I added the other three building names to the list of property Nan left me. And he still didn't respond, so I had to ask if he was still on the line."

Now McDougal was laughing. Removing his right hand from the steering wheel, he raised his arm and extended his index finger as if attempting to make a point. "You didn't tell him you were considering buying the firm did you?"

"No, but that thought crossed my mind when he said I wasn't thinking like a potential partner."

"We're here," said McDougal changing the subject as he turned off the street and into the parking garage.

The nervousness Sara had felt earlier returned as her thoughts focused on what was about to happen. McDougal pulled up to the valet, and Sara heard her door open. Upon exiting the car, her lawyer led her into the building and to the elevator banks for the ride up to Robert Fleming's office.

The banker had been expecting them, and Sara and her lawyer were shown into his office.

Robert Fleming stood to greet his new client. Sara thought he looked like a banker, mid-fifties, balding, perhaps twenty-five pounds overweight and wearing a gray, three-piece suit. Wireframes with a half rim helped bring focus to his brown eyes. Fleming offered a friendly smile along with his hand. "Ms. Ferguson, it is a pleasure to meet you,"

Sara shook the offered hand, "Nice to meet you also, Mr. Fleming."

The banker then turned to her lawyer. "Mr. McDougal, it's nice to meet you, too. I know we've spoken on the phone, but I always find it nice to put a face to the voice."

"I agree."

"Please, won't you both have a seat," said Fleming as he motioned to the two burgundy leather chairs in front of his desk.

After Sara and McDougal took their seats, Fleming returned to his chair and sat. "We have a lot of paperwork to fill out; what say we get started?"

"That's why we're here," said McDougal and he opened his briefcase and removed a folder. The lawyer stood and handed the folder across the desk to the banker. "This is a certified copy of Mrs. Cavendish's death certificate, I'm aware you need that to initiate a name change as you transfer her account over to my client."

Fleming accepting the folder, opened it and scanned the form with a practiced eye. "Yes, everything seems in order. However, before we sign the forms for all that, there is one other matter I'd like to attend to first."

McDougal looked at the banker. "And that is?"

Fleming had another folder on the desk blotter in front of him. After looking at the portfolio, he turned his attention to Sara. "Ms. Ferguson, would it be safe to assume that it surprised you to find out your grandmother was a wealthy woman?"

"Surprised doesn't even begin to cover it, Mr. Fleming."

"Good, then perhaps you now understand that Mrs. Cavendish was rather good at keeping secrets."

"That, sir, is an understatement."

"Yes, I believe it is. Anyway, your grandmother knew of all the legal ramifications of things going through probate and having to transfer money, inheritance taxes and the lot, so she asked us to prepare a contingency plan."

"What exactly are you talking about?" asked McDougal.

"Just as I'm sure you were issued instruction by your client, we were as well. Upon being notified of her death, I was to wait sixty days to see if Mrs. Cavendish's will cleared probate court. If it did not, then I would be free to act upon her instructions."

Sara looked at the banker. "Act? And do what?"

Fleming opened the folder and removed an envelope much like McDougal had done yesterday. "If the will was still in probate or had been contested in any way, after sixty days I was supposed to contact you and give you this." Standing up, he handed it across to Sara, who took it and looked at McDougal. "Is this one of those other letters you were talking about?"

The lawyer shook his head, "I honestly don't know. The fact that there would be more letters was just a piece of information I was supposed to pass on. I don't know what that is."

"Please, open it," said Fleming offering Sara a letter opener.

As she had done yesterday, she opened the envelope and found a letter wrapped around another smaller envelope. When Sara unfolded the single piece of paper, Nan's handwriting again made her realize how much she missed her grandmother.

Dearest Sara,

If for some reason, the reading of my Last Will and Testament is delayed beyond what Mr. McDougal told me to expect, I don't want to leave you high and dry. This is a little rainy-day money I've put aside for you should the need arise.

Hopefully, Mr. McDougal was correct, and you will not need to use this. However, as I'm sure you have learned by now, I've tried to plan for everything.

Love,

Nan

Sara passed the letter over to her lawyer so he could read it. She examined the smaller envelope before opening it. Within the envelope, she found a blue Citibank saving account passbook. She opened the cover to find the account had been taken out in her name.

As Mr. Fleming looked on, he could tell she had a thousand questions. "We have lawyers, too, and accountants," said the banker. "we have taken care of everything over the years, so you don't have to worry about back taxes. At this point, the entire amount listed is yours, free and clear and as you saw already in your name."

Sara turned the page and looked at the printed numbers. After turning two more, she got to the last entry. Her eyes grew wide as she silently read the number printed on the bottom,

$1,638,259.63

Chapter 18

Sara continued to stare at the passbook. She reread the number before looking through the previous pages just to check there was no error. "Rainy-day money," she mumbled. Turning to her lawyer, she handed him the passbook thinking why not show him, I'm sure he knows more than he's letting on.

Sara sat back in her chair and crossed her legs. The skirt she was wearing rode up and offered the banker a view of the legs of the young woman he hoped would continue to allow him to manage her assets.

"Nan always said a woman needs some rainy-day money," said Sara. "When I was younger, we'd go shopping on rainy days. Nan always paid for everything. When we'd stop for lunch, she'd often take out her purse and hand me money, usually a twenty, but that became a fifty when I got older. She'd say put that away for a rainy day."

McDougal smiled as he returned the passbook to Sara. "Looks like you've got enough for the entire rainy season."

Fleming had sat, only listening for the past few minutes and now decided it was time to get back to business. "Now that's taken care of we can move on to the main reason for this meeting. The transferring of your grandmother's assets into your name." Fleming opened another folder and extracted a pile of papers. Sara noticed the red page tabs and the yellow 'sign here' stickers she was familiar with, having dealt with client contracts.

"Ms. Ferguson," continued Fleming. "We've filled out most of the paperwork for you and have also made several assumptions which I will discuss before you sign. If you wish to have anything changed, we can do that in a matter of minutes."

The banker handed the original document to Sara and a copy to her lawyer. "Our first assumption is that the assets would stay with Citibank. Do you find that acceptable?"

Sara thought sure why not, they're here now, and then she remembered Nan's first letter and looked to McDougal to see if he had an opinion. The lawyer offered a slight nod. "Yes, that's fine. I see no need to move anything at this time."

"Thank you for continuing to trust Citibank," he said. "Now we have that covered, the other thing we need to discuss is who you would wish to be your asset manager."

Sara had seen the way Fleming had glanced at her legs which was more the look of a connoisseur than a voyeur, so she asked a pointed question, much as she had posed to Jeff about McDougal. "I don't know. You've been doing this for a while, are you any good?"

Fleming sat up in surprise at the question as McDougal stifled a laugh. "She is without a doubt Rose Cavendish's granddaughter," he mumbled under his breath.

"I would say so, Ms. Ferguson. In the fifteen years, I've had this account I've been able to secure an average of nine percent growth. And that takes into account the market crash after the housing market bubble burst in 2008. I hope you would view that as a good resume."

Sara didn't need to look to see if McDougal approved of this choice, she'd heard him strangle that laugh and mumble to himself when she asked Fleming the question. "Once again, I see no reason to change what my grandmother had put into place."

Fleming beamed at Sara's response. He'd kept the account at Citibank and in his portfolio of clients. "Thank you, Ms. Ferguson. I'm glad you will allow me to continue managing your account. I'm sure you will never have cause to question your decision."

"I'm sure I won't, Mr. Fleming. You've managed this account for fifteen years through good times and bad. If my grandmother didn't find fault with you, I'm sure I won't either."

McDougal had been reviewing the paperwork as Sara continued to talk with Fleming. Once he finished, he placed his copy on the desk. "Sara, everything appears to be in order, I see no issues with the paperwork. I would recommend you sign on each of the pages as required."

Fleming walked around to the front of the desk and produced a pen for Sara to use. He showed her where to sign, and Sara affixed her signature to the documents that would legally transfer the account.

Fleming completed the process by countersigning all the documents as the bank's representative, then flipped the divider in the folder and handed Sara an account sheet. "Ms. Ferguson, this is the account status as of this morning. You will notice three figures, cash, bonds, and asset-backed securities. It represents them as percentages in the pie chart. It lists the total at the bottom."

Sara took the sheet and looked at it with a careful eye. After the surprise with Nan's rainy-day fund, she wasn't as shocked when she saw the number. $37,657,000.00. Sara smiled as she handed the paper back. "I can understand why you're happy to keep this in-house."

The banker blushed, "Thank you again for placing your trust in me, Ms. Ferguson. Unless you have any further questions you would like to discuss today, that completes everything we needed to do."

Without a clue where to even begin Sara followed McDougal's lead. "Mr. Fleming, I think Ms. Ferguson will need time to plan a series of questions for you. I would imagine you are busy so we won't take up any more of your time trying to figure out what to ask. May I suggest we schedule another appointment for discussing any additional items my client is interested in?"

"Yes, that sounds like an excellent idea. Should you need anything before then, please call." Taking two business cards from the desk holder, he wrote a phone number on the back of each. "This is my direct number. When would you like to meet again?"

McDougal looked at Sara as he offered the banker a timeframe. "Shall we say two weeks?" Sara nodded her approval.

"That's fine. Would you like us to contact you with dates and times?"

"Please," said McDougal as he produced one of his own business cards. "Contact my office, and we'll coordinate with Ms. Ferguson."

"With pleasure. Ms. Ferguson, it was nice to meet you. I look forward to a long and prosperous relationship," concluded Fleming as he offered his hand as a parting gesture.

Sara shook his hand, "Thank you, Mr. Fleming. I'm sure we'll be seeing each other on a regular basis. Goodbye."

McDougal shook Fleming's hand. "Thank you. We'll be expecting your call," he said as he turned and led Sara out of the office and back to the elevators.

On the ride back down to the parking garage, Sara looked at McDougal. "That went well," she said.

"I would say so. Are you still nervous?"

Sara shook her head, "Not anymore, I think I'm getting used to this whole idea that my grandmother was full of secrets and somehow amassed a fortune."

"I'm glad you've accepted the facts being divulged to you without fainting."

"Come on, Mr. McDougal, that's not fair. I mean what would you have done if suddenly you found out you owned four apartment buildings in Manhattan?"

The lawyer let out a chuckle, "I don't think I'd have fainted, I might have had a heart attack, but I wouldn't have fainted. You're not nervous anymore, that's good. How *do* you feel?"

"Hungry. Do you have time for lunch?"

"Of course, is there any place special you like to go?"

"Since we're already downtown, how about back to Vesuvio?"

"Excellent choice."

When the elevator arrived at the garage level, they exited and walked to the valet stand. McDougal handed the parking ticket to the young man at the podium who ran off to retrieve the Bentley. As the car pulled up in front of the couple, the attendant exited the vehicle and held the door for McDougal while the other valet opened Sara's door. The lawyer thanked the attendant and slipped him a ten-dollar bill as he got behind the wheel.

"Thank you, Sir. Enjoy your day," said the valet.

McDougal drove out of the garage and into the bright sun. Sara noticed how the light danced off the polished wood surfaces inside the car's cabin. "I didn't say this before, but I have to tell you, this is a beautiful car."

"Thank you, I'm glad you like it."

Sara ran her hand over the soft leather of the seat, "Like it? I love it."

"You want one? The dealership is on 11th Ave and 51st Street. We can stop by after lunch."

"Umm, no thanks, I'll pass for the time being," Sara said while trying to imagine walking in, picking one out, and making arrangements to have it paid for out of her rainy-day fund.

Chapter 19

Sara enjoyed her lunch at Vesuvio. Today she had the fish special, which was red snapper and several glasses of wine. McDougal repeated his order from the last time they had been there and had the veal chop. While they ate, the conversation was about many things but not about the remaining business they needed to complete. When they had finished their meal, the lawyer turned the conversation back to business.

"I would suggest we return to my office and go over the next item on the agenda we need to deal with."

"Which is what?" asked Sara.

"To visit Walter Fitzsimmons. He was your grandmother's broker at Merrill Lynch. Just like with Citibank, we need to transfer everything over to you."

Sara peered at McDougal over the rim of her wineglass. "And what surprise will Mr. Fitzsimmons have for me?"

McDougal shrugged his shoulders. "I can't answer that question. As you saw in the letter, there are things your grandmother kept to herself." The lawyer leaned forward, "What do you know about your grandmother's investments?"

"Probably not much more than she told you. She said Grandpa Bill made several good investments when they were married and that they turned out to be very profitable. She mentioned IBM and Polaroid. But that's about all I know."

"Did she ever tell you what William Cavendish did for a living before going off to war?"

Sara shook her head, "No, she never did. She didn't talk about him much, and when she did, it was just about their short time together and how he got killed in Korea."

McDougal took a sip of his coffee as he prepared to tell what little he knew. "Rose told me your grandfather was a stockbroker. And yes, he did make some good buys when they were together." He continued as he placed his cup back on the table. "I'm sure we'll both find out more interesting facts about Mrs. Rose Cavendish when we meet with Mr. Fitzsimmons tomorrow morning. What say we finish up here and get back to the office? I want to offer you some options to consider for the road ahead."

"Okay, I'm ready to go whenever you are."

"Let me pay the check, and we'll be on our way." McDougal flagged down their waiter and handed him his black visa card, "Frank, just close it out and bring me the receipt," he said.

The waiter accepted the card and bowed slightly, "Yes, Mr. McDougal, right away."

The bill folio was returned several minutes later. McDougal scribbled some numbers down on the tip line and signed the bill. "Shall we go?"

Sara nodded, "Yes, I'm ready."

As they walked out, Sara took her lawyer's arm, smiling at the older man. She began to feel closer to him, as if he was becoming the father or grandfather figure she'd never had in her life. "Thank you for lunch, it was very nice."

"You're welcome, and yes, I agree it was nice. I'm glad you suggested we have lunch."

Chapter 20

Janet Collins was waiting for them when they returned to the office. "Welcome back," she said as she offered to take Sara's coat. "Mr. McDougal, would you like me to have coffee sent in?"

McDougal looked at Sara to see if she wanted some, and she politely shook her head. "No thanks, Janet. We're just going to go over some things about tomorrow's meeting with Merrill Lynch and what remains to be done. Please come join us when you've finished what you were doing."

"Yes sir, I'll be back in about ten minutes."

McDougal ushered Sara over to the conference table in his office and held a chair for her while she took a seat. "Let me just get the folder from my desk then we can begin," he said. He returned to the table and took a seat next to Sara.

"Sara, before we go any further, please allow me to ask how you're coping with all these revelations?"

"Disbelief would be a good word," she said. "Before Nan died, I was a creative director at Charles, Jasper, and Williams. I went to work every day, and I worked hard. Last year I made two hundred and seventy thousand, including bonuses, not a fortune but a good salary. I had sixty-five thousand in savings. Now the day after my grandmother's will is read, I'm sitting here the owner of four apartment buildings."

Sara opened her handbag and removed the Citibank passbook as if she needed to offer herself proof of what had happened. "I've got a rainy-day fund of one point six million, a bank portfolio worth another thirty-seven million, and we're not done yet."

As she placed the passbook back in her handbag, she looked at her lawyer. "Yes, Mr. McDougal, I think disbelief probably describes how I'm coping. After everything I've seen so far, I don't think there is much left to find out that could shock."

McDougal opened the folder and looked over several documents before he began. "As we had discussed previously, there were three people we needed to see to complete the transfer of everything over to you. We've completed Citibank and tomorrow morning we will meet with Merrill Lynch. That will leave one more meeting, and that will be with Mr. Thomas Moskowitz. Would you like to get this all finished up tomorrow? We could see him in the afternoon."

"Sure, I guess that would be okay, then we would be finished with all three. Who exactly is Mr. Moskowitz?"

"He's also an asset manager much like Mr. Fleming, only he's with Bank of New York."

Sara looked over and burst out laughing, "Johnny, please show us what we have behind door number three." Turning in her seat so she faced McDougal, Sara regained her composure. "Sorry, I just find all this almost hilarious. I mean it's like a treasure hunt. Isn't it?"

The lawyer nodded, "Yes, I guess in a way it is, and as with today, I can lead you to the chest, but I don't know what you'll find in it. And, to be truthful, it's funny you should make that analogy, this being like a treasure hunt."

"Why's that?"

McDougal flipped the folder to the last section moved the metal tabs of the fastener and removed a small blue envelope from the folder. "When we go to see him, you must bring this with you," he said, offering it to Sara.

"What's that?"

"It's the key to a safe deposit box. You'll need it to claim whatever property is contained within the box."

Sara accepted the small key holder and looked at it with a certain amount of curiosity. "First the will, then the letter and the bank accounts, now a safe deposit box. I'm not even going to guess what is in there."

Sara held the blue envelope out and placed it on the table in front of McDougal. "Since you're taking me to meet with Mr. Moskowitz tomorrow, would you please hold on to this for me?"

McDougal retrieved the key holder and returned it to the folder. "Yes, I can do that."

"Then you'll have someone contact him so we find out if we can meet tomorrow afternoon?" Sara asked.

"Of course. We'll attempt to set it up for mid-afternoon that way there will be plenty of time to go through everything that will be required at Merrill Lynch."

"Okay, so what else is there that needed to be done today? You said you wanted to talk about options for moving forward."

"I was going to talk to you about ensuring you have a good accountant to ensure all your tax liabilities are taken care of as well and setting things up to be paid for automatically. But that can all wait since you reminded me we still have a lot to uncover. I would suggest it's best to find out exactly what the whole of your estate comprises before we get you some help in managing it in its entirety."

"I like that idea. Besides, you remember the letter. When we're done here, Nan wanted me to go to England to meet with her old friend."

"I remember that. Have you called her yet?"

"No, I haven't. I found her number on Nan's cell phone. I'm just waiting until we're done here before I set up the trip."

"Let me know if you want us to help make the arrangements for the trip. Janet can get one of her people to handle everything."

Sara thought about that for a moment because her whole concept of business as usual had changed dramatically over the past few days. "Thank you, that would be good. I must remember to check my passport when I get home to make sure it's still valid."

"We can discuss that further tomorrow since after we meet with Mr. Moskowitz, you will have done everything your grandmother wanted you to complete before you go over there."

After he arranged all the papers and closed the folder, McDougal returned to their conversation from earlier in the day. "You never finished telling me about your phone call from Jeff. You left off after you said you told him you now owned four apartment buildings and he became quiet. What happened after that?"

"I believe he started seeing dollar signs," replied Sara. "He started the whole bit about 'I hope this doesn't change things between us because he cares for me.' Blah, blah, blah. I reminded him there no longer was an *us* and told him when I finished doing what I was doing, I'd let him know if I was coming back to work."

"How do you feel about that idea? Will you go back to work?" asked McDougal.

"I don't think so. It was hard enough keeping Jeff away from my door when I was just a creative director. Now that I'd be an independently wealthy one, I'm sure the scent of money would be hard for him to ignore. The last thing I want is to be courted by someone who looks upon me as a walking checkbook."

"At this point, you'll be able to do whatever your heart desires."

Sara sat back in her chair. "I hadn't thought about that, but you're correct. I can do whatever it is I want to do. That will take some getting used to."

As Sara contemplated what it was she would like to do, Janet returned to the office. Janet noticed Sara had a faraway dreamy look in her eyes, "What's happening? Did I miss something big?"

"No, Sara and I were just talking about what she would do in the future now that she no longer needs to work for a living."

* * *

AS THEY LEFT MCDOUGAL'S OFFICE Sara heard a familiar voice coming from one of the offices. Turning to Janet, she asked, "Is that Dr. Randell?"

"Yes, it is. It seems we had some trouble transferring the money your grandmother left him into his account. There was an issue with the bank's routing number."

"I'd like to say hello to him."

"Certainly," said McDougal, who led Sara into the other office.

"Hello, doctor," Sara said as she moved alongside the neurosurgeon.

Dr. Randell turned to see who was speaking. When he saw Sara, he offered a warm smile, "Hello yourself, Ms. Ferguson. How are you?"

"I'm well, thank you for asking. Janet said there was some problem with transferring the funds. Is everything okay?"

The doctor looked down at his feet for a second, before raising his eyes to look at Sara, "Yes, now it is. It seems I'm capable of performing the most delicate procedures currently being used in brain surgery, but I couldn't copy the bank numbers down correctly."

Sara smiled back at the doctor, "I guess it's a good thing you're a neurosurgeon and not an accountant."

"Yes, I guess it is."

As she stood there, that devilish urge overtook her again. "Dr. Randell, would you consider it forward of me if I asked if you would like to go for coffee? I seem to recall the last time we met and you had a coffee, you had to return to work."

"Yes, that was a hectic day. If I remember correctly, once I got back on the floor, I never even got the chance to drink it."

"Then that settles it. If you have the time, we should go for coffee."

"I have the time, I'm off duty until tomorrow."

Michael McDougal interrupted the moment. "Sara, I'll pick you up in the morning. Same time as today so we can make our next appointment."

"Thanks, Mr. McDougal, I'll see you then," said Sara.

Janet returned to the office carrying Sara's coat. Dr. Randell put his hands out, offering to take it from Janet, so he could help Sara put it on. Sara slipped her arms into the sleeves of her coat and buttoned it up. "Goodbye, Mr. McDougal, I'll see you tomorrow. Janet, thanks for everything you continue to do."

After both lawyers acknowledged her comments, Sara took Dr. Randell's arm. "Shall we go, doctor?"

Chapter 21

Dr. Randell said he'd seen what looked like a quaint coffee shop with an attached bakery half a block away from McDougal's office when he came on Sunday for the reading of the will. He couldn't attest to the quality of the products because it had been closed.

"I'm game," said Sara. "Besides, if I get food poisoning, I've got a doctor with me."

"Thank you very much, but suppose I'm the one who gets food poisoning, what will you do then."

"I'll call 911," she said with a giggle.

As they sat and talked, Sara noticed Dr. Randell looking at her with a kind of peculiar smile. She wasn't sure what he was thinking about, but they seemed to be running into each other on a regular basis.

"Okay, Dr. Randell, out with it. Why the enigmatic smile? What's going on in that brilliant mind of yours?"

"I'll tell you on two conditions."

"Ah, so we're setting conditions now are we?" she replied playfully.

"But of course. Any relationship usually has ground rules."

"Then tell me, doctor, what are these rules."

Dr. Randell offered a smile. "The first condition is that you call me George. While I may be a doctor, I'm not your doctor, and this isn't a professional setting."

"That's simple enough. Okay, George, what is your second condition?"

"You can't laugh when you hear what I'm about to say."

"Okay, that's a deal."

"Right, here goes. If I had known you would wind up being my landlady, I wouldn't have moved."

Sara mulled over his statement for a moment before she replied. "If you'd have known I would be your landlady. I have no idea; what are you talking about?"

"Two years ago, I lived on West 65th Street, just off Amsterdam Avenue. Right by Juilliard. But the travel time up to the medical center was getting me down, especially when I was on call. So I moved uptown closer to the hospital."

"Okay, George, what's that got to do with it?"

"Because the building on 65th is called *'The Stratford.'* It's one of the buildings your grandmother left you."

* * *

THE NEW FRIENDS TALKED for several hours until George suggested perhaps it was time they left. Sara agreed it was getting late, and she had another long day ahead of her tomorrow. When they walked outside, George hailed a cab. He opened the rear door allowing Sara to enter first. "I'll have you dropped off at home on the way."

"That'll work," replied Sara, and she moved closer to George.

As they continued on, George Randell looked over at her, "So, since you don't have to worry about me asking for a reduction on my rent, what would you say if I asked you to have dinner with me one night?"

Sara smiled, "I would say that sounds like fun. Let me have your phone."

George dutifully unlocked his iPhone and handed it over. Sara took the phone, brought up the phone directory, created an entry, and entered her number. Once she had completed the task she slid her finger across the screen once again locking it.

"There you are Dr. Randell; you now have my number."

"Thanks. Did you put it under Sara?"

"No."

"Ferguson?"

"No."

George gave her a puzzled look. "What then?"

"You'll figure it out. But right now, I think I'm home," she said as the cab pulled to the curb.

The doctor exited the taxi and let Sara out. Once she was on the street, she leaned over and kissed him softly on the cheek. "Thanks for the coffee, I enjoyed myself. Call me."

"I enjoyed myself, as well. Bye for now. I'll get my new duty schedule day after tomorrow. Once I get that, I'll call to set a date." The doctor still had his phone in his hand, so he raised it to where it was eye level with Sara. "I say I'll call, of course, that is, if I can figure out where you put your number."

"You're an intelligent man, I'm sure you'll figure it out," replied Sara.

The handsome doctor gave her a peck on the cheek, "I better go, I'll be talking to you soon," he said as he got back in the taxi.

Sara hadn't realized how tired she was until she walked into the building. Recognizing the new owner and by extension, his employer, the concierge ran to open the front door allowing her unimpeded access to the lobby.

"Good afternoon, Miss Ferguson. I hope you're well."

"Hello, Charlie, I'm okay, just tired. Have a good night," replied Sara as she walked straight to the elevator bank and got into the waiting car for the ride to the fourteenth floor.

* * *

GEORGE RANDELL SAT IN THE BACK of the yellow cab as it made its way uptown to take him back to his apartment. As he looked at the phone in his hand, he wondered where in his directory Sara had secreted away her phone number.

It didn't take long before curiosity got the best of him and he unlocked the phone. Once he brought up his directory, he checked under Sara. She was correct, it wasn't there. Or under Stratford, or Ferguson. George then ran his finger across the screen to scroll thought the entries until he found what he was looking for under the E's. The doctor let out a small chuckle and shook his head, Sara Ferguson had most assuredly gained his attention. As he continued to look at the screen, he laughed at how she had titled the entry for her phone number. Ex-Landlady.

Chapter 22

As promised, Michael McDougal pulled up in front of Highgate at 10:00 a.m. Since it was a sunny day, Sara was standing under the awning waiting for him to arrive. Once he maneuvered the large car close to the curb and stopped, Sara got in.

"Good morning," she said, with an upbeat tone.

"Good morning to you, too. How are you today?"

"I'm doing well. I'm excited to see what things we will find out today."

The lawyer agreed. "Yes, it should be an interesting day. We were successful in setting a meeting with Mr. Moskowitz, we'll be meeting with him at 2:00 p.m. I've also brought the safe deposit box key like you asked."

"Thanks. Mr. McDougal, would you mind if I called you Michael? It looks like I'll be needing a lot of help to figure out the legal aspects of all this and as Nan suggested, I'd like to get your advice."

"Not at all. Please, feel free to call me Michael. I'll do what I can to assist you as we get more parts of the puzzle."

"That's good. I was thinking about some things last night and I wanted to talk to you about them."

McDougal glanced over as he was driving, not wanting to take his eyes off the heavy traffic, "Sure, what's on your mind?"

"The first thing was the letter. How often did Nan rewrite that letter?"

"I've been in possession of that letter for five years. But I think I understand what you're asking. It's about the part concerning her knowing the other person had not died before she did. Am I correct?"

Sara nodded, "Yes, that's exactly what I was thinking."

"Simple answer really. Every time we met, she told me the contents of the letter were still valid. I would guess she had some way of knowing. Perhaps she got that information from Mary O'Riley when she called her."

"That makes sense. Okay, the second thing that's bothering me will be a harder one to answer. And that is, how did my grandmother amass such a fortune. I don't ever remember hearing anyone talk about her working except the job she had in England at the aircraft factory during the Second World War."

McDougal shrugged, "That one I don't have an answer for, but hopefully today's meetings with the broker and banker will shed some light on that."

"I sure hope so. I mean, so far, I've discovered almost forty million and cash, bonds, and securities. I have no idea how much the buildings are valued at, and we still have two more people to see."

"We're here," said McDougal. "I guess we can find out more from Fitzsimmons and Moskowitz. Hopefully, they can put some of how she did it into perspective for you."

* * *

THEY FOUND WALTER FITZSIMMONS WAITING for them when they arrived at the front desk of Merrill Lynch's main office on Liberty Street. Based on what Sara had seen of her grandmother's advisors so far, Fitzsimmons didn't fit the mold. Maybe thirty-five to forty years old. His six-foot physique looked like he spent a lot of time at the New York

Athletic Club. A full head of jet-black hair topped a tanned face and piercing blue eyes.

As they approached him, he smiled and introduced himself. "Ms. Ferguson, Mr. McDougal, I'm Walter Fitzsimmons." Once the formalities of the introductions were completed, the broker offered them each a visitor's badge he had prepared in advance. "If you will please follow me, we can go to my office."

The party of three walked to the elevator and rode it to his office on the thirty-seventy floor. Once they arrived and everyone was seated, McDougal produced a folder similar to the one he'd given to the banker at Citibank. It contained all the legal paperwork and a copy of Rose Cavendish's death certificate. Fitzsimmons quickly reviewed the items in the folder while McDougal looked on, and Sara enjoyed the view of New York from the high vantage point.

Fitzsimmons looked up as he closed the folder on his desk. "Everything appears to be in order. Before we proceed are there any questions you would like to ask?"

Sara spoke up, "Yes, I have a few."

"Certainly, Ms. Ferguson, what are your questions?" He replied, focusing his attention on the woman.

"How long have you been managing my grandmother's portfolio?"

The broker smiled. "As the principal manager, only for five years, but I was an assistant to the former manager for seven years before that. I guess you could say I was being groomed to take over."

"I see, and why did you take over?

"The previous manager retired five years ago."

"Who was the previous manager, and how long had he overseen the portfolio?"

"The previous manager acted as the primary on Mrs. Cavendish's account for about thirty-five years before retiring," replied the broker as his smile grew wider. "His name was Walter Fitzsimmons, Junior. I'm Walter Fitzsimmons, III."

Sara's eyes went wide again, "So you took over for your father."

Fitzsimmons' smile didn't fade, "Yes, I did just as he took over the account from his father, Walter Fitzsimmons, Senior."

Sara went silent, as McDougal allowed himself a small chuckle before he spoke. "Your family has overseen this account through three generations. Yet another surprise from Rose Cavendish."

The broker looked at Sara, "I imagine you are now wondering about the how and why for all this family history."

"You have my full attention," said Sara as she sat back and crossed her legs.

"Mine, too," added McDougal.

"Certainly," said Fitzsimmons as he put his pen down. "When I tell you, you'll see it has a rationale behind it. It all goes back to my grandfather who was a broker with Shearson Hammill & Co. I'm sure you've heard of them."

McDougal nodded, "Yes, that's going back some years to the original company, before the name changes."

"Correct, as I was saying my grandfather worked for them. And when he was there, he had a friend named William Cavendish."

"Grandpa Bill?"

"Correct again. My grandfather and your step-grandfather were friends. They went to Columbia together and started with Shearson after they graduated."

McDougal sat back, "Well now I've heard everything," he said in a laughing tone. "And here I was, thinking after being Rose Cavendish's lawyer for forty plus years I knew her. She's got more secrets than the Vatican."

"Then I gather after Grandpa Bill died, your grandfather took over as the primary manager."

Fitzsimmons nodded his agreement. "That's right. Senior oversaw the transactions within the account while William was away. After he was reported killed in action, Mrs. Cavendish requested Senior continue to manage the account."

Sara shook her head before she spoke. "Well that answers the question I had concerning your age. Everyone I've dealt with so far who were entrusted with my grandmother's affairs has been older and with her for years." Pointing to the broker, she continued, "However, you Mr. Fitzsimmons get the longevity award for generations of service."

The portfolio manager placed his right hand over his heart and gave a slight bow. "It's been my family's pleasure to serve your family. Is that the only question you had before we proceed?"

Again Sara shook her head. "No, I have a few more. For one, can you explain how my grandmother built a portfolio I'm sure you will tell me is worth millions of dollars?"

Fitzsimmons crossed his arms and leaned forward on his desk. "The first thing I can tell you about your grandmother is that she was what we affectionately refer to as a mule. And by that we mean she was very systematic and dependable with her investments."

"I don't follow. What's that mean?" asked Sara.

"For years, probably decades, she made systematic deposits, everything went in, nothing was taken out."

"So you're saying Rose reinvested any dividends she received," said McDougal.

"That's correct. It wasn't until recently, maybe five years ago Mrs. Cavendish started having dividends transferred to Citibank."

Sara looked at her lawyer and smiled, "I'll bet if we look at those transfers, they will match the deposits to my rainy-day fund."

"Sounds plausible," agreed McDougal.

"What about the investments in general? Nan always said Grandpa Bill made some smart buys that turned out well like IBM and Polaroid."

Fitzsimmons removed a thick folder from his desk drawer, opened it and looked back at the beginning of what was a complete history of the account. "That's true, that was the start of the account. But there were other excellent buys that added a great deal to her bottom line." After flipping through several pages, he looked at Sara. "I remember a conversation with your grandmother years ago when I was learning the ropes. She told me that Bill always told her two things relating to how he viewed new stocks. And that was technology doesn't go backward, and people will always spend money to buy things."

Sara understood what he had said and replied. "I didn't know about the technology part. However, I heard Nan on several occasions say something about people will always be willing to spend money they don't have."

The broker again looked at the folder. "I guess Grandpa Bill's words had a lasting effect on her. And I say that because much of what is in your grandmother's portfolio are unsolicited buys."

Sara offered the broker a puzzled look, "I don't follow."

Fitzsimmons offered Sara a look as if begging forgiveness for his fellow traders. "You've seen the movies where a broker calls a client and says, listen, I've got a line on ABC Corp, we hear they will break out a new product that will send the stock soaring."

"Yes, I have."

"Well, according to the history in her file, your grandmother usually contacted us and said buy so many shares of XYZ. I'll give you an example," he said as he looked through the folder for the item he wanted. "Here it is. Back in nineteen seventy-two, my father received a call to buy three hundred shares of a new company stock that was selling for six cents a share. Your grandmother never let that stock go. Over the years that stock split two-for-one nine times." Fitzsimmons looked at both people sitting across from him before he went on. "Allow me to do the math for you. Three hundred, doubled nine times, comes out to one hundred fifty-three thousand six hundred shares. And that's without reinvesting the dividends."

No one said anything as they waited for the portfolio manager to provide the rest of the information. "That penny stock your grandmother instructed my father to buy three hundred shares of for the price of twenty-one dollars including sales commissions was for a small company that wanted to expand, and by going public they floated the capital to expand. You may have heard of this company. It's called Walmart."

Sara's mouth fell open. "Walmart, a hundred and fifty thousand shares of Walmart."

"Fitzsimmons typed some information into his desktop computer, looked at what the result was and turned to Sara, "Two hundred seventeen thousand, four hundred sixty-eight to be exact. And the last dividend it paid out was fifty-one cents per share."

McDougal thought about that for a second before he turned to Sara, "That's over a hundred thousand dollars in dividends."

"That's correct," said the portfolio manager, "and as of today's current price of ninety-one dollars and fifty cents, it has a value of twenty-one point two million dollars. Not bad for a twenty-dollar investment." Fitzsimmons changed his focus from Sara to her lawyer, "Mr. McDougal, do you remember the old commercials for E. F. Hutton?"

"Sure, something about my broker is E. F. Hutton, and they say… which caused everyone to stop what they were doing and attempt to listen in on the conversation. Then a voice-over followed, and someone said when E. F. Hutton speaks everyone listens."

Fitzsimmons applauded. "Correct, well when Rose Cavendish spoke, we all listened. She made a lot of money for herself and for those who gambled on her hunches. There were losers, too. Mainly in the tech stocks like Lucent Technologies. And K-Mart on the retail side, but she saw the writing on the wall based on the dwindling dividends and sold off all of that while others were still buying, hoping for a turnaround."

Sara was speechless. Everything she thought would happen did, but the magnitude of the discovery surpassed her expectations many times over. Perhaps Fitzsimmons could answer the question she had asked Michael earlier today. "Mr. Fitzsimmons I have one more question, and hopefully you will be able to answer it for me."

Once more, the broker gave her his undivided attention.

"Back to what I asked earlier about building the portfolio. I understand how it grew once things were purchased, and my grandmother just let them grow. Can you tell me where the money came from to make the buys?" Sara offered a knowing smile as she continued. "I mean, I'm sure there were many purchases over the years that cost over twenty dollars."

Fitzsimmons nodded, "There were. As I said earlier the money that started going out went to Citi. But the money that came in for purchases always came from the Bank of New York."

Sara turned to Michael and raised her eyebrows, "I guess we've got another piece of the picture. It will be interesting to see what we discover when we go there this afternoon."

The lawyer nodded his agreement then spoke to the portfolio manager. "I believe Ms. Ferguson has asked everything she wanted to ask at this time." Turning to Sara, she confirmed his statement with a nod. "Now, as you said, everything is in order so we can sign the accounts over. Can you inform us as to the current value of the portfolio?"

The broker looked to Sara for approval of the lawyer's request.

"Yes, it's okay."

"If you will give me a moment to bring the entire portfolio up, I'll be happy to give you that information." Typing on the keyboard, he entered some commands then clicked on several items on the screen. "With everything actively trading, at the moment the total value of the portfolio is just south of one hundred seventy-nine million."

Sara smiled, but it was more a look of disbelief than of joy. "A hundred and seventy-nine million." As she raised her eyes to the heavens, Sara thought about her Grandmother. Nan, I don't even know where to begin, but don't worry, I'll do what you asked me to do in your letter.

Chapter 23

After they left Fitzsimmons' office, they returned to the lobby and walked to the parking garage where McDougal had left the Bentley. Sara hadn't spoken ten words since her portfolio manager gave her the current total figure for the assets it contained. The lawyer looked at his client instinctively knowing she needed time to process everything that was happening to her. He was sure she hadn't spent her life wondering what it would be like to be an heiress to a vast fortune. He saw her as being someone who just went through day-to-day life expecting nothing, only to find out a wealthy relative had passed on and left her a fortune.

The only difference here, he thought, was that she lived with that wealthy relative for years and never knew about the money. Now things were rapidly unfolding as all her grandmother's assets were being transferred to her and it overwhelmed her.

He likened this to waking up one morning to find out you had won the lottery, but you didn't know just how much you had won because the accounting hadn't been completed. Then his thoughts shifted back to Rose Cavendish, and he pondered why she had kept all her wealth secret. Did it have to do with the promise she had made so many years ago to some unnamed person? He thought about the letter Sara had allowed him to read. It urged Sara to find out who she was. There was obviously more to this than met the eye, but he hadn't known much more than Sara before they began making the rounds of the bankers.

The final piece of this part of the puzzle would be revealed in a few hours when they met the last of the three men who held the keys to the financial empire Rose Cavendish had left her granddaughter.

They had a little over two hours before they had to be at Thomas Moskowitz's midtown office. McDougal attempted to engage Sara in conversation. "It's only a quarter to twelve, we've got a while before we have to be at BNY-Mellon. Would you like to have lunch?"

Sara shook her head, "No, I don't think I could eat. I feel sick to my stomach."

"You want me to stop? Do you want something to drink?"

"No, thank you, I'm not sure that would help. Can we just go to your office and wait there?

"Of course, you just relax, try to close your eyes. I'll open the window so you can get some fresh air."

Sara slouched in the seat, putting her head against the well-padded headrest. McDougal opened the window about halfway, letting fresh air and noise into the luxurious cabin.

Sara wrinkled her nose, "I didn't realize how quiet this car was until just now."

"Yes, it's sort of like riding in your living room."

"It is," she replied as she sat up in her seat and turned toward the window to allow the fresh air to flow over her face. "That feels better," she said.

"I'm glad you feel better, we'll be at the office in about five minutes."

Turning in her seat, Sara looked at her lawyer for the first time since they'd gotten in the car. "Michael, what am I going to do?"

"Do? About what?"

"About two hundred million and counting. What am I going to do about all that money?"

"I'd say once we're done, we get you a reputable accountant to oversee your accounts. Then you really enjoy your life."

"Enjoy my life. I'm not sure how to do that. Normally my life consisted of working. Now I guess it's more like every day is Sat… Sunday." She smiled, "I was going to say Saturday, but I've spent a lot of Saturdays working on pitches."

"True, but you have to remember, the first thing you get to do is travel over to England to try to find out whatever it was your grandmother wanted you to find out."

"I've been thinking about that. I guess I could go next week. I checked my passport, it's good for another two years."

"Okay, then there's something to begin planning. We can get Janet's folks on that once we get back to the office."

"All right, we can do that. And maybe we can order something for lunch," she said, rubbing her stomach. "I'm beginning to feel better. I probably should eat something."

"We can do that, too."

* * *

SARA ATE HALF A ROAST BEEF SANDWICH on rye. She stayed away from the coleslaw and potato salad because she wasn't sure how the mayo would affect her stomach.

Janet had joined them for lunch as they ate in one of the small conference rooms. Michael mentioned that Sara was thinking of heading over to London next week to meet with Mary O'Riley in an attempt to find out what her grandmother's secret had been. Janet made some notes and said she would have someone make all the arrangements. As she put her pen down, she looked at Sara and smiled, "I assume you would like to travel first class."

Sara thought about that for a second before she offered Janet a smile of her own, "Why yes, I think I would. Now that will be an experience."

"Careful, we don't want you to get spoiled," said McDougal with a chuckle.

"Don't listen to him," said Janet. "He's not even willing to fly business class."

McDougal nodded, "She's right. Once you experience first class you're ruined. The only thing better is a private jet."

Sara leaned forward and placed her chin in her hand, "Hmm, a private jet. Nah, I'll stick with first-class. At least I'll have someone in the seat next to me I can talk to."

McDougal noted the time on the wall clock. "It's twenty-five to two, we better get going."

Sara looked at the two lawyers, a slight look of dread crossed her face as she agreed, "You're right. I've got to tell you, part of me doesn't want to do this. But this is the last one, right?"

"Yes, this is the last one." Replied McDougal. "Given what we learned from Fitzsimmons, perhaps this will shed some light on your questions."

"I hope so," said Sara as she leaned back in the chair.

"And this one is where the safe deposit box is," offered McDougal. "Maybe you'll find some answers there."

"One can only hope," replied Sara as she stood.

* * *

ONCE AGAIN, MCDOUGAL LED SARA into the offices of a person who had more of the answers she wanted. Answers required to fill in the missing parts of the picture Rose Cavendish had hidden away from her granddaughter and her loyal legal confidants for years.

150

When Sara met Thomas Moskowitz, she decided he was more of what she had expected one of her Nan's trusted agents to look like. He must have been in his late sixties. Tall and trim, salt and pepper hair that appeared freshly cut. Intelligent brown eyes that looked out through stylish but not youthful frames. The banker wore a charcoal gray suit with a chalk stripe; he most definitely presented an image of someone with a high place in the financial district.

Since she had already been through this process twice, Sara sat patiently as McDougal and Moskowitz went over all the paperwork and forms required to begin the transfer. After they completed everything, the banker smiled at Sara. "Ms. Ferguson, before we begin, please allow me to express my condolences on your grandmother's passing. I've managed her accounts for years, and as sad as it is, I have to say I'm glad I got to see her before she passed away."

Sara tilted her head as she tried to put the banker's comment into context. "Did you see her in the hospital?"

"No, I actually met with her on the day she collapsed. She said she wanted to talk to me about something and asked if I would be in the office."

"So she came here?" asked Sara.

Moskowitz shook his head, "No, I was spending the day uptown at the offices of another client. I told Mrs. Cavendish, I would have some time to meet with her at lunchtime if she wanted to make the trip up."

Sara looked at McDougal. "Well, at least we now have the answer to why Nan was uptown when she collapsed. That was something nagging at the back of my mind. 'Why was she there?'"

Moskowitz continued, "Yes, we had lunch and discussed what it was she wanted to talk about, then she went on her way. From what I know, she had the stroke not more than thirty minutes after we parted ways."

"Can you tell me what it was my grandmother wanted to talk to you about?"

"I can, but now that topic is rather a moot point. Your grandmother wanted to talk about creating another account in your name. I know you must have a list of questions you want to ask, but before we get to those, please allow me to tell you some things that you may find useful."

Sara took this all in stride and answered, "You can't imagine some of the questions that come to mind after everything I've learned to date."

"Perhaps, however, if you will allow me to share some processes Mrs. Cavendish had in place, it could help."

"Please, enlighten me," replied Sara. "So far, everything I've learned has been a shock, so I'm ready for the next one."

"Very well. Let me begin by saying BNY-Mellon was the bank that supplied Mrs. Cavendish with the money she used day-to-day."

"I already know that. Nan had a checkbook, debit, and credit cards. The works."

"We managed her account. On the first of every month, we credited her account with twenty thousand dollars, and we paid her credit card off."

Sara tilted her head as she spoke. "Okay, so you put twenty thousand in her account and zeroed out her credit card. Where does the money come from?"

"I'll get to that in a bit, but first, there's more." Moskowitz looked at the young woman whom he knew had no idea of what was involved. "Your grandmother's account, and now, by right of inheritance your account, has a low balance warning and automatic overdraft protection. If the balance dropped below the minimum fifteen hundred dollars required to be kept in the account, it was automatically refilled to the twenty-thousand-dollar level. And likewise, on the first of the month, whatever money remained in the account was adjusted up to the same threshold."

"The account is funded and automatically refilled? Okay, I think I can understand that. But I'll ask again, where does the money come from?"

Moskowitz looked at Sara and offered a simple answer, "We transfer it from what is now your savings account."

"Ah, finally!" said Sara. "Now we're getting somewhere. So the saving account funds the checking account, I can see that. And how much is in my savings account?"

"At the moment, almost three million dollars, but that number changes."

"Of course it changes, you're transferring money out of it to keep the checking account afloat," said Sara as she looked over at McDougal, thinking, and this guy's a banker.

"Yes, but when I was referring to the changing balance, I wasn't talking about the money transferred out to fund the checking account. I was talking about the electronic transfer of funds which are deposited quarterly."

McDougal spoke up, "You must be referring to money that now comes in from Mrs. Cavendish's Citibank account."

Moskowitz shook his head.

"Okay, then it comes from Merrill Lynch. It must be the transfer of the dividends," said McDougal.

Once again, Moskowitz shook his head, "No, I'm afraid that is also incorrect, the money transfer comes from another source, and it fluctuates."

"So, where does it come from?" asked Sara.

"The electronic transfer is from Barclays Bank, London."

Sara was once again dumbstruck as Moskowitz continued. "The sum wired is in British pounds and has to be converted, which is why the number of pounds received changes. It fluctuates to ensure the amount received in U.S. dollars remains constant."

McDougal looked at the banker and asked, "You said the dollar amount remains constant, can you tell us how much money is transferred quarterly?"

Moskowitz looked to Sara for approval to divulge the amount. Sara nodded, "Yes, please answer the question. How much money comes in quarterly?"

"One hundred thousand U.S. dollars."

Now it was McDougal's turn to be lost for words as he locked eyes with the banker. Once he regained his composure, he again began the conversation. "Let me see if I understand this. The account used to fund my client's day to day spending account gets its funding from England."

Moskowitz nodded, "That is correct."

"And at the present time, it is getting a quarterly electronic transfer to deposit the sum of one hundred thousand dollars."

The banker nodded again, "That is also correct."

Both men looked at Sara, who had taken a deep breath and prepared to ask her questions. "How long have these transfers been taking place?"

"Since Mrs. Cavendish started her account with us. However, please understand, the money transferred has not always been equal to the current amounts of deposit. It has increased over the years."

Sara took over the conversation as she attempted to wrap her mind around yet another unbelievable fact. "So, this account has always been funded by money transferred from England?"

Moskowitz nodded slightly, "Yes, Ms. Ferguson, as we already established, these transfers have been in place since the account was started."

"Which was when?" asked Sara.

Moskowitz opened the folder and looked for the information. "The account was opened in the name of Mrs. Rose MacDonald on August 22nd, 1945. Our records indicate the initial transaction was to convert two thousand pounds sterling to dollars. After the exchange, $8,530 was deposited.

Sara looked pale as she rose to her feet. "Excuse me, where is your restroom?"

Moskowitz also stood. "Certainly, it's down the hall, third door on the left. Ms. Ferguson, are you okay, you don't look well."

Sara nodded as she left the office. "I need a moment."

* * *

WHEN SARA STILL HADN'T RETURNED after fifteen minutes, Mr. Moskowitz sent his executive assistant to check on her. Ten minutes later, Sara returned to her seat in the banker's office, looking fresh and composed.

"I'm sorry, please forgive me, it's been a trying few days."

"No need to apologize," replied Moskowitz. "While you were away, Mr. McDougal and I completed all the paperwork for the transfer. Unless you want to make different arrangements, everything Mrs. Cavendish had in place regarding the disposition of funds into her checking account will remain in place." The banker produced a pile of papers and placed them in front of Sara. "All we need is your signature on these forms to complete everything, and we will order your checks, and bank cards."

Sara glanced over the forms and signed on the line, completing the last of the transfers. Moskowitz reviewed the arrangements to ensure everything was in order, then placed everything back into the folder. "There is one final thing we need to take care of today, and that is the safe deposit box."

Sara nodded as she looked at her lawyer. "Mr. McDougal has the key," she said as McDougal opened his briefcase and removed the envelope. Sara accepted the key and held it up for Moskowitz to see. "I guess we have to go to the vault and retrieve it."

"That's correct, if you follow me, we'll go down there now, and you can sign for the box."

McDougal stood and accompanied the two to the elevator and down to the vault. Sara signed the access form that had been waiting for them to arrive and followed the bank official into the vault. Sara handed her key to the banker who inserted it along with the master into the door lock of box 1437. The box wasn't that large, but it was one of the wide ones that would allow documents to be placed in it without folding them.

Moskowitz turned the keys and opened the door, allowing him to remove the safe deposit box from its location and handed it to Sara. "We have secure rooms so you can review the contents in private."

Sara looked at McDougal, "Michael, would you please come with me?"

"If you wish."

Sara handed the safe deposit box to McDougal and nodded as she turned to Moskowitz, "Which room would you like us to use?"

The banker pointed to the corner room. "Use number four. It has a larger table."

"Four it is then," said McDougal, and he led Sara into the room, closed, and locked the door.

* * *

MCDOUGAL PLACED THE SAFE DEPOSIT BOX in the center of the table as he and Sara sat down. Sara sat motionless, looking at the green box. Not wanting to touch it or even open it, she feared the unknown contents of the container. McDougal sat by quietly as he watched his client come to terms with the last piece of the puzzle he was charged with delivering. Sara's stare was unwavering, her eyes transfixed on the object in front of her.

Sara took a deep breath and reached for the small latch on the front of the box and flipped it over. As it clicked, she withdrew her hand as if she had received an electric shock. "I can't," she said.

McDougal didn't reply. He remained sedate and waited for Sara to calm down before he spoke. "Sara, it's just a box, whatever your grandmother placed in there will not hurt you." He turned the box around on the table, as if it's exterior would offer a clue. "We've already talked about this, perhaps it's more information to help you on the quest Rose has sent you on."

"What do you mean?"

"Simply this, the other two gentlemen told us about your grandmother's wealth, Mr. Moskowitz gave us information about how she managed to live so comfortably and the fact she was not, in fact, penniless when she got to the States. That's quite a different twist to the tale of her early days in America."

"Would you open it for me?"

McDougal followed his client's wish and turned the box so he could open the lid and peer inside. He released the cover, allowing it to rest on the hinge stop. The lawyer reached inside and moved things around so he could determine what was inside the container.

"What's in there?"

"Papers, cash with bank wrappers, looks to be twenty thousand dollars." In the back of the container, he found a stack of envelopes wedged under the rim. "I've got a pile of what looks like letters tied with a ribbon, a black velvet box, and one more envelope addressed to you. It's written in Rose's hand."

Sara spoke, her voice almost cracking as if she were about to cry. "May I have the envelope?"

McDougal handed it over as requested, and Sara placed it on the table in front of her. After a minute, she slid it across the table to her lawyer. "Please read it to me."

"Take a deep breath and relax while I open it."

Michael retrieved his reading glasses from his pocket and put them on. Carefully tearing the envelope open, he removed the handwritten letter. Once he looked it over, he was sure it was Rose Cavendish's handwriting.

"Are you ready?"

Sara nodded.

My Dearest Sara,

I'm sure you have been shocked by everything you have uncovered about the fortune I've managed to accumulate over the past sixty-plus years.

Some was accomplished by luck, some because Grandpa Bill was an excellent teacher when it came to understanding the stock market and a lot of it because of the provisions put in place when I agreed to keep a secret.

The fact you are reading this letter means you have reached the end of the road in America. The rest of the story is to be found in England. You will find more items in this safe deposit box that will provide you with clues. But once again a big piece of the puzzle will be uncovered when you talk to Mary.

Now that you have reached the end, if you have not done so already, it is time to make the call, and travel across to England to meet with her.

Please understand, I never meant to deceive anyone, but it had to be done. People needed to be protected, and I needed to ensure you were safe and would be well cared for if anything happened to me.

Everyone involved knew about the part they played in my affairs, but only I knew how everything fit together. Now you know almost as much as I did. It's time for you to find out the rest.

Love,

Nan

After he finished reading the letter, he placed it back on the table and pushed it in front of Sara. "There you have it. Not much of an explanation if that's what you were looking for, but now we know every person had a part to play in your grandmother's grand plan."

Sara picked up the letter and looked it over as she spoke. "Quite the story, and it's not over yet. It looks like I better make that phone call. Let's look at the other items in there, shall we?"

The first things McDougal removed were the bundles of cash bound with bank straps. Two packets of hundred-dollar bills totaling ten thousand dollars each. Placing the two packs in front of Sara, he smiled. "If you're up to going to dinner after this, you're buying."

For the first time today, Sara smiled. "Okay, I guess that's only fair. What's next?"

The lawyer removed the velvet box and handed it to Sara. "I say we see what's in the box."

Upon opening the box, Sara gasped as she saw the contents. A stunning diamond and sapphire brooch lay fastened to the blue velvet pillow contained within. The design was classic, smaller sapphires surrounded by diamonds all set in a pattern around a large sapphire center stone. Ornate white gold filigree connected the smaller stones to the larger one. Sara noticed the name of the jeweler on the inside of the box's top, *Toye, Kenning & Spencer, Great Queen Street, Covent Garden.*

Sara showed the brooch to her lawyer. "Have you ever seen Nan wear this?"

McDougal shook his head. "No, I don't think I've ever seen your grandmother wear anything other than a string of pearls, and some earrings. She wasn't at all about flash."

As she continued to inspect the brooch, Sara noted, "This would certainly fall into the flash category, I wonder where it came from. I mean, I wonder who gave it to her. Couldn't have been her first husband. You know, come to think of it, I'm not even sure what my grandfather's first name was. The only person

Mom ever knew was Grandpa Bill." Closing the cover on the brooch, Sara slipped it into her handbag. "When I go over there, I'll bring this along. If this place is still in business, maybe they can tell me who bought it."

"That's a good idea. If it was any kind of special order, they should have a record. The Brits are sticklers for records, especially in the upper classes. I guess it's important to know where something came from and who bought it, sold it, etc. Keeps things legal."

Feeling more relaxed now, Sara reached over and turned the box so she could look inside. "What else have we got?"

McDougal reached in and pulled the stack of envelopes out from under the ledge created by the top of the box that didn't open. When he removed them, he found his assumption had been correct. They were, in fact, letters tied into a bundle by a long piece of satin ribbon. The lawyer noticed two things as he looked at the envelopes: One, the ones he could see were addressed to Rose MacDonald. Two, they had stamps that appeared to be British.

Sara untied the ribbon and picked out one letter. McDougal's suspicion was correct when Sara saw the envelope was postmarked from London.

Once she removed the letter from the envelope, Sara noted the handwriting differed significantly from her grandmother's.

Highgate House
Eaton Mews, South
London, SW1

September 4, 1945

Dearest Rose,

I hope this letter finds you well. Not much to tell from this side. Now that the war is over, the rebuilding had begun in earnest. Unexploded bombs dropped during the blitz are still being found

Thoughts of you fill my dreams. I continue to look for a way to bring you back to England. Do not lose hope. Love always finds a way.

Eternally Yours,
T.

Sara held the letter up for McDougal to read. "I'm not sure if this is a love letter or what. The first part is rather cold, but the end talks about trying to get Nan back to England." Turning the page over, looking for clues, she continued talking to her lawyer. "I'm confused. Did Nan have a boyfriend right after her husband got killed? It sure sounds like he loved her."

"I can't answer that, but you've missed something that might be important."

Sara looked at the letter again, "What's that?" she asked.

McDougal reached over and pointed to the top corner of the letter. "The address."

"Highgate House. How did I not see that? Now that is interesting. You're right, it could be a clue for Mary O'Riley to help me with."

"I'm sure it's not pure coincidence that Rose named her apartment building Highgate."

"No, I'm sure you're correct about that. Everything we've seen over the past few days had been very well planned. Every move calculated and done with precision." Sara reflected on the letter Nan had left for her in the safe deposit box. Everyone knew about their bit. But not about the others. Even Michael, he was sort of the key. He knew the three men were important but not the extent of the information they controlled.

Sara tapped the corner of the letter where McDougal had shown her the address. "Hopefully, Mary O'Riley can tell me who lived at Highgate House."

McDougal laughed at her comment, "Or you could just go knock on the door and ask if T is home."

"I could, and all this jesting is all well and good. However, the one question I really want to be answered is, who's been sending money for more than sixty years, and a better question would be why?"

McDougal thought about Sara's comment as he leaned back in his seat,. "That is the million-dollar question, no pun intended."

Sara put stack of letters in her handbag. "I think we're done here. Like Nan said, this is the end of the road here in the States. Since I'm feeling better now, I think your idea about going for dinner is wonderful." Picking up the two straps of cash, she flipped through the end of one of the stacks. "This should cover dinner, don't you think?"

McDougal stood. "I should hope so, including drinks and tip."

Chapter 24

Michael knew of a quality steak restaurant that would be opened Once they were seated, the waiter took their drink orders while they looked at the menu. Sara had a dirty martini to start while Michael has a double Johnny Walker Blue label. They toasted the end of the journey they had completed, which transferred all of Rose Cavendish's wealth to her granddaughter.

Sara ordered the filet while Michael asked for the bone-in ribeye. While they waited for dinner to arrive, they talked about Sara's pending trip to England. McDougal knew Sara might need help navigating the legal and banking systems, so he thought about suggesting Sara get in touch with a barrister he had worked with on several cases.

"I've been giving some thought to your trip over to the U.K.," said McDougal.

"I have been, too. I need to go over there and talk to Mary O'Riley, but after that I'm not sure what to do next."

Glass in hand, McDougal swirled the whiskey in the glass as he offered his ideas. "I have a colleague in London that I've worked with on several occasions, I'd like to put you in touch with him."

"Great minds think alike," replied Sara. "I was going to ask if you could recommend someone over there who could help me out. I'm sure there will be things I'll be needing help with, like getting in to see the bank managers."

Dinner arrived, and all conversation about business ceased and turned to comments about the quality of the food and what an excellent selection had been made for the wine to accompany the meal.

* * *

AFTER THEY HAD FINISHED THEIR MEAL, the waiter cleared the plates and retired to his station to print out the bill. When he returned, he placed the bill folio in front of McDougal. Sara saw McDougal smile as she caught the waiter's attention. "Please," she said as she extended her hand, "I'll take that."

The waiter smiled as he changed directions and placed the leather folder in Sara's hands, "Of course, Madam, excuse me. Whenever you're ready."

"I'm ready now, just a second," replied Sara as she dipped her hand into her purse. She removed one bundle of cash and put it on the table while she opened the bill folder with her other hand. After reviewing the total, she looked at the waiter and nodded as if saying everything was in order. Sara counted off the proper number of bills required to pay the bill and leave a very generous tip. She pulled the currency out of the bundle, placing it into the folder and handed it to the waiter who stood there eyeing the pile of cash. "Thank you very much, the dinner was excellent and so was the service."

The waiter accepted the folder containing the money and accepted Sara's compliment with a slight bow. "Thank you for dining with us this evening. Please come again."

Sara returned the strap of bills back into her purse, offering a slight nod of acknowledgment to the waiter before turning to her lawyer. "Shall we go? It's been a long day."

"Yes, it certainly has been a busy day. This is one I'm sure I'll remember for a while."

Michael rose from his seat and moved to hold Sara's chair while she stood. Together they left the restaurant, walking to the valet parking stand where McDougal presented the ticket to the attendant. While they waited for the car, Michael looked at Sara and smiled but said nothing.

Sara noticed the look he was giving her. She began to feel self-conscious and offered a nervous smile in return. "What's wrong? Do I have spinach in my teeth or something?"

McDougal continued to smile as she shook his head. "No, Madam, everything is fine. I'd like to thank Madam for dinner."

Sara laughed as she attempted to provide her lawyer with a stern look. "Okay, don't you start with the Madam stuff, too. How old do you think our waiter was, twenty-one, maybe twenty-two? Someone his age calling me Madam made me feel really old."

"Sorry, I couldn't resist after I saw the look you gave him when he called you that."

The Bentley pulled to the curb, and the attendants opened the doors for the occupants. McDougal pulled into traffic and headed toward Sara's home. As they drove, he rekindled the conversation they had been having earlier about Sara's trip to England. "Sara, going back to what we were talking about earlier, it seemed you were agreeable to my contacting my colleague to assist you in England."

"Yes, I agree that it would be a good idea. How do you know this person?" she asked.

"I worked on another inheritance case that involved a naturalized American citizen who, like your Nan, immigrated to the States in the late forties." McDougal stopped for a second as he checked his mirrors to change lanes so he could turn left. "Sorry, as I was saying, this person bequeathed property located in England to his wife and family. The brother of the husband contested the will. He claimed that when his brother left England, he abandoned the property and that he had worked on keeping up on repairs and had paid the taxes."

"Sounds complicated," replied Sara.

"It was. The property was deeded to my client, and his brother never challenged the ownership before my client's death. Since this wound up in court, I needed to enlist a barrister to represent my client's interest in the proceedings. Reginald Cromwell is his name. He's a direct descendant of Oliver Cromwell. I'll put in a call to him tomorrow and see if he's available to assist, if not I'll ask him to name a suitable replacement."

"That sounds good."

"Would you like to come to the office tomorrow to go over the plans for your trip?"

Sara shook her head, "No, thank you, after the past three days, tomorrow I don't plan on getting out of my pajamas. I'm going to stay home, sleep, order in and probably sleep some more."

"And call Mary O'Riley?"

"Yes. I'll call her and let her know what's happened and that I'll be there in a few days. Once I get my itinerary, I can call her back and let her know when I'll be there."

"I'll have Janet call and email you a copy of the trip details."

"You know, I'm still expecting to wake up and find this has all been a crazy dream, and I'll be headed to the office in the morning."

"That's not going to happen," said her lawyer as he pulled the car to the curb. "This is all very real. Everything is true, and yes, it has actually occurred. Your grandmother is gone, and you are now a wealthy woman."

"And one with a task that will take me across the Atlantic in an attempt to uncover a secret that's been kept for over sixty years. I wonder what's waiting for me in London?"

"I don't know. But whatever it is, it was something your grandmother promised to keep secret, and she did just that. Don't worry about it now." McDougal shifted the car into park, then turned in his seat to better see his client. "Right now I think you should just go upstairs and do exactly what you described to me, and that's relaxing."

"Thanks, that sounds like good advice, and I think I'll add a long hot bath to the beginning of that list. Goodnight, Michael," said Sara as she exited the vehicle and disappeared into the lobby of the apartment building.

Chapter 25

Sara poured a glass of wine and carried it into the bathroom. The idea of having a long hot bath appealed to her. She opened the taps and allowed the large garden tub to fill.

The water was hot, just the way Sara liked it. It provided a therapeutic effect as it helped ease away the tension Sara had developed as the day wore on. The water also had a buoyant effect; Sara closed her eyes while she floated in a semi-weightless state.

Thoughts of the events of the past three days came to her in no order: the will, the meetings with the three men who were the keepers of a part of Nan's secret, the letters from her and the ones from T. And mostly the money, all that money over two hundred million dollars. Sara found that figure hard to fathom. It was the quarterly electronic transfers of one hundred thousand dollars that held her attention. Since Nan had never discussed the money in the bank or the investments beyond what she mentioned about Grandpa Bill, Sara wrote that off. What bothered her was the fact Nan had told her more than once that she was relatively penniless when she arrived in America was a lie. The fact she'd found out Nan had converted two thousand pounds into dollars and deposited over eight grand in the bank a month after she got here, had proven that simple statement to be a falsehood.

Thinking back to the first letter Mr. McDougal had given her to read, Sara tried to recall what it said about what she thought she knew of her grandmother's past was fiction. "What's the difference between fiction and a blatant lie?" she asked herself. Lies and half-truths, she thought. These are all things I'll have to sort through to find the answer Nan wants me to uncover. Based on her final letter I guess the rest of the answers are in London, waiting.

* * *

THE WATER IN THE BATH was turning tepid. Sara stood up in the tub and reached over to open the drain valve. After climbing out of the tub she donned her bathrobe and grabbed a towel to wrap around her head to absorb the water dripping from her long hair. After drying off her legs and feet, she turned off the lights and left the bathroom.

Sara refilled her wine glass in the kitchen then walked into the living room and stretched out on the couch. She closed her eyes for a moment, took a deep breath, then slowly exhaled, thinking how much better she felt after the bath. After reclining for a short time, Sara got up and headed to the kitchen to find something to eat. There wasn't much of a choice in the refrigerator. She decided two fried eggs and toast would suffice.

Since Nan had passed away, Sara had gotten into the habit of immediately rinsing off the dishes and placing them in the dishwasher. That way nothing remained in the sink or on the counter. One thing Nan had stressed was keeping the house tidy. Thinking about that simple thing Sara remembered she had just dropped her undergarments on the floor, and they remained there since she hadn't picked them up. Saga began feeling self-conscious, almost as if Nan was watching her, so she returned to her bedroom, picked up her undergarments and put them in the laundry basket.

Alone in what was now her living room, Sara contemplated the phone call she would make to Mary O'Riley, Nan's lifelong friend and confidant. Knowing Mary would know something had happened as soon as Sara explained who she was, she tried to figure out how to break the news to the old woman. Sara attempted to think things through; if I call from Nan's phone she'll probably think something's up since she hadn't contacted her in almost two months. Then again, maybe not. How often did Nan call her? When she called, did she call Mary from her cell phone or from the house phone?

Sara realized she didn't have the answer to any of the questions she asked herself. So she decided to call using Nan's phone, say hello, ensure it was Mary on the other end and take it from there. When Sara checking the time on the TV's DVR she saw it was 10:00 p.m., which made it the middle of the night there. The call would have to wait until the morning.

Now relaxed by the hot bath and having satisfied her hunger with the small meal she had prepared, Sara decided sleep was the next order of business. Moving from the couch, she walked into the bedroom and removed the towel from her hair, finding it was still damp. So she went into the bathroom and began to blow dry it by working the comb through her tangled locks. Fifteen minutes later she emerged from the bathroom and walked over to her bed. After pulling down the covers, Sara removed her robe and opted to sleep naked. As she sat on the side of the bed, she looked around the room. "No one here but me. I can walk around in my birthday suit whenever I want," she said. She slid her legs under the covers, adjusted her pillows, turned off the lights and settled in for the night. Her breathing settled into a slow rhythm, and dreamless sleep followed quickly.

Chapter 26

Since this was going to be a *Sara day*, she had not set the alarm clock before going to bed. Sara turned over after she had opened her eyes. The turquoise numbers showed it was only 7:00 a.m. True to her promise to spend the day relaxing, she turned back over and pulled the covers up to her chin.

Two hours later, she awoke again and decided it was time to get up. Sara pulled her bathrobe on and tied it closed with the belt. She noticed the plush carpet under her bare feet as she walked to the kitchen. "Was it like this yesterday?" she asked herself. "It must have been," she answered. "I must just be looking at the world with a different perspective now. Noticing things I took for granted."

When she got to the kitchen, the tile floor underfoot was cool, but not cold. Sara took out the coffee and measured out enough to make a half pot. After she pushed the start button, she began searching for her slippers. She found them partly under her bed. She slipped them on and returned to the kitchen.

"Ah, that's better, the floor wasn't that cold, but this porcelain tile is hard on the feet." Sara took the milk from the fridge, poured some into a mug and added a teaspoon of sugar while she waited for the coffee to finish brewing. After filling her mug, she found the file folder they kept on the counter next to the fridge. In there, Sara kept all the menus from the local delis and other restaurants that delivered. As she looked through the file, Sara kept another promise to herself, which was, the hardest decision she would make today would be what to eat. Since the clock was pushing 10:00 a.m. and figuring in delivery time she decided brunch items would be in order, so she pulled the menu for the local Jewish deli.

After she called and placed her order, she returned to her bedroom to get dressed. Now wearing a pair of royal blue silk pajamas and a white satin dressing gown, Sara was prepared for her day of doing nothing.

Winston called up to the apartment at a few minutes after eleven to inform Sara her delivery had arrived. "Send him up," she said.

"Certainly, Miss Ferguson. He's on his way," replied Winston as he hung up and allowed the deliveryman entrance.

Sara answered the door when the bell rang and let the young deliveryman into the apartment.

"Hi, Miss Ferguson, how are you doing today?"

"I'm doing okay, thanks for asking. How are you?" asked Sara who was familiar with the young man but couldn't remember his name.

"I'm good," he said as he moved the box containing her order. In doing so, he uncovered his name embroidered on the breast of his high school letterman jacket.

"That's good, Tommy. How much do I owe you?"

Tommy moved the bag inside the box so he could see the printed receipt. "That'll be $56.25, Miss Ferguson."

"Would you mind putting the box in the kitchen while I get my purse?"

"Sure, no problem."

Sara opened her handbag and found one bundle of cash with the bank strap still in place. She smiled to herself as she removed two one hundred-dollar bills from the stack. As she did, she thought I need to get some change. Cash in hand Sara returned to the front door where Tommy was waiting for her. "What was it again, $57.00?"

After Tommy repeated the correct cost, Sara asked an unrelated question that caught the young man off guard. "You're in college now aren't you?"

"Yes, that's right. I'm in pre-med up at Columbia."

"Pre-med, that's impressive. How's that going for you?"

Tommy smiled, "Pretty good, I finished my freshman year with the three-point seven GPA."

Sara returned his smile as he handed him the bills. "You keep it up, Tommy. Here, you go."

Tommy looked at the two hundred dollars, "Miss Ferguson, the bill was only fifty-six bucks."

"I know. I also know Columbia isn't cheap. Just keep your GPA up, I might need a good doctor someday."

"Thanks, Miss Ferguson. I'll do my best," replied the young man as he turned to leave.

"I'm sure you will, Tommy. Take care," she said as she closed and locked the door behind him. "That felt good. Maybe that's something I can do with some of Nan's money. Help kids that have the potential but not the resources. I'll have to talk to Michael about that. But that can wait, right now I'm starving."

Sara found the box on the kitchen counter where Tommy had placed it and dug into its contents. Finding the delicacies she'd ordered, Sara took out the packages and put them on the counter. Unable to wait for everything to be unwrapped she helped herself to samples of some of the items as she unpacked. Smoked salmon, chopped liver, brisket. Sara was in heaven; a feast for one was now laid out before her, and she assembled a plate to take to the dining room table.

Once she'd eaten her fill, she returned to the kitchen and cleaned up. The plates and cutlery went in the dishwasher. She closed the containers and place the rest of her order in the fridge. Once the chore of tidying up was completed, she walked into the living room and stretched out on the couch. "I've got a full stomach, and I feel like I could have a nap," she said to herself. Television remote in hand she turned on the set and flipped through the channels looking for something to watch. Nothing in the daytime lineup struck her fancy, so she tried the movie channels. The classic movie channel was showing *King Solomon's Mines* with Stewart Granger. The old movie reminded her of spending time with Nan, so she left that on, and it gave her a slight comfort that Nan was still with her.

* * *

SARA WATCHED THE MOVIE and didn't think she'd fallen asleep. The sound of her cell phone brought her back from her dream world. She opened her eyes to find Bogart on the TV screen. It took a moment for her to get her bearings. She realized the sound was her cell phone, she jumped from the couch to get it. Not recognizing the number, Sara was tempted to let it go unanswered. She imagined it to be someone who had gotten the word about her windfall and would ask her for money for something. Before it defaulted to voice mail, she reconsidered.

She pressed the accept button. "Hello."

A man's voice answered, "Good afternoon. Is this the woman who would have been my landlady had I not been so foolish and moved?"

After hearing the question, Sara recognized the caller's voice and gave an answer. "I don't know. Is this a certain doctor who decided personal convenience outweighed the desire to have an address in one of the nicest apartment buildings in Manhattan?"

"Touché," answered Dr. Randell. "How are you? I hope I'm not disturbing you. I promised to call once I got my duty schedule."

"I remember. I gather you got your schedule. Shall I assume this call is to make good on your dinner offer?"

"It is, and I must have been an excellent doctor because the department head who coordinated the schedule saw fit to give me a three-day weekend."

"Wow, now that is impressive."

"And as rare as hen's teeth. It is even more so since they've added Friday to the weekend, four days off, in a row even. Given my short release from house arrest, what would you say to dinner on Saturday?"

Sara had already said yes in her mind, but hearing Friday was on offer as a possibility she asked the question. "How about Friday? That gives you more time for other things."

George Randell moved the phone from his ear and glanced at it before answering, He'd just been given an alternative by someone who sounded rather eager to commit to this next meeting. "I'm good with that, I can do Friday. How about I pick you up at 8:00?"

"Sounds good. I'll be waiting. You have my number if anything comes up."

"Don't worry," replied Randell as he chuckled. "Nothing will come up on my end. After I get off shift on Thursday, I'm going to turn my phone off."

"Can you do that?"

"No," said the doctor with a heavy sigh, "But it's a thought."

"It's a date then, and should something come up, we can always reschedule for Saturday."

"Deal. I'll see you Friday night."

"See you on Friday then. Thanks for calling, George," replied Sara before she broke the connection. Now that she had a date with the handsome doctor who came into her world because of the tragedy that took Nan from her, she returned to the couch. Sara watched Bogie's image on the TV, trying to decide what movie it was. After a few seconds, another actor came into the scene and Sara recognized the distinct form and voice of Sydney Greenstreet. *"The Maltese Falcon,"* she said.

Sara sat back and put her legs back up on the couch and watched the movie. One of the guilty pleasures she had enjoyed with Nan was watching old movies. It didn't matter if they'd seen the film many times. There were certain ones they made a point to either watch or record when it came on. Nan was partial to the British actors, but like many women her age, Bogart and Gable were her favorites.

Once the movie ended, Sara turned off the TV and closed her eyes again. The freedom to do absolutely nothing was exhilarating. What was it Michael McDougal said, something about having the ability to do whatever it is she wanted to do?

That thought caused her to open her eyes. She wasn't free to do as she pleased, at least not yet. There were several things she had to do, and the first one was to make a phone call. Sara got up off the couch and went to her room to retrieve Nan's phone. Sara opened the phone's directory and scrolled through until she found the number for Mary O'Riley.

She hit the dial button. Several seconds elapsed before she heard the short, double ring, common to European telephone systems. The phone rang six or seven times before a female voice answered.

"Hello," came across the miles. A clearly spoken word, the polished accent she had heard so often in the old movies.

"May I please speak to Mrs. Mary O'Riley?" Sara asked.

"Speaking."

"Mrs. O'Riley, this is Sara Ferguson calling."

There was silence on the other end of the phone. Sara had figured revealing her name to Mary would be a hint something had happened. Sara then heard the person inhale as if gathering that steadfast British resolve that had seen them through the ages. "Rose has passed away, hasn't she?"

"Yes, she has."

"I knew the day would come. One by one, we're all leaving this earth. What happened to Rose? When did she pass?"

"Nan had a stroke. About seven weeks ago. She never recovered."

"I knew something had happened. Rose never missed a phone call. In all the years we've been in contact, you could set your watch by the day and time Rose would call."

"Mrs. O'Riley, Nan, left me an extraordinary letter…"

"I know," Mary cut her off. "When shall I expect you?"

"I'm flying to London on Monday. The arrangements are being made for me, and I don't have the details yet. I'll call again once I get everything set."

"That will be fine. I shall await your next call." That's a curt response, thought Sara. Someone who had been waiting for this call for years finally gets it, and it's like yeah, okay, I'll see you.

"Thank you, Mrs. O'Riley. I'll be in touch."

"I'm sorry you had to make this call Sara, but it was inevitable. I knew it would come someday. Part of me wishes I would have gone first, then the secret would likely never be known. But, that wasn't meant to be. Goodbye, Sara, we shall meet soon. There is much I have to tell you."

"Goodbye, Mrs. O'Riley."

Sara turned off the phone. "This is just crazy. First off, she sounds like the call is no big thing, almost like an annoyance, and then she changes her attitude, and it's almost like an apology. What is this big secret?" Sara thought about her trip to England. How long would she be there? What would happen when she met with Mary O'Riley? What did Nan mean when she said, "Find out who you are?" Questions only brought more questions, and Sara concluded that before she could attempt to walk through one door, she needed to close another.

* * *

THIRTY-FIVE HUNDRED MILES AWAY, Mary O'Riley sank slowly in the chair by her writing desk. Her now silent phone in her lap, she sat, looking out the window as tears rolled down her cheeks. "Oh, Rose, I knew something terrible had happened to you, my dear."

Mary O'Riley went to a sideboard, opened the drawer and removed a small black velvet box and opened it. As she fingered the item she had kept safe for years, Mary continued to cry. "Now Rose, after all these years, your story can be told. I pray your granddaughter will find peace and understanding in what I have to tell her."

She closed the lid on the box and placed it back in the drawer where it had been kept safe for years. "I'll keep my promise, Rose, just as you have done for all these years. I'll tell Sara everything I know. I hope it will help her."

Chapter 27

Thirty minutes later Sara retrieved her own phone and dialed a number she hadn't used in a long time. It was answered on the third ring.

"I was wondering if you would call."

"So was I. Can you meet me for a drink?"

"Where and when?"

"How about the Irish pub down by the Garden? Remember, we used to go there before the Rangers games."

"I remember. What time do you want to meet?"

"Give me two hours. I'll see you there," said Sara.

"Two hours, I'll be there."

As she disconnected the call, Sara felt as if this would be the last act of the play called *The Former Life of a Millionaire Heire*ss. Sara went into her room, stripped off her pajamas, and had a quick shower. She dressed in a pair of tight jeans and a loose-fitting multi-colored print top cut in a way to provide a fair idea of what lay hidden underneath. Black knee-high boots and a Navy-style pea coat completed her outfit. She grabbed her phone, keys, and handbag and set out to take the first step in establishing her new life.

* * *

SARA GOT TO THE PUB ON TIME. She knew he would be there early. The interior was dimly lit just the way she remembered it from those nights. Once her eyes adjusted to the darkness, she stood inside the doorway scanning the faces. She thought back to where they sat the last time they were there. Sara moved through the pub and found the three steps that led to the seating area in the back.

She climbed the stairs and made the turn. Sara found him sitting in the corner booth. He offered her a smile that said he was glad she called. As she approached, he stood and opened his arms to provide a welcome hug.

Sara stopped, just out of reach. "Hello, Jeff."

"What, no hug?"

Sara shook her head as she took a seat in the booth. "No hug."

Jeff returned to his seat and looked at Sara. "I hoped you'd call. When you rang my private number, I had the feeling things were going to change." He reached for her hand resting on the tabletop, but Sara moved it away. "I'm getting an obvious signal I was right. Things are about to change, but not in the way I hoped."

Once more, Sara nodded. "Yes, that's right. Things are changing. I'm not coming back to work. Consider this my notice. I'm leaving my position with the agency."

"You're quitting? Just like that?"

"Yes, Jeff, just like that. My world has been turned upside down, and now I have things I must do. Things that have to be done now. I don't know how long it will take me to finish what needs to be done. Next week I'm flying to England."

Jeff looked at her, a sign of desperation in his eyes. "Sara, you can't leave, not now. We've got contracts to work on."

Sara leaned against the back of the booth, increasing the distance between them. "Jeff, there are a lot of talented people in the agency. I'm sure you can persuade the clients to go with another person." She looked Jeff in the eye. "Listen, it's not like I'm jumping ship and trying to take my clients with me.

I'm done. Finished. No longer interested in banging my head against the wall trying to develop a pitch the clients will love."

Jeff nodded before he asked the question he already knew the answer to, but he wanted to hear her reply. "I guess that means there's no more *us* either."

"I thought that was pretty clear, given my actions when I stayed with you. There is no *us*, nor has there been an *us* for a long time. You had a chance, but you hedged your bet and kept me in the background. I don't want to be a mistress, waiting for your call."

"I guess that's it then. Do you want to come by the office and pick up your personal stuff, or should I have it packed and sent to you?"

"I'll come in, maybe tomorrow. There are some people I'd like to say goodbye to." Sara slid out of the booth, "Goodbye, Jeff," she said and walked away.

***

JEFF REMAINED SEATED as Sara walked out, his drink untouched as he thought about what had just occurred. All his plans of making Sara a partner to gain access to her cash reserves had gone up in smoke when she announced she was leaving. "Guess I'll have to dust off my dancing shoes because I'm going to have to pull off some fancy footwork to keep that new account Sara just landed." He knew the client had made it known that having Sara as the project lead was the only reason they agreed to the contract and signed with Charles, Jasper, and Williams.

As the senior partner, he needed his share of the injection of cash this account would bring in to keep himself afloat. It cost him a fortune to support Charlotte in the custom she was used to, in addition to funding his own living accommodations and lifestyle.

Jeff tossed back his drink and slammed the glass on the table. "I'll figure it out. I always seem to manage to pull through. Why should today be any different?"

He threw a twenty-dollar bill on the table, walked out of the bar, hailed a cab, and took the long ride home. Alone.

***

SARA WALKED ALONG THE STREET, sporting a small, almost undetectable smile, thinking about closing and locking the door on her past with both Jeff and the agency She was ready to move forward. She surprised herself at the ease with which she had informed him she was leaving the firm and how simple it had been to discount his supposed feeling for her. She was sure Jeff Charles had something up his sleeve to woo her into investing in the firm and also using her talents to ensure the new clients remained.

She was free to move forward, but still, Sara couldn't help but wonder where this new door would lead her. The destination for this trip was still unknown. Mary O'Riley held the key to unlock the information that would allow Sara to travel that road. Hopefully, that information would all be discovered next week. And what about Dr. Randell? What if anything would she find behind that door if she stepped through it?

Chapter 28

When Sara made the trip to Charles, Jasper, and Williams, Jeff was nowhere to be found. Bill Jasper and Martin Williams had taken the time to stop by her office while she packed her personal items. When Bill walked in, Sara gave him a hug. "Thanks for all the opportunities you've given me over the past few years."

"No need to thank me, you deserved everything you got. You and your creative team have been very successful in bringing in new clients and upping the budgets on others. We're sorry to see you go, but at the same time, we're glad you're not leaving to join another agency or start your own company."

Martin echoed those sentiments and also got a goodbye hug. After packing everything she wanted to take with her, she made a sweep through the art department and then visited the creative department. Everyone wished her well on her whatever and wherever her new adventures took her. Not wanting to seem cold and callous, Sara stopped by Jeff's office to see if he had returned.

Jeff's executive assistant greeted her.

"Hi, Candice, Has Jeff come back yet?"

Candace shook her head, "No, I'm afraid he's not coming in today."

Sara's smile turned inward as she heard his assistant's reply. He's a coward, she thought, he doesn't want to face me on my terms, so he's not going to show his face in the office today. Oh well, I'm not going to lose any sleep over this, I said goodbye to him yesterday. When she got back to her office, Sara picked up the small box of her belongings and left Charles, Jasper & Williams for the last time.

* * *

WHEN SARA RETURNED TO HER APARTMENT with her belongings, there was a message on the answering machine. "Hello, Sara, this is Janet Collins. I'm calling to let you know we have made all the arrangements for your trip. I've emailed you the itinerary for your approval. If there is anything that you would like to be changed, please call. Also, Michael has been in contact with Mr. Cromwell, and he will ensure someone will meet you at the airport. I've also arranged for a car to take you to JFK on Monday. I'll check in with you again later to ensure you've received everything. But please feel free to call if you need anything. Bye for now."

Chapter 29

Friday arrived, and Sara was pleased with the prospect of seeing George Randell again. It had been a while since she had dated anyone. The affair with Jeff had left her wanting a stable relationship. Pretending to be going to a client meeting so they could meet for an afternoon tryst didn't seem right. Neither did sitting home alone waiting for him to call and let her know if he could meet her as planned. That's the word that annoyed her about their relationship, *planned.* There was no spontaneity in their time together.

Since Jeff was married, he always had to make time for Sara. And since she wanted to be with him, her part of the bargain was to be available when he called. Now that she reflected on her past relationship with Jeff, she wondered what her Nan would have called her. Mistress? Whore? Perhaps fool would be a better word since no money was ever exchanged, and she hadn't been kept in the true sense of being a mistress.

Yes, she'd been a fool. Always wanting to believe he would leave his wife. Younger than him by eighteen years, she would have been wife number three. The trophy wife. "If we'd been together, I wonder if Nan would have changed her will?" she said to herself. "If not, then I would have been his gold plated, diamond-studded trophy wife. I'm glad I dodged that bullet."

Deciding her past relationship with Jeff didn't deserve any more of her time, Sara closed the book on him in much the same way she had closed the door on him when she had stayed with him after Nan had passed away.

Thinking about tonight's date, Sara didn't know where they would go for dinner. Would he take her to a swanky place in an attempt to gain the attention of a woman worth a small fortune? Perhaps he would choose a more casual dining experience in an effort to show her he wasn't impressed with her money. He hadn't given her a hint on what to wear when he called. Just that he would pick her up at 8:00 p.m.

Sara looked in her closet for different options. Jeans were out. Slacks and a blouse, maybe, I can dress it up with a jacket if needed. But that looks more like I'm ready for a business meeting. I think a dress would be the best option for tonight. Now, which one? After removing several options from her closet, she placed them on the bed. The navy was out, as was the black. Even though the little black dress is always appropriate, she'd been wearing a lot of black because of the funeral. So, since this was supposed to be a date and possibly the beginning of a new relationship, black was out for tonight.

She held the fitted burgundy satin one up in front of her as she looked in the mirror. "This is the one for tonight," she said. The dress had a three-quarter sleeve, and a tapered bottom that resembled a pencil skirt. The square-cut neckline wasn't overly revealing but rather more of a promise than an outright display of what could be offered.

Now that she had chosen the dress, what would she wear to accompany it? For the first time in weeks, Sara ventured into what had been her grandmother's room. After taking a seat at the dressing table she moved her grandmother's jewelry box to a spot in front of her. Sara remembered watching Nan get ready to go out on special occasions and open the antique box covered in embossed ivory-colored leather. When she raised the cover, it caused a drawer the same width of the box to slide out from the bottom. Red velvet lined the inside, and a satin-trimmed velvet flap covered the contents of the drawer.

Sara pulled open the flap and found what she was looking for. As a child, Sara had always been fond of her grandmother's diamond necklace. Nan had told Sara that someday it would belong to her. Nan had explained that the jewelry had been a gift from Grandpa Bill for their first wedding anniversary. After removing the diamonds from the drawer Sara wondered if that was, in fact, true or if it was one of those half-truths Nan had mentioned in her letter. Perhaps it was true because she kept it here in her jewelry box and not locked away in the bank vault as she had done with the broach.

Feeling she had selected the perfect outfit for this evening, Sara went about getting ready for her date. The first order of business was a shower and blow-drying her hair. After that was accomplished, she realized how early it was and that she had hours to finish getting ready. Sara returned to the living room, walked over to the small writing desk, and picked up the folder she had received from Michael McDougal to hold all the documents she had been collecting as they had made the rounds of the stockbroker and banks. Folder in hand, she walked back over to the couch.

Sara removed the three letters she had received over the past several days. The first from Mr. McDougal, in which Nan said almost everything Sara thought she knew about her grandmother, was a lie. The second one she received from Mr. Fleming, and the third one they found in the safe deposit box for her to discover. Did Michael know about that letter? He'd said there would be several along the way, and he didn't know about the one from Nan, which discussed the rainy-day fund.

Sara picked up the first letter and scanned it to find the part about Mary O'Riley. The old woman had said she had much to tell, so Sara reviewed what Nan had said.

> *"If anything should happen to Mary before you meet, I am afraid the first, and perhaps the most important part of the British portion of the puzzle will be lost forever."*

After reading it several times, she focused on one phrase. *The most important part of the British portion of the puzzle.* Mary only had a part of the puzzle; one-piece, though important, it would not provide the final answer as to what the secret was. That would require some detective work to figure out. As she thought about the quest her grandmother had asked her to undertake, Sara wondered if she would be able to decipher the clues to find the answer. Rose McDonald Cavendish had kept this secret for decades. Now it was up to Sara to be able to discover the truth.

* * *

A MIXTURE OF DAYDREAMING, thinking about the future and wondering what ultimate truth would be uncovered helped Sara pass the time. It was now 6:30 and time to finish getting ready for her dinner engagement with George Randell.

Once the make-up ritual was complete, Sara gazed at her reflection in the mirror. Happy with the result, she chose a lipstick color that would tie all the elements together. After selecting one she believed to be perfect, she applied the color to her lips, capped it, and placed it in her handbag. She slipped into her dress, and pulled the zipper closed before donning her heels. She was ready to go. All she needed to do was choose a coat to wear. Sara double-checked her handbag to ensure she had everything she needed, then got her black coat from the closet,

Sara saw that Charlie Wilkins was on duty in the lobby when she exited the elevator. "How are you tonight, Charlie?"

"I'm doing well, Miss Ferguson. It's nice to see you. It looks like you're going out for the evening. I hope you enjoy yourself."

"Thanks, Charlie, I hope so, too. It's been a while since I've been out to just have some fun."

"You're welcome, Miss. Are you expecting someone, or would you like me to get you a taxi?"

"I don't need a taxi. I'm being picked up. Thanks for asking."

Charlie nodded his understanding and returned to what he had been doing when Sara had exited the elevator. As soon as Charlie began typing into the building's computer record, a bright yellow late-model Corvette pulled into the space in front of the doors. Sara watched as George Randell opened the door and got out from behind the wheel. When she saw he was dressed in a suit and tie, Sara was glad she had guessed right.

Charlie opened the front door, allowing Dr. Randell to enter the lobby. Sara walked up to meet her date, who offered a polite hug and gentle kiss on the cheek. "Hello, Sara, you look lovely this evening."

"Why thank you, doctor. You clean up pretty well yourself."

"On my way over, I realized I never told you where we were going or how to dress. Please excuse my oversight."

"I'm glad I guess correctly."

"You're dressed perfectly. If you will allow me, I'll help you with your coat." Sara relinquished the hold on her coat, and George Randell assisted her in putting it on.

Once outside, Randell offered Sara a hand to assist her as she got into the low-slung car. Sara took her seat on the black leather expecting it to be cold. Much to her surprise, the seat was warm. As the doctor took his place behind the wheel, Sara commented about the car. "Nice car, George. I didn't take you for the sports car type."

"Thank you. I don't get to drive it enough. As for being a type, I guess being an unattached doctor in NYC, people have certain expectations. Besides, I always wanted one as a kid. Now that I can afford one, I got it, even if it sits in the garage most of the week."

"A guilty pleasure is normally the best kind."

"Do you drive?" asked George

"I don't have a car, I've got a license, but I've never needed to have my own car. I used to take the subway to work, a taxi, or an Uber to go other places, and if I were going out on a date, I would get picked up."

George looked in Sara's direction as he drove. "Used to take to work? It sounds like you've left your job."

"Yes, I gave my notice to the head of the agency yesterday."

"Very nice," replied the doctor. "What will you be doing now?"

"For the long run, I'm not sure. I'll give that some thought when I get back," replied Sara.

"Back? Where are you going?"

"I'm flying to London on Monday to look up an old friend of my grandmother's. Nan left me a letter that was part of her will. In it, she asked me to do something for her. To do this I have to go to London."

"So, you're off to London on an adventure. That sounds intriguing."

Sara looked over at the date. "You don't know the half of it."

"Perhaps when you get back, we can go out again, and you'll tell me all about it."

"My, my, Doctor Randell aren't we sure of ourselves," Sara replied in a joking manner. "We've been on this date for five minutes, and you're sure we'll have another."

"Hope springs eternal," he said with a broad smile.

"Where are we going tonight?"

"I was hoping you would be in the mood for a nice steak or perhaps seafood, so I've made a reservation at Del Frisco's."

"Sounds good. I'll give you a point for that choice," said Sara with a slight smile.

"Thank you very much."

"You're welcome. Besides, that point wipes out the minus one you started with tonight."

"Ouch. What did I do to start with a minus one?"

Sara reached out and touched his hand that was on the shift knob. "It was for not telling me how to dress."

"Noted, when we go out next time, I'll be sure to let you know what to wear."

"Why are you so sure there will be a next time?" asked Sara, an inquisitive tone in her voice.

"Because I'm hoping that you're asking me to go for coffee, accepting my dinner invitation, and then pushing it forward when I asked if Saturday was acceptable were all signs you were as interested in me as I am in you," replied Randell as he caught her eyes while they stopped at the red light.

Sara began to blush, "Was I that obvious?"

"Not at first, but they train doctors to look for signs and indications. Your suggestion to move it up so there would be more time available for the weekend made me take notice."

"Okay, Dr. Watson, I'll admit it, I am interested."

"Good, now that all this is behind us we can enjoy our dinner without having to wonder if each of us has any real interest in the other." As the doctor made the closing statement on the subject, they arrived at the valet line for Del Fresco's. "Shall we?" he said.

* * *

DINNER WAS EXCEPTIONAL. Sara ordered a filet mignon; George had the Surf and Turf. The food was excellent, the dry-aged steaks cooked to perfection. Everything was wonderful. George didn't ask about what happened after the reading of the will or why Sara had to go to London. Jeff never came up in the conversation, either.

George Randell talked a bit about his family and his childhood. He told Sara about growing up in Morris County, New Jersey. A rural setting where kids still rode bikes and played in the few remaining open fields. He'd gone to the local high school, played football, ran track, and was on the golf team. He'd gone to Saint Peter's College and didn't have a clear vision of what he wanted to do until his mother had gotten ill halfway through his second year of college. The long hours in her hospital room watching the doctors, nurses, and medical technicians come and go gave him the urge to help people. After graduating with honors, he'd been fortunate enough to attend Johns Hopkins University School of Medicine in Baltimore.

His desire to become a physician drove him to once again strive to be the best. After graduating number two in his class, he stayed on and completed his internship and residency at Johns Hopkins Hospital. Just as his mother's illness had driven him to medicine, it was her specific medical problem caused by a fall on the stairs that caused him to become a neurosurgeon.

Sara listened intently as George told her all about medical school and some of the people he'd met on the long road to becoming a doctor. "My God, you were in school forever, weren't you?" she asked.

"I was, but hey, if you had to have someone operate on your brain, wouldn't you want someone with years of training before they could even start?"

"Of course, I would. I'm sure most sane people would want the same thing. So how long were you in training?"

Randell leaned forward, putting his forearms on the edge of the table, his fingers interlaced. "All together – fourteen. Four years of college, four of med school, a one-year internship in general surgery, and finally, a five-year neurosurgery residency."

"Wow, that's quite a commitment," replied Sara. "I'd had enough after four years of art and design at NYU. I started a master's program, but work got in the way."

George sat back in his seat. "You seem to have done well for yourself while you were working. You were with Charles, Jasper, and Williams, right?"

"Yes, I was," said Sara as she moved closer to the table. "I managed to become a creative director and should have been up for a partnership after I landed the last contract."

"But instead, you quit the firm."

Sara nodded her reply.

"Why did you do that?"

"Because my boss said I wasn't thinking like a partner when I told him I wasn't thinking of coming back. Plus, there were other reasons."

George Randell thought about the comment for a moment but didn't ask what those reasons were. "Things seem to have a way of falling into place when the time is right. Tell me about your impending trip to England, you said you're going on Monday specifically to see an old friend of your grandmother's. How long are you going to be there?"

Sara shrugged, "I don't know, I have some things to sort out over there. It could take three days or three weeks. I won't know until I get to talk to the woman I'm going to see." Tilting her head, Sara offered her date a smile. "Is there a reason you asked how long I'll be there?"

George reached into his jacket pocket and removed a slim leather folio slightly larger than a checkbook and opened it. Sara could see the leather folder held a calendar. He held the open page to her, and smiled, "I was wondering how long you would be away because I wanted to plan our next date."

Sara reached out and took the calendar from his hand and flipped through several pages looking at what was written. After seeing several meetings scheduled, she turned back to the current week. She saw the page for today had *Dinner with Sara / 8:00 p.m.* written in. She saw the calendar's format displayed Saturday and Sunday on a shared the page on the right-hand side. Both days were blank. Sara removed the slim, gold pen from its holder, twisted the barrel on the writing instrument and wrote by the page dedicated to Saturday. *Lunch and '?' with Sara / 1:00 p.m.* She returned the pen to its storage space, turned the folder and handed it back to George. "What do you say to that?"

Randell looked at what she had written and smiled. "I say it's a date, but what's the question mark?"

"Didn't you say you wanted to know when to plan our next date?"

"Yes, I did, but–"

"Then I guess you better plan what we're going to do after lunch."

* * *

WHEN GEORGE DROVE SARA HOME, she directed him around the block to the underground garage entrance and had him park in one of the two spaces assigned to her apartment. Sara led him to the elevator, where she used her key card to activate the code that would allow it to open on the garage levels.

When they got to the fourteenth floor, Sara led George to her apartment and invited him in. Once inside, she realized this was the first time she'd brought a man home. Sure, she'd gone home with men in the past, but as she had done with Jeff, she never stayed out all night. It was also uncommon for her to get home at three or four in the morning. But now there was no one home. No reason to be quiet and no reason she couldn't have someone stay if she chose to do so.

After inviting George to take a seat on the couch, she removed her coat and placed it over the chair. "Would you like a drink or coffee?" she asked.

Turning on the couch so he could see her, Randell replied, "Coffee please, I've still got to drive home."

"Coffee coming up, make yourself comfortable. It'll be ten minutes," said Sara as she began setting up the machine.

"This is a nice apartment, it's huge compared to mine."

"I guess," replied Sara. "I've lived here so long, I never gave it much thought. Since my parents died, this has just been home."

"Well you can take my word for it, I spent weeks looking. It's not what I would consider a typical apartment in the city." George got up from the couch and walked around the living room as he continued. "Most of them are less than a thousand square feet for a two-bedroom, and for a one bed, you're lucky if you can find one larger than six hundred square feet."

"Coffee's ready. You take it black, right?" asked Sara as she carried two cups into the living room and placed one in front of George.

"That's right, you've got a good memory."

Sara took a seat next to George on the couch, kicked off her shoes and tucked her legs under her as she answered. "I had to. My job was listening to the customer and then trying to figure out what they thought they wanted and what they really wanted. And doing all that by what they said."

"Sort of like being a doctor and attempting to interpret a patient's symptoms by what they tell you."

Sara moved closer to the doctor, looking into his eyes as she reached out with her left hand and stroked the hair on the back of his head. "Exactly. But sometimes you also have to consider body language."

"I agree," replied Randell as he turned on the couch and moved toward her. Once he could reach her with both arms, he took hold of her waist and pulled her to him. "Sometimes body language gives you all the information you need." She responded by pressing her mouth against his and opening it, allowing his tongue to enter.

She responded further by wrapping her arms around his neck and pulling herself onto him, turning her body, so she was sitting on his lap, and he was leaning over her. Her arms pulled him closer, and he followed along willingly. She felt the heat rise in her as they kissed. It had been months since she'd been intimate with someone, and she relished the sensations flowing through her body.

His hands hadn't moved; he held her securely against him but allowed her the ability to move if she wanted to. She turned more to him, pressing her breasts against his chest. As she moved against him, he could feel her body, tight, firm, yet supple. She broke the kiss and buried her head in his neck. Sucking gently, she shifted again as she felt him swelling below her. He leaned back and allowed her to continue. His hold on her relaxed as he moved his hand down and ran it over the curve of her bottom. He grabbed a handful, squeezed and felt her tense.

Sara threw back her head, offering him the opportunity to attack her neck, which he did without hesitation. He could hear her ragged breathing as he nibbled on the soft flesh, and she continued to move her body against his. Time stood still as the two continued to kiss and rub on each other.

His hold on her relaxed even more, and he gently pushed her away, creating a space between them, "I think it would be best if I went home."

"Why? Aren't you having a good time?"

"Of course I am, can't you tell? A wonderful time, and what's even better is being here with you. But I think it's time for me to leave. Besides, I've got something important I have to do."

She looked at him with questioning eyes, "What do you have to do that's so important?"

He smiled and gave her a gentle kiss on the lips before answering. "I have to figure out what we're going to do after lunch."

"Ah, yes, I guess you do. I forgot all about that," she said, offering him a coy smile. Sara stood and helped him rise from the semi-reclined position she had forced him into while they were kissing.

"I told you it was important, didn't I? I better go." He said as he kissed her again. "How do I get back to the garage level?"

"Take the elevator to the lobby, and I'll call David and let him know you're on your way down. He will use his key to allow you to get to the garage."

He put his arms around her again, kissing her one last time. "I've had a very nice time tonight. I'm looking forward to seeing you again tomorrow."

She returned his kiss. "So have I, I'm glad you asked me to dinner. I can't wait to see what you come up with for tomorrow. Goodnight, George," she said.

"Goodnight, Sara. I'll see you at 1:00," he said as he turned and headed toward the door, stopping once he reached for the doorknob, "Oh, before I forget, please dress casually for tomorrow. Jeans and comfortable shoes would probably be best."

Sara smiled and nodded, "Okay, I can do that," she said as she let him out of the apartment. She continued to watch him as he walked toward the elevator and disappeared around the corner, then locked the door. Sara returned to the living room, picked up the cups and brought them into the kitchen. She still felt a tingling running through her as she rinsed the cups out. "George Randell, where have you been all my life?" she asked herself. "I sure hope I can sleep after that, or it's going to be a long day tomorrow."

Chapter 30

Sleep had come for Sara last night, but it was a dream-filled sleep. Nonetheless, Sara awoke rested, revived, and ready for what the day would bring. As she took a shower, her thoughts weren't of George but rather her upcoming trip to England. In two days, she would fly *across the pond,* as Nan used to call it, to meet with Mary O'Riley.

She hadn't given the trip much thought for the past few days simply because she had no idea what to think about. Since the phone call with Mary was almost as cryptic as Nan's letters, there wasn't much to go on. Not knowing where to even begin speculating, Sara decided she would just wait to find out what Mary had to tell her. Besides, Sara now had other things on her mind.

When she finished her shower, Sara dried herself off and put her dressing gown on. As she ran the brush through the long strands of her hair, she thought about the changes in her life. Nan was gone. She was finished with Jeff and the agency. She now had more money than she knew what to do with, and she was about to go to England. And finally she's met George. Life was full of changes. "Perhaps it's time for a change of hairstyle, too."

Since it was already Saturday, and she had a date, changing her hairstyle would be something to think about when she got back from London. Right now, her main concern was what top to wear with her jeans. After a search for the perfect top in her closet, she selected a medium-weight multi-colored knit top with a V-neck. She chose a pair of dark indigo jeans and lace-up ankle boots with a good sole for walking. Dressed in the outfit she had selected, she returned to the bathroom to apply some makeup. A glance in the mirror confirmed a little blush and some eyeliner was all she needed. A touch of lipstick, and she was ready to go. Sara grabbed a short leather bomber-style jacket from her closet, put it on but left it unzipped. She picked up her handbag from the hall table on the way out, pulled the apartment door shut and headed toward the elevator.

George was already waiting for her in the lobby when she arrived. She found him by the front doors talking with Winston who noticed her first as she walked toward them.

"Good afternoon, Miss Sara, how are you this fine day?"

Sara saw the smile on Winston's face as he looked at her, "I'm very well. Thank you for asking. How are you?"

"Miss Sara, if I was doing any better, I'd probably be arrested," he said in a laughing tone. "I was just talking to the good doctor here; I was asking him about his car."

"You thinking about getting a vette, Winston? I'd have thought you were more of a Cadillac man."

"Maybe. You never know, sometimes a little change is good for the soul," replied the concierge as he tipped his hat to leave. "You have a good day, Miss. You too, doctor."

"Thanks, Winston, it was nice seeing you again," replied George. Offering Sara his arm, Randell pushed open the door and led Sara outside. "You look very nice," he said.

"Thank you. I followed your instructions, jeans, and walking shoes."

"I see that. Let's go."

George opened the door for Sara and watched her slide smoothly into the passenger seat before closing the door. He jumped in, started the engine, and the throaty roar of the Corvette's big V-8 engine made him smile. He glanced over at his companion while clicking his seatbelt into position,. "Are you hungry now, or would you like to go for a ride first?"

"I'm not starving. What did you have in mind?"

George put the car in gear and pulled from the curb. "It's such a beautiful day I thought we could take the Henry Hudson and drive up to the Cloisters, have a walk around, and get something to eat up there. Or if you still weren't famished, we could continue on up to Tarrytown. I know several good restaurants up there. What do you think?"

Sara reached out and put her hand on top of his. "I think you did an excellent job of figuring out how to answer the question mark. Let's start at the Cloisters and play it by ear."

"Plan A it is," he said as he turned west and headed for the Henry Hudson Parkway.

There wasn't much traffic today, and they made good time traveling up to the Cloisters. George had the radio on, classic rock n' roll, which Sara also enjoyed more than the current trends in music. Sara watched George as he drove. She could tell he was enjoying himself guiding the sports car along the road. He said he didn't get to drive it often, so perhaps this trip killed two birds with one stone. He gets to spend time driving, and we both get the opportunity to leave the city.

As they got closer to their first destination, George lowered the volume of the radio so he could talk to Sara. "I picked the Cloisters because you're going over to England on Monday. I know it's not English architecture, but I thought you might enjoy seeing some medieval art and architecture."

"Thank you. I'm not sure how much time I'll have to do touristy things in London, but I hope to at least get to one or two of the museums and check out some of the sights."

George looked over, "You don't have a schedule. Once you're done with your business, you don't have to come rushing back. You're not working anymore so what do you have to hurry back for?" he asked.

Sara offered her date a coy smile before she replied, "Well, I'm not sure yet, but there may be one or two things I'd like to come back to and get on with."

George returned her smile and nodded, "Okay then, looks like we're here. Now let's find a place to park."

They took their time walking through the current exhibits as Sara took note of the architecture of the buildings. George held her hand as they wandered through the buildings and toured the grounds. Sara felt comfortable in his presence. They bumped together when they went through narrow passages, and George always ensured she was with him if he had gone through first. She put her arm around his waist as they walked, and he placed his around her shoulders.

Sara was enjoying being in his company. Everything seemed natural and not forced. Neither felt compelled to talk continuously or to comment on everything they saw. After about ninety minutes, Sara said she was getting hungry.

As George led Sara back to the car he asked, "Do you want to eat around here, or do you want to go to Tarrytown? It'll take about half an hour to get there."

"Let's go there, you said you know some good restaurants."

"I do. What are you in the mood for? There are a few good American bistro's, a nice little Korean place."

"It's getting closer to dinner time than lunch, so if you know a cozy little bistro, that sounds like the perfect place to go."

"I know just the place, and since it's cooling down, I'll bet they'll have the fireplace going."

"Very well, Dr. Randell, I leave myself in your capable hands. Let's go to this bistro you recommend."

Chapter 31

Sara wanted to cuddle against George for the short ride to Tarrytown, but the low bucket seats and center console in the Corvette made that impossible. Instead she settled for just holding his hand when it was free of the shifter.

George had been correct in his estimate of the time to get there, and twenty-five minutes later, he pulled into the parking lot of a small bistro on East Sunnyside Lane. The gray stone building with the leaded windows fit perfectly in the local setting. A large black awning over the entryway announced the presence of the bistro in the building's basement. The large hearth had a welcoming fire in it, and the heat warmed Sara who had left her jacket in the car.

George asked for an out of the way table, and the maître d' showed them to a small table for two in the back corner out of the traffic flow. After they were seated, their server came over and took their drink orders while they reviewed the menu.

"This is a nice place; how did you find it?"

George put his menu down on the table and looked at Sara. "I had a patient about two years ago who lived here in town. He recommended it as an out of the way place to take someone for a good meal outside of the city."

Sara placed her menu on top of his and leaned forward. "So tell me, do you bring all your dates here?"

A smile developed as she asked the question. "I've only been here once before, and yes it was with a special lady. My mother. She was visiting, and I brought her here for her birthday."

"Did she enjoy the food?

"She did, and so did I. Everything was excellent."

Sara picked up the menu again, "Any recommendations?"

"The duck ravioli was superb. A little rich, but quite decadent."

"Hmm, rich and decadent, sounds perfect," replied Sara as she gave George a devilish smile.

When the server returned to take their order, Sara stayed with George's recommendation while he chose the diver scallops.

Tonight, it was Sara's turn to tell George some things about her life. So, she began with the tragedy that caused her to live with her grandmother for the past fifteen years. A short history of her scholastic achievements and her athletic prowess followed that. Soccer and swimming were her passions. Sara admitted she hadn't played soccer in years, but she still used swimming to help keep her in shape.

George had noticed more than once that Sara had a trim and athletic figure with long, toned arms and legs. Last night when they were kissing and hugging, it was the muscular definition of her shoulders that had given him the idea that she was a swimmer. As Sara sat talking, George became even more captivated by her beauty. The way she moved when she spoke was almost a swaying of her torso, her long hair shifting one way then the other. Her hazel eyes caught the light from the candle on the table and appeared to be more of a green tonight. He drifted as she spoke, listening intently but not really hearing what she said.

Sara noticed the way he was looking at her and stopped talking for a moment to see what his reaction would be. The silence broke George's trance-like stare, and he recovered well by asking a question about something he had heard. "What was it like working in a high-powered ad agency?"

Sara smiled and answered his question with one of her own, "What's it like poking around in someone's brain trying to figure out why it's not working?"

George thought about that for a second before answering, "Frustrating as hell, and if we're lucky, rewarding as hell when we find the problem."

Sara smiled and nodded, "Bingo, same thing in an agency. It's just as frustrating because you have to get into the client's mind and figure out what it is they want and not what they tell you they think they want. Then rewarding when you figure it out, and they say you've nailed it."

"Sounds like you're not going to miss it."

"I will for a while, sort of like that nagging pain you get when you pull something during a workout. You know it's there, but it's tolerable. Then suddenly, one day, you notice it's gone, and you try to remember when it stopped hurting."

George laughed at the comment because he knew that analogy well from the times he played sports. However, he repeated it back as an example he had dealt with. "I've had patients like that. They never seem to get better while they are collecting workman's comp or unemployment, then suddenly, they're well enough to return to work when the benefits are about to stop."

As they ate, Sara made a comment about her dinner choice. "I have to say you're correct, the ravioli is excellent. How are you scallops?"

"I'm glad you're enjoying your dinner. The scallops are succulent and perfectly cooked."

After they had completed their main course, Sara sat back in her chair and finished her glass of wine. A contented look on her face, she just smiled at her companion before she spoke.

"I'm going to have to stop eating like this, or I'll be living at the gym."

"So, no room for dessert?" asked George.

"If you insist. I may be able to manage a little. Can we share?"

"Definitely."

George ordered the chef's special bread pudding with brandy sauce and ice cream. When the server brought it to the table, he flambéed the sauce and served it in the middle of the table. The size of the serving was large enough to share even though designated an individual dessert.

Sara tried the first spoonful. Once the creamy dessert hit her pallet, she closed her mouth and savored the flavor. She closed her eyes as she moved her tongue around the inside of her mouth, chewing the morsel. Different tastes filled her senses, hints of vanilla, cardamom, and mace made an appearance as did the butter and brandy. "Umm, oh my god, that is so good," she said as she opened her eyes and looked at George.

George was sitting and watching Sara while she ate. He hoped she wouldn't think it was freaky, but he was captivated by her. Her gentle laugh was charming. He enjoyed talking with her because she was interesting and understood many things. Being with her made him happy, and he was glad she had pushed their first date up a day because he got to see her twice in two days. He was sure Sara would be busy getting ready for her trip tomorrow, so he wanted to make today last. Sara wasn't sure when she would return from England, so he had to wait for her return and then hope she would be willing to go out again.

Sara tapped her spoon on the rim of the bowl containing the dessert. "I hope you don't expect me to eat all of this," she said.

"Oh no, I want my share," he replied. "I was just watching you enjoy it. The look on your face when you took the first bite told me it was a good choice."

"It was an excellent choice. I've never had anything that tasted like this."

"Good, then I hope you will add that to the list of things I did to successfully address the question mark you had written in my calendar."

"You, sir, have most definitely done well. You have met and exceeded my expectations for this date."

George placed his hand over his heart and offered a slight bow while he remained in his seat. "I humbly accept your assessment."

They finished the dessert, although Sara ate more. Once they paid the bill, George escorted Sara from the restaurant. As they climbed the stairs from the basement bistro, the cold air caused Sara to shiver. George placed his arm around her, providing her some of his body warmth. Sara responded by putting her arm around his waist, pulling him tighter to her.

When they got back to the Corvette, George helped Sara into the car. He started the car and turned on the seat warmers. Sara felt the warmth come through the leather and rubbed her back against the seat. "Whoever invented this is a genius."

"It helps when it's cold," replied George as he reversed out of the parking spot. As he pulled out onto the road, he glanced over at Sara. "I'm sorry to say that dinner was the end of my planned activities for today. So unless you have something in mind, I think it's time to head home."

"How about you take me home a different way?" offered Sara.

"What way would you like to go?"

"Oh, I don't know, surprise me."

"You got it," said George as he did a U-turn and headed north. "How about we go over the Tappan Zee, and I give you the tour of the one thing Jersey has that we don't?"

"What's that?" asked Sara.

"The view of the New York skyline."

Chapter 32

George drove the Corvette onto the Tappan Zee and stayed in the right lane so Sara could take in the sights. About halfway across Sara noted how wide the Hudson River was up here as compared to down in Manhattan. "I feel like we're driving out to sea."

"The river is a lot wider up here, the bridge is about two miles long."

Sara nodded her understanding but didn't reply. Once they got off the bridge, George continued on toward West Nyack, where he could get onto the Palisades Interstate Parkway and head south toward New Jersey. As they crossed into Jersey, the road moved closer to the Palisades, and they could see the lights of New York in the distance.

"It's a clear night, we should have a good view as we travel down," said George.

"It sure is, I can see the lights of the George Washington Bridge from here. Is that where you're going to cross back over?"

"Sush," replied George. "You said to surprise you."

"Okay," said Sara in a laughing voice.

George continued driving, and as the G.W. Bridge grew closer, he looked for the exit he knew existed that would allow him to avoid having to take the bridge. After making the turn, he began going through some residential areas before driving under the overpasses for the bridge, emerging on the other side. Now headed through Fort Lee he took River Road south. As they drove south, the skyline grew larger with every mile. In the small town of Guttenberg the name of the road changed to Port Imperial Boulevard. Sara was enjoying the sight of all the buildings lit up against the black sky. A three-quarter moon had risen over the city and only added to the beauty of the scene.

George drove past the entrance to the Lincoln Tunnel in Weehawken and headed for Hoboken. Sara turned and told George what he already knew. "You missed the entrance to the tunnel."

"I know, we've got one more thing to see before we cross back over to the city."

"Okay."

The Corvette traveled down Park Avenue, and George made a left turn onto Fifteenth Street. Since they were now heading toward the Hudson River, the iconic shape of the Empire State Building rose in front of the car.

"I never tire of seeing that building," said George.

"That's New York," replied Sara.

"It certainly is," said George as he turned onto Sinatra Drive for another four blocks, before he turned and headed down Eleventh Street. As he drove back toward Weehawken, George followed the signs for the Lincoln Tunnel and drove back into Manhattan.

Now in New York, George drove across town to Madison Avenue and began the trek up to Ninety-Fourth and Park. Once they passed Eighty-Fifth Street, Sara turned in her seat and reached for George's hand. "That was a fantastic ride home. You get mad points for that one."

"I'm glad you approve. I told you I'd give you a good view of what the folks who live in Jersey have that we don't."

"True, but they only get to see it, we get to live here."

George rocked his head side to side, pondering Sara's statement. "Well there's good and bad with that, but then I guess there's good and bad with most things in life."

"There certainly is. We're almost there, you remember how to get to the garage, don't you?" asked Sara.

George glanced over, "Yes."

"Good, since you've done such an excellent job in planning today's outing, I think that deserves a drink or at least coffee."

"Sounds like an offer I can't refuse."

Sara smiled as she put her hand on his. "Well, you could, but I hope you won't."

George pulled up to the electronic gate, put the window down and reached for the keypad. He hadn't asked for the access code, so Sara sat and watched to see if he got it right. "Let's see if I remember this. Six-eight-four-one-seven," he said as he punched the keys. After pressing the last number, the roller door began to rise.

"Very good, Dr. Randell, I was wondering if you would remember," said Sara.

"I've got a good memory for numbers, I guess it's because of all the passwords and things I've always had to remember."

"Well, whatever the reason, I'm impressed."

George drove to the parking space with the number that corresponded to Sara's apartment, parked the Corvette, quickly exited, and helped Sara out of the vehicle.

Sara produced her keycard and activated the elevator's garage access. George placed his arm around her shoulders as he'd done when they left the bistro. Sara looked up and smiled as he leaned over and kissed her full on the mouth. She responded by putting her hand on the back of his head and pulling his mouth closer. The kiss lingered, and both parties were fully engaged when the elevator bell dinged. George broke the kiss and laughed as he shook his head. "They say timing is everything."

When they arrived on the fourteenth floor, Sara led George down the hallway to her apartment while taking her key from her purse. She opened the door and walked in, pulling him with her as she went. George closed the door and turned to find Sara standing in front of him. She had dropped her handbag on the floor and stood close, looking into his eyes.

"Now, where were we?" she said as she kissed him on the mouth.

He wrapped his arms around her. He pulled her close and held the kiss for a moment. George broke the kiss, pulling his head back to create a space to speak. "I think that's close to where we were."

"I agree. Now please remember that place because I'm sure I'll want to go back there in a little while. Make yourself at home," said Sara as she removed her coat and dropped it on the chair. "What will it be, coffee or a drink?"

"How about a drink? I see the bar; would you like something also?"

"I'll have a dirty martini, please help yourself to anything you see. I've also got beer in the fridge."

"One dirty martini coming right up." George made the drink for Sara and poured himself a small glass of bourbon and brought the drinks over and placed them on the coffee table in front of the couch.

Sara returned to the living room. George noticed she's changed out of her knit top in favor of a loose-fitting cotton one that had buttons down the front. The top three remained undone. Curling up on the couch next to him, she reached for her drink and in doing so provided him with a beautiful view down the inside of her blouse. George could see the swelling of her breast and the way her nipples pressed against the cloth. It was obvious she had removed her bra.

Drink in hand, she took hold of his arm, raised it over her head, and placed it around her shoulders. "Umm, that's better," she cooed as she took a drink.

George turned, pulling her closer, allowing the hand he had on her shoulder to move lower. No one spoke as he took his other hand and began stroking her face, tracing his fingertip down her face across her nose. She kissed it each time he came in contact with her lips. He then moved his finger up the side of her face; he continued until he reached her forehead where he ran his fingertips through her hair.

"You can do that all night," she purred as she slid a little lower against him.

George put his drink on the side table, bent over and kissed her on forehead, the tip of her nose, and then the lips. Again she pulled his head toward hers, and she began biting his lip. After several minutes in this position she turned toward him now, pressing her body against his. Their kissing became more passionate, and she felt warm all over. Thinking she must be covered in a bright red blush, she broke the kiss for a moment and changed position again. Now straddling him she kissed him on the mouth then pulled his head down to her breast.

His hands were on her back as he also pulled her closer. He pushed the cloth aside with his nose as he kissed the swelling of her breast. His lips searched for her nipple, but he was denied the delight because of the next button on her shirt. He couldn't undo the button as she continued pressing herself closer. Happy with what was being offered, he continued to kiss her breasts, neck, and lips.

She took her turn. Using his hair to pull his head back, she attacked his neck, nibbling on the soft flesh and then nipping softly on his ears. He closed his eyes, allowing her to do whatever she wanted. The sensation was pleasurable and satisfying, although thoughts of a more intimate interaction were running through his head.

Since they both enjoyed the intimacy, no one was keeping track of the time. Time wasn't important at the moment. Tomorrow was Sunday, and he wasn't scheduled at the hospital, and she wasn't leaving for England until Monday night. Not having any idea how long they had been kissing, he glanced at his watch. 12:30 a.m.. They have been going at it for almost two hours.

George didn't want to rush things and felt today's festivities would probably not proceed any further, so he decided it was time to call it a night. Since she would be getting ready for her trip to England, tomorrow would be an R & R day for him. Time to sleep in and just kick back and maybe watch some basketball or pre-season baseball. He knew he would call her later to wish her safe travels and plan to get together when she returned.

"It's getting late, I think I should be going. I know you've got a full day tomorrow as you get ready to head over to England."

"I have to pack."

"Still, you'll be busy trying to figure out what to bring. I hear that you can have all four seasons in one day, so you may need a little of everything."

"Nan used to say something similar. She'd say, 'dress in layers so you can add or subtract throughout the day,'" said Sara as she got off his lap and returned to her former position, partly laying in his arms. "Guess I'll follow that advice. You never can tell what the weather will be."

"Sounds like you've got it all figured out. Listen, I think I'm going to go, so you can get some sleep." At his urging Sara moved back to an upright position.

"What are you going to do tomorrow?" she asked as he stood.

"I plan to not do much of anything, just take it easy."

Sara jumped up from her seat and walked over to where she had left her handbag and began fishing for something. "You could do that here if you wanted," she said as she found what she was looking for. "We could do brunch. I can order some things from my local deli. That way, we could just hang out here. That is if you wanted to."

Her comment surprised George; he'd never dated the same woman three days in a row. Usually there were a few days in-between dates. This situation was different. He'd gotten four days off in a row, and she was leaving the country for an unknown number of days. Maybe this was a good thing. He's already decided he wanted to see more of her once she returned. She obviously wanted to see more of him before she left.

After kissing him on the lips, she held up the spare keycard she had removed from her purse. "Here, take this," she said. "It will allow you to go directly to the garage without stopping in the lobby. And tomorrow, it will give you access to come straight up when you arrive."

He returned her kiss as he accepted the key. "Thank you, I was going to call you tomorrow and wish you well on your trip and ask about a plan to go out again once you got back. That would have given me time to plan out the next outing." As he slipped the card into his pants pocket, he asked, "What time is brunch?"

"I'll have it delivered for 11:30. Does that sound good?"

"Yes, that sounds great."

Sara offered George a sly smile. "And as for something to do. Let's leave that open, shall we? We're both clever people, I'm sure we can come up with something to do."

"Without a doubt," replied George as his smile broadened. "I'll see you tomorrow then."

"I'll look forward to it. See you then," she said as she kissed him goodbye.

George palmed the keycard as he kissed her goodnight. They both lingered with their goodbyes until George broke the cycle. "Okay, I'm really leaving now. Goodnight," he said as he turned and opened the door to leave without offering one last kiss.

"Goodnight," she said to his retreating form as he walked down the hall. It had been a fun day, and Sara had enjoyed her time with George. She found it interesting that they had talked about a wide assortment of topics during the day, but he never asked about anything relating to the money her grandmother had left her. If nothing else he knew she now owned four Manhattan properties worth tens of millions if not more. But the subject was never raised. I'm not sure Jeff would have acted the same.

Sara returned to the bar, made herself another drink and went back to the couch. As she sipped her martini, she thought about next week and the meeting with Mary O'Riley. She had found Mary's comments fascinating. Mary knew something had happened to Nan, but she had followed her instructions and not called. Everyone seemed bound to follow their instructions from Rose Cavendish. Nan always seemed so sweet and agreeable. Now I find out she had plans in place for years and people who saw to it they carried those plans out to the letter. "I guess those kinds of relationships require a different level of trust than anything I'm used to in advertising. People will steal an idea for a pitch as soon as look at you," she said to herself. "But Nan's secrets were kept for decades. Regardless of the fact she had made the pact, it's nice to know there are people in the world you can count on."

After finishing her drink, Sara clicked on the TV and turned to the classic movie channel as she got up from the couch to bring her glass into the kitchen. Her back was to the screen as she walked away, but she heard the familiar voice of Basil Rathbone, one of Nan's favorite actors, as he said, "Come, Watson, come! The game is afoot."

"Ah, my dear Mr. Holmes," she said as she began to laugh. "I think I may need your assistance to help unravel the case of the secret promise."

* * *

GEORGE EXITED THE ELEVATOR in the parking garage. As he walked to his car, he thought about how much he liked Sara. She was fun to be with. She was intelligent and had a quick wit, which had probably served her well in her advertising job. He found it interesting that she was pursuing him even more than he was her. Sara had initiated the first meeting for coffee and pretty much made every move since then.

George got into the car, started the engine and pulled out of the garage. Along the way home he thought a lot about Sara. The look on her face when he'd told her, her grandmother had passed away. The way she looked when he saw her in the hospital cafeteria. The gleam in her eye when they met at the lawyers that day he was getting his account information squared away. And tonight as she had straddled him while they kissed. He was glad he had accepted her invitation to coffee because this was turning out to be a fantastic four-day break.

Chapter 33

George Randell woke up at 7:00 a.m., enjoying the fact he had another day off. Since he wasn't due at Sara's for hours, he chose to just remain in bed for a while. Typically, his regimented lifestyle on workdays had his feet hitting the floor within seconds of the alarm going off. His morning routine as hectic as his shift at the hospital.

After thirty minutes of listening to the oldies station on his clock radio, he decided it was time to get up. Peeking out the window, he saw it was a sunny day. After dressing in sweats, he donned his socks and running shoes. Another check of the clock confirmed he had plenty of time to get in a good run this morning. Maybe I'll do ten miles, he thought, haven't done ten in about a month. Before he headed out he stopped off in the small galley kitchen, opened the fridge and took out a canned protein drink, shook it up, popped the top, and downed it.

George grabbed his phone, his Bluetooth headphones and his house key and left the apartment. Once he arrived on the street George set the phone to a favorite running channel off the iHeart Radio app and slipped it into the arm sleeve holder. Though not a fan of Techno-Dance or Disco music, he found they both had an excellent beat to help him keep a good pace as he ran. George spent five minutes stretching out his hamstrings and Achilles tendons. He decided to run north toward where he and Sara had spent time yesterday. The Hudson River Greenway was one of his favorite places to run because it provided the long stretch of road he needed for a good run. George had never enjoyed running around in circles on a track or having a short route that required running the circuit multiple times to achieve the miles you wanted. George preferred the up and back one-time approach.

It didn't take long for him to settle into a good rhythm. George turned up the volume on his earphones and began to zone out. Everything faded into the background. The beat of the music the only thing he focused on. An hour later he returned to his starting point. The GPS fitness monitor on his wrist told him he'd run ten point two miles in sixty-one minutes. His heart rate was one hundred ten. George watched his heart return to its normal fifty-three beats per minute as he walked up and down the block to cool off. Since it was time to start thinking about getting ready for his date, he headed back to his apartment.

* * *

SARA AWOKE AT 8:55 A.M., five minutes ahead of the alarm, but stayed in bed until the music started. Thoughts about the future filled her head, in particular what today would bring. George Randell was definitely at the forefront. Nan's passing had brought him into her life in a most unusual way. Could Nan have known? That was a silly thought, but still Mr. McDougal had said he'd never seen a will with such a peculiar codicil.

Sara threw the covers back, rose from the bed and put her dressing gown on before venturing into the kitchen. Coffee was on her mind, as well as thinking about what to order in for her brunch with George.

Once she finished making coffee, Sara called the deli, placed her order and asked to have it delivered at about 11:30. "Well, that should be everything, time for a shower."

* * *

GEORGE USED THE KEYCARD Sara had given him to gain access to the underground garage and parked in one of the spots designated for Sara's apartment. After locking the car, he used the card to call the elevator to the garage level.

Once it arrived, he got in and pushed the button for fourteen as he thought about Sara. His thoughts were interrupted as the chime dinged, and the doors opened on the lobby level. A young man wearing a letterman jacket got in carrying a cardboard box containing several bags.

"What floor?" asked George as the young man's hands were full.

"Fourteen, please."

"Already going there."

George looked over at the younger man and eyed the contents of the box. "By any chance, is that a deli delivery for Ms. Ferguson?"

Tommy looked up. "It is. How did you know?"

"Because she invited me over for brunch. If you don't mind, I'll make the delivery."

Tommy looked at the other man. "Gee, I don't know, mister…"

"Randell, Dr. George Randell," he said, taking a card from his pocket. How much is the order, I'll pay for it?"

"Ms. Ferguson already paid with her credit card."

"Okay," said George reaching into his pocket and extracting a wad of bills. He removed two twenties and held it out in front of Tommy. "I'll take the box and make the delivery, and you take this. I think that's a fair trade. Don't you?"

"Thanks, Dr. Randell," said Tommy.

"No problem, and if anyone asks, this was my idea."

The elevator arrived on fourteen, and George stepped off while Tommy pressed the button to return to the lobby. George walked down the hallway to Sara's door and rang the bell. As he did so, he held the box low and out of sight, hoping Sara wouldn't see it through the peephole.

When the door opened, Sara stood there smiling, "Well now, if it isn't my favorite neurosurgeon," she said with a smile.

George held up the box he'd taken from Tommy. "And delivery man," he added. "I've heard there's a beautiful young woman who lives in the apartment, and I hear she's a good tipper, too."

"Is that right? Well, allow me to reassure you I do, in fact, tip well but only for superior service. Why don't you put that box in the kitchen while I close the door?"

George looked at Sara. "Yes, ma'am," he said as he took the box through to the kitchen

Sara closed the door, walked into the kitchen, stood behind him and put her arms around his waist. "Don't I get a hello?"

George took her hands in his, pulled her around in front of him, picked her up, and sat her down on the counter. "Hello," he said, kissing her full on the mouth.

Sara responded to his kiss by pulling him closer and wrapping her legs around him. Their kiss lasted for several minutes; both were breathless when they parted.

George lifted her chin to look into her eyes, "How was that for a hello?"

Sara gave him a quick kiss on the lips. "Very nice. Now, if you'll let me down, I can plate the food so we can eat."

"I could do that," George replied with a sly smile, "or, I could do this." He kissed her again.

There was passion and fire in their kiss that lingered after they again parted. Sara felt lightheaded and took a deep breath. "I think we better eat, or this food might turn into leftovers."

George laughed as he helped her down off the counter. "That sounds like a plan. I've been waiting to eat. Besides, I'm hungry after my morning run."

"If you would make some more coffee, I'll get everything ready. You'll find the coffee in that cabinet." Sara pointed it out to George.

"Sure, no problem. Glad to help." As he took the coffee down from the cabinet, George watched Sara move about the kitchen. She had dressed in a pair of loose harem pants and a wrap shirt that tied on the side and exposed much of her well-toned midriff. Her movements were smooth, almost like those of a dancer. And George admired the view.

"Okay, I think that's everything. I'll put it on the table, and we can start as soon as the coffee is ready. Care for a mimosa with brunch?"

George offered a broad smile. "Hmm, you're not trying to get me drunk, are you?"

Sara responded with a sly tone. "Why, Dr. Randell, the thought never crossed my mind."

When the coffee finished brewing he took the carafe from the machine, "Coffee's ready. Let's eat."

Sara produced a bottle of chilled champagne and two flutes to make the mimosas. "If you open this, I'll get the OJ."

George did as Sara asked and popped the cork. Sara poured some orange juice into each of the flutes, then George topped them off with the champagne and handed one to Sara.

"What shall we drink to?" she asked.

"How about a successful trip to London and a quick return to New York?"

Sara smiled and nodded. "To a successful trip."

They clinked their glasses together and drank to the toast. Then they began to eat, each sampled the delights Sara had ordered for brunch.

"My God, Sara, there's a ton of food here what are you going to do with all of this since you're leaving tomorrow?"

"It's a long time until tomorrow. I thought we could just nosh from time to time while you're here today. I hope you don't have any plans for later."

George put his fork down and looked at Sara. "Plans? No, my schedule is completely open. I seem to remember we both decided that we could come up with something to fill the time."

"That we did, and now, I think the plan is that we sit here and eat and drink our fill before we figure out what's next."

George's eyes gleamed as he put a morsel of food in his mouth and took a sip of his drink. "I'm all for that. This food is delicious."

Their conversation seemed to have a focus on food; they shared stories about their past that had something to do with food. George reminisced about his discovery that you didn't have to be Jewish to eat at a kosher deli. Sara talked about how the Sunday deli run had been a staple in her life for as long as she had been living with Nan.

Brunch lasted for an hour as they talked and picked at different foods. The mimosa's gave way to straight champagne and a second bottle was opened.

They were halfway through the second bottle when Sara decided it was time to move out of the dining room. "I think we've eaten enough for the moment. I'll put the rest of this away for later."

"I was wondering when you'd suggest that. I don't think I've stopped nibbling. Everything is so tasty. I have to admit this isn't my normal brunch."

Sara stood and began gathering the plates. "What would you have eaten today if I hadn't suggested brunch?"

George followed suit and followed her into the kitchen. "I would have had a protein shake after my run and then maybe some Chinese takeaway later in the day."

"That doesn't sound very appetizing. I glad I suggested we have brunch together."

"So am I."

The food was all put away, and the dirty dishes rinsed and placed in the dishwasher. After Sara wiped down the countertop, she picked up the champagne bottle, took George by the hand and led him back into the living room. They returned to the couch they had been sitting on last night. George sat in the corner, and Sara curled her legs under her and sat next to him, leaning against his side. George put his arm around her shoulders and slid down some to bring himself closer to her.

"Umm, this is nice," said Sara in a soft tone.

"Yes, it is. I've got a full stomach, a glass of champagne, and you sitting next to me. Couldn't ask for a better day off than this."

They continued to snuggle for a while. George stroked her hair. "Hey, don't get too relaxed. You need to pack for your trip."

Sara sat up and laughed. "Sure, spoil the moment," she said.

"Hey," said George, holding up his hands in mock surrender. "Don't shoot the messenger, I'm just repeating what you said you had to do."

"You're right. Once that's done, I'll be free for the rest of the day. I've already started pulling stuff out to pack." Sara rose from her seat, picked up her champagne glass, and started to walk off. She stopped and turned to George. "Are you just going to sit there? Why don't you come give me a hand? I could use a big strong man to help get my suitcase down off the top shelf."

George got up and also took his champagne glass with him as he followed her into her bedroom.

"The suitcase is in that closet," she said, pointing to one of the doors in her room.

George put the glass down and walked to the closet and opened the door. When the lights came on, he looked up and saw several cases piled on top of each other. "Which one do you want?"

"The largest one, please. You can just put it on the bed."

George obliged and then picked up his drink again as he watched her move around the room, bending and stretching to take things out of drawers or off shelves. The material of her pants moved with her; at times it clung to her slim form, other times, it danced seductively. Her movements hypnotized him. Every once in a while she would catch his eye and smile in a way that said: "I know you're watching."

George stood and walked around the bed to where she was taking things out of her dresser. He put his glass down on top of the chest and kissed her neck. As she turned, he wrapped her in his arms and gave her a deep passionate kiss that seemed to last forever. He broke the kiss and gave her a gentle push to increase the distance between them so he could look her in the eyes. They stood, motionless, recovering from the last kiss. She pulled his head down and kissed him with the same passion he had displayed. She pulled him down, pulling him into her. As they kissed, he kept moving forward as she pulled him to her.

They lost their balance, realizing they were falling onto the bed. But the kiss wasn't broken. As they now lay amidst the folded clothes and the empty suitcase, they began to move. Hands roamed everywhere. He found the knot that held her blouse closed and tugged to release it. It came undone, and he pulled it across, opening it, revealing her breasts. He broke the kiss and moved his mouth to her breast as she urged him on.

She pulled his hair in an attempt to redirect his mouth, and she attacked his neck. She bit him gently and heard him moan. He pressed against her, and she had wrapped her legs around him to pull him closer.

She tore at his shirt, opening the buttons and clawed his chest and back.

He pushed back, allowing himself space to remove his shirt as she pulled her arms from her blouse giving him total access.

He kissed her again, rolling her over, so she was on top of him, and she took control. She reached for his belt, undid it and opened the fasteners and zipper. She wiggled as she tugged and pushed his pants below his waist.

He responded by pulling on the elastic waist of the harem pants and pushing them down over her hips, exposing her bottom. After grabbing a cheek in each hand, he squeezed and tried to regain control. He pulled her back down onto him, he rolled her over again as she pushed her folded clothing onto the floor. She kicked the suitcase off the bed as they wrestled for control. He wasn't sure if it was his superior size and strength that allowed him to regain control or if she had allowed him to do so. It didn't matter because once again he was on top pulling at her pants forcing them lower on her thighs exposing everything she had to offer. As he moved them lower, he began to slide off the bed, pushing his mouth lower as he went. When he had her pants off, he was in the perfect position to provide her the pleasure she desired. His attack was slow, deliberate, moving from place to place, probing, infiltrating, urging her to surrender.

But she fought back by sitting up and pulling him to a standing position.

She took her turn by removing his underpants, then began fondled him, urging him onto the bed next to her. He followed her direction and allowed her to give him what she offered.

As she continued on him, he began to move on the bed. Turning and angling for position. Finally, he got where he wanted to be and pulled her close. Once again, he attacked her with his mouth and tongue. Their passion continued unabated. They broke and repositioned themselves. She mounted him and took him inside her. As he slid deep into her, there was an instance of pleasure, and everything stopped for a moment. The moment lingered as they both experienced a feeling of euphoria. But that passed as her desire began to grow.

He began to move under her. By raising his hips, he could lift her off the bed, causing her to press down harder because of her weight. This kindled her fire and she began to make a series of rapid movements that brought them both close to the point of ecstasy.

He matched her rhythm as she increased the speed of her thrusts.

It wasn't long before her moment of release came as the rapture overcame her. The fireworks she felt in her head seemed to explode in perfect synchronicity with the spasms that coursed through her body.

Panting, she stopped moving and placed her head on his chest while he kept up the pace. "Stop, please stop. I don't think I can take any more."

He rolled her off of him, as he continued to stroke and nuzzle her.

As her breathing began to return to normal, she kissed him and reached down to entice him once more.

"Again?" she whispered.

He kissed her again, and she shifted position once more allowing him unimpeded access to the treasure she had to offer.

He accepted the offer, again entering her. As he probed deeper, he came to rest on top of her and they lay together intertwined as one.

The rippling sensations of pleasure again began to build inside her, as he allowed her to set the rhythm of the dance.

The tempo increased as their passion built; hand in hand they climbed the mountain of pleasure. The slope becoming steeper as they approached the top, yet they persisted and gave their all. Muscles tensed, straining to remain in control as they clutched each other in the throes of the ultimate pleasure. They felt the moment arrive. Both knowing they had given all there was, they let go, surrendering themselves to each other.

He pulled her close and rolled onto his back taking her along with him. Now once again resting atop her lover, she put her head down on his chest and breathed, "That was incredible."

"It certainly was." He continued to hold her and stroke her back as she relaxed. Feeling himself beginning to get drowsy, he rolled her onto her side, so they were lying face to face. Holding each other in a gentle embrace, they fell into a deep, restful sleep.

Chapter 34

For the rest of that Sunday, Sara and George found lots of ways to entertain each other, and none of them involved clothing or packing Sara's suitcase for her trip to England. They continued to snack on the rest of the food from the deli while also consuming more champagne and each other.

All Sara's frustrations and pent-up desires had been removed. As they lay together, Sara looked at the man next to her. George was nothing like Jeff. Everything about him was different. The way he touched her, the attention he provided to her needs and desires as they made love. Thinking back to the start of her affair with Jeff, she tried to remember if he had ever put her first. Nothing came to mind. The fact he was still married meant their time together was measured in stolen moments.

After spending time with George for three days in a row, Sara began to realize this was what a relationship was supposed to be like; going out, having fun, making love. All without having to look at the clock or worry if Jeff's phone would ring with his wife asking where he was.

Now that it was Monday morning, their time together was ending, at least for the foreseeable future, as Sara went to England to find the answers to the question of who she really was.

As she slipped out of bed, she took her silk robe from the hook in the bathroom and left the room to go make coffee.

As it brewed, Sara made up a plate of leftovers from yesterday's feast and put it on a wooden tray. When the coffee finished , she poured two large mugs.

When she returned to the bedroom carrying the tray, she found George was still asleep. Sara set the tray on her dresser, removed her robe and walked over to the edge of the bed. A mischievous moment overcame her, and she took a step back and jumped on the bed startling George awake.

George's body spasmed, and he almost fell out of bed as the shock woke him. "Shit, what was that?" he said, looking around.

"Sorry, I didn't mean to scare you like that," said Sara apologetically, and she laid her body on his.

Catching his breath after being startled, he pulled her over to lay next to him. "Now that you've jump-started my heart, I guess I can say good morning."

"Good morning," she said, kissing him. "I'm sorry I did that. Something just came over me and said, 'go jump on the bed.'"

George laughed and returned her kiss. "Didn't you get enough of the jumping on the bed game yesterday?"

Sara smiled and rolled her eyes, "I sure did. But that was yesterday. Today I'm leaving for England, so it's going to be awhile until we can do that again." Batting her eyes at him, she continued. "That is assuming you'd still like to see me again after I almost scared you to death just now."

"Hmm," said George as he pondered his choices. "That's a tough question. I guess it depends."

"On what?"

"On whether that's coffee I smell."

"It is, and I've also brought food," replied Sara as she rolled over to get off the bed. Sara retrieved the tray from where she's left it, walked around to the other side and laid it in the center of the bed before she took her place under the covers.

"Breakfast in bed, now that's not something I'm used to getting."

Sara lifted the plate of food, offering George a choice of delicacies. "You mean all your lovers don't offer you something like this after a night of fun and games?"

"Nope," replied George as he gave Sara a coy look. "Usually, they just want more of the fun and games we took part in the previous night."

"Really, I'm certainly willing to engage in more of the jumping on the bed game, but I thought before I asked for more, I'd at least feed you."

"You are a kind and caring soul, Sara Ferguson. Guess I better hurry and eat. We're running up against a hard deadline. Isn't that what you call it in the trade?"

"Yes, that's right, so I suggest you finish your coffee and let me have your best pitch."

George almost spewed his coffee across the sheets when she said that. "I'll give it my best," as he put his coffee down. He picked up the tray and put it on the floor, then put his arm around her waist and pulled her down from her sitting position onto the bed, so she lay flat. "We start with a close-up," he said as he kissed her deeply.

Her response was immediate, pulling him onto her. They spent the morning making love. Again it was George who pointed out to Sara that the clock was ticking, and she needed to pack for her trip. Now sitting up in bed, Sara surveyed the carnage their lovemaking had reeked upon the clothing she had already selected to take with her.

"Okay, as much as I don't want to admit it, I guess I better get up and start packing, or I'm just going to be traveling with my toothbrush."

"I can help if you'd like. Believe it or not, I'm handy at packing, and if needed, I'm a master of the steam iron," replied George as he stood and pulled on his underpants.

"Before I do anything, I think I need a shower. How good are you at washing backs?" Sara asked with a devilish grin.

"I'm not sure," replied George as he offered her his own version of a devilish grin. "But I'm willing to give it a go. You decide if it's something I should add to my repertoire."

Sara walked around the bed and took him by the hand and led him to the bathroom. "Somehow I have a strong feeling I won't be disappointed."

Part III

*I went to the woods because I
wished to live deliberately, to front only
the essential facts of life, and see if I
could learn what it has to teach and
not, when I came to die, discover that I
had not lived.*

Henry David Thoreau

Chapter 35

George helped Sara bring her luggage downstairs, and together they waited for the car to arrive. The car pulled up in front of Highgate at 5:30 pm. Sara gave George a hug, and he kissed her gently on the lips. "Have a good flight. I hope everything works out, and you'll come back with all the answers you were looking for."

"So do I. I've got no idea what I will find, but after everything else that's been revealed to me, I think I'm just about ready for anything."

Charlie Wilkins was on duty tonight and carried Sara's bags to the waiting limo as George Randell escorted her to the car.

"Take care of yourself," said George as he kissed her again.

"You too, I'll be back as soon as I can."

"Don't worry, I'll be here waiting for you to get back. Hopefully, after your trip, we can pick up where we left off." Giving Sara a final hug he let her go as Charlie held the rear door of the limo open for her.

"Safe travels, Ms. Ferguson," said the concierge.

"Thanks, Charlie."

Charlie closed the door after Sara took her seat, and the limo driver pulled away from the curb as she waved goodbye.

The ride took forty minutes in the evening traffic, but Sara arrived in plenty of time to check-in. The limo delivered her to the Delta Air Lines first class check-in line where her luggage was taken and tagged as Sara produced her passport and ticket.

After clearing the TSA checkpoint, she made her way to the Sky Club to wait for her flight to board. Sara was no stranger to flying, though she admitted that premium economy was her normal travel mode. This first-class experience was new to her, and Michael McDougal wanted to ensure she had all the privileges and perks available, so he'd arraigned a club membership for his client.

The notice board showed that Sara's flight was preparing to board, so she left the Sky Club and made her way to the gate.

As she arrived, the man at the desk announced, "Delta Flight 402, non-stop service to London Heathrow is ready to board our first-class passengers."

Sara walked up to the attendant, presented her ticket, was checked in, and admitted to the jetway. Once she arrived at the cabin door, the flight attendant again looked at Sara's boarding pass and directed her to her seat. Sara put her small carry-on in the overhead bin, moved across the aisle to her window seat and sat down. No sooner had she found the end of her seat belt when another attendant arrived.

"May I offer you something to drink?" she said.

A stranger to first class, Sara hesitated before asking, "Can I get a glass of champagne?"

"Certainly, I'll be right back."

Sara moved about in the wide reclining seat, which looked more like an individual seating pod than the regular two or three-seat sections she was used to seeing. I could get used to this, she thought.

The flight attendant returned with Sara's drink and pushed a button to extend the tray table. Sensing Sara was not accustomed to the amenities of first class, the attendant removed a card from the holder and handed it to Sara. "Everything you need to know about the seat and your personal entertainment center is in this pamphlet. If you have any questions, please press the call bell."

Sara smiled at the middle-aged woman. "Thank you, I haven't got a clue what's what in this seat."

The attendant smiled and nodded before leaving to see to her other passengers.

The flight took off on schedule. Once the plane began its gentle climb out to cruising altitude, Sara reclined and began to relax.

Sara figured out the intricacies of her seat without help. She watched a movie, enjoyed her chef prepared meal, and had two more glasses of champagne before reclining the seat its full hundred and eighty degrees to create a flat bed. The attendant delivered a pillow and a blanket. Sara fell asleep thinking of George Randell.

* * *

FOUR AND A HALF HOURS LATER, the cabin lights came on, and the attendant announced they would serve breakfast.

Sara woke and stretched out on the reclined seat. As she opened her eyes she thought, now that's a new experience, actually being able to sleep like a real person on a flight. A small amenities kit was delivered, and Sara took it and went to the lavatory to wash her face and freshen up. She took a few minutes to put on a little make-up, then returned to her seat.

The flight landed at 7:20 a.m., and Sara enjoyed being able to be one of the first off the plane. She also discovered that getting off quicker meant she had to wait longer at the baggage claim.

Once she cleared immigration, she collected her luggage and proceeded through customs and out onto the main concourse. Janet had mentioned that she would be met as she exited customs, so Sara scanned the limo drivers holding signs awaiting their passengers. Sara found the person waiting for her and began walking in his direction. Once she made eye contact with the driver, he began to move toward her.

"Ms. Ferguson?"

Sara nodded, "Yes."

"Good morning. My name is Raj, Mr. Cromwell has sent me. May I take your bags?"

Sara relinquished the hold on her suitcase. "Thank you, Raj."

"Please follow me, Miss The car isn't far."

Sara followed the driver through the throngs of people present on the concourse as they headed for the parking garage. Raj removed the remote from his pocket and pushed the button. The trunk of the black Bentley opened, and the driver placed the luggage in with an ease that only comes with years of practice. He closed the trunk lid and opened the rear door allowing Sara to enter.

Sara slid across the buttery soft leather seats and smiled to herself as she adjusted her seat belt, thinking, so this is what the *back seat* of a Bentley is like.

Raj took his place behind the wheel, then turned to address his passenger. "It will be about forty-five minutes to an hour to get to your hotel. There are drinks in the cabinet. Coldwater in the small cooler in the center armrest. If you would prefer, I've also filled the small pressure vessel with hot coffee."

"Thank you, I think I'm good for the moment."

Raj drove the car down the ramp, exited the parking garage, and guided the limo north on Tunnel Road until he came to the entrance of the M4. An hour later he pulled to the curb in front of The Royal Horseguards Hotel on Whitehall. Raj exited the vehicle and opened the rear door for Sara before removing her luggage from the trunk. The doorman opened the door allowing Sara and her driver to enter the historic building, which had been converted to a lovely boutique hotel.

When Sara approached the desk, the clerk became very attentive. "Good morning, may I help you?"

"I believe I have a reservation; the name is Ferguson."

The desk clerk entered some information into her computer. "Yes, certainly, Ms. Ferguson, we have you in the Library Suite for five days with a confirmed extension should you require a longer stay."

Sara nodded and signed the registration forms.

"Thank you. I have a message for you from Mr. Cromwell. He said he would meet you for afternoon tea in the lounge at 4:30 this afternoon."

"4:30; can I schedule a wake-up call for 3:45?"

"Certainly. Amit will show you to your room. We hope you will enjoy your stay with us at the Royal Horseguards."

"Thank you, I'm sure I will," said Sara as she left the desk and followed the bellman across the lobby and up a short flight of five stairs that led to another hallway where the elevator was located.

The bellman led Sara down to the door of the suite, opened the door, and placed the room keycard into a slot inside the door, turning on the lights.

Sara tipped the bellman. "Thank you, Amit. I can take it from here."

"Yes, ma'am. If you need anything, please ring the front desk."

Sara rolled her suitcase across the room and parked it by the standing wardrobe. "I better unpack now, or I'm going to fall asleep, and it won't get done."

After she had finished putting her clothes away Sara stripped down and went into the bathroom to remove her make up before heading to bed. Once that was done, she pulled down the covers on the bed and slipped between the crisp linens.

* * *

THE CHIRPING OF THE BEDSIDE PHONE woke Sara, and she reached for the handset. "Hello."

"Good afternoon, Ms. Ferguson, you requested a 3:45 wake-up call."

"Yes, thank you," she said as she hung up. It took Sara a second to realize a real person had actually called. "Now that's different," she said to herself as she got out from under the covers.

After a quick shower, Sara redid her make-up and dressed for her meeting with Mr. Cromwell.

Sara took the elevator to the lobby and followed the signs to the lounge. When she entered, she was met by the maître d'.

"Will you be joining us for afternoon tea?" he asked.

"Yes, but I'm supposed to be meeting someone. But, I'm not sure if he's arrived."

"Would that be a Mr. Cromwell?"

"Yes."

"He has arrived, please follow me."

Sara followed the maître d' across the room to a small table against the window. Cromwell rose when he saw Sara approach. Sara saw the man rise and smiled as she got closer.

"Ms. Ferguson, it's a pleasure to meet you. Mr. McDougal speaks highly of you." Cromwell was of average height and weight. His dark red hair showed signs of gray around the temples. Unlike many of the British natives she had already encountered, his skin was tanned, and Sara assumed it showed he was successful enough to enjoy time abroad.

Sara offered her hand. "Nice to meet you, as well." Shaking hands with the barrister, she continued, "Please allow me to return the compliment, Mr. McDougal also has nothing but praise for you."

Cromwell released Sara's hand and placed his right hand over his heart, bowing slightly. "Your humble servant, Ma'am."

Sara took her seat, and Cromwell followed suit.

"Ms. Ferguson, please tell me how I can be of assistance. I'm afraid Mr. McDougal was vague on his request to assist you."

Sara explained some of what she had uncovered about her grandmother's holdings and how Nan had received a quarterly payment from Barclay's Bank since the 1940s. She then produced the letter she had retrieved from the safe deposit box and showed it to him.

Reginald Cromwell took his reading glasses from his jacket pocket and read the letter.

"No name and no street address. I'm assuming you want to know who lives at Highgate House." Cromwell removed his glasses as he returned the letter to Sara.

"That would be a start." Sara folded the letter and placed it back in her handbag. "But that will be after I visit my grandmother's friend, Mrs. O'Riley. I'm going to call her again in the morning and set up an appointment to meet. My grandmother's letter was very cryptic and said I needed to speak to Mrs. O'Riley to get the first clue as to who I really am. I still don't understand what she meant."

"I can certainly inquire as to the ownership of Highgate. I'm not sure how successful we will be at gaining information from Barclays. Bankers have their own rules for client confidentiality. However, I have some contacts in the bank. Perhaps we can find out something of use."

"Thank you. I'm confident any assistance you can render will be of use. As you can imagine, I feel as if I'm trying to assemble the pieces of a jigsaw puzzle without a picture to guide me through the process."

The waiter arrived with a serving trolley containing all the elements of a proper afternoon tea and began to place them on the table.

Sara sat and watched as the waiter set everything up. While she had on occasion had afternoon tea with her grandmother, this was different. This was the real deal, served on multi-tiered trays, elegant gold embossed tea service. A proper English Tea.

After everything was set, and the tea was served, the waiter left.

"Shall we?" asked Cromwell.

"Indeed," replied Sara.

As they enjoyed their tea, the conversation turned to other things as they began to grow more comfortable in each other's company. It was 6:00 when they finished up, and Mr. Cromwell departed. Sara returned to her room and began to develop a list of things she would do next. Top of the list was the call to Mary O'Riley.

Chapter 36

When Sara woke in the morning, she felt as if she hadn't slept. The clock on the bedside table said it was 8:30 a.m., and Sara did a quick calculation. "It's only 3:30 back home," she mumbled. Then she thought, I wonder what time Mary O'Riley wakes up. I wouldn't want to disturb her.

As she lay in bed, Sara began to envision the conversation she would have with Mrs. O'Riley. She was sure it would start with Mary saying she was sad to hear that her friend had passed away. Then she would give Sara the information she had held for all these years, just waiting for the day she would get the call.

Fifteen minutes later, Sara tossed the covers off, went into the bathroom, and started running the shower. Once the temperature was to her liking, she stripped out of her nightie and climbed in. The warm water ran over her body and began to wash away her tiredness. After washing her hair, she set about using the luxurious washcloth. She grabbed a towel for her hair as she climbed out of the shower and donned one of the plush terrycloth robes the hotel had provided.

By the time Sara had dried her hair, dressed, and put on some makeup, it was 9:50. Sara left her room and took the elevator back down to the lobby and made her way to the restaurant. After being seated and ordering tea, she pondered the choices offered on the menu. Yesterday's meeting with Mr. Cromwell had offered her an opportunity to experience afternoon tea. Today she decided she would opt for another staple of British cuisine. When the waiter returned with her drink, Sara ordered a full English breakfast.

Though blessed with a healthy appetite, Sara was astonished at the amount of food delivered to her. As she looked at what was on offer, she thanked her parents with also blessing her with a high metabolism and getting her into a regular exercise regimen, both of which helped her maintain her trim figure.

Helpings of eggs, bacon, sausage, mushrooms, tomatoes, and beans covered her plate and served along with a side order of toast. Sara smiled as she thought of her grandmother. "Here's to you, Nan," she whispered as she began to dig in.

Having finished most of her breakfast, she returned to her room and removed the phone diary from her bag. "I've come all this way, no sense in putting this off any longer," she said as she picked up the receiver of the room telephone and began to dial the number.

When the call connected, that same proper English voice answered the phone. "Hello."

"Mrs. O'Riley, it's Sara Ferguson."

"Hello, dear. I'm glad you've arrived safely."

"Yes, I arrived yesterday. I'm calling to see when it would be convenient to meet."

"Would it be possible for you to be here today at 4:00 p.m.?"

Sara looked at the clock to see what time it was. "Yes, certainly. I have the street address I copied from Nan's book. Are you still there?"

"Yes."

"I'll see you then."

"Until then, Sara, I look forward to meeting you."

"Thank you. Goodbye, Mrs. O'Riley," replied Sara as she hung up the phone. "It's only 11:15, I should go for a run and work off some of that breakfast."

Once she had changed into her running gear, Sara gathered wat she needed and headed out.

After stretching out for about ten minutes, Sara began her run by heading across Whitehall gardens and toward the River Thames. After crossing over the Golden Jubilee Bridge and continued to follow the river until she came to Tower Bridge. The GPS in her watch said she'd covered almost three miles on the outbound leg. She decided that was far enough for today and turned around to retrace her route back to the hotel.

Once she returned, she again showered and prepared herself for her meeting with Mary O'Riley. Sara wondered what Mary would have to say. What was the great secret Nan had taken to her grave? After uncovering many of Nan's other secrets Sara was convinced this one must be one for the ages since Nan has asked Sara to travel to London to meet with her friend.

Chapter 37

The taxi ride from the hotel to the home of Mary O'Riley gave Sara a view of some sights of London. Since she had time before her appointment, she had asked the driver if he wouldn't mind giving her a short tour on the meter. The driver agreed, noted the time, and set off. He exited Horse Guards Parade and headed south on Whitehall past the World War One monument known as the Cenotaph and across the Westminster Bridge. He turned north and drove past the giant enclosed Ferris wheel called the London Eye and crossed back over the Thames River on Waterloo Bridge.

The driver continued down Victoria Embankment to Northumberland Avenue and followed that to Trafalgar Square. From there he drove down the Pall Mall, past the Palace of Saint James and up to Piccadilly. Driving into the heart of Mayfair, he turned onto Charles Street and stopped in front of an immaculate white stone-fronted building.

"Ere' you are, Miss, 'Olborne 'Ouse," he said, dropping the H's in his pronunciation of the name.

Sara paid the fare and added a generous tip for the driver, who thanked her. As she exited the taxi, she looked at the other properties on the street and realized Mary O'Riley, like Nan, wasn't poor by any stretch of the imagination.

Sara walked to the door, rang the buzzer, and waited. After a minute or two, she thought to herself it must be a long way to the front door since it was taking so long for Mary to open it. Much to Sara's surprise, a butler answered the door.

"May I help you?" asked the butler.

"Yes. My name is Sara Ferguson, I'm here to meet with Mrs. O'Riley."

The butler winced at the sound of the name before replying. "Yes, Miss, Lady Holborne is expecting you.

Sara looked confused. Who's Lady Holborne, she wondered.

"If you will follow me, her ladyship will receive you in the morning room," replied the butler as he stepped aside, allowing Sara to enter the home.

Sara dutifully followed the majordomo as he led her through the house to the morning room.

"Please be seated. I shall inform her ladyship you have arrived," said the butler as he bowed slightly and exited the room closing the doors as he left.

Sara didn't take a seat. She was mesmerized with the room, almost afraid to sit. Instead, she walked around, taking in the beauty of this classic English residence. The tall glass doors opened into an impeccably manicured back garden. The bushes and topiaries had been trimmed with military precision. Spring flowers were coming into bloom, providing a variety of colors. Fresh-cut flowers filled vases in several locations in the room. The furniture looked to be in the same style as Nan's bedroom, so Sara assumed it was from the Regency period. After looking at the chairs and the rest of the surroundings, she decided they must have been original and not reproductions.

A large oil painting of a woman hung on the wall above a sideboard. Sara wondered if that could be Mary O'Riley. Her question was answered when the doors to the morning room opened, and the live representation of the painting walked in. Mary O'Riley was a tall, silver-haired woman in her late eighties. Dressed in a beautifully tailored, blue tweed suit and a white blouse, she oozed style and grace.

"Mrs. O'Riley?" asked Sara in a questioning tone.

The old woman smiled. "Yes, but that was a long time ago, my dear. My name now is Holborne. I remarried many years ago after my first husband died. I am now married to Admiral Sir Charles Holborne."

Feeling like *Alice Through the Looking Glass*, Sara tried to imagine what to say next. She remembered those old English movies she had watched with her grandmother as she addressed the other woman. "I'm sorry, your ladyship. I had no idea. I followed the instructions my grandmother left about contacting you when she passed away."

"Don't concern yourself with those trivial details, Sara. To Rose, I was always Mary O'Riley even after I remarried, and they knighted the Admiral. Please, just call me Mary," she said pointing to a chair, urging Sara to sit. "Would you like tea?"

"Yes, please, tea sounds like a wonderful idea at the moment."

Lady Holborne walked to the fireplace and pressed a small button on the wall. Sara assumed this to be a modern version of the pull cords that rang bells in the servants' area to inform them someone needed assistance. Before Lady Mary crossed the room and took a seat by Sara, the doors opened, and the butler entered.

"You rang, your ladyship?"

"Yes, Jenkins, please bring us tea."

"Of course, your ladyship," replied Jenkins, taking his leave.

Once she had returned to her seat, the woman once known as Mary O'Riley sat back and looked at Sara. "You remind me of your grandmother," she said. "We were friends for years before the war. Did you know we were in school together?"

Sara shook her head. "She never spoke of you. In fact, I never heard your name mentioned until it showed up in the letter Nan left me as part of her will."

"Rose Beardmore *was* superb at keeping secrets. Beardmore was her maiden name."

"You don't know the half of it," said Sara, as she looked at Mary. "Or maybe you do. Are you aware of the fortune she had accumulated?"

"Somewhat. Rose sometimes mentioned the odd stock transaction. In fact, Charles and I have enjoyed the benefit of some of her advice."

Conversation ceased when Jenkins returned with the tea and set it down on the sideboard. Turning to the mistress of the house, he asked, "Shall I pour, ma' Lady?"

"No thank you, Jenkins, we'll see to ourselves."

"Very well, ma' Lady," he said as he left.

Mary rose from her seat and went over to the tea service. "How do you take your tea?"

"Just lemon, if you please."

Mary nodded her head as she turned her back on her guest to pour the tea. "Just like Rose." Returning to her seat carrying two cups, Mary set them down on the small side table between the chairs. After they both had taken a sip of their tea, Mary returned her cup to the table and folded her hands placing them in her lap.

With a gentle smile, she looked at the young woman across from her. "Where shall we begin?" she asked.

Sara picked up her handbag and removed the first letter she had received and passed it to Mary. "Perhaps you should read this. Then you'll know how much I know. Or should I say, think I know."

Mary took the letter and opened it. "I'm afraid I'll need my glasses for this," she said as she stood and walked over to another table next to a large comfortable looking armchair. Lady Mary picked up her glass case, returned, and sat down to read the letter.

Sara watched as her grandmother's lifelong friend read what she had penned long ago. Mary's facial expressions said much. Some showed joy, some pain, and some possibly related to her telling Sara she had wished she had passed on before Rose. Upon finishing, she placed the letter in her lap and looked at Sara. "The best place to start is at the beginning. Now that I've read this, let me ask you, what is it you *think* you know about your grandmother's past?"

Sara sat back for a moment before she spoke. "One thing I just found out wasn't true was that Nan said she was penniless when she arrived in America. Since we have converted all her financial accounts to my name, I discovered that not long after arriving in New York, she converted two thousand pounds sterling into American dollars and opened a bank account."

Mary nodded her understanding. "Go on."

"Not long after that, she began getting quarterly deposits from Barclays Bank in London."

"What else did Rose tell you of her early days?"

Sara looked confused. "I'm not sure, her letter says just about everything I believe to be true is a work of fiction or only partly true. The story she always told and never changed was, during the war, she worked in an aircraft factory, got married to a soldier who was killed in the closing days of the war, and when she landed in America, she was an eighteen-year-old pregnant widow. And she was poor, which has already proven to be false."

Lady Holborne put her glasses on again and looked at the letter once more. "Rose always had the most beautiful penmanship," she said in a soft tone.

Sara looked at the old woman who was now smiling as she looked at the handwritten pages, wondering if perhaps Mary suffered from a mild form of dementia.

"Even when we were children, her handwriting was always perfect. Rose was the one the teachers always called on to write the lessons on the blackboard."

Mary O'Riley paused, then looked in Sara's direction, but she wasn't looking at Sara. It was as if she was watching her own memories play out in front of her. "Did you ever consider it takes a person with perfect penmanship to write horribly? Think about that for a moment, dear. If your handwriting is nothing more than a scribble, how could you ever be expected to write in a clear, legible hand? However, if you were able to pen a perfect letter, you would probably be able to scribble."

"I'm not following you. What does this have to do with her past?"

Lady Mary removed her glasses as she passed the letter back to Sara. "Your grandmother didn't work in an aircraft factory during the war.

"What?"

"In fact, Rose worked right here in London."

"What did she do?"

"She wrote. She used her penmanship skills to assist in the war effort."

"I'm sorry, I still don't understand what you're trying to say."

"She was a forger, dear. Rose and I were in the Women's Royal Naval Service, they called us Wrens. We worked for Military Intelligence. Rose and I worked together in the documents office, creating forged documents for our operatives."

Mary's disclosure stunned Sara. A look of total disbelief overcame her.

Mary O'Riley smiled. "We call that look *gobsmacked.*"

Chapter 38

Sara blinked the disbelief from her eyes, but her words betrayed the fact Lady Mary's statement hadn't convinced her. "You're telling me my grandmother was a forger… for Military Intelligence? You're joking."

"After discovering the secrets you have already uncovered about her, is this so impossible to imagine?"

Sara let out a heavy sigh. "No, I guess not."

"Do you know who Major William Martin was?"

After thinking about that name for a while, Sara replied, "No. Should I?"

"Not really. Not unless you are a student of World War II history. Rose's letter said you spent many afternoons watching old English movies."

"We did," replied Sara. "Especially in the winter or on rainy afternoons."

"Do you recall ever seeing a movie starring Clifton Webb, called *The Man Who Never Was*?"

Sara pondered the question for a moment as she searched her memory. "Not that I can recall. What was the movie about?"

"It was about the allied invasion of Sicily and how we got the Germans to believe it would happen somewhere else."

"Ah, yes, now that you've told me about it, I'm pretty sure I've seen that movie. My grandmother was part of that?"

"She was. British Intelligence devised a plan they called *Operation Mincemeat*. If you remember the movie, the way they achieved this deception was through the use of a dead body carrying a briefcase containing specific documents that made the duplicity seem plausible."

"Major William Martin was the name they gave to the body of the person carrying those documents," added Sara.

"Correct. Rose created all his identity documents and some of the papers he was carrying. Others were true originals signed by the real people named in them but containing false information."

"Wow, Nan was part of a famous operation that saved the lives of a lot of people. I wish I would have known that when she was alive. What about the rest of her story about the war and coming to the States, is any of that true?"

"Partly," replied Lady Mary. "First of all, Rose wasn't eighteen when she went to America. She was twenty-one."

"Really? Why do you think she lied about that?"

"I don't know, perhaps telling everyone she was only eighteen made her seem more vulnerable and in need of assistance. Something as far from the truth as her telling everyone she worked in a factory." Mary replied as she took another sip of her tea. "Next, yes, it was true that she was with child when she left England. Was she a war widow? Not exactly."

Sara listened carefully as Mary continued. Maybe this was the secret.

"You referred to me as Mrs. O'Riley when we first spoke, and O'Riley was what Rose called me for years. When we were in school, she called me Mary McDonald."

"McDonald! That was my mother's maiden name. That's the name Nan used to open the bank account in New York. Are we related?" asked Sara, a hopeful look in her eyes at the possibility of still having a family.

Mary shook her head. "No dear, we're not blood. This is another bit that is partly true and partly contrived. There really was a Capt. Robert McDonald. He was my older brother. Robert was four years my senior, and it is true he was killed two days before the German surrender."

"So, okay, there was a Robert McDonald, and he was your brother. Who was the Robert McDonald Nan was married to?"

"There isn't one. I've already told you Rose was an expert forger, and we worked together in the documents department of Military Intelligence. Your grandmother wanted to leave England because she had been in love with someone. She got pregnant and didn't want to remain here. I don't know the reason, but it is my understanding that the person she was in love with, your real grandfather, wouldn't, or perhaps couldn't, marry her."

That's it, Sara thought, that's the secret. Picking up Nan's letter, she looked at the last page she had written.

I cannot stress how important this first meeting is. If anything should happen to Mary before you meet, I am afraid the first, and perhaps the most important part of the British portion of the puzzle will be lost forever.

Sara's face showed she now understood. "So together, you came up with the idea to forge a marriage license between your deceased brother and my grandmother."

"That's correct. Since Rose was immigrating to America, the use of Robert's name on a marriage license, or your mother's birth certificate would never be recorded in any official records here in England."

"That was Nan's secret, she wasn't really a widow, and my real grandfather wouldn't or couldn't marry her. Not much of an uncommon occurrence in today's world, but I guess it was scandalous in 1945."

Sara leaned back in her chair and smiled. She had discovered the family secret. But why was Nan so cloak and dagger about the whole thing? Why did she make her come to England to find out? "So that's it then, now I know the deep dark secret," said Sara as she gently shook her head.. "Thank you for that information. Now if you would please be so kind as to tell me. Who is my real grandfather?"

Lady Holborne looked toward the ceiling. "I'm sorry, I can't tell you that."

"Oh no, that's enough with all the secrets. Now I know Nan wasn't married. Please tell me the rest. Who is my grandfather?"

"I can't tell you because I don't have that information. Rose never told me who he was."

The elation Sara had felt only moments before, was gone. Nan was playing with her, and she didn't like it. She picked up the letter again to read the part about why it was important to see Mary.

Sara apologized to her grandmother's livelong friend "I'm sorry for my outburst." She held the letter up as a flag of truce. "Now that I've reread the letter, I see you were only to provide the first clue. My hunt for the answer isn't over yet."

With a nod, Mary replied, "Now you will better understand why I said I wished I had passed away before you contacted me. Had I done so, you never would have found out that Robert McDonald was not your grandfather."

"Where do I go from here? I know Nan wasn't married, but I..." Sara stopped dead. "The other letter. That's it. The one from Highgate House."

Now it was Mary O'Riley's turn to look confused. "Highgate House... letter... what *are* you talking about, child?"

Sara removed the other letter from her handbag and passed it to Mary. "Read this. It's one of a stack of letters Nan had in a safe deposit box. It talks about trying to get her back to England. I think this could be from my grandfather."

Mary began by reading a portion of the address. "SW1, that's a pretty big area. But I'm willing to bet Eaton Mews South is either in Belgravia or Westminster. Whoever wrote this probably comes from money."

"I should think so," replied Sara as she pointed to the letter. "Whoever it is can afford to send British pounds equaling four hundred thousand dollars to Nan's bank account in hundred thousand dollar increments every three months."

Sara removed the velvet case that held the sapphire brooch and passed it to Lady Mary. "Not to mention this little trinket that was in the safe deposit box with the letters."

Lady Holborne opened the box and looked at the brooch. "Hmm, Toye, Kenning & Spencer, very high-end jewelers."

"It's obvious you've heard of them?"

"Indeed I have, and for several reasons. The first being this," she said, extending her left hand. "Charles bought me this diamond wedding ring from them for one of our anniversaries." Lady Mary rose from her seat and walked to a table where she picked up a framed photo of her husband in his dress uniform. "The other reason I'm acquainted with them is that they do all the gold embroidery for the military insignia of rank." Mary handed the photo to Sara and pointed to the Admiral's sleeve. "When Charles was promoted to full admiral, I ordered all his sleeve braid, shoulder board insignia, and cap badges from them."

Sara handed the photo back to her ladyship. "Do you think they could tell me who they made this for?"

"Perhaps, if it was a custom order, they should be able to tell you who commissioned it to be made. But when you go there, and I'm assuming you will, you will see they have many beautiful pieces like this one on display for sale. I'm sure it is the same in New York, as it is in London and probably every major city in the world. There are times when a man or possibly a woman in today's society may need a special piece of jewelry to apologize for an indiscretion."

Sara smiled, "I'm sure, although I've never been the recipient of such an offering."

"Give it time, Sara," she replied. "What will you do with the information you now have?"

"I guess I'll go to Covent Garden to the jewelry store and see if they have a record of the sale. And as Mr. McDougal suggested, I'm going to go to Highgate House and find out who owns it, unless you know," she said, looking at Mary for further clues.

"I'm sorry, I can't help you. However, I can contact Mr. Toye and let him know you're coming."

"That would be wonderful. Thank you very much."

"Since we are speaking of jewelry, before you leave, I have something I've kept in my possession since the end of the war. I'm sure your grandmother would want you to have it." Lady Mary rose from her seat and walked to the sideboard below her portrait. She opened the top drawer and removed the small, black velvet box she had taken out after Sara's first call.

As she returned to her seat, she said, "I'm sure you are familiar with the British custom of having letters after one's name, perhaps the most common one being OBE, for Order of the British Empire."

"Yes, I've seen that on some television programs I used to watch with Nan. When they interview people, and they put their name in the caption, the letters show up."

Mary O'Riley handed the box over to Sara. "Your grandmother was entitled to have the letters BEM after her name because she was awarded the British Empire Medal for her work on *Operation Mincemeat*."

Sara opened the box and looked at the bronze medal depicting the image of the helmeted figure of Britannia. The magenta ribbon was faded from age, but the medal was bright and said, 'For Meritorious Service.' Sara ran her finger over the award and began to realize her Nan had been a war hero whose work saved countless lives.

"The King himself awarded that medal to Rose," said Mary O'Riley.

"I never would have guessed she had been involved in anything like that. Why would she keep something like that a secret?"

"Probably because it didn't fit into the story she told everyone about her life and the events that brought her to America."

Sara sat silent, looking down at the items she held in her hand and on her lap and concluded everything Mary O'Riley had to tell her had been said. This part of the mission was accomplished. However, none of that information had provided Sara the answers she was looking for. "Thank you again, Mary, you've been very helpful, now I have to move on. I've got more investigating to do to complete the task Nan sent me on. Guess it's time to contact Mr. Cromwell and see what help he can offer."

Mary O'Riley stood. "I'm not sure what else I can do to assist you in the next part of your search for your grandfather. If I think of anything, or if you have any more questions, please don't hesitate to contact me."

"Thanks again. You've given me a lot to think about and places to look for answers. I'll let you know what, if anything, I find out."

Offering Sara a hug, Mary smiled, "Regardless of what happens, I hope to see you again before you leave England."

"You will. It's the least I can do since you provided me with so much information about my grandmother's past."

"I'll have Jenkins call a taxi to take you back to your hotel."

"Thank you. I'll just make a call to the barrister while I'm waiting." Sara fished her phone out from her handbag, found Mr. Cromwell's private number, and hit the call button. Sara smiled as she heard that strange double ring used on the phone system in England as she reminded herself that this was now part of her heritage. Funny, she thought, having tea with Lady Hollborne, and calling a barrister who is a descendant of Oliver Cromwell. These were very different roads she was walking, but somehow, she didn't feel out of place.

"Good afternoon, Miss Ferguson," said Cromwell.

"Good afternoon, Mr. Cromwell. I've just finished meeting with Mrs. O'Riley, who is, in fact, no longer Mrs. Mary O'Riley but rather Lady Mary Hollborne," said Sara, looking at the older woman and offering a smile. "Lady Mary has given me more information. Now, I think I'll need your help to further investigate my grandmother's past."

"Certainly, Miss Ferguson. How would you like to proceed?"

"I'd like to begin by going to the address on the letters we found in my grandmother's safe deposit box. I believe that is the most direct approach."

"I agree. I have an appointment tomorrow morning. I should be free by half-ten, excuse me, that's ten-thirty."

"No apology required, I understood what you meant. Shall I meet you at your office?"

"If that is convenient, if not, I will arrange to pick you up at the hotel," replied Cromwell.

"Yes, that'll be fine, I'll come to your office. I'll be there at 11:00. That will allow you to finish up your meeting, and it will give me more time to explore London."

"Eleven it is. I shall expect you then. Have a good evening, Miss Ferguson."

"Thank you, Mr. Cromwell. I'll see you in the morning."

Sara noticed Jenkins enter the room and approach Mary, "M' Lady, Miss Ferguson's taxi is waiting."

"Thank you, Jenkins. Sara, your taxi is waiting. I wish you well on your quest."

"Thank you, Lady Mary, I'll be speaking to you soon. Goodbye," said Sara as she left the room and went to the waiting taxi.

As Sara sat in the back of the taxi for the ride back to her hotel, she began to review everything Lady Mary had said about her grandmother. She'd been a WREN who received a medal from the King. A forger for the Intelligence Service. A woman of twenty-one, not a child of eighteen. Why was all this information kept secret? I have no idea where this quest will lead me, but I promised Nan I would find the answer. It looks like I'm in it for the long run. Hopefully, with Mr. Cromwell's assistance, I will be able to complete this and find the truth Nan wanted me to uncover.

Chapter 39

ady Holborne returned to the morning room after Sara left and took a seat at the small desk she used to address her correspondence. Lady Mary opened a side drawer, removed a small wooden box and placed it on the tooled leather top. She paused and looked at the container for several moments before opening it.

As she removed the lid, she looked at the photograph placed on top of the other contents. As she picked up the photo, Lady Mary smiled at the memory it brought. Taken in the summer of forty-four, she and Rose Beardmore stood together proudly, both wearing the uniform of the Women's Royal Naval Service. The stripe and curl insignia of a Third Officer displayed on their sleeves. They carried the canvas bags containing their gas masks and steel helmets.

Lady Mary spent some time looking through the rest of the photos. As she did, thoughts of her life as Mary O'Riley began to return. She and Rose had been friends since childhood, and the memories flooded back. Thoughts of Rose had never been far from her mind, and she enjoyed the regular phone calls with her friend. Rose always called with a bit of news about something or other, and the friends kept each other informed of even the most mundane things as friends have a tendency to do.

Mary O'Riley vowed to assist Rose in any way she could and agreed to be Rose's intermediary when the time came, even though she didn't have the answers. Rose Beardmore had been very good at keeping her secret and at times, that made Mary angry. Not because she wanted to know, but simply because she knew if the time came, Sara would ask questions she could not answer. So what was the purpose?

"Oh, Rose, you were a devil, but I loved you."

Lady Holborne put the photos down and removed the letters Rose had written in the early years after she settled in America. The letters had been fairly regular in the late forties and early fifties. The phone calls became their means of communication in later years.

Then it happened. Rose missed her first regular contact. Mary realized something was amiss when the call didn't come. She checked her social schedule to confirm the date and time and found it to be correct. As every day passed, she began to fear the worst. When a month passed without hearing from Rose, she began to await the inevitable call from Sara. Every morning brought her the thought, 'Would today be the day I find out what happened to Rose?'

Now that she met with Sara and told her what she knew, Lady Holborne had offered to assist in any way possible. Would they ever find out who Sara's grandfather was?

Lady Holborne opened the small side drawer of her desk and removed her personal phone directory, picked up the receiver and dialed the number.

"Good afternoon. Toye, Kenning & Spencer. How may I direct your call?"

"Good afternoon, this is Lady Holborne. May I please speak to Mr. Toye?"

Chapter 40

The taxi dropped Sara off at the barrister's offices five minutes ahead of her scheduled appointment time. When she entered the old building, she thought about the first time she'd gone into Mr. McDougal's offices. Bookcases full of legal books lined the walls. The matching bindings made Sara think they were perhaps of the most extensive set of encyclopedias in existence.

After introducing herself to the receptionist, she was escorted to Mr. Cromwell's offices and turned over to his private secretary, who asked her to please be seated while she contacted the barrister.

Five minutes later, Reginald Cromwell came out and invited Sara into his office. "Good morning Ms. Ferguson. I hope you are well," he said offering his hand.

"Yes, I am, thank you for asking," replied Sara as she walked past him and entered his office.

"Would you like me to have tea bought in?"

"That would be nice, thank you."

"Claire, please have tea sent through."

"Certainly, sir," replied Claire as she stood and left the office to fulfill her boss' request.

"Please, Ms. Ferguson, let's sit over here. It's a tad less formal," he said pointing to a couch and chairs off to the side of his office.

Sara took the offered seat and withdrew a small electronic tablet from her purse, where she intended to write any information she received.

"That won't be necessary, Ms. Ferguson. I've got copies of everything for you. But, at the moment, I'm afraid there isn't much."

As she returned the tablet to her purse, Sara gave Cromwell a quizzical look. "What's wrong?"

Cromwell took a folder from the table and opened it so he could report on his findings. "Unfortunately, without a street address, I've been unable to locate Highgate House. I've checked with the post office, and there isn't an address in Eaton Mews or anywhere else in the SW1 postcode that uses that name."

"I'm not sure I follow."

"It's quite simple, wherever this property is, the current owners no longer call it Highgate House."

"So that's it? We can't find out who owned it?"

Cromwell flipped back a few pages further. "No, that's not an impossible task. We need someone to go back through the sale records of the properties and find out who the last owners of Highgate were, who owns it now, and who owned it during the time he wrote the letters to your grandmother."

Sara crossed her legs, then her arms showing her impatience. "How long would you expect that to take?"

Cromwell closed the folder, "I can't say, maybe a day if we get lucky, longer if we're not. Remember, the search of the sale records has to cover every property in the confines of what is now and what had been Eaton Mews during the period we're talking about."

Sara uncrossed her arms as she shifted in her seat. "I'm sorry for being short with you, Mr. Cromwell. But none of this is turning out to be an easy task. Based on my grandmother's letter, and the importance she placed on my meeting with Lady

Mary, I would have thought she would have been able to give me the answers to many of the questions that remain unanswered."

There was a knock on the door announcing the arrival of their tea, and Cromwell told Claire she could enter.

After tea was served, Sara asked her next question. "Any luck getting us in to meet with someone at Barclays Bank to find out about the wire transfers?"

"I've arranged for us to meet with one director tomorrow afternoon. I wouldn't get my hopes up as to the result. As I said previously, they take their client's confidentially very seriously. But we shall see if we can't get something of use from the meeting."

"Okay, I guess we'll see what happens."

"Right then, leave it with me. I'll see what further information I can find out. I'll pick you up at your hotel tomorrow at 2:00 p.m. and we will go together."

Sara stood and picked up her handbag. "Thank you, Mr. Cromwell. Until tomorrow then. Hopefully, our search will yield something of use."

Cromwell nodded. "Good day, Ms. Ferguson. I'm sure we will get there. Enjoy the rest of your day. You've got good weather to explore some sights."

Sara left the barrister's office and walked out onto the street. Once she got her bearings, she headed off in the direction of the underground to catch a train to the Bond Street station, which was only a short walk to Oxford Street and Selfridges. "Might as well go shopping while I'm here," she said to herself.

Chapter 41

After spending an enjoyable afternoon shopping in some famous high-end stores, Sara returned to her room at the hotel with her new purchases swinging from the different colored cords of the shopping bags. She placed her purchases on the desk, removed her coat, sat on the edge of the bed and kicked off her shoes.

Once she removed her skirt and blouse, she fixed the pillows on the bed so she could sit up. Now that the process of shopping and trying on different pieces of clothing was no longer at the forefront of her mind, she began to think about the series of events from the past two days. Her experience with Lady Mary and Mr. Cromwell reminded her of Nan's letter. Nothing is as it seems.

Her grandmother had asked her to find out who she really was. She knew who she was. She knew who her parents were, but that wasn't the answer she was chasing down a series of dead ends. It was finding out who her mother's father had been. Whatever the answer was to that question wouldn't make Sara different person. Because of this, there was a part of her that wanted to just leave things as they were and return to New York. The status quo had existed since nineteen forty-five, and no one seemed the wiser. The wheels appeared to be continuing to go around as they had for the past seventy-odd years. So, in reality, what did it matter? When her mother died over fifteen years ago, she thought Capt. Robert McDonald had been her biological father, and William Cavendish had been her stepfather until he'd been killed.

A slow anger began to build in Sara as she reviewed everything that had happened in the past two months. "Shit," she shrieked as she punched the pillow. "Nan, why did you do this to me? You've left me all this money, and yet you've left me alone. Alone and searching for an answer that probably won't have any impact on my life. But you asked me to do this, and I promised I would, so I'll keep at it until I find the answer."

As Sara continued to think things through, she remembered she wasn't completely alone. George Randell had walked into her life at the same moment she'd found out Nan had been taken from her.

As she thought about George, she realized she hadn't had time to think about him since she'd arrived. Sara needed a friendly voice to talk to at this moment, so she got up from the bed, walked over to her handbag, and removed her cell phone. Returning to her position on the bed, she checked the local time, calculated the difference between London and New York, and decided it was a good time to call.

Sara unlocked her phone, brought up her phone book, and pressed the screen to start the call.

George Randell had just gotten out of the shower when the phone rang. Since today was his on-call day, he answered the phone as he would at work. "Dr. Randell."

Sara heard his voice, and it raised her spirits. "Hello, Dr. Randell, I was wondering, do you make house calls?"

George smiled at her question. "I have been known to do so. However, unless I'm mistaken, at the moment I believe you're a bit too far away for a home visit."

"Oh, darn," replied Sara. "And here I was hoping I could get you to come over and give me a thorough exam."

"I would be happy to do that for you, but I'm on call and have to be available in forty-five minutes or less."

"Perhaps another time."

"That's a deal. In fact, I'll credit you for one exam to be collected at a later date."

Sara giggled, "It's nice to hear a friendly voice."

"It's nice to hear from you, too. What's wrong, don't they have friendly voices in England?"

"They do," she said with a huff, "But no one has given me the information I need to solve the puzzle."

"Why not? Wasn't that the whole purpose of you going over there? To meet with the people who would give you the answers."

"That's what I thought, too. I was expecting Lady Mary to give me the info that Nan said was important."

"Wait, you lost me," said George as he tried to follow along. "Who's Lady Mary?"

"Ah," she laughed. "That was the first surprise. Lady Mary Holborne is, in fact, Mary O'Riley. It seems she remarried years ago, but Nan insisted on calling her by her former name."

"People resist change, it's normal, besides if Lady Mary didn't mind, then it's okay. What else isn't going your way?"

"Pretty much everything at the moment, including almost getting hit by a car twice today because I keep looking the wrong way when I cross the street."

"Careful, I'd like you back in one piece," said George.

With a giggle, Sara replied, "Don't worry, I've got it figured out. I just have to look down at the street before I cross."

"Look down at the street, you've lost me again."

"They have 'Look Right,' painted on the street at the crosswalks. I guess it's not just the Americans that look the wrong way. Oh, by the way, I've also learned to 'Mind the Gap.'"

"I have no idea what you're talking about."

"On the Underground, that's the subway to you Yanks," she said using a British accent. "It means to watch out for the space between the platform and the train car."

George laughed at her attempt to sound British. "Are you going native? Eating fish and chips off a street vendor and all that kind of stuff."

"Not yet but give me time. London is a nice city, I've seen some sights, and I think I'd like to come back here solely as a tourist and spend some time looking around and taking in the culture."

"You certainly have the means to do so now. But let's go back to what we were talking about before you told me about almost getting hit by a car. You said nothing was going right for you. What else is wrong?"

"Mr. Cromwell could not locate the building known as Highgate House. He said that the name isn't used anymore. And we don't have a street address."

George continued to listen as Sara downloaded all her frustration onto him. There wasn't anything he could do, but he felt being there as that 'friendly voice' was something Sara needed more than anything at this point. "Given all the setbacks, what's the plan from here?" he asked.

"Tomorrow, Mr. Cromwell has arranged for us to meet with someone from Barclays Bank to see what we can find out about the wire transfers. But before that I'm heading over to Covent Garden to go the jeweler that made the brooch. Hopefully that will give me a lead to find 'T.'"

They continued talking for another twenty minutes until George pointed out that he needed to get ready to go to the hospital to do his afternoon rounds. Sara was reluctant to let him go since she was enjoying talking about nothing of importance.

"Listen, I better go, or I'm going to be tempted to talk to you for as long as you want. I'm on nights for the rest of the week, so anytime you need another helping of a friendly voice' call me."

"That's a deal, Dr. Randell. Thanks for listening. You can bet I'll be calling again."

"I'll be waiting. Have a good night, Sara. Talk to you soon."

"Thanks, George, bye for now," replied Sara as she hung up.

After she put the phone down on the bedside table, Sara slid down on the bed and turned on her side to have a nap. As she relaxed she tried to clear her mind of all the roadblocks she was running into and thought about what she would do for dinner tonight. George's comment about fish and chips from a street vendor popped into her head. "Fish and chips, why not," she said. "That's as good an idea as any other."

Chapter 42

Since her appointment to go to Barclays' with Mr. Cromwell was not until 2:00 p.m., Sara decided to visit Mr. Toye at the jewelry store that had supplied the brooch she had found in the safe deposit box.

Sara exited the taxi at the Covent Garden address. When she entered the store, a well-dressed shop attendant approached her.

"Good morning, madam, welcome to Toye, Kenning, and Spencer. How may I be of assistance?"

"Good morning, my name is Sara Ferguson, I believe Mr. Toye is expecting me."

"Thank you," replied the assistant with a polite nod. "If you will excuse me, I'll let him know you've arrived."

Sara looked around the store while she waited. The wall cabinets were filled with large serving pieces made of sterling silver as well as an assortment of candelabras and flatware samples. They arranged the counter displays in a way she had seen before, which was by gemstone. All the rubies were in one case, the sapphires in another and so on. The more expensive the stone, the deeper in the store.

Finally, her eyes came to rest on a small corner counter level display case. While she looked at the exquisite pieces in the display, she thought of what Lady Mary had said about having an occasion to need a special piece to pay for an indiscretion. As she continued to browse what she decided were the "Oh gee, Honey, I'm so sorry for, whatever," pieces, a tall, distinguished gentleman emerged from the back wearing a three-piece, dark gray chalk stripe suit. He exuded charm and elegance Sara associated with the movie stars of the golden age.

"Ms. Ferguson, please allow me to introduce myself. I'm Charles Wallingford, I am one of the senior directors. I'm afraid Mr. Toye was called away on urgent business. He has asked me to assist you in any way I can. It will be my pleasure to do so."

Sara smiled at the jeweler as she thought it's good to have important friends. "Thank you, Mr. Wallingford, I appreciate your taking the time, but I don't know if you can help."

"Let us not say all is in vain until we look at what you have brought. If you follow me to my office, we can continue to talk in private."

Sara agreed and followed Mr. Wallingford into the back of the store and up a flight of stairs to the private offices.

"Please have a seat, Ms. Ferguson."

Sara sat and removed the jewel case from her handbag. "This is the piece in question," she said, handing the box over. "I'm hoping it was a custom order and you can tell me who bought it."

Mr. Wallingford opened the box, removed the brooch and began his inspection. Sara sat and watched as the jeweler examined the piece before removing a jeweler's loupe. He turned the pin over in his hands as he inspected it, then nodded slightly, "Yes, this most certainly is our work."

He pointed to something on the back of the brooch using a small pair of tweezers. "We hallmark all our work so we know it's ours." Mr. Wallingford removed the loupe from his eye and placed the pin on the black velvet pad on his desk. "All the stones are intact and definitely genuine."

"What else can you tell me?" asked Sara. "Can you tell if it's a custom piece?"

Mr. Wallingford picked up the loupe again and looked further. "I am sorry, I'm afraid it isn't a custom order. Every piece we make that is custom has a number that can be traced to the original purchase order. But there is one more thing I can tell you that may be of help."

Sara's ears perked up at that statement. "What's that?"

"There is a line of fine engraving on the inner rim."

"Really, I didn't notice that," replied Sara as she leaned closer. "What's it say?"

Once more, Mr. Wallingford used the small tweezers to point out the area to Sara. "It says T.S. to R.B. There is a small heart and a date 12-25-44."

"T.S. to R.B. December twenty-fifth. Sounds like it was Christmas present," said Sara.

"Quite a special gift. Someone thought highly of your grandmother."

"I'll say, white gold, diamonds, and sapphires. I bet that cost a pretty penny."

The jeweler glanced at the back. "Even more so, Ms. Ferguson. This is not white gold, it's platinum. I have a piece similar to this currently in my inventory, priced at seventy thousand pounds."

"Seventy thousand. That certainly would be an extraordinary Christmas present."

Mr. Wallingford took a calculator from his desk along with a sheet of paper containing a list of numbers. He ran his finger down the column until he found what he wanted, then punched numbers into the calculator. "Given inflation, fluctuations in the pound's value, etc., this brooch would have sold for approximately sixteen hundred pounds in nineteen forty-four." The jeweler took another quick look at the numbers on his sheet. "That would equate to about six thousand five hundred US dollars."

Sara filed all this information away. She would make notes later as she tried to make sense of everything that was happening. "Thank you, Mr. Wallingford. You've been very helpful. While you couldn't provide the information I'd hoped for, you have shed more light on the questions I'm trying to answer. Now I know the mysterious 'T' has a second initial, 'S.' I also know this brooch was a gift and given the date, more than likely a Christmas gift to R.B. which were my grandmother's initials. And finally, since you have inspected the stones and assessed the value of the piece, I can add that information to what I already know and deduce that T.S. comes from a prominent family."

The jeweler returned the brooch to its original box and handed it back to Sara. "I'm sorry I couldn't have been of greater assistance. However, I am pleased I could provide you with more information than you had when you arrived. May I be of any further assistance at this time?"

Sara thought for a few moments while she returned the brooch to her handbag. Sara shook her head gently, "No, Mr. Wallingford, you've been very helpful. Thank you for your time."

"It was my pleasure. It was also nice to meet you. If you should see Lady Holborne again, please tell her Mr. Toye sends his regards and offered his apologies for not being here to assist you," said the jeweler as he offered his hand.

"I will do that, thank you again."

"If you will follow me, I'll take you back down to the sales floor, and you can be on your way."

Once Sara left the jewelry store, she decided to catch some of the sights and sounds of Covent Garden. As she strolled along, her mind was trying to assess the new information she'd gained. T.S., hmm, not much to go on, but a hundred per cent more than I had when I walked in there. I also know this brooch isn't a knockoff, put in a fancy box. Sixteen hundred pounds in forty-four. I assumed as much given the fact that Nan started getting quarterly transfers of cash from Barclays.

"Okay, T.S. I'm one step closer to finding you if you're still alive. Or, at least finding out who you were if you've passed on. Now all I have to do is find out what the 'S' stands for. Hopefully, Mr. Cromwell will give me that information when he finds out who owned Highgate House."

Chapter 43

s Sara meandered through Covent Garden, she stopped in several of the shops and looked at the goods on display for sale. Window shopping was an art form Sara had perfected while living in New York. Browsing the stores for bargains had been something she really enjoyed doing. Another favorite was hitting the high-end shops at the outlet mall. She had once picked up a twelve hundred dollar Armani top for two hundred dollars. Since it was a chic black beaded number, she didn't care if it was last year's design. Black never went out of style.

She realized that given the current change in her financial situation, she could buy whatever she wanted. Then she wondered if she would continue to hunt for bargains or if her approach to shopping would change as drastically as her life had.

After having lunch at a small café, she hailed a cab for the return trip to the hotel to await Mr. Cromwell.

Once she arrived at Royal Horseguards, Sara returned to her room to freshen up before meeting the barrister.

When she returned to the lobby, she realized she was ten minutes early. Sara decided she would do a bit of exploring in the hotel while she waited. As she wandered around the lobby area, a round blue plaque mounted above an ornate sideboard caught her attention. Her curiosity got the best of her as she walked across the room. The first thing that she noticed was the name 'Mansfield Cumming,' then she saw the smaller letters on the top of the plaque saying, 'English Heritage.' Finally, she was close enough to read the entire inscription which said;

Sir

Mansfield

Cumming

1859-1923

First Chief of

the Secret Service

lived and worked here

1911-1922

Sara let out a slight laughed. After everything that had happened so far, she thought, this just gets crazier as the days go by. I find out my grandmother was worth millions. She worked on a top-secret operation in WWII that saved a ton of lives. She got a medal presented by King George VI, and now my hotel was once the home and office of the chief of MI-6, the British Secret Service. What's tomorrow going to bring?

***

SARA WAS DEEP IN THOUGHT when the barrister entered the lobby. "Good day, Ms. Ferguson. How are you keeping today?"

"I'm well, Mr. Cromwell. Thank you for asking."

"I'm glad to hear that. You appeared lost in your thoughts."

Sara pointed to the English Heritage plaque. "Yes, I guess I was. I'd just finished reading the plaque about Sir Mansfield, and I thought about what a strange turn of events my life had taken in the past several months."

"I can imagine. From what Mr. McDougal told me, you had no idea about the vast amount of wealth your grandmother had amassed during her lifetime."

284

"You don't know the half of it. As we drive to the bank, I'll fill you in on what else I've learned since arriving here in England."

"I'm at your disposal, Ms. Ferguson, my car is outside."

As they made their way through London's afternoon traffic, Sara recounted the information she'd gotten about her grandmother from Lady Mary and what Mr. Wallington had told her about the brooch.

Mr. Cromwell asked several questions about what Sara had discovered. As a barrister, he was curious by nature and wanted to know as much as Sara was willing to tell him to better assist her in her quest for information.

Sara seemed almost pleased to share the information she'd gotten, especially about the medal Nan had received from the hand of the King.

The trip from Sara's hotel to Barclays' main offices out on Canary Wharf took just over half an hour. When they arrived, Mr. Cromwell led Sara over to the reception desk, where he produced a business card and handed it to the young woman behind the glass.

"Reginald Cromwell, Q.C., representing Ms. Sara Ferguson, of New York City," he said. "We have an appointment with Mr. Cedric Montague."

"Certainly, sir. I'll ring his office and let them know you've arrived."

Cromwell nodded and smiled at Sara while they waited. Sara's thoughts turned to her encounters with some other banking types she'd dealt with over the past two weeks. Turning to her lawyer, she asked, "Do you think we'll be able to get any information that will be useful?"

"One can only hope."

The receptionist replaced the handset of the phone to its cradle. "Sir, Mr. Montague is expecting you." Pointing across the lobby, she continued. "Please take the elevators to the twenty-seventh floor. Someone will meet you there and escort you to Mr. Montague's office."

"Thank you. Shall we go, Ms. Ferguson?"

Sara nodded, and together they walked across the lobby to the elevator banks. When the elevator doors opened on the twenty-seventh floor, they were met by a young man who led them to the offices of Mr. Cedric Montague, Executive Vice President, International Accounts.

One thing Sara had discovered during her time with Charles, Jasper, and Williams on Madison Avenue was that each profession seemed to have a "type." It involved a style that told you this person was in a particular business. Sure, it was easy to pick out doctors when they wore white lab coats or nurses who walked around in scrubs. But she had developed a sense that allowed her to differentiate between bankers, lawyers, and executives.

Cedric Montague was most definitely a banker type. Clothed in a well-cut suit in a color Sara knew was called 'banker gray,' he stood there, a bastion of the banking system. The starched white shirt and perfectly knotted burgundy tie showed he'd had many years of practice in donning the uniform of his profession. His graying hair didn't really give a hint as to his age. He wore eyeglasses of a modern design that caused you to focus on his gray eyes. As she watched the man in gray standing before her, Sara didn't get a good feeling about what was to transpire.

No smile greeted them; Montague was all business. "Ms. Ferguson, Mr. Cromwell, please come through," he said, turning his back on them and returning to take his seat behind his desk.

Sara and her lawyer took the seats across from Montague, who sat without speaking to his visitors. Cromwell looked at Sara as if asking permission. Sara gave him the slightest nod, and Cromwell stated his case.

"Mr. Montague, on behalf of my client, I'd like to thank you for seeing us today."

The banker nodded acceptance of the thanks before speaking. "What is it I can do for you?" he asked in a tone which sounded as if they had intruded on his valuable time.

"My client has become the heiress to a substantial fortune left to her by her grandmother, Mrs. Rose Cavendish, formally Mrs. Rose McDonald."

"Congratulations, Ms. Ferguson. I wish you good luck with your newfound wealth. Now, I'm sure you haven't traveled here solely to inform me your client has inherited money from her grandmother."

Cromwell pursed his lips for a moment as he thought to himself, so that's how it's going to be. "No, Mr. Montague, we are here because, as part of her inheritance, my client is now the owner of a bank account with Bank of New York, Mellon. Said account was started by then Mrs. McDonald back in nineteen forty-five. And since shortly after its inception, this account had been getting quarterly transfers of funds from Barclays. At the moment, the quarterly transfers are in British pounds equivalent to the sum one hundred thousand U.S. dollars."

Montague leaned forward in his seat. "And?"

Cromwell looked at Sara, who was having a hard time remaining quiet.

"And…I'd like to know who the benefactor is that's been funding this account for all these years," said Sara in a tone that said she expected an answer.

Montague placed his elbows on his desk, steepled his fingers, and tapped the tips together. "Fair enough, I suppose I could have a look for you," he said. "Would you have the account number we transfer the money into?"

Sara nodded and removed the passbook from her purse and handed it to Montague. "This is it. You'll see the date of the last transfer is there. It was two months ago."

After taking the passbook from Sara's hand, the banker fingered the keyboard of his computer to bring up the proper program to display the information. He typed in the date, amount, and destination and waited for a reply. When the report appeared on his screen, he checked the numbers against what Sara had provided. Once he was satisfied, he made several notes on his small desk pad and turned off the computer.

"I'm sorry, Ms. Ferguson, there isn't much I can tell you." He returned the passbook to Sara.

"What do you mean?"

Montague looked at his notes. "I can confirm we made a transfer equivalent to one hundred thousand U.S. dollars on the date shown in your passbook. I can also confirm that the money went to the account number listed on your book."

"Okay, so if you can confirm that, it obviously came from here. Who sent it?"

"That I'm afraid I can't tell you."

"Why not? Is it a secret?"

The banker nodded. "In a way, it is. The money was sent from a blind trust set up in nineteen forty-five."

Sara looked at the bank book and placed it back in her handbag. "All right, I understand the money is in trust. The trust had been paying out to the account in my grandmother's name. Now that she's passed away, what happens to the trust?"

"I'm afraid I can't answer that, either. Whoever administers the trust, meaning the trustees or whoever may have been given a power of attorney to manage the trust, have full discretion over the assets. Your grandmother and now yourself because of inheritance as the trust beneficiary are not entitled to have knowledge of how much or what holdings remain in the trust.

Nor do you have any right to intervene in their handling of the trust."

"What you're telling me is that I have no control over this, and now that my grandmother is dead, the quarterly deposits could stop?"

"Yes and no. It depends on what the trustee wants to do. If they choose to stop the payments, they will do so. If for some reason, the trust was set up to continue to pay out in perpetuity as long as it remains solvent, then the payments would continue under the rules originally set."

"And I can't stop it?"

"That's correct. If the trust remains in force, you have no say in the matter. However, once we deposit the money, you have full discretion on what to do with it."

Sara couldn't think of another question. Her mind was overloaded. More money coming down the spout, and the banker said there was no way to turn it off. A blind trust set up to ensure Nan would be taken care of for the rest of her life. I'm sure T.S. had been the one who set this up to take care of her and her child. I'm going to find you T.S. Nan has asked me to do so, and I won't let her down.

Mr. Cromwell had been listening to the conversation and decided it was time to end the meeting. His client was being overwhelmed with information, yet not getting the answers she'd hoped for.

"Thank you for your time, Mr. Montague, you've been accommodating. I believe my client has enough information for the moment. If we need anything else, we will be back in contact."

"Yes, thank you," echoed Sara.

Once they had gathered their belongings, Cromwell and Sara left the banker's office and returned to the elevator banks. Sara stared into the polished chrome of the elevator door and remained silent while they waited.

After they entered the elevator, Cromwell spoke. "Ms. Ferguson, I'm sorry Mr. Montague wasn't able to be more forthcoming with the information on the account."

"It seems my life is full of dead ends. Nan's letter said I might think the task sounded simple. Go see Mary O'Riley, she said. It's important, she said. I did that, only to find out Lady Mary didn't have the answers. Highgate House is a memory; the money comes from a blind trust. What else won't I be able to find out?"

As they left Montague's office, Sara's frustration was clear, so the barrister let his client vent until they arrived in the lobby. After exiting the elevator, Mr. Cromwell led the way back to the street where his car and driver were waiting.

Once they had taken their seats in the car, Cromwell received a phone call, which gave him some information he relayed to his client, offering her a ray of hope during this dark moment.

"That was James Corry on the line. He's the estate agent I've had looking into the records to see what could be found on Highgate House."

"Did he find something?"

"Yes, but he said it needed to be further investigated and explained. He's requested we come to his office."

"This may be the first solid lead we've gotten. Can we go there now?"

"Of course. John, please take us to Broadwick's on The Strand."

The driver touched his fingers to the brim of his cap and set off to their next appointment.

A thousand questions passed through Sara's mind as they drove, but she had heard the ten-second conversation, so she understood Mr. Cromwell probably wouldn't have any answers for her.

Chapter 44

When they arrived at the estate agent's office, James Corry was waiting, folder in hand.

"James, my good man, what do you have for us?" asked Cromwell.

"Not a lot, I'm afraid. But, I've made progress in finding a street address for what was once Highgate House." Corry handed over a listing sheet to the barrister. "There's the address. As you can see, the house is now called Wil-Bern."

"Anything else you can tell us?" asked Sara.

"Not at this time, Miss, but now that I have a firm address, I can go back through the files and look for all records pertaining to the sale history for that property. I should be able to have everything available in the public records for you in a day. Two at the most."

A smile came to Sara's face for the first time today. Perhaps this was the break she needed in finding out who T.S. was. "Thank you, Mr. Corry, you've been a big help."

Sara opened the folder and saw the facade of the building once known as Highgate House. The white stone was similar to Lady Mary's residence, Holborne House, but this one was a corner property. Sara offered the sheet to Cromwell. "Is it far from here?"

While the lawyer looked at the address, Corry answered. "It's in Belgravia, probably only a twenty-minute drive."

"Would you take me there now?" asked Sara.

"That could be arranged," replied Cromwell. "I believe you've waited long enough to at least see the home you've been searching for. I'm not sure how helpful the current owners will be, but we can ask."

Taking the folder James Corry provided them, they left the estate agent's office.

"Good luck," said Corry.

The trip only took fifteen minutes. As they exited the car, Sara stood and looked at the impressive home. "This is about twice the size of Lady Mary's," she said to Cromwell. "Whoever T.S. is, he certainly didn't come from the poor side of town."

"I would agree with that assessment. What say we knock and see if anyone is home?"

Chapter 45

The tall windows of Wil-Bern House were covered with heavy drapes that denied any chance of seeing inside. The entry was above the street level. An ornately carved marble stairway contained ten steps and led to a portico supported by six carved Corinthian columns. The entry door was painted gloss black. A polished brass plate on the wall announced this was, in fact, Wil-Bern House.

Cromwell opted to use the large bronze knocker instead of the doorbell. As they waited, Sara wondered if this butler would be as severe as Jenkins had been when she told him she was looking for Mrs. O'Riley. Her thoughts came to a halt as the door opened.

The man standing there wore tight, jade green leather pants, an orange paisley shirt open to the waist. A burnt orange scarf tied around his neck. A mop of green hair hung down as he looked at the intruders through a pair of purple granny glasses.

Before the visitors could speak, he let loose. "Well, it's about bloody time. You're two hours late, now get upstairs and get your clothes off. Everyone's waiting."

Sara froze, unable to speak. Cromwell answered. "Sir, Ms. Ferguson, is my client—"

"Ferguson, you say?" he balked. "I don't care if she's Mary, bloody Queen of Scots. She's late, and we're behind."

Cromwell raised his hand to object. "See here, my good man—"

"Oh, sweetie, I'd be your good man in a heartbeat," he said, removing his glasses. "But that's for another time. Right now we've got to get this shoot done, or we'll miss the deadline. If that happens, no one gets paid."

Turning to Sara, the man tried to prod her along. "Chop, chop, dearie, time is money."

"You've mistaken us for someone else," Cromwell said.

The man with the green hair put the tip of the arm of his eyeglasses in his mouth. "You're not from the agency?"

"I'm afraid not," replied Cromwell.

The man continued staring at Sara, who still had not spoken. "You're quite attractive," he said as he took a step back to get a better look. "Certainly not mutton dressed as lamb. And from what I can see, you've got a good body. Want to make five hundred pounds for two hours work?" he asked.

Sara shook her head as she found her voice. "Thanks for the offer, but I think I'll pass."

"Too bad, I bet you'd look bloody gorgeous in the outfits. Since you're not who I was expecting, please excuse me for a moment."

"Certainly," replied Cromwell.

The green-haired man took a few steps into the house and barked orders to some unseen person upstairs. "It's not them! Someone call the bloody agency and find out what's going on."

Cromwell smiled as they waited.

The man returned to the two strangers on his front porch, "Sorry about that. Now, if you're not from the agency, what brings you to my door?"

Cromwell began. "As I tried to explain, Mr...."

"Doolan, William Doolan."

"Ah yes, Mr. Doolan. As I was saying, my name is Reginald Cromwell." He presented his card as he continued, "And this is Ms. Sara Ferguson from New York."

Doolan looked at that card. "Please come in, I'm sure a member of the Queen's Council isn't used to conducting business on the doorstep."

Doolan led the way into one of the front reception rooms. Sara was once again reminded that Wil-Bern house was of a different class from Lady Mary's home. While Holborne House was beautiful, it didn't have the same feeling of being the ancestral home of members of the aristocracy or the landed gentry aspiring to gain title through appointment of a life peerage.

Once they were seated, Doolan again asked. "What is it that brings you to my door?"

"We are interested in the history of this house," said Cromwell. "How long have you owned the property?"

"Bernard and I bought it almost twenty years ago."

"And you changed the name from Highgate to Wil-Bern?" asked Sara.

"No, love. It was called 'Sherborn' when we purchased it."

"Sherborn? Are you sure," she asked.

"Absolutely. We got a great deal on the house. The owners had just about gone bankrupt trying to do the house up during the time they owned it. They started all the big renovations. They redid the wiring, installed air conditioning, and replaced the Victorian era plumbing."

Cromwell asked, "Do you know who they purchased the property from or if it was called Highgate prior to their ownership?"

"Sorry, no. Bernard and I were chuffed at getting this property, we didn't ask a lot of questions. We've turned some upstairs rooms into photo studios. Bernard is the creative genius behind the lens. I'm the jack of all trades."

Feeling as if someone had pulled the rug out from under her yet again, Sara drew a deep breath. "Thank you for your time. Since you don't have any knowledge about the house when it was called Highgate, I'm afraid you can't help me on my quest to find out who lived here during the war and has the initials T.S."

"Sorry, love, can't help you there. Listen, we really are behind, and I must find out what's keeping that bloody cow from the agency." As Doolan stood, he gave Sara the once over, "You sure I can't interest you in doing a little modeling work."

Sara stood and shook her head. "No, I'm sure. I've done my time in advertising and have no desire to be on the other side of the cameras." Sara smiled and batted her eyes at Doolan. "But I'm flattered you asked."

"Sorry to have bothered you, Mr. Doolan. Ms. Ferguson and I will be going. Thank you for your time."

"Anytime, Mr. Cromwell… Anytime," replied Doolan, offering his hand to the barrister.

Cromwell shook Doolan's hand and got a wink from the co-owner of Wil-Bern House.

Chapter 46

Mr. Cromwell's driver delivered them back to Royal Horseguards Hotel, where the barrister released him for the evening. "Thank you, John, I won't be needing the car any more this evening. You can pick me up in the morning as usual."

The driver tipped his hat, acknowledging his employer. "Very good, sir. I'll be waiting as always. Good night, Ms. Ferguson. Good night, sir." John returned to the vehicle and left.

"May I interest you in a working dinner?" asked Cromwell. "We can go over the information we've gathered today and try to fit that together with everything else you know. Perhaps that will give us an idea of how to lay out a plan for our next move."

"That sounds like a good idea, but if you don't mind, can you give me twenty minutes? I'd like to freshen up before we go."

"Of course, I'll wait for you in the bar."

* * *

THE BARRISTER WAS LOOKING THROUGH THE FILES he had in his briefcase when Sara returned. He stood when he saw her enter. "Welcome, may I get you a drink before we have dinner, or would you prefer to go through to the dining room and get one there?"

"I think I'd prefer one here. That way, we can sit for a moment."

"Not a problem. What would you like to drink?"

"Normally I like a dirty martini. But seeing I'm in London, I'll have a gin and tonic."

Cromwell smiled at her comment, nodded his head as he went to the bar to order the drinks. After he'd told the bartender what he wanted, he returned to his seat. "The drinks will be here in a few moments. Now, where would you like to begin?"

Sara considered his question before she answered. "Barclays. You're a barrister. Is there any legal way you know of that would allow us to find out about who funded the trust?"

"Not that I'm aware of, at least not in your case."

"What do you mean in my case?"

"The money that has been and continues to be paid into your account was meant as a means of support. I would assume that money came from the person you believe to be your grandfather. It's not money that's being moved or used for nefarious means."

Sara made a face. "So you're saying there's no credible reason for us to get the information we'd like to have."

"Correct. If it were dirty money, we could have the records unsealed. I'm afraid the suspected crime of providing support to the woman who mothered your child out-of-wedlock doesn't quite meet the threshold of national security."

Sara sighed heavily. "Okay, so that's out. And like Mr. Montague said, I have no control over whether the payments continue. I wonder if they're even aware my grandmother has passed away."

Mr. Cromwell was about to speak when the drinks arrived. He paused until the barman withdrew from the table. "Let me ask you a question. You probably don't know the answer, but I'd like you to consider this as a possibility." Cromwell closed the folder, leaned back, crossing his legs. "We know that your grandmother had regular contact with Lady Holborne after she left for America. It would be safe to assume this contact began as written correspondence until it became practical to make a telephone call."

"That makes sense, I'm sure that's what happened, but I can ask Lady Mary to confirm."

"You showed me the letter written to your grandmother signed 'T,' which was how you came to discover there was a Highgate House here in London. This was another small piece that fit into the puzzle. But you mentioned this letter was one of a stack of letters to your grandmother written by 'T.'"

"That's correct, but why is that important?"

"Indulge me for a moment and allow me to ask you a question. Since your grandmother's contact with Lady Mary switched from written letters to telephone calls, wouldn't it be plausible to assume if this mysterious T.S. was sending your grandmother letters…"

"That they also remained in contact by telephone?"

"Exactly," replied Cromwell. "May I please see the letter your grandmother left you?"

Sara removed the envelope from her handbag and passed it over to the lawyer. Cromwell unfolded the pages as he scanned the perfect penmanship for the part he thought he'd remembered. "Ah, here it is," he said. "Ms. Ferguson, when your grandmother wrote this, she stated, 'Since I know at the time of this writing the other person has not predeceased me.' There must be a way she knew this. And since Lady Mary doesn't know who T.S. is, your grandmother's knowledge of that he was still alive could not have come from her."

"Wow, I never would have thought of that. I would think that's possible. But if they were in contact by telephone, we don't know if Nan used her cell phone or the home phone. And I didn't bring her cell phone or address book along with me."

Cromwell thought about how they could get around that small problem while Sara was thinking of another possible answer.

The barrister was attempting to sort through things logically when Sara spoke. "Mr. Cromwell, wouldn't it be possible my grandmother knew this person was still alive because his death hadn't made the news?"

"Pardon, I'm sorry, I wasn't listening."

It was Sara's turn to give her idea on the subject. "We've been to Wil-Bern House, you've seen the size of that property. Whoever T.S. is, either he or his family owned that property during the war. So whoever they were, it's clear they were a prominent family."

Cromwell gave Sara his full attention as she continued. "We also know the trust fund is currently paying out four hundred thousand dollars a year. And we know it's been in place providing quarterly payments since nineteen forty-five. So again, this person comes from money, and by the looks of it, a lot of money. I would assume whoever this person is, he's probably someone well known in his community. A person of means whose death would be reported in the news or the papers. Perhaps not in London unless it was in the business or society pages. But perhaps it would be bigger news where this person was from originally. Highgate House may have just been where they came for the social season."

Reginald Cromwell, Q.C., gave careful consideration to the counterargument being made from the other side of the table. Years of trial experience had taught him to never dismiss an opposing point of view.

"Then you believe that perhaps personal contact was discontinued years ago, but your grandmother kept watch to see if the death of this person was ever mentioned in the news."

Sara shrugged, "I don't know, I'm just talking off the top of my head trying to figure out how we can find out who my grandfather is. That way, I can do what my grandmother asked of me."

"I should think at this point, our best hope of finding that out lies with Mr. Corry," replied Cromwell as he returned his papers to his briefcase. "Now that he has a physical location of what was once Highgate House, it will make his search for the previous owners much simpler."

"I guess you're right. No sense worrying about it right now. Mr. Corry said he hoped to have an answer in a day or two. I've never given much thought to who my grandfather was since Nan told me he died in the war. Now I guess I can wait a bit longer to find out who he really was," said Sara as she finished her gin and tonic. "Nothing else to do today, so I think I'm ready for dinner."

Cromwell stood, offered Sara his arm, and escorted his client into the dining room.

Chapter 47

After breakfast, Sara checked in with Mr. Cromwell to see if there had been any further developments on the search for the owners of Highgate. The barrister relayed what Mr. Corry had reported late last evening, and that was the search was still on and he was hoping to have something soon.

Not wanting to spend the day sitting in her room in the hopes the phone would ring, Sara ensured Cromwell had her cell phone number. She promised to be on a phone tether for the rest of the day should anything develop.

After she hung up the phone, she dressed in a casual outfit of pants and a sweater and began to plan her day. Since this would be a day of nothing important she put on low shoes which were best for walking.

Happy with her outfit, Sara took her coat, left her room and went to the lobby to get directions to some major tourist attractions. Since she was familiar with the Big Red Bus hop-on, hop-off tours from NYC she also asked directions to the nearest stop.

Armed with her map and a plan to have a fun day, Sara began walking to the closest bus stop. As she was leaving the hotel, she noticed a crowd gathering a short distance down the road at the entrance to the Horse Guards Parade. "I wonder if it's time for the changing of the guard?" she said to herself.

As more people continued to gather, Sara decided that would be her first stop on today's tour. She made her way into the parade ground and found a good spot to watch the action. Military tradition was the focal point of the ceremony, which was entertaining, even though Sara wondered how the soldiers managed to walk in those thigh-high boots made with soles so thick, the foot part of the boot barely bent. Not to mention all the metal armor they wore. "That can't be very comfortable to wear," she said to the woman standing next to her.

"I'd have to agree with you," the woman said. "But don't they look magnificent all decked out like that?"

"Yes, they do. I'm sure they must have to volunteer for this kind of duty."

"I'll bet. It takes a special kind of person to do what these young people do."

As Sara took several photos, the troop of guards exited the building and came out onto the parade ground. The ceremony was impressive as the inspecting officer came out, sword in hand and gave each of the troops the once over before they took their positions.

Once the changes were made, the crowd disbanded, and Sara headed back to the bus stop to wait for the Big Red Bus.

As she waited, she pulled out her map to see where her first stop would be, and she decided on Trafalgar Square. Since it was only about a quarter mile away, she looked down Whitehall and discovered she could see Nelson's Column, so she walked.

Sara walked into the square, taking it all in. She'd always thought New York was a fabulous city, but London seemed to have so much more to offer. She wasn't able to put her finger on the difference, but it just felt that way. The architecture was older and a lot more ornate, so maybe that was it. After she walked around for a while, she found a place to sit and just watch the people go by. Much like New York, there was a mix of tourists and those just trying to make their way to wherever it was they were going. Sara enjoyed watching the chaos as people made their way through the crowds.

"Time to go," she said as she walked across the square to the Church of Saint Martin-in-the-Fields. One thing Nan had loved was classical music, and Sara could remember hearing the announcer giving the title of the piece and saying it was being played by the Academy of St. Martin-in-the-Fields Orchestra conducted by Sir Neville Marriner.

Sara entered the church and took a seat near the rear of the church and marveled at the intricate work done on the ceiling. Nan never spoke much about going to church, and in the time Sara as lived with her, Nan only made the pilgrimage on the holidays of Easter, Christmas, and other special occasions. So now as she sat in this church built before the time of the Revolutionary War, Sara wondered if Nan had ever been religious. "Funny what goes through your mind at times," she mumbled to herself.

When she left the church, Sara abandoned all her other plans and headed across the street to the National Gallery. Once she entered the museum, she became immersed in looking at the art on display and spent the rest of the day divided between the main gallery and the National Portrait Gallery. Sara lost all track of time as she wandered through the different galleries and rooms. When she heard the announcements that the museum would close in twenty minutes, Sara realized she had spent most of the day in there.

"That was fun," she said to herself. She couldn't remember the last time she'd had a day to herself where she had just gone out to a museum and spent the day admiring the artworks of the masters.

Sara removed the map from her purse, oriented it to her current location and began walking toward Leicester Square which would lead her to her desired dinner location in Chinatown. As she walked through the square, she stopped to take a photo of the Charlie Chaplin statue she'd read about in the tourist brochure before continuing on to the Dim Sum restaurant she'd chosen.

After Sara finished her dinner, she took a leisurely stroll back to her hotel. She surmised that since she had not received a phone call from Mr. Cromwell that today had produced nothing of substance on the former owners of Highgate.

When she arrived back at the hotel, she stopped in the bar and had a drink before returning to her room and settling in for the night.

Part IV

*The problem of our age is the proper
administration of wealth, so that the ties
of brotherhood may still bind together the
rich and poor in harmonious relationship*

Andrew Carnegie
Wealth: from the North American Review
(June 1889)

Chapter 48

The phone rang at 9:15 a.m. and woke Sara from a sound sleep. Sara knocked the phone off its cradle and onto the floor while groping for the handset in the semidarkness. She sat up in bed cursing softly and retrieved the handset by pulling on the wire.

"Hello."

"Good morning, Ms. Ferguson. It's Reginald Cromwell. Sorry to wake you, but I have received a call from Mr. Corry."

The barrister's words caused her to become fully awake. "What did he have to say?"

"He said he has news about Highgate and asked when we could meet him in his office?"

Sara got out of bed. "That depends on how quickly you can get here to pick me up."

"Can you meet me outside your hotel in half an hour?" asked Cromwell.

"Yes, that won't be a problem. I'll see you then."

"Thank you, Ms. Ferguson, I'll see you shortly."

Sara put the phone down and left a trail of her pajama top and bottoms as she went into the bathroom to get ready. A quick wash was accomplished in five minutes. Another five minutes was spent brushing her teeth and making her hair presentable. After pulling an outfit from the wardrobe, she almost jumped into her underwear and clothing. As she slipped her shoes on she removed her lipstick from her purse. A quick application of red gloss, and she was ready to go.

As she grabbed her handbag and coat, Sara did a quick scan to see if she had forgotten anything. Convinced she had everything she needed she took her room key and headed for the lobby.

Cromwell's car pulled to the curb just as Sara exited the building, and the doorman opened the rear door for her. As she slid into the back seat it was clear to Cromwell that Sara was ready to hear what he had to say.

"Good morning, Sara."

Sara's anxiety caused her to dispense with formalities as she forewent responding to Cromwell's salutation. "What did Mr. Corry say? Did he give you any information?"

"I'm afraid not. The only thing he said was he's uncovered some information that you needed to know. I would assume since he said, 'needed to know' that he's discovered who owned the property during the time in question."

"That would be a major discovery. I would think it could lead me directly to T.S."

"It very well could. But we must see what information he has for you."

Sara thought about that as they drove the rest of the way to the estate agent's office. The missing piece of the puzzle could be the one that provided all the answers Nan had asked her to find.

The car stopped in front of Mr. Corry's office, and Cromwell and Sara exited the vehicle.

James Corry was in his office talking on the phone when Sara and Cromwell appeared at his door. He directed them to the chairs in his office while he quickly finished the call. As he hung up the phone, he smiled at the people sitting across from him.

"I've got good news, Ms. Ferguson. I can now give you the missing pieces of the history of Highgate House."

Sara nodded. "That's great. What can you tell me?"

Corry opened a folder on his desk. "As you already know, William Doolan and Bernard Faircloth are now the owners of Wil-Bern House, which they claim they purchased approximately twenty years ago. This is in fact correct. They purchased the property twenty-one years ago from Jacques and Marie DeChambeau. At the time of the purchase the property was known as Sherborn. But again, you already know that."

"Yes, I do. Since you've called us, I'm assuming you can add to that information."

"I can. Jacques and Marie DeChambeau came here from Paris in nineteen fifty-three. They were looking to purchase a summer home. They found the property known as Highgate House that was for sale. At the time of the sale, Highgate was unoccupied. The records show in nineteen fifty-one there was a fire at the property that caused extensive damage to the kitchen and much of the downstairs and first floor. According to the sales records, this damage was never repaired, and the property remained unoccupied. Given the amount of damage to the property the DeChambeau's were able to secure the house for a very reasonable price."

"Then it was the DeChambeau's who undertook the restoration that Mr. Doolan spoke of that caused them to almost go bankrupt," said Cromwell.

That's correct. Now here's the part that is the key to your puzzle Ms. Ferguson. At the time of the fire and the twenty-five years before the sale to Mr. DeChambeau, a William Sandbourne owned the property."

"Sandbourne. That's the 'S' I'm looking for," said Sara. "Who is he?"

"From what I can find William Sandbourne, OBE was a wealthy industrialist from Sheffield. Steel mills and coal mines were where he made all his money," replied Corry.

"Any chance he's still alive?" asked Sara.

"I'm afraid not. He was born in eighteen eighty-five and died in nineteen seventy-two at the age of eighty-seven."

"Eighteen eighty-five, that means if it was him, he would have been sixty when Nan got pregnant. It's probably not him. Did he have any children?"

Corry turned some pages in the file. "Yes, he has two sons, Andrew and Edward."

"No one with the initial 'T'? What about a middle name?" asked Cromwell.

Corry shook his head. "I'm afraid not. The boys are Andrew Henry and Edward Phillip."

"Anyone else, perhaps another son who died," asked Sara, her frustration beginning to show again.

"No," said Corry. "Mrs. Sandbourne died in nineteen thirty-five. There is no record of Mr. Sandbourne ever remarrying. Nor can I find anything that would suggest he had an illegitimate child. Andrew and Edward both married. Andrew in forty-five, Edward in forty-nine."

Sara's mind was running through everything she'd just been told, trying to think of another question. "What about a brother? Did Mr. Sandbourne have a brother? It could be a cousin or nephew? Anyone with the initials T.S.?"

"Not that I can find in the public records. There are no other leads on the Sandbourne name that ties to the initials T.S." replied Corry.

"How about a nickname? Ted or Teddy is common for Edward. Did they call Edward Teddy?"

Corry shook his head, "Once again, Miss, not that I can find anywhere."

"Then we've run down another dead end at the moment," said Cromwell.

Silence came over the room as the occupants tried to come up with an alternative hypothesis.

"Is it possible that T.S. wasn't a member of the family but perhaps a member of staff," asked Corry.

"Not unless they paid their staff princely wages," replied Sara. "The brooch that was given to my grandmother as a Christmas present would have cost sixteen hundred pounds back then. No member of staff would have been able to afford that, let alone to fund the trust account. No there has to be someone else."

"Are the Sandbourne brothers still alive?"

"They are. Sir Andrew and his brother are both in their nineties."

"Sir Andrew?" asked Sara.

Corry nodded, "Yes, Lord Sandbourne received a life peerage from Her Majesty in nineteen eighty-eight."

"Do you have an address for Lord Sandbourne or his brother?" asked Cromwell.

The estate agent flipped through some pages in the open folder he had on his desk, removed a sheet and passed it to the barrister. "They live together outside of Sheffield on the family estate Sandbourne Manor."

Cromwell looked at the sheet Corry had given him. It contained a photograph of the property and an address he then passed it to Sara. "It appears a trip up north is in order wouldn't you say?"

Sara looked at the page Cromwell had passed her. The looming Victorian structure known as Sandbourne Manor stood out amidst the surrounding green fields. The manor house looked like it could be the home of a person financially capable of doing the things she had discovered over the past weeks. But none of the men in the Sandbourne line seemed to have the initials T.S.

Since this all happened during the war, was it possible T.S. was a friend of the Sandbournes? Maybe someone else with a surname beginning with 'S' visited. Perhaps he was in the war and lived with his friends at Highgate while he was in London. As Sara realized there were still more questions that needed to be answered she looked up from the paper in her hand.

"Yes, I agree. I think it's time we visited Sheffield and called on Lord Sandbourne and his brother."

"I have several appointments this afternoon that I need to attend to, but I can have my secretary clear my schedule for tomorrow. We can go then if that's acceptable," replied Cromwell.

Sara nodded in agreement. "That's fine. I'd like a bit of time to see what I can find out about Lord Sandbourne and his brother Edward. Maybe there's something on the internet that will help me figure out who T.S. could be."

James Corry closed the folder he had on his desk and handed it to Sara. "Ms. Ferguson, please take this. It's everything I've been able to find out about Highgate House, the Sandbournes, and their business empire."

"Thank you, this will give me a starting point for my internet searches. If they are that wealthy, I'm sure there's a lot more out there."

Mr. Cromwell glanced at the clock on the wall of the estate agent's office and commented, "I'd say this has been a very productive morning. Since I know I woke Ms. Ferguson from a sound sleep, I'm certain she hasn't eaten yet. May I recommend we adjourn this meeting and reconvene at one of the local pubs for lunch?"

"I wouldn't say no to that suggestion," said Corry.

"Neither would I," agreed Sara. "You're correct, I've not eaten, and now that I've heard we have some solid information, it can also be a mini-celebration of sorts. I feel we're beginning to finally get some data that brings us closer to an answer."

"Mr. Corry, since this is your patch, where would you recommend we go?"

"Unless you really want to go to a pub, I'd suggest we call for a table at Simpson's or the Savoy Grill."

"Do you have a preference Ms. Ferguson?" asked Cromwell.

"I've heard of the Savoy Grill; let's go there."

"The Savoy it is," said Corry as he picked up the phone and called his assistant. "Felicity, please call the Savoy Grill and see if you can get us a table for lunch."

* * *

AFTER LUNCH AT THE SAVOY, Mr. Cromwell's driver returned Sara to her hotel at 3:00 p.m. Sara returned to her room, set up her laptop and logged into the hotel's Wi-Fi. She began her search by opening three windows and typing in one of the following names to each. 'William Sandbourne, OBE, Lord Andrew Sandbourne, and Edward Sandbourne.

The search on William returned much of the information Mr. Corry had imparted to Sara. A wealthy industrialist who made his money from coal and steel. He'd also been a soldier in the First World War. A captain in the infantry who saw action in France. Nothing specific that pointed to awards for gallantry. Just one who served, did his time, and was lucky enough to return home.

The search on Sir Andrew had more information. Born in nineteen-nineteen, graduated from Oxford. Served in the RAF as a fighter pilot who flew Spitfires with the Forty-One Squadron out of RAF Coningsby, Lincolnshire, during The Battle of Britain and it said he also flew air support missions for the troops during the evacuation of Dunkirk. They promoted Sir Andrew to the rank of Squadron Leader. They had awarded him the Distinguished Flying Cross and a host of other medals during the Second World War. And he had fourteen confirmed enemy kills, making him a double Ace.

"Now that's impressive," Sara said to herself after reading the page. "I could see Nan falling for a guy like this. Hell, I'd fall for a guy like this, too."

Sara pulled up the last search. The one for Edward was similar to Andrew's. Edward was born in nineteen twenty-four, which made him five years younger than his brother. He was too young to fight in the early part of the war. But like his brother he had graduated from Oxford and then joined the military and flew with the RAF during the campaign in Burma.

Both returned from the war and went into the family business, with Andrew taking control from his father when he retired.

Sara looked at the pictures that were part of the data pull and looked for any sign of resemblance with her mother or herself. There weren't any she could see. She looked at their bio's again, she did the math on their ages. In nineteen forty-five, Andrew had been twenty-six, Edward, twenty-one. Nan had also been twenty-one. Therefore either of the brothers could have been Nan's lover.

As she looked through the information again, especially the photographs, nothing jumped out at her that caused her to lean one way or the other. The photos of the two brothers in their RAF uniforms, brought about the same thoughts of them being handsome and how she could see Nan or any other woman falling for either of them. They had the same good looks Sara had seen in movie stars like George Sanders, Errol Flynn, and Peter O'Toole. The eyes that would drill into your soul and a smile capable of melting even the coldest heart. However, the biggest hurdle was that while their last name began with 'S,' neither of them had the initial 'T' in their names. As unlikely as it was that their widowed father had been Nan's lover, William George Sandbourne didn't have an initial 'T,' either.

* * *

AFTER THREE HOURS, Sara had compiled more information on the Sandbourne family and saved it to a folder on her computer. Nothing she had found provided a hint who 'T' could be. As she closed the laptop, she decided nothing was to be gained by mulling over everything she'd been able to gather. Tomorrow she would make the trip to Sheffield and with luck, get to meet Sir Andrew and his brother Edward. Hopefully they will be able to provide more information.

As she packed up her computer, she thought about giving George a call. She missed hearing his voice, and she thought he'd be interested in hearing what had been discovered so far. However, she made another call first.

Sara listened as the call connected, and the double ring came through the line.

"Hello, Sara, how are you, dear?"

"Hello, Lady Mary. I'm doing well, thank you. I've been making some headway."

"That's marvelous. What have you been able to find out?"

"To begin with, Mr. Wallingford at the jewelers found an inscription on the back of the brooch. I now know that the mysterious 'T's initials are T.S. We've also been able to discover who owned Highgate during the time in question. It was a family named Sandbourne."

"Sandbourne? That fits nicely with your discovering the second initial."

"Yes, it does," agreed Sara. "However, I can't find any records of a T. Sandbourne. During the time the Sandbourne's owned the home, I can only find the names of three adult males. William, who was the father, and his two sons, Andrew and Edward. Do any of those names sound familiar to you?"

"Sandbourne… No, I don't recall Rose ever talking about someone by that name."

"They were both in the RAF, they were fighter pilots. Did Nan ever mention anything about seeing someone in the RAF?"

"No. Rose and I would often go to the service clubs, but I can't say I remember anyone in an RAF uniform she took a fancy to and went off with."

Her hoped dashed once again, Sara shared the one remaining card she had to play in her quest with Lady Mary. "The Sandbourne family has an estate outside of Sheffield. Mr. Cromwell and I are going there tomorrow in the hopes of speaking to Sir Andrew and his brother Edward."

"I wish you well, Sara. Please let me know if you discover more information. After keeping part of Rose's story secret for all these years, I must admit, I am curious as to where this secret will lead you."

"Thank you, Lady Mary. I'll be in contact when I have something new to pass on. Goodbye."

"Goodbye, dear," replied Lady Mary as she broke the connection.

As she held the now silent phone, Sara reflected on the events of the day. Thinking back to the photos of the Sandbourne brothers, she remembered how handsome they had been in their youth. Her thoughts then switched to the image of another handsome man, the one who had recently come into her life, and she made the phone call she had intended to make earlier.

When George answered, Sara, smiled at his salutation.

"Dr. George Randell here, personal physician to the rich and famous. How may I be of service?"

"I'm not sure, I already know I'm too far away for a house call," Sara said laughingly.

"How are you doing?"

"I'm doing well, thanks. It's been an interesting few days. A lot has happened since the last time I called."

"Hopefully, it's all been good."

"Yes and no. I've gotten a great deal of information from different sources. We've found Highgate House, and I now know who owned it at the time the letters were written."

"That is good news. Then you've been able to locate 'T.'"

"No, I haven't," said Sara as she again began to recount everything she'd learned during her visit.

"I guess you must be getting frustrated."

"If you only knew. Every time I think I'm getting closer, the trail stops. I feel like I'm standing in line for a ride at Disney World. Just when you think you're getting close the path changes direction, and I'm headed away from where I think I want to go."

"What's your lawyer say about all this?"

"Not much he can say or do for that matter. We're going to call on the former owners tomorrow."

"Do you think one of them could be your grandfather?" asked George.

Sara let out a sigh, "I don't know. As I said, neither one has the initial 'T' in their name."

"Have faith, I'm sure everything you've found out so far will help you get the answer you promised your grandmother you would find."

"Thanks, George, it's nice to have someone to talk to. What's the latest from NYC? Anything exciting going on? I haven't even watched the news or picked up a paper since I've gotten here."

George filled Sara in on everything he knew about that was going on in the city, which wasn't that much. Then they talked about things in general for a bit longer before they hung up.

After talking with George, Sara felt better. She thought how much different her conversations with him were as opposed to the ones she used to have with Jeff. Then she realized there was no comparison between the two.

Chapter 49

Cromwell's car arrived at Horseguards Hotel at 8:00 a.m., and Sara was waiting. Upon entering the rear seat, the smell of fresh coffee greeted her. "I wasn't sure if you had eaten breakfast. It will be a long ride, so I had John pick up some coffee and pastry for the trip."

"I had something a while ago. Thank you for bringing coffee along, it's certainly appreciated since I didn't get very much sleep last night."

"I can understand your feelings of trepidation with this entire situation. Hopefully, someone in the Sandbourne home can fill in the missing pieces to this mystery."

"I hope so, too. Since I never knew what I thought to be the truth was a series of well-fabricated lies, none of this ever mattered. But even having kept her secret for seventy-odd years, I'm sure my grandmother wanted me to know the truth. If for no other reason than to set the record straight."

Cromwell looked over at Sara, who slumped down in her seat. "Whatever the reason, we'll see what we can find out. Why don't you try to get a bit of sleep? It's a three-hour ride to Sheffield."

"I'm not sure I can, but I'll try," said Sara as she closed her eyes, leaned back against the side of the car and drifted off.

* * *

THREE HOURS LATER, Reginald Cromwell reached out and touched Sara's shoulder. "Ms. Ferguson, we're almost there."

Sara stirred at both the touch and recognition someone was calling her. As she opened her eyes, she remembered where she was and straightened herself in her seat. "Are we close?"

"Yes, we're just outside Sheffield. It should be about another ten to fifteen minutes until we arrive. Would you like a coffee? It's still hot."

"Yes, please. It'll help clear some fog from my brain."

Cromwell's driver pulled the car onto the extended access road leading to Sandbourne Manor. Sara looked out the window and took in the view. The photo on the fact sheet provided by Mr. Corry hardly paid this house the homage it deserved. The style and grandeur of the stone façade showed this was the home of someone who was a very prominent person in the history of Sheffield. Although the Sandbournes were not originally among the members of titled nobility, William Sandbourne was undoubtedly a highly placed member of the landed gentry. Even with the decline of the coal and steel industries that brought Sandbourne his wealth and power, the current appearance of the home and surrounding grounds provided evidence that the family fortune had withstood the economic downturn that affected much of Sheffield.

Cromwell turned to his client. "I'm not sure how well they will receive uninvited guests. Please allow me to do the talking until we get inside."

Sara nodded, "Okay, I can do that."

"Excellent."

John opened the rear door of the car and allowed his employer and his client to exit. Then he closed the door and remained by the car as they walked toward the front door. Cromwell rang the doorbell, and the two visitors waited to see what would happen next.

A well-turned-out butler answered the door and looked over the strangers with a well-practiced eye. When the butler viewed the car and driver parked in the forecourt and the cut and fit of the clothing the visitors were wearing, he determined they weren't here soliciting for something and addressed them accordingly. "Good morning, sir, madam. May I help you?"

Cromwell presented his card. "Reginald Cromwell, Q.C. I don't have an appointment, but I was wondering if it would be possible to have a word with Sir Andrew or Edward Sandbourne."

"What is the nature of your business, Mr. Cromwell?"

"It's rather a delicate matter, and it would be best if it were possible to speak to one or both of the Sandbourne brothers."

"I see," replied the butler in a cautious tone. "Please come in. I'll see if someone is available to speak with you."

"We made it inside," said Sara once the butler walked off.

Cromwell nodded his agreement but didn't offer a reply.

The butler returned several minutes later. "If you will follow me, they will receive you in the library."

They did as requested, following the butler down the hallway and into the well-appointed library. "Please be seated," said the butler.

Once more, doing as had been requested of them, they sat and waited. Sara looked around, taking in the room's opulence. She ran her eyes across the shelves of books noting the different colored bindings. As she continued to scan the room, Sara wondered two things. One was how does someone amass such an incredible library. She was sure this room didn't start as walls of empty bookcases, filled one volume at a time. And two, does anyone ever read any of these books or were they merely a statement of status. Another case of 'look what I've got.'

As Sara pondered the questions of how people displayed uncounted wealth, the door opened, and a tall man she judged to be in his sixties entered the room, pushing a much older man in a wheelchair.

Cromwell and Sara stood as they entered.

"Good morning, I'm William Sandbourne," said the tall man. "This is my uncle, Edward. I'm afraid father isn't here. He's currently in London attending meetings at the House of Lords."

Cromwell approached the two men. "Thank you for taking the time to see us. Please allow me to introduce my client, Ms. Sara Ferguson of New York."

"Nice to meet you, Ms. Ferguson. Please take your seats. Mr. Carstairs said you wished to discuss a delicate matter with my father and uncle. What exactly is this business you wish to discuss with us?"

"It concerns a woman named Rose Beardmore. Miss Beardmore left England at the end of the Second World War and settled in America. At the time of her departure, she was pregnant and unwed. Rose Beardmore was the recipient of funds being transferred from a trust set up with Barclays Bank from nineteen forty-five until the time of her death several months ago. We've also discovered that the trust remains in force and will continue to pay out a specified sum in US dollars every three months."

"That's all very interesting, but what does it have to do with my family?" asked William.

"Are you aware of anyone in your family with the initials T.S.?" asked Cromwell

"Yes, my cousin Theresa, Uncle Edward's daughter."

"Any *male* relatives, perhaps other members of the Sandbourne family?"

"Not that I'm aware of. Uncle Edward, do you know of anyone?"

The old man shook his head.

"No, he doesn't know of any either. Why do you believe someone from my family is the father of this child?"

Sara produced the note and the box with the brooch. "I found a stack of letters like this one in a safe deposit box after my grandmother passed away. You'll notice the address was Highgate House. Your grandfather was the owner of Highgate at the time these were written."

William took the letter from Sara and began reading it as she opened the box containing the jewelry. "The brooch is engraved on the back, T.S. to R.B. with a heart and the date 12-25-44. I've taken it to the jeweler who sold it. While he could not tell me who purchased it, he confirmed it was from their store, the stones were, in fact, genuine and that an estimated cost to purchase the piece in nineteen forty-four was sixteen hundred pounds."

William took the brooch from Sara after handing the letter to his uncle. "It's a beautiful piece, and I see it's from Toye, Kenning, and Spencer. The only thing I can tell you is that they have been our family jewelers for as long as I can remember. However, there is no male member of this family that I know of who had the initials T.S."

Cromwell noticed Edward was looking at the letter with interest but hadn't said a word. "Mr. Sandbourne, is there something familiar about that letter?"

Edward Sandbourne looked up and smiled. "Yes, I remember."

Sara got excited. "What do you remember, Mr. Sandbourne? Do you remember my grandmother?"

"Highgate House, I live there. We all live there, mum, dad, Andy. We have so much fun there. It's a wonderful place, come visit us," he said.

"You must forgive my uncle," said William as he took the letter from his uncle's hands. "His memory is failing, but occasionally he gets a moment of clarity when something stirs a memory."

"Mr. Sandbourne," Sara said in a soft tone. "I've been to Highgate House recently. And yes, I agree it is a wonderful house. But what about Rose? Do you remember Rose, Rose Beardmore?"

The old man's smile faded as he drifted back into the clouded recesses of his own mind. He looked around at the people in the room. "Who are you?" he asked.

"I'm sorry, Ms. Ferguson, it appears you've come all this way for no reason," said William as he returned the letter to her.

"Maybe your father could provide us more information," said Cromwell. "Would you give us his address in London? Perhaps we could call on him."

"Yes, I can do that, but please call first. While father doesn't suffer from the same ailment as my uncle, he tires easily."

"Don't concern yourself, Mr. Sandbourne, Ms. Ferguson, and I will be considerate of your fathers' advanced age and the value he places on his time."

William walked over to the writing desk and pressed a button before he began writing something on a sheet of paper. The doors to the library opened, and Mr. Carstairs, the butler, entered. "Yes, sir."

"Carstairs, please return my uncle to his room while I show our guests to the door."

"As you wish, sir," replied the butler as he walked over and began wheeling Edward back to his room.

"Goodbye, Mr. Sandbourne," said Sara.

Edward Sandbourne peaked out from behind his affliction and smiled. "I hope you'll visit us at Highgate House. We'll be there beginning in May."

"I'll do my best to visit," offered Sara as the butler wheeled Edward out.

William folded the note in half and handed it to Cromwell. "That's my father's London address and his phone number. I'm not sure what he can add to what I've already told you, but I wish you well on your quest."

They followed William out of the library and to the front door where they said goodbye. Sara and Cromwell returned to the car and John once again opened the rear door allowing them entry. Once they were in the car, William Sandbourne turned and closed the front door of Sandbourne Manor.

"He was rather sociable. Wouldn't you agree?" asked Cromwell.

"Yes, considering our questions were asking which one of your relatives got my grandmother pregnant and refused to marry her."

"You Americans can be blunt."

"I'm sorry, Mr. Cromwell, but we're not getting anywhere with our inquiries. I would say we contact Sir Andrew; ask him the same questions we've asked his son. If we don't get an answer or a firm lead on who T.S. is, I'm going to call it a day."

"If Sir Andrew can't help, you will stop looking for T.S.?"

"That's right. We have a saying in America. 'I really enjoy beating my head against the wall, but it feels so much better when I stop.'"

"I should think so."

"Look, Mr. Cromwell, you've been very helpful. And so has Mr. Corry. He uncovered the owners of Highgate at the time the letters were written. You've helped me track down the trust that had been paying into my grandmother's account since nineteen forty-five. I now have hundreds of millions of dollars in property, stock, and cash. A trust I have no control over. A stack of letters and a brooch that T.S. gave to my grandmother as a Christmas present.

"What I don't have is a clue to who T.S. could be. So it's a simple matter of logic. If we've exhausted all the clues and the only living members of the family who owned Highgate don't know who T.S. is, then we've run out of road. There's nowhere left to go. So I'll call it a day. I can honestly say I tried to find the answer."

"I must admit you are correct. Without further clues, the road does come to rather an abrupt end. But there is still one last person to speak to, and perhaps he will help."

"We'll see, Mr. Cromwell, but I'm not holding out hope."

Chapter 50

John returned them to Mr. Cromwell's offices by four that afternoon. The barrister had commented to Sara that he wished to contact Sir Andrew today to see if they could agree on a date and time to meet. Sara wanted to get this over with as soon as possible; therefore, she agreed with Cromwell.

"The sooner we meet, the sooner I'm on a plane back to New York."

"I'll make the call then, and we'll see what happens."

Sara nodded, "I guess we will."

Cromwell opened his briefcase and removed the slip of paper William Sandbourne had given him. After choosing speaker mode, he dialed the phone number. The phone connected and began to ring. It didn't take long before someone answered.

"Lord Sandbourne's residence."

The barrister provided a formal introduction of himself before asking. "Is it possible to speak to his lordship?"

"I'm sorry, sir, his lordship is out for the evening. I'm not sure when he will return. May I take a message? Perhaps your number?"

"Yes, that would be acceptable." Cromwell provided his phone number before giving the message to the butler. "Please tell his lordship I've been to Sandbourne Manor and spoken with his son, The Honorable William Sandbourne. It was he who provided me with his lordship's address and phone number."

"Yes, sir, I understand, is there more to your message?"

"Yes, I'd like an opportunity to call on his lordship and bring my client along to discuss a matter we are investigating. We are hoping Sir Andrew will provide us with more information beyond what we received from his lordship's son and brother Edward."

"I'll pass this on to his lordship's secretary."

"Thank you," replied Cromwell as Sara listened. "I'll wait to hear from him. Oh, please add that we should like to meet within a day or two since my client is returning to the States in several days."

"Yes, sir. I will add that information to your request. I'll ensure Mr. Clarkson gets this message."

"Thank you again," replied Cromwell as he disconnected the call.

"What do you think?" asked Sara.

"I think we must wait and see if Sir Andrew will grant us an audience. At this point, I'm not thinking much beyond that. As you said he's the last link in the chain, and if he can't give us anything I would assume as do you, this search is at an end."

Sara crossed her arms. "Not much more we can do tonight, is there?"

"No, I'm afraid not," said Cromwell as he glanced at his watch. "And it's much too early for dinner. What say we find a pub and go for a drink? It's been a long day."

Sara agreed, "It sure has. I know I could use a drink after all this running around."

"Right, then. Allow me to help you with your coat, and we'll go. Perhaps a drink will help soothe your headache."

"Headache?" Sara questioned.

"Yes," replied the lawyer as he continued in a laughing tone. "The one you claim comes from repeatedly banging your head against the wall."

Chapter 51

Sir Andrew's private secretary, Mr. Rupert Clarkson returned Cromwell's call early the next morning. Since the barrister was not in his office, his secretary provided Mr. Clarkson with Cromwell's private cellphone number.

The barrister was en route to an appointment at the Old Bailey, which is the Central Criminal Court of England and Wales when his cellphone rang.

He didn't recognize the number on the screen as he answered. "Reginald Cromwell."

"Good morning, Mr. Cromwell, this is Rupert Clarkson calling. I'm the personal secretary to Sir Andrew Sandbourne."

"Good morning, sir. I assume you received my request for my client and myself to meet with Sir Andrew."

"I have. However, his lordship has a full schedule today."

"I see. Would it be possible to meet tomorrow or if possible this evening? My client is due to return to the States in a matter of days, and we're trying to bring closure to a personal matter."

"May I ask what it is you wish to discuss with his lordship?"

"We're attempting to find the individual whose initials are T.S. and may have been staying at Highgate House during nineteen forty-four. It is our understanding that none of the male members of the Sandbourne family have those initials. Therefore, we are hoping Sir Andrew could enlighten us as to the identity of this person."

"Thank you for that information. Mr. Cromwell, please allow me to speak to his lordship and see if he would be free to speak with you. I'll call again when I have an answer."

"Thank you. I'll inform my client and let her know we're awaiting your call."

"One last thing. Would you tell me your client's name?"

"It's Ferguson, Ms. Sara Ferguson. She's the granddaughter of Mrs. Rose Cavendish, formally Miss Rose Beardmore, of London."

"Thank you," was all Clarkson said as he broke the connection.

Cromwell looked at his phone for a moment as he wondered why his client's name was necessary. Surely Sir Andrew's son would have imparted that information to his father when he called to let him know he'd had visitors at the manor house. He also would have let his father know he'd given the visitors his London address and phone number.

Cromwell dialed the number to the Horseguards Hotel. He wanted to let Sara know Sir Andrew's secretary had been in contact with him.

As Sara spoke to Cromwell, she decided she couldn't sit in her hotel room all day long waiting for his call, so she ensured he had her cellphone number and told him she was going out for the day.

Now dressed in comfortable clothing, Sara headed back out to hit more of the sights she wanted to visit. Since her last outing comprised a walk to Trafalgar Square and spending the rest of the day in the National Gallery, she opted for something different. Today, the Tower of London was on the top of her list, as were the Houses of Parliament.

* * *

RUPERT CLARKSON CALLED CROMWELL back at 4:00 p.m. "Mr. Cromwell, I've spoken with his lordship and informed him of the nature of the subject you and Ms. Ferguson wished to discuss. Sir Andrew is agreeable to a meeting. Would you and Ms. Ferguson be able to meet his lordship at 10:00 a.m. tomorrow morning?"

"I believe so, I must contact my client to confirm. However, since this is an issue of great importance to her, I would not think that will be a problem."

"I'll inform his lordship that you will be here in the morning at the appointed time. Do you have the address?"

"Yes, we have the address, we received it when we visited Sandbourne Manor."

"Very well. I'll expect you tomorrow morning. Good afternoon, Mr. Cromwell."

"Good afternoon, Mr. Clarkson, and thank you," replied Cromwell as he hung up.

Cromwell found the number he'd written down earlier and called Sara to tell her the final hurdle was about to be crossed.

"Hello," she said.

"Sara, it's Reginald Cromwell. We have an appointment to meet with Sir Andrew tomorrow morning at 10:00 a.m."

"That's wonderful. Now I'll either find out who T.S. is, or we'll have exhausted all leads. If that happens, I'll return to New York with more information but without a definitive answer."

"I'm afraid that's correct. But don't lose hope just yet. Perhaps Sir Andrew will fill in the missing piece."

"I hope so, Mr. Cromwell, but I'm not holding my breath."

"Very well, Ms. Ferguson. I'll pick you up at 9:30."

"Thanks, I'll be ready," replied Sara as Cromwell broke the connection. "Well, tomorrow's the day," Sara said to herself.

As she walked along the streets of London, she thought about everything that had happened, the revelations she'd learned about her grandmother's past. Sara looked at the buildings and tried to imagine what it must have been like living through the "Blitz." Taking shelter deep in the tunnels of the London underground, then coming out to look upon the devastation caused by the German bombs and missiles.

Chapter 52

Sara waited for Mr. Cromwell to arrive to take her to yet another appointment that could provide her with the answer. A simple question that lay buried under seventy years of lies and secrets.

Sara pondered the possible outcomes of the meeting with Sir Andrew. In reality, there were only two. Either his lordship knew who "T.S." was or he didn't. But then she realized if he did, in fact, know who "T.S." was, would he be willing to provide that information to Sara or was he also sworn to some secret pact?

The barrister arrived on time and seemed almost excited at the possibility this would be the day his client had been waiting for since she came to London.

"Good morning, Ms. Ferguson. Are you ready to call on Sir Andrew?"

"As ready as I'll ever be. This is the end of the road, and we'll either get an answer, or the road will just drop off the edge of a cliff, leaving us with nothing but empty air."

"You don't sound very hopeful."

Sara shook her head. "It's that whole banging your head against the wall syndrome. Nothing we've uncovered to date has given me a reason to be hopeful."

As they arrived at Sir Andrew's residence, Sara took a deep breath. "Let's do this."

"Agreed," said Cromwell.

A man in a dark blue suit answered the door. By his demeanor, Sara decided he wasn't the butler.

"Good morning, Ms. Ferguson, Mr. Cromwell. I'm Rupert Clarkson."

The three exchanged pleasantries in the entrance hall. A maid appeared and took their coats as Sir Andrew's private secretary led them into one of the reception rooms.

"If you will wait here, I will inform his lordship you have arrived. Please make yourselves comfortable."

Sara sat in an armchair by the large fireplace. She scanned the room, trying to figure out what period the décor of the room was. The only frame of reference she had was her grandmother's Regency-style furniture and what she saw in Lady Mary's home and Sandbourne Manor.

Sara caught Cromwell's attention by asking. "What period would you say this room is done in?"

"That mantle is certainly Victorian," he paused in thought. "As are some other pieces in here. But I believe it's also an eclectic mix of periods. Why do you ask?"

"No reason. It's just that homes like this are so different from anything I've ever been in. I'm just intrigued by the culture and the style."

"This isn't a normal home."

Sara laughed. "I'm sure it isn't."

The door opened, and Sir Andrew entered the room, followed by his private secretary. Clarkson performed the introductions as Sara and Cromwell stood.

Sara looked at his lordship and thought back to the photos she saw of him in his RAF uniform, medals prominently displayed on his jacket. Unlike his brother, Sir Andrew stood erect, the posture of a soldier. His dark gray suit custom made on Saville Row. A full head of silver-white hair and a Van Dyke beard of the same color. His gray eyes were clear, taking in everything in the room as he entered.

"Your lordship, it is very kind of you to receive us this morning," said Cromwell with a slight bow.

Sir Andrew nodded without speaking as Sara held his gaze.

"Your lordship, my client is in search of some information. We were hoping you may be able to provide the answers that would allow Ms. Ferguson to bring closure to the task she has been asked to perform."

"What is it you hope to find out, Ms. Ferguson?" asked Sir Andrew.

Sara opened her handbag and removed the letter and the black velvet box containing the platinum brooch. She opened the letter and held it out for Clarkson to hand to Sir Andrew. "This letter is one of a group I found in a safe deposit box after my grandmother's death. As you will see, the return address was Highgate House."

Clarkson handed the letter over to his employer, whose eyes remained fixed on Sara.

"And you think I may know who wrote this because Highgate House belonged to my family."

"Yes. If you look at the letter you will see it's signed with the letter 'T.' Having done some research, I could not find any male member of the Sandbourne family whose initial is 'T.'"

"Why do you think the 'T' belongs to someone named Sandbourne?"

Sara opened the box and removed the brooch. "It's purely speculation. But it's based on the engraving on the back. It says T.S. to R.B. with a heart. It's dated 12-25-44."

"May I see the brooch?" asked Sir Andrew.

Sara rose from her seat and delivered the brooch. As she did, she locked eyes with Sir Andrew, and a chill flowed through her body.

Sir Andrew took the brooch from Sara's hand. As he looked at it, his expression changed to a faraway gaze in his eyes as if remembering some past event.

Cromwell watched how Sir Andrew's gaze never left Sara as she walked. Sara took her seat, and the barrister asked. "Sir Andrew, my client had been looking into her grandmother's affairs, one of which has been a trust fund established in nineteen forty-five which has been paying out a quarterly stipend and continues to do so to this day. Currently, it is providing an annual sum of four hundred thousand U.S. dollars to an account established in Ms. Ferguson's grandmother's name."

A small smile came to the old man's face as he heard about the trust, and he nodded. Sir Andrew's eyes shifted back to Sara. "Your grandmother was Rose Beardmore. Seeing you standing there, you remind me so much of her," he said, looking at the brooch again. "T.S. to R.B. with love. December twenty-fifth, nineteen forty-four."

Sara was stunned. "You know? Sir Andrew, you know who T.S. is? Don't you?"

"Rose called him 'Twink.'"

"Twink? The 'T' stood for Twink? Was that some sort of nickname?"

"It was. Rose called him that because she said his eyes twinkled like the stars when they were together."

"Whose eyes, Sir Andrew? Who is Twink?"

Chapter 53

Sara waited for Sir Andrew's reply, but his lordship remained silent. She rose and walked to him. "Sir Andrew, my grandmother sent me on this journey because she thought it was important for me to discover the truth about her life and find out who my real grandfather was. It's obvious you know who Twink is."

Before the conversation continued, Sir Andrew turned to his secretary. "Mr. Clarkson, please go into the kitchen and instruct the butler to bring tea."

"Yes, your lordship."

Sara put her hand on Sir Andrew's arm. Her voice softened as she made a final plea. "You're my last hope of finding him. It seems like you have fond memories of my grandmother. If you do, please help me. Who is Twink?"

Sir Andrew looked into Sara's eyes. "I am."

Sara froze, at the revelation.

Sir Andrew looked at Sara as he continued to finger the jewel encrusted pin. "I loved your grandmother very much. But I was betrothed to someone else," he said as he looked at the back of the brooch.

Sara stared at the man she had just discovered to be her real grandfather. "I never knew the truth about Nan's life. Now I know everything I've learned in the past few weeks is the real story of her life. Nan left me a letter in her will that asked me to find out who I really was. That's why I came to London to find out Nan's great secret."

"It has been a secret for many years. But now that Rose is gone, it no longer matters," said Sir Andrew.

"I'm not here to judge you or my grandmother for what happened during the war, but I would like to know the whole story about the two of you and why your identity was secret for all these years."

Clarkson returned with the butler pushing a tea trolley. After the tea was served, Sir Andrew dismissed the butler and his secretary so he could speak to his guests in private.

"Since you said you've uncovered the truth behind Rose's early life, I suppose you know that she was a Wren during the war."

"Yes, I learned that from Lady Holborne. If you didn't know, Mary O'Riley is now Lady Mary Holborne. But that's not important at this point. Anyway, yes, I learned all about what she did during the war."

Sir Andrew took a sip of tea as he recalled the past. "I met Rose in one of the service clubs. I was on leave from the squadron," he said looking for signs that his granddaughter understood.

"I know you were a pilot in the RAF, I looked you up on the internet," she said.

"As I was saying, I was on leave when I met Rose. We hit it off from the first moment I asked her to dance. She was beautiful and charming. A carefree soul, full of life. I guess we all were back then. Life had a different meaning during the war. You had to get what you wanted at that moment because you never knew if you would live to see tomorrow."

Sir Andrew placed his teacup on the table, stood, and walked to the fireplace. The erect posture he had displayed when he first entered the room seemed to waver as placed a hand on the mantel to steady himself. "I fell in love with Rose, but there was another. My fiancée was in Ireland, away from the Blitz and the air raids. She didn't know what was going on.

But my father did. He wanted me to end it with Rose. It should be obvious I didn't adhere to his wishes and continued to see her. I seriously thought about marrying her when the war was over. I intended to distance myself from my fiancée, then cancel our engagement. Then I would be free to marry Rose."

"What happened?" asked Sara. "Why didn't you follow through and marry her?"

"I had already returned to the squadron when I found out she was with child. I couldn't go back to London. The war had moved to the final stages, and we were being sent forward to support the allied troop movements as they prepared to invade Germany."

"But the war in Europe ended in May of nineteen forty-five," said Cromwell.

"And Nan arrived in the States in July of forty-five. You could have married her," added Sara.

Sir Andrew's chin dropped to his chest. "I could have, I should have, but for selfish reasons, I didn't. My marriage was to be for the good of the family. Elizabeth's family was one of political power and influence. Father wanted access to everything our union would bring with it. He threatened to disown me if I married Rose. But he said if Elizabeth and I were wed, he would see to it Rose and his illegitimate grandchild would be taken care of for the rest of their lives. But there were conditions."

"And that's why the secret pact was put in place?" asked Sara.

"Yes," replied Sir Andrew. "And there was another. To secure the financial future for herself and her child, Rose had to leave England and never return."

Sara stood and walked over to the fireplace and put her hand on her grandfather's shoulder. "I've read the letters you sent her, it seems like you were trying to bring her and my mother back to England."

"I tried to persuade father to allow her to come back. Things were never good between Elizabeth and me. We were both foolish and made our choices based on money, not on love. We made do with the lives we had chosen."

"If your father was the problem, why didn't you do something after he died." Sara raised her voice as she spoke. "You're the oldest son. I'm sure you inherited pretty much everything."

Sir Andrew nodded, "That's true. I could have changed the trust. However, Rose objected. By the time my father died, your mother, Sophia, was a grown woman who had gone through life thinking her last name was McDonald and that her father had been killed in the war. Sophia and Rose had a wonderful relationship having grown close as they made a life for themselves in America. The trust ensured Rose never had to work again unless she wanted to do so. Your grandmother dedicated herself to raising Sophia, in much the same way she raised you after your mother was killed."

"Was it Nan's decision to remain in the States?" asked Sara.

"Yes, much like she did with you, she continued the lies about her past to avoid confusing everyone for no reason. The stability of her daughter's life was more important to Rose than her own happiness."

"I guess I never realized what a strong woman she was. When she left England, I know you wrote to her for a while. I have all the letters she kept. What happened after the letters stopped?"

"We spoke on the phone occasionally. Normally when something of importance happened," said Sir Andrew. "Wait here for a moment, I've got something to show you."

As Sir Andrew left the room, Sara returned to her seat and looked over at her lawyer. "I'm shaking," she said. "After all the dead ends, I never expected this to be the outcome."

"They say confession is good for the soul. Perhaps seeing you standing in front of him has given him the conviction to reveal the truth."

"What happens now? I wonder if he'll tell his son. What about the trust? Maybe he can stop it now that everything is out in the open?" Sara's mind was running through different scenarios as she verbalized some of her thoughts.

"Sara, take a breath, slow down. You've just gotten the answer you've been searching for since you read grandmother's letter, which was who you really were. Remember, you were ready to give up the search if this meeting didn't provide you with an answer. Now that you've discovered the final truth, you need to process the implications of what you've found and how you will deal with your newly acquired family."

"Where do I begin?" she asked.

"That is something I can't advise you on. That will be between you and your grandfather."

The door opened again as Sir Andrew returned, carrying a burgundy leather binder under his arm. After taking a seat on the couch he motioned to Sara. "Please, come sit next to me."

Sara took the seat next to him as he opened the binder for the first page. There she saw a photo of her grandmother and her infant mother. "Rose would send me things to a private address I gave her. Sophia was about six months old in this picture," said her grandfather as he passed the binder across to Sara.

Sara placed the book on her lap. As she slowly turned the pages, she watched her mother's life unfold before her. "I never knew."

"Sara, I can't even claim I understand what you are feeling at the moment because I can't. I've been privy to information about your mother and yourself, yet you had no idea I existed."

"Sir Andrew, I always thought I knew who I was. Now everything has changed. My heritage, my financial position. Since you seem to know so much, can I assume you also know that Nan left me millions of dollars?"

"Yes, I'm aware of that."

"Now that you've told me you are, in fact, my grandfather, what happens next?"

"I will have a talk with William and his family when I return home. He needs to know I have another granddaughter."

"You can tell him not to worry, I don't want or need anything from you or your estate."

"William and his family will not be short of money. You needn't worry about them. As for you Sara, arrangements now in place will remain as they are in perpetuity."

"Do you mean the trust that sends money to the account in America?"

Her grandfather nodded. "The trust is solvent and should remain so for years to come. The trust's current value is fifty million pounds. It will continue to pay out quarterly. The amount of the payouts will increase based on inflation."

Sara protested, "I don't need your money."

"It's there for you. If you should marry and have children, then my great-grandchildren shall benefit from the trust."

"Nan's estate is valued at over two hundred million dollars. Grandfather, I really don't need the money," said Sara as she realized she had just acknowledged their relationship.

The old man smiled as the young woman from America called him grandfather. He nodded his understanding as he took her hand. "Sara, my dear, I can't change the past. What I did, what Rose did is all behind us. The money is of little consequence at this point in my life. As I've said, William and his family will be very well off and will not suffer any financial loss. You can't mourn the loss of something you never had. The trust your great grandfather put in place to ensure Rose and Sophia were well taken care of has served its purpose. Now you can decide what to do with the money."

"All right, if you won't cease the payouts, I have to give a lot of thought to what to do with it. Perhaps I'll discuss it with my lawyer when I get back to New York."

Sara and her grandfather continued talking for several hours. Mr. Cromwell had excused himself earlier, citing other appointments scheduled for the afternoon. Sir Andrew ensured the barrister that his driver would take Sara back to her hotel or wherever she wanted to go when they finished their conversation.

After lunch, Sir Andrew led Sara back to the room where he had revealed that he was, in fact, T.S., and they resumed their private conversation.

"What made you decide to tell me that you were my grandfather?" asked Sara.

"William called to inform me of your visit and the particulars of your quest. I knew you would call for an appointment. I had no intention of telling you I was 'T.' When I saw you, I saw Rose." Reaching across the space that separated them, once again he took his granddaughter's hand. "My Rose, young, beautiful, and loving. It was at that point I decided if you asked the question, I would give you the answer you were searching for. It was as if Rose had returned to me, and I had a chance to do the right thing."

"I was about to give up all hope of finding the answer. The fact that you are still alive and told me who you really are is a bonus. If you had denied all knowledge of the person I was looking for, I would have gone away without finding the truth."

Sir Andrew released Sara's hand and sat back in his chair. "Now that you know, will you be staying in London longer? I think William would like to meet you properly."

Sara shook her head, "No, I'm going to return to New York as planned. I think the discussion you are going to have with your son about your illegitimate granddaughter will be interesting enough on its own without me standing beside you. But now that I do know I would like to come back very soon. Hopefully, if

William goes into shock when you inform him there's another relative out in America, it will have worn off by then."

Sara took her grandfather's hand and held it to her cheek. "When I do come back, maybe I'll also be able to tell you how I intend to use the money your trust provides."

"I would like that. Please don't wait too long to come back, I'm not getting any younger," replied her grandfather. As he smiled, Sara saw what her Nan saw all those years ago. That twinkle in his eye and the smile that made women melt.

Chapter 54

Once Sara left her grandfather's residence, she returned to Mr. Cromwell's office to wrap up their business. The barrister decided Sara appeared more in need of a drink than another cup of tea. "I would say you have discovered everything your grandmother wanted you to do in her letter. Perhaps a small celebration is in order. May I pour you a brandy?"

Sara walked over and took a seat on the leather couch. "Yes, please. And make it a large one."

Cromwell obliged and poured a healthy amount of Louis XIII into a crystal balloon. "Here you are."

Sara accepted the glass and nodded a thank you as she thought through everything that had occurred in the past few hours. After she took a long swallow of the aged spirit, she finally verbalized her thoughts to her lawyer. "It's amazing, almost crazy. Nan lived her cover story until the day she died. She also gave up the chance to go back to England to protect the narrative she told everyone."

Cromwell had taken a seat opposite Sara. He was swirling the tawny liquid around his glass as he listened to his client. Once again, he offered a counterargument for his client to consider. "Suppose we look at this from your grandmother's point of view."

Sara took another drink as she listened. "What do you mean?"

Cromwell placed his glass on the side table and leaned forward in his chair. "First off, your grandmother had been forced to build a life for herself and your mother in America. She had to do this on her own, without the support of a husband or a family.

Granted, she wasn't left without the financial means to do so, but she was forced to do it without physical assistance."

Sara nodded her acceptance of Cromwell's statement.

Once Cromwell saw that Sara was following, he continued. "The years passed, and your mother grew up, believing both her father and stepfather had died in the wars. Your grandmother told her this was their family history, and your mother came to understand who she was." The lawyer stood and continued to present his argument. "Now, consider the fact you were born. As you got older, your mother passed your family history as she learned it, on to you."

Sara added her part of the storyline. "When my parents were killed, I was old enough to understand my family history and believe everything my mother had told me about them."

"Also, please consider this," said Cromwell. "At the point in time Sir Andrew's father died, many years had passed. Mentally and emotionally, they were not the same people. They had lived different lives. Your grandmother had forged a secure life for you while using the money provided to build her own personal fortune. Sir Andrew lived the life he'd chosen. He had opted for money and security over love."

"Still," said Sara, "my grandfather offered her a chance to return to him and be together once again."

"Okay, for argument's sake, let's say your grandmother accepted. You knew her, how do you think she would have explained that to you. 'We're leaving America because an old flame of mine has invited us to return to England to live there?'"

Sara took exception to Cromwell's characterization of her grandmother. "That's not fair. My grandmother was a wonderful person."

"Sorry, I'm not disputing that fact. I'm merely asking how you think your grandmother would have presented a case for leaving America after all these years to return to England. To return to a place and people who were unknown to you?"

"I don't know," replied Sara as she lowered her head. "Nan would have come up with something."

"Sara, here is a final point I'd like you to consider. Let's assume your grandmother chose to uproot everything you had in the States to move to England. What would be the consequences if things didn't go well? It's entirely possible they would have not been happy. After all, a wartime fling is not the same as fifty years of marriage."

* **

WHEN THEY FINISHED THEIR BUSINESS, Cromwell and Sara said their goodbyes, and the barrister instructed his driver to take Ms. Ferguson back to her hotel.

The first thing Sara did was phone Lady Mary and let her know she had discovered T.S.'s identity. When Sara told her Sir Andrew Sandbourne was her real grandfather Lady Mary was surprised. She said she now remembered having met Sir Andrew at a function in the past. She told Sara she had found him charming. Sara provided details of her new family history uncovered while talking with Sir Andrew.

After her call to Lady Mary, Sara thought about beginning to pack for the trip back to New York. She realized the day's events had taken a lot out of her and decided to just rest for a while. She pulled down the bed covers, revealing the crisp linen. She rolled onto her back and stretched out on the bed.

Sara closed her eyes. A smile developed as she softly whispered, "I did it, Nan. Now I know who I really am."

Chapter 55

Delta Flight 4358 from London Heathrow to JFK, landed on time at 4:20 p.m. Sara had contacted both George and Janet Collins to let them know she would be arriving. Sara had asked Janet to send a car to pick her up and if it wouldn't be too much trouble to have George picked up from Highgate and brought to the airport to greet her. The lawyer who had also become a friend assured Sara that wasn't a problem, and she would see to everything.

When Sara exited customs and walked out onto the main concourse, she spotted George front and center on the railing waiting for her. As she walked toward him, her smile grew as her pace quickened. Reaching the exit Sara released the hold on her luggage and grabbed the man she'd been thinking about for the past thirty-six hours. Their kiss was passionate and they didn't seem to care that they were out in public.

George broke the kiss and held her tightly. "Welcome home."

"Thank you, it's good to be home. I've missed you."

"I've missed you, too," said George as he gave her another kiss. "So, tell me what happened. During our last conversation, you said you were coming home, but you never told me if you found what you were after. Did you ever find out who T.S. was?"

Sara nodded and kissed him again, "Let's get out of here. Where's the car? I've got a lot I want to share with you, and I can begin on the ride home."

George led Sara out of the terminal to the waiting limo Janet had arranged for them.

Sara gave George all the critical details that led to her discovering who her real grandfather was. She explained how frustrated she'd been and the fact she was about to abandon her search if Sir Andrew hadn't been able to provide an answer. George stopped her right there.

"Sir Andrew?" he asked, with a surprised look. "Do you come from royalty?"

"No, it's not that kind of title. My grandfather was knighted by the queen, so it's called a 'Life Peerage.' A title for life, like Sir Mick Jagger or Sir Paul McCartney, but it's not passed on after his death."

George gave her a quick kiss on the lips. "Ah, okay, I understand. For a second there, I thought I was dating a duchess or something."

"No, sorry, I'm still plain ordinary Sara."

George pulled her closer. "Honey, there's nothing plain or ordinary about you. Sorry for the interruption. What else did you find out?"

Sara continued to explain what she'd learned. She told him about the trust and how her grandfather told her to find a way to use the money because it was now hers to do with as she saw fit.

"Now you have an opportunity to do good with the money. Have you given it any thought?" asked George.

"There are a few ideas I've been toying with since I found out the payments from the trust would continue. I will talk to Mr. McDougal about them and get his opinion," she said as the car arrived at Highgate.

Once again, Charlie Wilkins was on duty when the limo with Sara and George pulled to the curb. Charlie opened the rear door, saw Sara, and greeted her. "Miss Sara, welcome home. I hope you had a good trip."

"Thanks, Charlie, I did. It's fun to travel, but it's always nice to come home and sleep in your own bed," she said as she turned her head to George and offered a sly smile.

The limo driver had removed Sara's luggage from the trunk, and Charlie brought it into the building and placed it by the elevator. "You need a hand getting the luggage upstairs, Miss Sara?"

"No thanks, Charlie. Dr. Randell and I can take it from here."

"Yes, ma'am. It's good to have you back," replied Charlie as he tipped his cap and returned to the desk.

When the doors opened, George followed Sara into the elevator, pulling her wheeled suitcase behind him. After Sara pushed the button for the fourteenth floor, she turned and put her arms around his neck, pulling his head down for another kiss.

"I'm sure you'll enjoy sleeping in your own bed again tonight," said George.

"Oh, I will certainly enjoy being in my own bed, but I'm not sure how much sleep I will be getting. When is your next shift at the hospital?"

George looked at his wrist to check the time as he watched Sara's smile fade, "Let's see it's almost 7:00 p.m. That gives us just…about…forty-five…hours."

Sara slapped his chest. "Oh, you, I thought you would say forty-five minutes."

"I knew you were coming home, so I swapped shifts."

"Then I'm certain there won't be much sleeping going on tonight," said Sara, as the doors opened on the fourteenth floor.

* * *

GEORGE WOKE UP FIRST and went to the kitchen to make coffee. Returning to the bedroom with a cup for Sara, he set it on the nightstand then sat on the side of the bed. George pushed the hair from her face, leaned over, and kissed her. "Good morning."

Sara stirred and opened her eyes. "Hmm, good morning," she said as she rolled onto her back. "What time is it?"

George looked at the alarm clock on the nightstand. "A little past 11."

"I'm starving," said Sara as she sat up against the headboard. "It's Sunday, isn't it?"

"Yes."

"It's Sunday, and I'm starving. You know what that means."

"That you want to order food from the deli?" asked George.

"Excellent diagnosis, doctor. What would you like?" she asked as she let the covers drop to her waist, revealing her breasts.

"Whatever you want to order is fine with me. However, you don't need to get enough food for the week."

Sara's lower lip jutted out in a pout, and she picked up the covers she had dropped. "Don't you want to be barricaded in here with me for the rest of the week?"

George bent over and kissed her. "I'd love to do that. However, I have to get back to work."

With a pensive look, Sara thought about that for a second. "Ever think about going into private practice. I know someone who would love to have you as her personal physician."

"Remember when we had coffee? I asked you to call me George because I wasn't *your* physician. If you're the person you were referring to, then I'm afraid you would have to call me Dr. Randell again. Personally, I much prefer this relationship."

"Point taken, *George*." She said as she threw the covers off and got out of bed. "I'll go phone in the order."

When Sara returned, George was in the shower, and she joined her lover.

* * *

SARA WAS BLOW-DRYING HER HAIR when the bell rang. "George, that's probably Tommy with our order, would you mind getting the door? I've already paid for it, but you can tip him."

"Okay, I got it," replied George as he put on his trousers and grabbed his shirt.

George opened the door and saw the young man he'd met in the elevator a few weeks back. "Hello, Tommy. How are you doing?"

"Fine, sir; it's Dr. Randell, isn't it?"

"Correct. I'll take the box. How's school?" George asked as he put the box down and reached into his pocket to tip the delivery man.

"To be honest, sir, it's kicking my butt. I need to work to help pay the tuition, but that takes time away from studying."

"How are your grades?"

"I'm hanging in there. I'm still carrying a three-point five, but I'm not sure how long I can keep that up as the coursework becomes more complicated."

"I can understand what you're going through. I know it's difficult, but the reward can be significant. If that's what you really want to do, then stick with it. I'm sure things will work out for you." George removed a wad of bills from his pocket and handed Tommy a fifty. "Here, add this to the kitty."

Tommy looked at the bill. "Thanks, Dr. Randell, but sir, a tip like that isn't necessary."

"How about you let me be the judge of that?" replied George as he smiled. "Thanks for the delivery. I'm sure I'll be seeing you again."

"Yes, sir, thanks again, Dr. Randell," said Tommy as he turned to leave.

George closed the door, picked up the box, and carried it into the kitchen. "Brunch is served."

"On my way."

George was already unpacking the items from the box when Sara walked into the kitchen. "Did I hear you talking to Tommy?"

"Yes, I asked him about school. He said it was getting harder, which is no surprise, but he said working was cutting into his study time, so he hoped he could keep his grades up."

Sara hopped up on the counter and took a bagel off the plate. "Really?" she said as she took a bite. "He seems like a nice kid. I hope things work out for him."

"I'm sure they will. Things have a way of sorting themselves out. If he wants to be a doctor, he'll make it happen."

Sara didn't reply as she got down from the counter and helped George bring the food through to the dining room.

George could see Sara had something on her mind while they ate, so he let her process whatever it was with little interruption. After brunch, they returned to the bedroom and spent the rest of the day playing catch up.

Chapter 56

Monday arrived just like it was supposed to, and George was preparing to return to work as planned. For weeks now, Sara had been giving thought to what she would do with all the money she had inherited from her grandmother. But what was now at the forefront of those thoughts was how to best use the money that would continue to be paid out of the trust her great-grandfather had created to take care of Nan.

Sara realized that whatever it was she did, it would most likely involve a lawyer to draw up all the legal documents. Nan's guidance for Sara's life was pretty simple, and that was to ask the advice of Michael McDougal before she did something extraordinary. While George showered and got ready to leave for the hospital, Sara called the offices of McDougal, McDougal & Slone and asked to speak to her lawyer.

Since Mr. McDougal was in court today, they connected her to Janet Collins.

"Sara, welcome back. How was the trip?"

"Frustrating and tiring. However, I accomplished everything I set out to do. I've answered the question of who I am and discovered my real grandfather."

"That's wonderful news. Michael got some details from Mr. Cromwell, but he deferred to fill in the major facts saying he thought he would leave it to you to decide what you would tell us."

"That's exactly why I'm calling," replied Sara. "I'd like to set an appointment with Michael to let him know what I discovered concerning both my heritage as well as where the quarterly money transfers come from."

"Michael is free tomorrow morning. Would you be able to make it? Let's say 10:00 a.m."

"Yes, I can make that. Would you be able to be there also? I'd like you to hear what I've got to say as well. I also want to discuss several ideas with both of you."

"Why yes, of course, I can be there. Thank you for including me," said Janet

"You're welcome. The way I figure it, both you and Michael have been there for me from the start. You helped get things sorted out for the funeral, not to mention the will and everything that transpired afterward. I'd like you both there with me as I go forward and do the things I want to do."

"That won't be a problem. We'll see you tomorrow morning at ten. Would you like me to send a car for you?"

"No, thanks. I can manage. I'll see you then." Sara went to find George.

George had finished showering and was dressing in the clothing he'd brought with him when he picked her up at the airport. He had anticipated spending the weekend at Sara's. When he'd finished dressing, Sara walked up behind him and wrapped her arms around his waist and rested her head on his back. "How did Monday get here so quickly?"

"Same way it always seems to, days off fly by."

"Then you need more days off."

George pulled Sara around in front of him and gave her a hug. "I'll be sure to tell the department head that next time I see him."

"I wouldn't complain if you had more time off."

"I'm sure you wouldn't. However, right now, I've got to leave if I'm going to make it to the hospital on time."

Sara was reluctant to let him go. She understood his commitment to medicine and knew that would be his profession for years to come. Yet, given the time they'd spent together, Sara hoped she could carve out a place for herself in his life. Things could work out for them as long as they both had something else to fill the hours they were apart. George had medicine; now Sara needed to decide what it was she would do not only with her inheritance but, more importantly, her time.

After George left the apartment, Sara sat at the writing desk and took out a pen and paper. She made two columns and began writing down the ideas she'd come up with and wanted to discuss with Michael and Janet.

* * *

MICHAEL MCDOUGAL AND JANET COLLINS were waiting for Sara when she arrived at the office.

McDougal stood as his secretary ushered Sara into his office. "Good morning," he said, offering his client a warm smile. "It's good to see you again."

"Thank you, Michael. It's good to be home."

"From the little we've been told by Mr. Cromwell, it sounds like you had quite the adventure over in England," added Janet.

"It certainly was interesting, frustrating as hell, but interesting. I was able to find out everything my grandmother wanted me to learn about her past. I may have uncovered more than she expected me to, but now that I know the truth, I see her in a different light. I'd always thought my grandmother was a remarkable woman. However, after what we've discovered here in New York and what I found in England, I'd have to say Rose Beardmore McDonald Cavendish could be considered a legend."

McDougal walked around his desk and led the two women out of his office. "Let's go into the conference room, I'll have coffee brought in, and you can fill us in on all the details Mr. Cromwell left out."

Sara agreed and followed. She occupied the same seat she had for the reading of Nan's Last Will and Testament and waited for everyone to be seated.

McDougal leaned forward in his chair and smiled at his young client. "Based on the bits of information Mr. Cromwell has passed on to me, it would appear you have a lot to share should you choose to do so."

"I do, but the place I'd like to begin is with the trust that currently makes the quarterly deposits to BNY-Mellon."

"Given your statement, I'm assuming those deposits will continue," said McDougal.

"Correct. The trust is set up to pay out for perpetuity as long as it remains solvent. My grandfather told me that at the moment, it's valued at about fifty million pounds."

Janet scribbled some numbers down on her pad. "With no changes or growth, that's more than a hundred and fifty years."

Sara nodded, "That's right. Since I can't stop the flow, you can understand why I want to do something good with that money."

"We can certainly handle all the legal aspects for anything you want to do," said McDougal.

"I was hoping you would say that."

"Do you have an idea of how you want to utilize that money?" asked Janet.

Sara leaned back in her chair and smiled. "As a matter of fact, I have been giving it a lot of thought. This is what I am thinking…"

Chapter 57

Michael McDougal's Bentley was parked at the curb as he awaited his client's arrival. Winston opened the door for Sara. She exited Highgate and found it to be another beautiful day.

As she took her seat in the hand-built car, she exchanged pleasantries with its occupants.

"Good morning, Sara," said Janet Collins from the rear seat.

"Good morning," replied Sara as she twisted in her seat to see the female lawyer. "And good morning to you too, Michael."

McDougal smiled as he looked over at Sara. "It is a good morning, isn't it? Are you ready for this?"

"I certainly am. Let's not keep them waiting, shall we?"

"Of course," replied McDougal as he put the car in drive and pulled into the morning traffic.

The conversation remained light on the ride across town. As they neared their destination, Sara asked. "What do you think will happen?"

"I think it will be an interesting conversation," replied McDougal.

Sara smiled as she thought back to her conversation with McDougal several months ago about now having the ability to do whatever it was she wanted to do. "I think it will be even better when the details are known."

"You can count on that being true. We've set everything in motion, as discussed. Someone will meet us when we arrive," said Janet.

"Perfect," replied Sara.

* * *

ONCE THE BENTLEY HAD BEEN TURNED OVER to the parking valet, the trio took the elevator to the lobby where they were to be met.

Their party was awaiting their arrival and handed out the security badges to his guests before escorting them to the elevator for the ride to the nineteenth floor. Since it was only 7:45 a.m., the normal level of activity in the offices had yet to begin, which allowed them a certain level of freedom from prying eyes as they walked through the office space to the executive conference room.

Coffee service had arrived shortly before they did, and each of the four enjoyed a cup in silence. Several minutes later, another member joined the group. He said his hellos before also pouring a cup of coffee and taking a seat at the table.

Michael and Janet had removed several folders from their briefcases and distributed them around the table to the participants and placed one more at the empty spot for the last person they expected. Once that was done, the two lawyers compared notes, and Michael made several notations on his legal pad. Everything was ready.

At 8:30 a.m., the last person they were waiting for entered the room, accompanied by his executive assistant.

As Jeff Charles strode toward the conference table, he called out, "Let's get this show on the road, we've got things to do!"

When his executive assistant looked around the room, a smile came to her face.

Jeff stopped short, obviously perplexed by what he saw. "What's going on?" he asked. "Bill? Martin?"

It was Sara who answered. "Hello, Jeff. Have a seat, this shouldn't take long."

Epilogue

Tommy Robertson was exhausted when he got home. As usual, it had been another very long day. He'd had three hours of lecture beginning at 8:00 a.m., followed by a two-hour class in the laboratory. After completing that, he had gone to the Columbia University Library to transcribe his scribbled notes into clear and meaningful ones he would use to study.

All he'd eaten today was a slice of pizza devoured on the run as he made his way to the deli. Tommy had worked until the deli closed at 9:00 p.m. and headed home to eat whatever his mother had cooked for dinner before beginning to study and prep for the next classes on the schedule for the week.

When Tommy walked into the living room, he found his mother sitting in her usual spot watching TV. "Hi, Mom, what's for dinner?"

Elizabeth Robertson turned off the TV and stood. "I've got some roasted chicken, mashed potatoes and gravy and steamed broccoli for you."

"Good, I'm starving."

"Go wash up. I'll get everything ready."

"Okay," replied Tommy as he went down the hall to the bathroom. Fifteen minutes later, he returned and took his seat at the table.

"How was your day? How's school?"

"My day was okay. School was hard. I got a B-plus for my last lab project."

"That's a good grade. Are you happy with that?"

"Happy, yes," said Tommy as he began eating dinner. "Satisfied, no. I was sure it was an A."

"Well, I'm satisfied. You're taking a full load. Working on top of that. You're doing more than a lot of kids are doing nowadays. I'm proud of you and if your father were still alive, I know he'd be proud of you, too."

"Thanks, Mom. I love you."

Elizabeth Robertson looked at her son for a moment before she spoke. "Tommy, is everything okay?"

"Yeah, mom, dinner is fine."

"No, I mean with you. Are you okay? You're not in any kind of trouble are you?"

"Trouble? Not that I know of. Why? What's going on?"

Elizabeth stood and walked to the counter. "You got a special delivery letter today," she said as she handed the envelope to her son. "It's from a lawyer."

Tommy opened the letter. His mother watched his eyes as he began to read.

The Law Offices of McDougal, McDougal & Slone
1166 Park Avenue, Suite 700, New York, NY 10036
Tel (212) 555-7500 Fax (212) 555-7501

Mr. Thomas C. Robertson
242 East 86th Street
Unit 403
New York, NY 10028

Dear Mr. Robertson,

Greetings. We are pleased to inform you that you have been selected to receive a grant to complete your studies. This grant is provided by the Beardmore-Sandbourne Educational Trust.

As a recipient of this grant, you must adhere to specific academic standards to continue to benefit from the award.

A)   You must remain a full-time student in good standing.
B)   You must retain a minimum Grade Point Average of 3.25 on a 4.0 scale.

The grant will be paid directly to your university and will be sufficient to cover all tuition and expenses to include any and all fees incurred for your course of study.

You will also receive a cash supplement to purchase any books and or equipment required to complete your studies.

Finally, you will begin to receive a monthly stipend to offset your living expenses, thereby allowing you to leave your current place of employment and focus on your studies.

On behalf of the Trustees, and myself as Executor of the Trust, we congratulate you on your selection and wish you much success in the future.

A representative of this office will be in contact with you shortly to collect the final details and make the arrangements for the payments.

Warm regards,
Michael J. McDougal, Esq.
Senior Partner